MISSION
CRITICAL

EDITED BY
JONATHAN STRAHAN

ALSO EDITED BY JONATHAN STRAHAN

Best Short Novels (2004 through 2007)

Drowned Worlds

Eclipse: New Science Fiction and Fantasy (Vols 1-4)

Fantasy: The Very Best of 2005

Fearsome Journeys

Fearsome Magics

Godlike Machines

Life on Mars: Tales of New Frontiers

Science Fiction: The Very Best of 2005

The Best Science Fiction and Fantasy of the Year: Volumes 1-13

The Book of Dragons (forthcoming)

The Infinity Project 1: Engineering Infinity

The Infinity Project 2: Edge of Infinity

The Infinity Project 3: Reach for Infinity

The Infinity Project 4: Meeting Infinity

The Infinity Project 5: Bridging Infinity

The Infinity Project 6: Infinity Wars

The Infinity Project 7: Infinity's End

Universal Robots (forthcoming)

The Starry Rift: Tales of New Tomorrows

Under My Hat: Tales from the Cauldron

Year's Best Science Fiction 2019: The Saga Annual Anthology of SF (forthcoming)

With Lou Anders

Swords and Dark Magic: The New Sword and Sorcery

With Charles N. Brown

The Locus Awards: Thirty Years of the Best in Fantasy and Science Fiction

With Jeremy G. Byrne

The Year's Best Australian Science Fiction and Fantasy: Volume 1

The Year's Best Australian Science Fiction and Fantasy: Volume 2

Eidolon 1

With Jack Dann

Legends of Australian Fantasy

With Gardner Dozois

The New Space Opera

The New Space Opera 2

With Karen Haber

Science Fiction: Best of 2003

Science Fiction: Best of 2004

Fantasy: Best of 2004

With Marianne S. Jablon

Wings of Fire

MISSION **CRITICAL**

EDITED BY
JONATHAN STRAHAN

First published 2019 by Solaris
an imprint of Rebellion Publishing Ltd,
Riverside House, Osney Mead,
Oxford, OX2 0ES, UK

www.solarisbooks.com

ISBN 978 1 78108 580 6

Cover by Adam Tredowski

Selection and "Introduction" by Jonathan Strahan.
Copyright © 2019 by Jonathan Strahan.

Page 461 represents an extension of this copyright page.

10 9 8 7 6 5 4 3 2 1

A CIP catalogue record for this book is available from the
British Library.

Designed & typeset by Rebellion Publishing

Printed in Denmark

ACKNOWLEDGEMENTS

My sincere thanks to my editor, David Thomas Moore, and the whole Solaris team for their support and for their hard work on the book you now hold. My sincere thanks, too, to all of the writers who sent me stories for the book, whether I used them or not, and to everyone who wanted to be part of *Mission Critical*. As always, my thanks to my agent, Howard Morhaim, who has stood with me for all of these years, and extra special thanks to Marianne, Jessica, and Sophie, who really are the reason why I keep doing this.

CONTENTS

Introduction, Jonathan Strahan   9

This is Not the Way Home, Greg Egan   13

Rescue Party, Aliette de Bodard   43

Devil in the Dust, Linda Nagata   81

Hanging Gardens, Gregory Feeley   111

The One Who Was There, John Barnes   135

By the Warmth of their Calculus, Tobias S. Buckell   163

Mutata Superesse, Jason Fischer & Sean Williams   195

The Empty Gun, Yoon Ha Lee   215

Genesong, Peter F. Hamilton   245

Something in the Air, Carolyn Ives Gilman   279

Lost in Splendour, John Meaney   315

The Agreement, Dominica Phetteplace   345

The Fires of Prometheus, Allen M. Steele   371

Ice Breakers, Kristine Kathryn Rusch   399

Cyclopterus, Peter Watts   427

WHEN THINGS GO WRONG

JONATHAN STRAHAN

MISSION CRITICAL COMES out of a moment where I was sitting in a cinema in my hometown of Perth watching *The Martian*. Matt Damon's character realises that he's been abandoned on Mars. Everything has gone wrong and if he's going to survive, he's going to have to pull something miraculous out of the hat; he's going to have to 'science the shit out of it,' as he says. Which he does.

Sitting there, my mind spun off for a moment to stories of real-life crises where it'd all come down to brains and bravery, where one or two or three or more people had to buckle down and pull a solution out of thin air if they were going to survive. Like the moment that came five and a half hours into Apollo 13's flight in April 1970 when an oxygen tank exploded and left three astronauts almost certainly doomed and how they went on to find a solution and to get themselves home.

And I began to think, there could be a book that collected

stories, where people, human or otherwise, were working on a mission or plan and something went terribly wrong. Where the mission went from being under control to critical. The stories could take place on Earth or in space, in our solar system or far out in the stars. But the constant would be that moment and how to come back from it.

When I got home from the movies that day, I immediately sat down and contacted my editor and he was just as excited as I was. It took a little time to make it happen, but it wasn't too long before I got to reach out to fifteen writers whose work I've loved over the years – John Barnes, Toby Buckell, Aliette de Bodard, Greg Egan, Greg Feeley, Jason Fischer and Sean Williams, Carolyn Ives Gilman, Peter Hamilton, Yoon Ha Lee, John Meaney, Linda Nagata, Dominica Phetteplace, Kris Rusch, Allen Steele and Peter Watts – and ask them to tell me stories, stories of brains and bravery, of things going wrong and how they might just be made right.

One by one, over a year, stories came in. Stories set out in the rings of Saturn, on a ship around a distant star, on a colony world, on Earth's moon, on Mars, on a ship slingshotting across the solar system, during an ice storm, on a hostile moon by a giant volcano, and at the bottom of Earth's oceans; stories that saw captains and engineers, pilots and passers-by faced with a moment and trying to see if they can find a way that will see them make it through and get to the next day and to the next mission.

Mission Critical is, for me, the spiritual successor to the *Infinity* books that I spent much of the 2010s working on. Smart, well-written science fiction, mostly hard science fiction, that shows everything the genre can do. I hope you'll love the stories here as much as I have and that I'll get the opportunity to take you to other worlds soon.

Jonathan Strahan
Perth, 2019

THIS IS NOT THE WAY HOME
GREG EGAN

1

When Aisha spotted Jingyi through the window, for a second she thought she was seeing a reflection in the glass. Suited to the neck but bareheaded, her helmet gripped in one hand by her side, Jingyi had to be standing behind her, facing away from her into the room.

But she wasn't.

Aisha knelt on the floor and wept. It was Jingyi who had kept her from giving in to despair. It was Jingyi who had shaped the plan into something real and found the strength to pursue it. But when she'd faltered, when she'd fallen into doubt herself, all of Aisha's attempts to lift her spirits and restart the virtuous circle of encouragement that had kept them both sane and striving for close to a year, had come to nothing.

Aisha sobbed until the grief loosened its hold on her, long enough to grant her a choice: follow Jingyi into the darkness, or step back and try to skirt around the edge of the abyss. She rose to her feet and returned to the crib, then lifted Nuri into her sling. *She could not afford to be crushed. Not by this, not by anything.* Her daughter was fast asleep; Aisha even managed to put their shared suit on without waking her. Then she went out to pack for the trip.

The buggy's trailer, with its open tray, looked like something she might have hired back in Dunedin to move a few pieces of furniture between share-houses in her student days. She didn't shy away from the memory; she pictured Gianni beside her, smiling and teasing her as she fretted over the placement of each item in the tray. The struts were all short enough to fit, but she didn't want them rolling back and forth. She hunted around in the workshop and found some cable ties, then she stood patiently binding the struts into a set of linked bundles that she could anchor to the tray at the corners.

She'd already folded the sheet of glistening silica fibers that she and Jingyi had spent the last four months weaving, but even in this compact form it was so bulky that when she squatted down to pick it up, it blocked her view completely. She fetched a sled with a pull cord, flipped the bundle onto it, then dragged it across the workshop floor and out onto the regolith.

As Aisha glanced up at the crescent Earth, Nuri woke and started crying. "Shh, shh!" It was impossible to stroke her through the suit, but Aisha managed to nudge breast and baby together, and once Nuri clamped her mouth in place, she stopped complaining and just fed, more or less contentedly. "We're going for a drive," Aisha explained. "How about that?"

Jingyi was facing west: the way they'd planned to travel together, chasing the sun. Aisha saw no reason to lay her friend to rest; she must have locked the suit's joints to keep her body upright, so she'd clearly had no desire to end up horizontal in the dirt.

Nuri stopped feeding to grizzle with displeasure, then pungently defecate, but her diapers were as magical as Aisha's and there was nothing to be done but endure the smell.

Aisha finished packing, then she covered everything on the trailer with a tarpaulin and started pulling the straps into place.

When she was done, she looked up at the Earth again. She'd always been good with landmarks; one glimpse of a distant spire and she could find her way home. But she was about as close to home right now as she could ever be on this world, and the idea of climbing into the buggy and driving until pretty much the opposite was true felt suicidally wrongheaded. How mortifying would it be if a rescue team finally arrived, a mere twelve months late, only to end their mission cracking each other up just by whispering, "She headed for the *farside*?"

Jingyi's memorial statue remained resolute. "All right, I'm sticking to the plan," Aisha told her. "Just like you should have done."

2

"A HONEYMOON IN Fiji! Thank you!" As Aisha embraced her father in gratitude, he interjected testily, "There's more in the envelope. Have a proper look."

Aisha flushed and did as he'd asked, wondering if the airline ticket and hotel booking were accompanied by some needlessly lavish spending money. But the extra slip of paper she'd missed was another kind of ticket entirely.

"I checked with Gianni before I bought it," her father informed her. That had been prudent: the lottery's prize was strictly for couples, and if she'd won only to find that her husband really couldn't face the journey, it would have made both of them miserable. Better not to have a ticket at all.

That night, as she and Gianni lay in bed, she'd talked down their chances. "One in a hundred thousand," she'd mused. "I'd have better odds of getting into the astronaut training program."

"Only if you applied."

"Yeah, well." Going into space was the kind of thing that was easier to imagine at twelve than at twenty-seven. She was touched that her father recalled her childhood ambition, but he seemed to have taken it more seriously than she had herself. "And really, there's no chance of us winning. They'll give it to a Chinese couple."

"Why? Just because China and America are squabbling doesn't mean the company's going to start blacklisting people from every other country."

"No, but it's a marketing gimmick. 'Honeymoon on the Moon!' Who else are you going to target but your biggest market?"

Gianni was bemused. "It's a lottery with *thousand-dollar* tickets. If you mess with the outcome, that's not marketing savvy, it's fraud."

And then, after all her cynicism and carefully managed expectations, the company live-streamed the draw. Five digits plucked from the hiss of the cosmic microwave background determined the winners, and the marketing department would just have to live with it.

Aisha's class of moonstruck nine-year-olds gave her handmade bon voyage cards, with postscripts ranging from impressively specific requests for certain kinds of lunar minerals to pleas for photos of various action figures (enclosed) posed on the surface. She and Gianni passed their health checks and were whisked away to the Gobi Desert, where the centrifuge rides and spacesuit training felt more like scenes for a mockumentary than anything that would really serve them in their role as spam in a can. But Aisha let the company's PR machine drag them along its strange conveyor belt, all the way to the launch pad.

"This is like being prepped for an operation," Gianni decided, as they waited in their flight suits for the car that would take them to the *Chang'e 20* itself.

Zhilin, the pilot, was amused. "Only if you mean the kind of brain surgery where you're awake the whole time."

"Are you ever afraid?" Aisha asked him.

"I was afraid the first time," he confessed. "It's a strange thing for a human to attempt, and it's only right that it feels unnatural. But that's true for anything our ancestors didn't do: driving a car, flying a plane."

"Walking on a tightrope between skyscrapers," Gianni joked. Aisha wanted to punch him, but Zhilin just laughed.

From the gantry, looking out across the stark gray plains,

Aisha waved cheerfully, knowing that her father and her students would be watching, but once she was strapped into her seat in the tiny cabin, she gripped Gianni's hand and closed her eyes.

"It'll be fine," he whispered.

She waited for the engines to ignite, wondering what had ever made her yearn to leave the Earth. She didn't need a pale-blue-dot moment to convince her that her home world was a fragile oasis. And if she couldn't inspire a love of science in her students without an overblown stunt like this, she was the worst teacher ever born.

When the moment came, she could hear the inferno unleashed beneath her, a wild conflagration that rattled all the flimsy structures that stood between the flames and her flesh. When Gianni squeezed her hand, she imagined the two of them spinning away into the air, lighting up the desert like a human Catherine wheel.

In the flight simulator, she'd watched the simulated rocket's progress on a screen in front of her, helping her translate every burst of noise and thrust into the language of stages and separations, but now she shied away from interpreting the cues, afraid of getting it wrong and convincing herself that the worst was over when it was only just beginning. The force of the engines and the shaking of the cabin made her teeth ache in ways she'd never felt before; this wasn't brain surgery, it was some kind of gonzo dentistry.

And when everything seemed still and quiet, she refused to trust her senses. Maybe she was just numb to the onslaught, or she was blocking it out in some kind of dissociative state.

"Aisha?"

She opened her eyes. Gianni was beaming madly. He took a pen out of his pocket and released it; it floated in the air like a magic trick, like a movie effect, like her phone doing a cheesy AR overlay. She'd watched *2001* a thousand times, but this couldn't be happening to her in real life.

He said, "We're astronauts now. How cool is that?"

3

THREE DAYS LATER, when they disembarked at Sinus Medii, Aisha was jubilant. She summoned up her twelve-year-old self to gaze in astonishment at the blazing daytime stars and the ancient fissured basalt stretching to the horizon, then she waddled precariously forward across the landing pad like her grandmother performing water aerobics. She *knew* that if she did X, Y, or Z, she would instantly die a horrible death—but she was no more likely to enact one of the fatal blunders she'd been warned against than she'd ever been inclined to open a window in a tall building and jump out.

Medii Base was a sprawling complex of factories and workshops open to the vacuum, but the sole pressurized habitat was about the size of a small suburban dwelling, albeit with a greenhouse in the back. Zhilin introduced the honeymooners to the staff: Jingyi, botanist and medical doctor; Martin, roboticist and mining engineer; and Yong, geologist and astrophysicist. These double-degreed geniuses all looked about thirty, and Aisha was intimidated at first, but that soon gave way to a kind of relief: envying them would be like envying an Olympic athlete. She wanted to enjoy the experience for what it was and emerge without any delusions or regrets: there'd be no *if only she'd done a PhD*, or *it was not too late to leverage her flight hours as a passenger into a new, interplanetary career*.

Jingyi sketched the whole complex system of nutrient and energy flows supporting the hydroponic crops, responding patiently to all the questions Aisha's students had passed on to her. Martin showed them the solar-thermal smelter that was processing basaltic rubble into useful materials—albeit, so far, mostly just the silica fiber for Yong's baby. The Moravec skyhook was a rotating cable, its length a full third the width of the Moon. Yong had spun it up to the point where the low end swung backward above the surface so rapidly as to momentarily cancel out the velocity due to its orbit. It was like a spoke on a giant wheel rolling around the Moon's equator—except that the imaginary track it was rolling on was several kilometers above their heads, so there was no risk of decapitation even at the top of the most exuberant bound. One day the hook would grab vehicles and supplies and sling them away toward Mars. For now, it was just a beautiful proof of concept, a tireless, hyperactive stick-insect doing cartwheels over their heads.

Back in their room, Aisha Skyped her father. The three-second delays were impossible to ignore, but she'd had worse between continents.

"You're healthy?" he asked. "You're not sick from the journey?"

"Not at all." She'd done all her vomiting in the ship.

"I'm so proud of you. Your mother would have been so proud!"

Aisha just smiled; it would have been heartless to protest that she'd done nothing more than accept his gift.

When they finished the call, she flopped back in her chair and sighed. "Where are we, again?"

"Are you jealous of my sister scuba diving on the reefs?" Gianni joked. They'd given her the Fiji holiday; it would have been greedy to take both.

"No." Some commentators had written sniffily that a smelter was hardly a tourist attraction. But in truth, nothing could be mundane here.

"They won't have put cameras in the room, will they?" Gianni asked. Aisha hoped he was joking; whatever their role, it was still a notch or two above contestants on reality TV. But she shut down the computer anyway, just to be safe.

They kissed tentatively, wary of performing some simple movement that would lead to a pratfall here. Anything that wasn't velcroed or magnetically locked to the floor might as well have been a banana skin.

She said, "Once we're inside the bag, we should be all right." They undressed each other, trying not to laugh, unsure just how quiet they'd need to be to keep their neighbors from hearing.

"When your father asked me if I'd go on this trip, I almost said no," Gianni admitted.

Aisha frowned. "Well, that's a real turn-on."

"I was trying to be honest."

"I'm joking!" She kissed him. "I almost chickened out a dozen times myself."

"Then I'm glad we both stuck with it," he said. "Because I'm pretty sure this is going to make us happy for the rest of our lives."

4

AISHA HAD SWITCHED her watch's default display to Dunedin time, so she wouldn't miss her appointment to talk to the school. She woke around six, showered, then stood by the sleeping bag and prodded Gianni's shoulder with her foot.

"Do you want to get up and have breakfast?"

He squinted at his own watch. "It's two a.m.!"

"Only in Beijing. Come on… you need to be sitting next to me when I call the kids, or they'll just spend the whole hour asking me what you're doing."

When they'd eaten and made themselves presentable, they sat down in front of the computer and powered it up. It booted without any problem, but when Aisha opened Skype, it told her that she had no connection to the internet.

"Maybe we're out of view of the dish," Gianni suggested.

"I thought they had us covered around the clock." There were ground stations in Mongolia, Nigeria and Honduras, and no one in the training camp or on the base had mentioned a particular time window for contacting Earth.

Gianni frowned. "Did you hear that?" The gentle thump had sounded like the airlock's inner doors closing.

They walked out into the common room. Martin had just returned from outside; he was still suited and holding his helmet.

"We're having communications problems," he said.

"Oh." Aisha hesitated. "Is it going to be easy to fix?" Forget about her disappointed students; Martin and his colleagues were stuck here for another four months, and if they didn't have the right replacement parts on hand, the link could remain broken until the new crew arrived.

"I don't know," he replied. "There's nothing wrong at our end."

"Okay." Aisha wasn't sure why his tone suggested that this was bad news. "So when we switch over to a different dish...?"

Martin said, "We should have been through one handover already."

"So the problem's at mission control?" Gianni suggested.

"No." Martin sounded harried. "We should be getting carrier from the dishes themselves, whatever's happening at Dongfeng."

Aisha was bewildered now. "How can there be two separate problems at two different dishes, halfway around the world?"

Martin shook his head. "I have no idea."

The other members of the crew joined them one by one, either woken by the conversation, or alerted by their own devices to the broken link. Yong talked over the technical issues with Martin, then went out to perform some supplementary tests. Aisha gathered that Martin had successfully established contact with a portable, self-contained transceiver that mimicked the protocols they would normally be following with a ground station. Medii's own antenna required no active measures to keep it aligned; the Earth was essentially a fixed target, with all the careful tracking delegated to the other end. But Yong had a theory about some obscure defect that might still blind them to a distant transmitter without stopping them connecting to the proxy.

Gianni tried to make light of it all. "At home we just flick our modems on and off, but here you need to check in case we've jumped into another dimension where the dinosaurs stayed in charge down on Earth."

Only Zhilin laughed, but then, he'd once flown commercial airliners. He had to be accustomed to setting his passengers' minds at ease—no matter what was going on inside his own head.

Yong returned. "It's not us," he declared. "The problem's back home."

Jingyi and Martin gazed down at the dining room table, but Gianni couldn't tolerate silence. "So maybe the Americans hacked all the Chinese ground stations? In some kind of… preemptive cyberattack?" He stopped short of spelling out the reason, but the recent tensions had revolved around rumors of weapons in orbit.

Aisha said, "I didn't think things had got that serious."

Yong turned to the couple. "You had some sightseeing scheduled, and I'm already suited up. The next dish won't be in view for five hours, and there's nothing we can do just by sitting here worrying."

Aisha and Gianni got into their suits and the three of them cycled through the airlock together. Aisha did her best to surrender to the spectacle and concentrate on perfecting her regolith gait. Never mind that the ground around them looked like it had been melted in a nuclear blast, and the claustrophobic confines of her suit made her think of fallout protection gear.

Yong was in the middle of explaining a theory that the farside had fewer maria than the nearside because a collision with a second, much smaller satellite had thickened the Moon's crust there, when Aisha noticed a high-pitched, metronomic beep.

"Does anyone else hear that?" she asked. She was afraid it was some kind of alarm, though she'd been told that even a malfunctioning suit would always manage to give a polite, informative message in the occupant's preferred language.

"Sorry, that's the beacon from the skyhook." Yong did something, and the sound went away. "I listen in to it sometimes, just to reassure myself that it's still up there."

"How could it not be?" Gianni wondered.

"A micrometeor could cut it in two."

"So what would a micrometeor do to us?"

"Don't worry, we're much smaller targets."

By the time they were back inside, the wait was almost over. Martin sat hunched over the console in the common room, gazing at the screen. Aisha tried to prepare herself not to take another dose of dead air too hard; there might be an entirely innocuous reason for it that hadn't occurred to any of them.

"Nothing," Martin announced. "They're all down."

Gianni said, "Can you try tuning in to one of the NASA dishes?"

"They won't be pointed at us."

"What about TV broadcasts?"

Martin grimaced impatiently. "The only antenna sensitive enough to pick up that shit is on the farside, precisely so it doesn't have to listen to it."

Gianni nodded, chastened. "Okay. So, what's the upshot? We should just relax and hope they get things working again soon?"

"Sure," Zhilin replied. "No internet for a couple of days. That never hurt anyone, did it?"

5

As THE SILENCE stretched on, Aisha found herself equally committed to two ways of viewing the situation. On the one hand, for her and Gianni the inability to communicate with Earth was just a mild inconvenience—and in the short term, at least, that was probably also true for the base's longer-term residents. And assuming that the problem with China's network of ground stations wasn't being treated as a state secret, no one's relatives would have reason to be worried about the lack of contact. Her father would still be anxious, but at least he'd know why he hadn't been able to talk with her.

On the other hand: short of hostilities, cyber or otherwise, what could have happened at three separate sites that was taking so long to repair? And if Beijing and Washington were merely sulking with each other, that shouldn't have stopped the ground stations in Spain or Australia showing enough good will to step in and make contact with Medii, just to let them know what was going on.

But even while being alone with Gianni, Aisha stuck to version one, and shut down any pessimistic speculations. "We won't need clearance from Earth to take off and head home," she reminded him. "It's not like it's so crowded out here that we need a flight plan approved by air traffic control." Zhilin would probably prefer to get a weather report before he took them all the way to Dongfeng, but in principle, they could still make the journey even if Earth's whole population had ascended in the Rapture, and the last soul to depart had turned off the lights.

AISHA WOKE TO the sound of Gianni repeating her name. "Something's happening!" he whispered. "They've been sitting in the common room, arguing, and now some of them have gone outside."

"Arguing about what?" Aisha wasn't sure she wanted to know, but Gianni seemed too agitated to be told to stop worrying and go back to sleep.

"I don't know, they were speaking Chinese."

She said, "Maybe someone realized that the problem is at our end, after all, and they've gone to fix it."

"I'll go and find out."

"No, just..." It was too late, he was out of the sleeping bag. Aisha watched him dress by the red glow of the safety lights. She was tired of the constant undertone of anxiety and paranoia, but in two more days, they'd be heading home, and in five, all their questions would be answered.

He left the room, and she heard him talking to Jingyi. At first, their words were too soft to make out clearly, but then Gianni started shouting. "You're fucking kidding me!" he bellowed.

"Please, don't try anything!" Jingyi implored him.

Aisha clambered out of the bag and went to join them. Gianni was pacing the room, hugging himself.

"What's happening?" she asked.

"*They're going home!*"

"What?"

Jingyi said, "They're afraid that if things are difficult, Earth might not send another ship for a long time."

Aisha was stunned. The *Chang'e 20* could only take three passengers and the pilot, so all six of them could not return together, but the idea that Earth would abandon the base's crew seemed deranged to her. "So we're the ones stranded here instead?"

Jingyi shook her head. "You're guests; you're here to make the company look good. They'll try much harder for you. But we signed up for one year, and we've trained for longer stays. There won't be the same pressure on them to help us."

Aisha was torn between indignation and a degree of sympathy: maybe the deserters' logic was sound. But if five days of silence really did mean that things were going badly on Earth, she very much doubted that all it would take to resurrect billions of dollars' worth of sabotaged infrastructure would be a little extra pressure on the public relations front.

Gianni said, "I'm going to stop them." He walked over to the airlock and began putting on his suit.

Jingyi turned to Aisha. "You need to talk him out of it. It's too dangerous for anyone fighting out there."

"I'm just going to talk to them!" Gianni retorted angrily.

"You can talk to them here," Jingyi replied, gesturing toward the console. Gianni ignored her, but Aisha went with her and sat down at the microphone.

"Yong? Martin?" she tried. There was no response. "Please. Can we discuss this?"

Gianni had everything but his helmet on. "They're not going to turn around and march back in because you asked them nicely!"

"So, what do you think you're going to do to change their minds?"

"They can't ignore me if I'm standing right in front of them."

Aisha said, "I don't think it's a good idea to confront them." The suits didn't exactly tear easily, but she did not want any kind of altercation in the vacuum. "They're probably inside the ship by now, anyway."

"We'll see." Gianni fixed his helmet in place and stepped into the airlock.

Aisha felt numb. If she went after him, would that just make things worse? When she heard the outer door close, she hit the button beside the microphone. "Gianni?"

"What?" He was breathing heavily, as if he was trying to run. The launch pad was five hundred meters away, but there was no way that he could overtake the men who'd left ten minutes earlier.

"Just leave it. They'll probably send another ship within a week."

"Fuck that! This is our ride home, and they don't get to take it."

"Just come back!"

Gianni did not reply.

"I have to go and get him," she decided.

As Aisha was putting on her suit, Jingyi looked on forlornly. Why hadn't she left with the others? There was room for her on the ship. Maybe they'd decided to draw straws to pick a babysitter to stay behind. Or maybe she was just too decent to walk out on a pair of novices who might not survive for one day on their own.

When Aisha emerged from the airlock, she saw Gianni in the distance, bounding across the rock like a kangaroo wrapped in tinfoil. She couldn't make out any figures moving around the launch pad.

"Come back, you idiot!" she implored him. "We'll be fine here!" Even if the wait turned out to be a year or two, Jingyi knew how to keep the crops growing and the base habitable.

Gianni kept running. Aisha waddled forward as briskly as she could, resigned to the fact that she'd never catch up with him.

When he reached the launch pad, she waited, hoping he'd accept the evidence of his own eyes. Zhilin would be going through the final system checks, and nobody was going to step out to debate their plans. Maybe the pricks would end up in prison for this; Aisha was unsure of the legal issues, but she recalled a sea captain being jailed for leaving his foundering ship while his passengers remained trapped below deck.

Gianni climbed the ladder to the hatch. Aisha couldn't make out exactly what he was doing, but she assumed he was pounding on the hull.

"I'm not leaving until you come out!" he shouted.

"Give it up!" Aisha begged him.

She heard the rattling first through his radio, then she felt the slight vibration of the ground through her boots. She stared at the lander; she couldn't discern any flames from the engines, but maybe they were too diffuse.

"You need to get down," she told Gianni, hoping he'd heed the note of terror in her voice when he'd ignored all her other entreaties.

"They're bluffing!" he retorted. "They're not going to take off."

"Jump and run, or I'll never forgive you!" She could see a ghostly blue light now, flickering around the base of the lander. "*Jump!*"

"Shut off the engines and come out," Gianni commanded his adversaries. Aisha had once watched him stand, immovable and unflinching, in front of a carload of thugs, ordering them to step out and face him after they'd shouted insults at her. When he thought he was right, he thought he was invincible.

The lander ascended: five meters, ten meters. Aisha emitted an involuntary sob, then held her breath as Gianni finally let go of the railing. Free-falling, he parted from the spacecraft with a dreamlike lethargy, tumbling slowly into the blue fire of the exhaust.

6

THE BUGGY NEEDED sunlight, so Aisha kept it moving at a sedate sixteen kilometers an hour; there was no point in outracing its energy source. With the sun all but frozen in the sky, the subtle changes in the light to which she'd grown accustomed were held in abeyance, leaving her with a sense of stasis that was only rendered stranger by the flow of the terrain. She watched the vehicle's progress on the GPS, and tried to distract herself by attempting to match her ground-level view of a crater or rille beside her with the corresponding features on the satellite map, but after a few days the endless variations on the same theme began to make her feel as if she were stuck in some barren, procedurally generated computer game. The verisimilitude was stunning, but she wanted someone to slip up and insert a shock of greenery, a building or two, a human figure.

Nuri mounted sporadic protests against her own, far more monotonous view. Aisha tried to soothe her without implying that the screams were unwarranted; no one should accept this kind of sensory deprivation, even when they had no choice but to endure it.

The suit recycled as much water as it could, and Aisha piped in liquid meal replacements from the tank at the back of the buggy. When she told the suit to make her faceplate opaque, it wasn't hard to sleep, at least when Nuri was in a cooperative mood. The buggy had plotted a smooth, safe path across territory that had been mapped down to the centimeter, and which probably hadn't changed in a billion years. It was not as if they were at risk of hitting an animal or going aquaplaning.

As they approached ninety degrees longitude, Aisha looked back at the Earth suspended above the horizon. Whatever the idiots had done, she doubted that they'd managed to render thc whole blue world uninhabitable. Maybe they'd lost the means to send a radio signal—let alone a rocket—to their nearest neighbor, but that had been true for most of human history. So long as the air was still breathable and crops could still grow, to return would be worth the struggle.

"WHY DOESN'T THE skyhook come lower?" Aisha had asked Yong. A gap of six kilometers above the base seemed excessively cautious.

"Because if it came much lower here," he'd explained, "it would strike the ground at other points in its orbit. There are six locations where one hook or the other comes swinging down; the orbit needs to be high enough that all of them have some clearance."

Six months later, when Aisha and Jingyi had been gestating the plan, they'd contemplated tweaking the skyhook's orbit into an ellipse that came in low over thc base while still avoiding the highlands of the farside. But the hub's ion engine would take months to execute the change—and in just two weeks the farside and nearside would rotate into each other's former locations.

So instead of making the orbit eccentric, they'd kept it circular but shrunk it as much as the safety margins hard-coded into the hub's navigation system allowed. At the point on the farside opposite Medii, the bottom of the cable would come within ten meters of the ground.

When the buggy reached its destination, Aisha looked up into the star-filled sky, trying not to cower into her seat at the thought of the thousand-kilometer-long whip tumbling toward her.

Nuri woke and started crying. "I know," Aisha commiserated. "Your mother stinks, and you're tired of staring at her chin."

She climbed out of the buggy and walked around for a few minutes, just to let her muscles know that their enforced idleness was over, then she unhooked the trailer and set to work.

She detached the roll cage from the buggy, undoing all the bolts and lifting off the tubular frame. Then she took the sheet of woven silica from the trailer and maneuvered it into the buggy, carefully positioning the loops of the connecting cords around the holes where the cage would re-attach.

She took twelve of the struts from the trailer and assembled them into a rectangular tower half a meter high, fitted two extra bars across the top, then had the buggy drive up onto it. If she hadn't practiced the whole thing a dozen times back at the base, she would have been panicking already, but by now this part seemed as unremarkable as automatic parallel parking.

Nuri redoubled her wails. "Shh, my darling, it's going to be fine," Aisha promised. "Just think of it as monster trucks meets Lego."

She attached a second tower to the first and made it a full meter tall. The buggy crossed over without complaint; it knew its own abilities well enough to assess her request and decide it was achievable. The integrity of the tower, though, was outside its domain of expertise; it was up to the builder to ensure that the structure was sound.

Level by level, she raised the scaffolding, and the buggy followed. When the tower was seven and a half meters high, she climbed down and stepped back to inspect it. Jingyi had seen her get this far in the rehearsals, but apparently that hadn't been enough to convince her to come along for the ride.

Aisha went to the trailer and fetched the magic box Jingyi had found in Yong's workshop. She woke it from its sleep and checked the status of the skyhook. It was due to make its next pass over the site in about twenty minutes.

If the lunar GPS was still accurate and both she and the skyhook were employing the same coordinates, the magnetic hook at the bottom of the cable would descend directly over the buggy, stop half a meter above the top of the roll cage, then ascend again. With the magnet switched off, the buggy wouldn't move a millimeter, but she had to be sure that the encounter really played out that way. She climbed the tower again and turned the dash cam on the buggy up toward the sky.

As the time approached, Aisha lay flat on the ground. The hook could not be coming down so low here as to strike the rock; the effect on the whole cable would have been unmissable. But if the real safety margin turned out to be less than advertised, she might be none the wiser until the proof smacked her in the head.

Nuri turned her face toward her, though they couldn't make eye contact. "You're my beautiful girl," Aisha declared soothingly. "You know you are."

She waited a few minutes, in case the timing was off, then rose to her feet; the suit did its best to help.

The tower remained standing, the buggy undisturbed. Aisha had the suit access the dash cam and play back the footage in slow motion.

Her faceplate went opaque, then filled with stars. "Skip forward until something changes," she said.

A circular silhouette moved toward her, growing, blocking out the stars. It slowed as it approached, as if she were looking down at a very large frisbee tossed into the air, approaching the top of its arc.

She froze the image when the silhouette began to retreat. From the apparent size, the height was close to what she'd expected, but the thing was off-center by about six meters. She'd have to take the tower apart and rebuild it in the right location.

She took her time, instead of rushing to try to get the job finished in one orbit; if the tower collapsed and flipped the buggy, that would be the end. She hummed to Nuri as she worked; singing would have been nicer, but it made her throat dry.

Five hours later she was done, strapped into the buggy, perched high above the rock. She told the hub to power up the hook's electromagnet and programmed the switch-off time to the millisecond. Now the whole process was out of her hands.

Nuri was asleep. "We're going to see your grandfather," Aisha whispered. "Very soon."

She sat watching the countdown projected in red onto her faceplate. At T minus two, she was ready to believe that nothing would happen, and she'd stay stranded forever. By T plus two, the feeling of half her Earth weight pressing her into the seat had already gone from a shock to a kind of ecstasy.

The landscape was falling away around her ever faster, but the buggy hadn't yet tipped by any perceptible angle; the hub was still an unimaginable distance above her.

Nuri woke, but she did not seem troubled. Perhaps she found the greater pressure against her mother's skin more comforting. Perhaps she'd always known that she needed more weight, more force, more friction if she was ever to thrive.

Aisha talked to her, explaining what was happening, then hummed for a while as she fed. Ten minutes into the upswing, the ground lay to her left, a sheer wall of gray rock like a distant cliff face. But down was still down in the buggy; the centrifugal force overwhelmed mere lunar gravity. And as the cliff slowly receded and tilted into an impossible roof above the dark slab of the magnet, she finally perceived the whole world of her prison as a mere disk in the sky again. Whatever happened now, at least she was free of it.

A few degrees past upside down, the magnet switched off and the buggy fell away into the void. Aisha grabbed at the seat, at the dashboard, but then the weightlessness lost its sense of danger, and once the magnet was out of sight, there was nothing to tell her she was moving.

Nuri grizzled half-heartedly, then went quiet and contemplated the change. "We're astronauts now!" Aisha told her. "How cool is that?"

7

THEY'D LEFT THE Moon traveling faster than most rockets, and the blue world grew more rapidly than it had diminished on the journey out. The buggy rotated slowly, taking hours to complete a turn, and each time the Earth rose over the dashboard, Aisha could gauge its increased width against the instruments below.

The suit saw no difference between the lunar surface and deep space; it kept scrubbing the air and keeping the temperature tolerable. The liquid meals had transcended their distinctive unpleasantness and blended into the general background of itchiness and filth. Aisha's stomach had bloated like a famine victim's, but she wasn't famished.

Two days after the hook had released them, the Earth filled almost half the view. Whatever errors she'd made in her calculations, at least she hadn't dispatched the buggy straight into the sun. She gazed down at Africa and took heart to see the cities lighting up as night fell.

She'd been afraid of cutting off the solar power prematurely, but as she followed the continent below into night, she started unfolding the silica sheet and drawing it around the buggy. Inside this strange tent, she could just make out the objects around her by the lights from the dashboard.

They needed to scrape through the air where it was dense enough to slow them down and keep them from escaping the Earth's pull, but not so dense that it would melt the improvised heat shield. She and Jingyi had pooled their knowledge and done their best with computer models, but the base had no local copies of any reference work that dealt with atmospheric density profiles—and even with perfect knowledge of the subject, they could never have accounted for the vagaries of mesospheric weather.

Aisha felt the first trace of heat through her gloves where she was touching the buggy's chassis. As she drew her hands in, the drag force itself came to her aid, pushing the seat firmly away from her so she strained against the belt like a passenger hanging upside down after a car crash. In front of her, the sheet began to glow a dull red, and radiant heat shone into her faceplate; the suit would be desperately sequestering thermal energy in its phase-change alloy, but that would only help for a while.

Nuri grew restless, but not distressed. Aisha was not in pain yet, but it felt like the times she'd lain too close to an electric radiator on a cold night, and the initially comforting warmth edged toward something damaging.

The force eased off; the glow faded. Aisha checked the data on the buggy's accelerometer. The whole spike had lasted four minutes: not as long as her calculations had predicted.

She fed the numbers into her model. The buggy had shed enough velocity for the Earth to capture it, but it would swing out to an apogee some hundred thousand kilometers away. And though it would come in close again, it would be moving more slowly than at the first encounter, so the drag would be less. The model showed an excruciating succession of incremental changes, taking sixty-three orbits in almost fifty days before they were low enough to parachute down.

To remain in Medii, hoping for rescue, had been untenable. Any gamble had seemed worthwhile—even if the narrow path home would be flanked by fiery death and slow starvation. But now she understood why Jingyi had made her own choice: what she'd feared most was watching her friend, and the child she'd delivered, perish beside her as the food ran out, the water dried up, the air went stale.

Aisha gingerly opened the tent to give the suit a chance to radiate some heat away. Maybe there were errors in the model still to unfold, in her favor. She felt Nuri shift and nuzzle against her, the broken skin of a rash on her daughter's cheek warm against her own skin.

Chance wouldn't save them. If she left this to chance, they would die.

She watched the planet slowly recede. Their speed and altitude the next time they entered the atmosphere were immutable now. Which left… what? The drag would depend on their shape, and the area they presented to the airflow. The sheet was much bigger than the buggy's frame, in preparation for its later role as parachute, but if she tried to trail it behind her at this point, the unprotected buggy would fry. If she'd brought half the struts from the tower, she might have stretched the sheet out into a larger shield, but they were all sitting uselessly back on the farside.

Nuri slept and woke, fed and shat, oblivious. Aisha could not have faced her dying as a three-year-old in a medical emergency, as a teenager in Medii's slide into disrepair, or, if the machines all proved resilient, as the loneliest centenarian in history.

But she could not face this either.

She closed her eyes and pictured the beautiful fabric she and Jingyi had toiled so long to weave, billowing out above her as the buggy drifted gently toward some green field or calm sea. Spread out by the force of the air alone. But when they grazed the unbreathably thin mesosphere… how much pressure would it take, *from within*, to puff the tent out like a balloon?

Not a lot.

Aisha opened her eyes and did some calculations. It was possible. She believed she could spare it and survive.

She forced herself to wait until the perigee was just an hour away, to keep the batteries charging as long as possible. Then she spread the sheet around the buggy and knotted the cords as tightly as she could around the hole at the back. It would not be a hermetic seal, but it only had to retain its contents for a few minutes.

She checked the time, then told the suit to start venting.

The tent remained limp and crumpled.

"Vent more," she commanded.

"That would put reserves below safe levels," the suit replied.

Aisha placed her gloves against the side of her helmet and turned it. The suit tried to dissuade her, but Jingyi had proved that it could be done. As the seal was breached, the air hissed out and the tent inflated, the fabric taut against the vacuum.

Aisha reversed the twist. She took a breath. It felt inadequate. She took a deeper one; she was dizzy, but she was not suffocating.

The silica balloon began to shudder, buffeted by the thin, fast air outside. Aisha felt the growing heat on her face, breaking through her light-headedness.

The drag pushed her forward: a little weaker than before, but much more than her dire calculations had predicted for the status quo. She watched the time pass, until she was weightless again. *Three minutes.*

She crunched the accelerometer data. Six more orbits, and

they would be spiraling down to Earth.

Nuri started babbling happily, making sounds Aisha had never heard before. Aisha let herself weep, for Gianni, for Jingyi, for whatever havoc she was yet to find below.

Then she composed herself and started singing softly to her daughter, waiting for the time they could look into each other's eyes again.

RESCUE PARTY

ALIETTE DE BODARD

KHÁNH GIAO HADN'T expected to be preserved.

She came home to Xarvi, a city she only saw in fits and snatches, to its dizzying towers built from the carcasses of reclaimed spaceships and failed orbitals and wide avenues offering an ever-expanding array of personalised environments, from quaint brushed metal bunkers of the Landfall era to riotous colours of the faraway Đại Việt court, with vague plans. She came home because she needed some planet time lest her bones break, because the mining station needed iridium to fuel its machines—and because her girlfriend An Di had asked her for some black sesame pastries and pandanus extract for their shared kitchen.

Nothing happened on the first night. But on the morning of her third day, Giao opened the door to her compartment, thinking of grabbing a noodle soup from Double Happiness Plaza with Cousin Linh and Linh's infant children—and found oily, inky blackness waiting for her. At its centre were vermillion letters: her own name and avatar ID, and the paintbrush and pine tree seal of the Ministry of Culture and Education.

The Repository.

A memory, sharp and merciless and inescapable, from a New Year's Eve two or three years ago: Cousin Tâm, smiling at her, the bots in her hair gleaming in the lights of the compartment—her face sharp and cutting, the magistrate's one before she ordered an execution. *Do you think yourself better than us, lil'sis, because you don't live here any more? The city doesn't let go. It'll weigh your usefulness against the value of your memories, and find you wanting in the end. It always does, with us.*

Always.

She didn't remember what she'd answered Tâm: she'd been drunk, trying not to count the missing places at the large banquet table, or the greyed-out holos on the ancestral altar—trying very hard to forget what it meant, to be Rồng in Xarvi, to be other. She must have laughed. She must have said something about not needing to worry about preservation or the Repository.

So drunk, so carefree. So wrong.

And of course, Tâm was gone now, preserved into the Repository like much of Giao's family and so many of her friends.

On the threshold of her own house, Giao opened her mouth to speak, to protest, and the darkness rose and leapt inside, leaving a taste on her palate like charred star anise—moments before it swept over her face and everything froze and rushed away from her.

* * *

GIAO WOKE UP in darkness, groggy and struggling to clear her mind. She sat up: the floor beneath her was hard and cold, and—

There was something in her mind, like a stray thought or something on the verge of recall—an always present shadow in her thoughts. She shook her head—rubbed her face with her hands, struggling to recall something of the past few moments, but nothing made it go away. She got up, shaking—and felt it skitter across her scalp, a touch like ten thousand burning bots. There was nothing in her hair. Or on her scalp. But when she moved again, it happened again, that same skitter—except it started in her scalp and moved deeper—and as it did so, a vast shadow dimmed her field of vision, a shroud thrown across the entire world.

She—she needed to think, to focus, but every time she tried to do so, the shadow would cross again, and her hands would come up to her head, hunting for the bots that didn't exist, until her nails burnt and ached, gummed with dry skin and broken, brittle hair.

Where—

What—

Focus.

Focus.

Something within her was moving, slow and vast and ponderous: a memory, long hoarded, of Grandma, her mother's mother, kneeling by her side, who'd been preserved so long ago. *Remember, child. If the Repository takes you,*

they'll trawl through your mind to satisfy their visitors.
Third Aunt had said something about muscle relaxants and
opioids, but Grandma had shaken her head. *That's irrelevant.*
Remember this, child. Reflexes are hard to eradicate
altogether, and muscle memory goes deep.

They will kill me, Giao had said.

Grandma's smile had had nothing of joy in it. *Life is*
sacred, she'd said. *You're preserved, not accused of crimes.*
They won't kill you.

It hadn't been reassuring, even at the time.

Giao brought her hands together. Slowly, carefully, she
stretched, bringing her arms up to the Heavens—and then
back down again, lowering them all the way to the earth.
Then she crouched, drawing an imaginary bow left and right
until her calves burnt and she felt her arms vibrate as though
she'd truly been loosing arrows into the darkness. And, with
each step—with each completed figure, the shadow receded—
until it was once more a faint tingle at the back of her hand,
and not the endless string of bots nibbling at her brain.

Bots.

Giao didn't have her bots any more, or rather…

They hung like dead weights, coiled in her topknot and
at the shoulder-seams of her jacket—their metal legs locked
together so tightly she'd have to break them to make them go.
Deactivated, or worse, killed off by the Repository, because
why would those preserved ever need personal comforts?

She ran her hand over them, feeling the familiar surfaces
under her fingers. Some of them had been purchases—the
newer, sleeker ones she'd got prior to leaving for Perse and

the mining station. Some of them had been gifts. *For the fifteenth return of the apricot flowers*, the one from Mom said. The one from Cousin Linh was rowdier, a wish for a sexual partner: *to the swallow looking for her oriole*. The one from Cousin Tâm was cool and businesslike, much like Tâm herself, with barely any hint of poetry. *Let this light scatter the blackness of ink and the darkness of space*. Letters so often read she knew them by touch, inscriptions fingered so much while walking in the corridors of the station or operating a drone in the depths of an asteroid, like prayers to the long disappeared.

And now the bots were gone too.

How dare the city deprive her of them?

"I'm sorry," Giao said aloud to the bots, but of course they couldn't hear her any more—and what would they have said, even if they could? They were the simpler and non-sentient kind, and had never been equipped to process emotional turmoil. Her voice was rough, her throat parched. What had they given her, when they'd grabbed her? The tingle was still there. She rubbed her hands against her cheeks, and her scalp. It didn't completely go away. It wasn't ever going to. And she hadn't bought herself much time with the khí công forms; just enough to walk a little further.

She'd never see Linh or her nieces again. An Di. She'd never see An Di again, never stand around in their small kitchen, feeling the heat of An Di's body against hers as they passed each other to fetch ingredients. She'd never feel again that thrill in her bones as An Di kissed her and Giao's entire heart seemed to beat in her lips. She'd never know what she and

An Di would have become: if there was a chance, any chance that what they had would turn into something deeper.

All of that was gone.

Giao was on the landing of a vast staircase. The letters of her name shone, briefly, on the floor as she moved—and so did the seal of the Ministry, and with it a brief flash of the halls on the other side: the continuous flow of visitors going through the Repository, being shown the history and culture of Asphodele—everything the city thought they needed or craved—Landfall, the first satellites, the first hydroponics farms, the first cities outside the domes. For a moment, as she set foot on the first stair leading down, Giao stared through what seemed like a vast window into another room. Sleek metal walls, displays in avatar space—and one particular visitor, a fifteen-year-old girl with pale skin and uncannily dark eyes, and small bots in her pupils: a child of Augmented parents. The room shimmered and became the custom display the Repository had chosen for her: a potted history of Asphodele that lingered longest on the troubled decade prior to Giao's birth, the labour rights riots, the sentience trials—and the inexorable way Asphodele had found its natural order again. A rebellious girl, then, one who needed to be reassured that straining against authority was futile.

"The Long Haul," the girl whispered, touching the last of the displays the Repository was showing her, the faraway planet orbiting its sun in the shadow of Asphodele's burnt-out wormhole gate. *Home,* Giao thought, as her chest tightened with a feeling halfway between grief and longing—except that Tuyết Ngọc was her ancestors' home rather than her own, wasn't it?

The stairs flickered as something rose from their depths, a vast and ponderous intelligence that sought everything it had, every person it had preserved that could best answer the question. The tingling in Giao's brain intensified—she dropped into the stance of the archer again, drawing the bow again and again—again and again as the shadow rose and the staircases hovered on the brink of disappearing altogether.

Following its independence from Asphodele, Snow Jade was mired in tensions between factions which devastated the planet's ecosystem and its economy. Faced with little choice, and with the wormhole gate destroyed in the independence war, some of the natives chose to leave on slow-moving ships in search of better opportunities: a journey named The Long Haul that would form the beginning of Asphodele's diaspora...

Slow-moving ships. Such a glib way of saying the mindships they'd painstakingly put together, their only hope at matching their colonisers' fast space-travel, had died one after the other on the journey, tearing apart half the ships as they did so, and slowing what should have been a fast journey down to a crawl. Every Rồng had ancestors among the dead of the Long Haul—and other dead, too, the rescue ship sent fifty years later that had simply gotten lost in deep space, too far away to be salvaged.

In Giao's mind, the Repository's systems raked claws of ice through her memories—the same ones that flickered, briefly, on the window that separated her from the girl: running with Tâm under the impossibly faraway tables of Mom and Third Aunt's restaurant, in that brief moment after naptime when the place was empty and everyone was in the kitchen— a New Year's Eve with Tâm and Linh helping Mom set up the kumquat tree while Third and Fourth Aunt counted new clothes, making sure every child would be able to change into them come New Year—everything so vivid and so present it brought her, shaking, to her knees.

The Long Haul ended when the remnants of the Rồng flotilla reached Asphodelian space, where they were hauled to safety by our cruisers. The corpses of their ships were towed to the scrap-heap to be recycled—the distinct architecture formed the basis of the Rồng Quarter, and one can still see the curvature of the ship's hulls in the distinctive window patterns.

Those Rồng who survived found a planet much changed from colonial times: a bright and shining metropolis with plenty of opportunities for hard-working migrants, to which they brought their customs...

"Whatever." The girl shook her head and moved on. The claws of ice opened, and Giao struggled to rise, to breathe— to compose herself. Below her, the huge shadow at the bottom of the stairs was fading away. Each landing was empty. She glanced around her but saw no one else where she was. Above her... Above her were only stars, a set of constellations she couldn't pinpoint, a pretty-looking, suitably arrayed set of constellations...

No.

She did know the stars, because she'd been staring at them

for so long—nothing much else to do on Perse when they were on energy-saving periods. They were the stars above Xarvi, except slightly distorted and out of place: the constellations above the city, as they had been at Landfall.

Such a surprise.

Breathe.

Giao was preserved in the Repository—trapped for all of eternity, her blood injected with the nanites that would keep her alive, that would make her part of the city's living memory. She had pitifully few choices: use the khí công forms to snatch some brief periods of awareness, or to simply sink back into a never-ending fugue of memories called up at need. She had no future, and soon her past would forever overwhelm her, sucking her dry until only a husk was left.

She should have been afraid, but all she had, rising through her, was a cold, cold anger that made her shake. How dare they. How dare they do this to her, to her family? She was twenty-four: preservation didn't happen so young, so soon.

Not to ethnic Asphodelians, of course, it didn't—not to the favoured scions, those who had been here for generations, who kept expecting people like Giao to give way for them. But it was a different story for migrants and their descendants; always would be—whether it be Rồng or any of the others.

Giao's family didn't have much, but they had researched. They had given what little money they had to ex-government officials and informants, desperately trying to understand the secrets of the Repository.

Downstairs was the heart of the Repository, the resting place of the artificial intelligence that controlled the entire building, and sent its tendrils out, to mark the people it chose to be preserved: those of interest to Asphodelian history who no longer meaningfully contributed to society. Downstairs was a chance at an appeal.

Never mind that no one, in living memory or otherwise, had ever left the Repository.

Ancestors, watch over me. And another, brief prayer to people who couldn't hear her: to Cousin Linh and her wife, who had to be sick with worry by now, waiting for the updated preservation lists to be published; to An Di, whom she couldn't contact, who was still new in her life and whom no one in the family would think of, when it came to news. *Hold on, little sisters. I'm coming back.*

THERE WAS NOTHING left in the world but these endless landings: empty flights of stairs, the metal resonating under Giao's feet, and each landing opening on a different room of the Repository, with a different flow of people staring at displays that kept flickering, Giao catching in a heartbeat a glimpse of all the different ways the Repository was filling them, all the different facets of history it was presenting to people.

The first few hundred years after Landfall were a difficult struggle against the planet's alien fauna and flora. But gradually, settlers were able to introduce food crops and to come to an uneasy truce with the local environment. A thousand years after Landfall, Xarvi, the capital city of Asphodele, rises proudly above the forests, though metal always remains at a premium...

Hard work and its value, justice and its inevitable arc, a society always seeking to be more progressive, more inclusive...

Various migration waves arrived at Asphodele, drawn by the promise of a new life. In today's cities, various quadrants pay homage to these: Galactic Town, Tinsel Streets, Dragon Island, the Rồng Quarter... And though the Việt mindships that travelled between the stars were always considered people, the sentience trials finally enshrined the rights of self-aware bots...

At some of the landings Giao would feel, again, the Repository rooting in her brain—but nothing quite as hard or as vivid as on the first one. Perhaps it just got easier, after a while.

Or perhaps that was just the way they kept everyone from escaping.

It was a fist of ice tightening around her entrails. And it was followed by another chilling thought that tightened her entire skin around bones that suddenly felt too sharp and too brittle.

Where *was* everyone?

There were hundreds, thousands of the preserved just in Giao's lifetime—her relatives, but also older people like Jean-Mae or Mer or all the teachers she'd had at university, and Ron's parents, and Meiluan's granduncles... And... Mom and Fourth Aunt and Cousin Tâm and every Rồng the Repository drew on for the history of the Long Haul. The Repository was, in so many ways, a mausoleum, a spider's web of a building that kept drawing more and more into its bowels. But here was this vast, echoing building with no trace of anyone. Faint, ghostly images on the landing that were dispelled as soon as Giao set foot on them. No *people*, not even their avatars.

Metal was always a problem: the scant mines in Asphodele didn't provide enough to sustain even the dome cities. Maker machines could split atoms into many things, but metal produced that way remained unstable and hazardous to human health... Hence the civic need to always carefully preserve metal, to respect the sharpening and recycling schedule for all blades, including kitchen knives...

At the second, or third landing after the history of metal, Giao saw the corridor.

It was lit with faint wisps of translucent radiance: not lamps, but iridescent butterflies that moved in slow, graceful patterns in the darkness. It couldn't have been signposted more clearly. But really, what did she have to lose?

She closed her eyes and breathed in—drawing the bow in her head again, against the raking of the Repository's assault on her memories. Then she followed the corridor, being very careful to count every pace she made, so that she'd be able to go back to the stairs if she needed to.

Two hundred and fifty-five paces in, the corridor flared into a large, huge room with rows and rows of...

She'd have said shelves, but they were coffins.

They looked like the sleeping berths Giao had seen on the Repository's reconstructions of the Long Haul—when she'd gone there as a child with her school cohort, back when she'd not understood yet what the building would come to mean to her. But there were too many of them, stacked on top of each other in endless rows and columns that ran all the way to the top of the vast, cavernous room, every berth labelled with an ID number and a place number. On the walls of the room was another number, one that kept blinking in and out of focus. *Ten thousand, three hundred and six.* It meant—it meant it wasn't the only room. Of course it wouldn't be.

Giao walked to the closest berth. It was white, opalescent plastic; but not transparent enough to let her see what was in it. Under her touch, it was faintly warm, pulsing like a beating heart; and bots crawled over it, a sleek metallic kind she'd never seen before. The newest ones, private to the highest ranks of government officials? But no, something about them felt… off.

There was an open berth further down the line, lit by butterflies. The message was clear and unsubtle: that one was meant for her. Giao didn't even want to get close to it.

"Hello, Cousin."

Tâm hadn't changed. Three years now—Giao may not have remembered which New Year's Eve they got drunk at, but she'd kept track of all the family's preservations with the same care as death anniversaries. She still wore her hair in that absurdly impeccable topknot, a hairstyle more suited to their great-grandparents and the Long Haul than to Asphodele, and wore the Asphodelian suit; a tailored jacket with dragons embroidered on the sleeves, and a set of matching trousers with leaping carps.

"Long time no see," Giao said. She moved away from the berth—and as she did so, someone somewhere queried the Repository, and the light flickered and a memory of folding dumplings in Grandma's kitchen overwhelmed her for a brief moment—before Tâm's hand on her shoulder brought her back to reality. "Breathe. In and out with each gesture. That's it. In, out."

When Tâm withdrew, Giao bit her lip not to grab her cousin's hands. "You've been here all this time?"

A grimace. Tâm pulled something from the air—a flat oblong box she opened, revealing the shimmering texture of Fisherman's Opals. She spread the paste on her neck, with the same poise she'd had when alive. "Some things help," she said.

"Like being intoxicated all the time on imaginary drugs you pull out of thin air?" The words were out before Giao could stop herself. "Sorry. The others—"

"The others don't come out any more." Tâm's voice was a sigh. She gestured, wordlessly, to the berths behind her. "It's easier to just sleep."

Drugged to the gills as well? "Big'sis..."

A shrug, from Tâm. "Truth? I wouldn't have come out either. I was... nudged." Another sigh. "It's always easier if it's someone you know welcoming you."

"Welcoming." Giao tried to keep her voice from shaking, and didn't succeed. "Like a party."

Tâm held out the box of Fisherman's Opals. "I can probably pull out tea and dumplings, if you insist. The dumplings will taste just like the ones Grandma used to make."

"Because it's inside the Repository. Because *Grandma* is inside the Repository. In one of those berths." Which one? She couldn't see the ID number, but of course there were so many berths, and so many other rooms.

Another shrug. "Mostly because we are here. That's

where the vividness of the memory is coming from, not from Grandma's recipe. Are you going to be choosy?"

"I want to get out," Giao said, chilled. Three years Tâm had been there. Unchanged, she'd thought, except everything had changed.

"You know as well as I do that no one ever has walked out."

"So you tried."

Tâm looked away from her. "I'm not going to stop you," she said in the same tone of voice she'd used when Giao had said she wanted to leave for the mining station. She thought it was futile—that Giao would always come back to her family, that the city would never forget her. That it would always be waiting.

"You wanted me to leave," Giao said.

"Of course. And I knew you wouldn't." Tâm sighed, her hands closing the clasp of the Fisherman's Opals box. "Home," she said in Rồng—a word that meant hearth and kitchen and everything within, everything loved and cherished. Their ancestors had once used it to mean Tuyết Ngọc, before its meaning irrevocably changed. Some in the family had left Asphodele altogether—a fraught and expensive undertaking, for Asphodele was so far away from other settled systems— but so many of them hadn't. Because it was their home and their family's home. Because, like Giao, they kept coming back to their hearths. "Home," Tâm said again. "Here." She laid a finger on Giao's chest, a sharp, almost painful touch that seemed to stab through the cloth of Giao's shirt. "Where you are. Where your family is."

Where the Repository was. Giao stifled a bitter laugh. "Where you always keep coming back." Perse... Perse wasn't that yet; perhaps it would have been one day, if her relationship with An Di had become more... But of course, that had been cut short.

"Where else?" Tâm said. "But yes. I wanted you to be safe."

"And I you." Giao closed her eyes for a brief moment, struggling to breathe.

"We don't always get what we want," Tâm said. "Except the Repository, of course. It always gets what it wants. What's best for us."

"And it wants me to get in there," Giao said, pointing to the empty berth.

Another shrug. "Actually, that's up to you. The Repository won't force you, and it'll always be there waiting for you."

Oh, so the Ministry had *standards*. Freedom of choice. Sanctity of life; the same lies they told in the classrooms, as if they meant something. She hadn't thought she could become even angrier. "You mean I'll beg to go into it when it becomes unbearable?"

Nothing from Tâm, not even a pitying look. "Are you even there?" Giao asked. "Physically?"

"Does it make a difference?" Tâm asked. "That's such a regressive attitude. Next you'll be telling me that shipminds have no rights because they can only project an avatar down into Asphodele." She moved, and when she did so, something shimmered, like the projection of an avatar into physical space.

Giao's heart missed a beat. "Are you... are you even my

cousin?" The Repository had all the memories, and it would be so easy, wouldn't it, to simulate something passingly familiar? Much easier than waking up Tâm—assuming the preserved could even be woken up, that these berths weren't simply final resting places. "Big'sis…"

Tâm spread more Fisherman's Opals on her neck, the way she always did when she was stressed—she'd have one hell of a headache and sense of thirst in the morning, except that who knew if any of that still applied, where they were. "I am your cousin." And, in smooth and almost too fast to follow Rồng, *"I'm the one who told you to stay away from Xarvi."* A sharp, amused smile. "Remember what Grandma said? The Repository hadn't quite worked out the hang of dialectal variations on Rồng. It always spoke that kind of weird version of the language that sounded off."

Giao didn't move. Because it was true, it had happened—and Tâm's voice and accent were uniquely hers, with nothing that sounded weird—but it proved nothing. "Perhaps it's learnt."

"I don't know how I can prove anything to you."

"Drop the avatar," Giao said.

"She won't want to do that," another voice said.

Its accent was pure Repository: something that Giao had never heard anywhere else—except in some of the newer dramas that came from Tuyết Ngọc, the hauntingly disturbing ones that were both familiar and utterly alien, coming from a culture that had diverged from them in the years after the departure of the Long Haul. Its owner, too, was dressed like nothing Giao had ever seen: a mix of Asphodelian fashions and traditional Rồng ones, from the embroidered jacket to the wide, flaring skirts. Behind them was a second person whose gender was equally indeterminate, wearing the jacket of an ao dai with the large panels of cloth falling over their hips, and slimmer trousers with kumquat flowers.

"I'm Trần Thị Hải San. You may call me San," the person said. "And this is Nguyễn Sinh Kim Ngân." San used feminine pronouns; Kim Ngân gender-neutral ones—except that they weren't the ones Giao would have expected. They were brutally simple, with none of the nuances of respect and age group she was used to.

"Pleased to meet you," Giao said, smiling to cover her confusion. Who were they, why were they injecting themselves in the conversation—how had they even known where to find her?

Kim Ngân smiled. "You're the only people here having an argument."

"We're not having an argument," Giao said between gritted teeth. "Now if you'll excuse us..." And, to Tâm, or the thing that pretended to be Tâm: "Drop the avatar. Now."

"She won't," San said in that same pleasant tone. "Because if she did, she'd have to show you what she's become."

That stopped her. She looked at Tâm, trying to breathe through a chest that suddenly felt constricted by a vice of metal. "Cousin—"

Tâm smiled. She turned to San, with a smile Giao knew all too well, a thing of teeth and vicious satisfaction, the same face she'd shown Giao on New Year's Eve. "You're wrong." And to Giao, "Here. You wanted to see."

It was... a shambling thing with shrivelled limbs and

blood-red muscles beneath translucent skin, a thing that shouldn't have been able to stand or walk without its bones snapping—except that its—no, her—her hollowed-out face with too-large eyes was Tâm's, almost unchanged. No, that wasn't quite true, because Giao suddenly saw that the whites of Tâm's eyes were the same colour as the berths.

"Preservation liquid," Tâm said, with a shrug she was trying to keep casual. "It does seep into everything." The avatar shimmered into existence again, hiding the horror beneath while Giao was still trying to conjure words.

"You—" Giao said.

Tâm's gaze was shrewd. "I wasn't strong enough. Are you truly going to reproach me for that?"

Three years in a berth. Three years being worn down to the bone, body shrivelled and faded, and all the while the mind being queried, repeatedly, for every scrap of memory the Repository could use to satisfy its visitors...

Giao swallowed back words—because she was angry, but not at Tâm. "I have to get out," she said, and it was almost pleading now. The words she wasn't saying hung in the air: before the Repository got her too. Before she became like Tâm, like her forever silent family members, those same worn-down bodies locked in opalescent berths. Before it was too late.

Tâm was staring at her. "Downstairs," she said, finally, and this time she didn't sound angry or distrustful, but merely tired. She gestured towards San and her companion Kim Ngân. "San knows the way. Remember what we gave you, lil'sis."

Kim Ngân was already waiting for Giao at the exit to the

room, their ao dai silhouetted against the door. San was still by her side.

"Wait—" Giao said. "Who are they?"

But Tâm was already turning away. "They're like you," she said. "They want to get out."

Giao knew a dismissal when she saw one. But, nevertheless… "Big'sis, please." And, before Tâm could move away, she hugged her hard—feeling every brittle bone and atrophied limb, every exposed muscle and hollow where the skin had melted away. "Thank you."

An amused snort. "Thank me when you're outside. If you ever are."

"YOU HAVEN'T TOLD me who you are," Giao said to San.

They were going down landing after landing. It was harder than it had been, closer to the top. The Repository didn't want her to get down—not further than where her berth was. Every landing brought her to her knees, squeezing the breath from her lungs and replacing it with an unending parade of past memories. San and Kim Ngân were the ones who gently guided her out, reminding her of where she was—of who she was, of how to breathe so she wouldn't choke on her own thoughts.

Sometimes, after she'd lost count of the gruelling descent— after an ageing government official asked about integration policies, and the Repository brought up lion and unicorn dances in the wide tree-lined streets, and kumquat trees and the lemongrass chicken they used to have when Mom worked late nights—that Giao finally got her nerve or lost her patience, or both.

"Comrades," San said, with a laugh.

"Seriously." Giao glared at Kim Ngân, who had the grace to look embarrassed.

"We're the rescue party," they said.

"I don't understand," Giao said.

When Kim Ngân spoke again, it was in the voice Giao had heard earlier that sounded almost like the Repository. "We set out fifty years after the Long Haul, when the flotilla's distress calls finally reached Tuyết Ngọc." An expansive shrug. "Radio waves are slow. There was a lot of debate in Parliament. Your ancestors weren't popular, making that decision to leave us and seek their fortune with our old colonisers, but we could understand their desperation. Finally, it was agreed to send a single mindship to see who or what could be salvaged. One that worked, this time. It took us fifty years, but we finally understood how the Đại Việt Empire made theirs work, and we used that as the blueprint for our own ships."

"The rescue ship," Giao said slowly. "You're the rescue ship. But you never made it here. You—" It was like a gaping hole opening, even worse than Tâm. Because at least the horror beneath Tâm's face had been expected. Dreaded, but in the way death was: utterly predictable and mapped. "Why are you in the Repository? Why have we never heard about you?"

"Oh, younger sister…" Kim Ngân shook their head. "Isn't it obvious? History is written by the winners, and the Repository has been winning at that game for a long, long

time. Our ship landed and was taken apart for scrap metal—
and every crew member taken for the Repository. We had no
use to Asphodele, and so much of value to teach you about
the culture of Tuyết Ngọc." Their voice was full of irony.

"You—you've been in the Repository ever since?" That
wasn't possible.

Kim Ngân bowed ironically. "As we breathe."

Fifty years after the Long Haul. A century. Three or four
generations of Rồng. Giao opened her mouth, shut it, because
she couldn't think of any words to make it better. "I'm sorry."

"Don't be," San said.

"A little." Kim Ngân's smile was wide, mocking. "The
Repository is the sum of everything you consider history. Of
all the lies you tell yourself."

The lies they told themselves? As if she'd been the one to
decide her family would be preserved—to single them out in
life and afterwards. "Because Tuyết Ngọc is better?"

"Of course not," Kim Ngân said. "But we don't eat our
own and call it justice… not any more."

"Younger sib." San laid a hand on their arm. "Of course
we do. We just do it in different ways." It sounded like an
old, old argument, rehashed until it lost its bite and heat.
"This is not the time."

Kim Ngân subsided, but they looked unhappy.

"Then tell me something," Giao said.

"As you wish."

"You could have walked downstairs yourself. To appeal."

"Ah." Kim Ngân's smile was bright. "I think you'll find
that… appeals"—she managed to make the word sound

utterly fictional—"are reserved for Asphodelian citizens. Certainly not for aliens from a former colony who've turned up in a suspect but highly desirable vessel."

"So you need someone to appeal for you."

Kim Ngân nodded.

"I can't be the first person you've walked with downstairs."

"A lot of them don't understand us," San said. "Or don't trust us. Or prefer the berths, anyway." A snort. "But no, you're not the first. A lot of the Rồng are sympathetic, and some of the other non-Asphodelian ethnicities."

"And you've never got out."

"No. But you already know that no one has, don't you?" Kim Ngân's voice was hard, with nothing of irony in it.

"And if I asked you to drop the avatars..."

A shrug from San. "You'd see much the same thing. We've never gone into the berths. We're not mined much. Not many people want to know about Tuyết Ngọc, other than us being desperately poor and fighting each other to extermination." Another snort. "No one seems to ever ask *why* we're poor, or why our planet was stripped of all its natural resources and its cultures set at each other's throats to make us easier to control. Asphodelians, still hiding from the truth."

"What's downstairs?"

San's face was hard. "I don't know. We're never allowed inside. And it seems to be different for every person. What I can tell you is that everything you can think of has already been tried. And everything your family has thought of, most particularly."

Because her family was nothing more than a weapon the

Repository had turned against her. "You think I'm going to be scared?"

Kim Ngân cocked their head. "No," they said at last. "You don't scare easily, do you?"

Giao would have laughed, but she suspected if she did, she'd never stop. She'd just sit there on the landing and let the Repository root through her brain. A wave of raking hit her—being sixteen at university, the overt mockeries of childhood becoming polite nods and unexpectedly sharp words in conversations.

Rồng and other minorities are faced with disadvantages, but they have transcended them. Where the first generations of Rồng did menial work, their descendants turn away from the restaurants and gruelling food industry jobs, and complete university courses for bot-makers, architects, or anything to do with the making and maintenance of wormholes.

Demons take them. Of course they didn't want to run restaurants any more. Mom and Third Aunt had never taken a holiday in their life, and even the best doctors couldn't straighten out their spines or the repetitive wrist strains from directing the bots in the kitchen.

"Younger sister. Breathe. You've got this. Breathe." They spoke to her but didn't touch her. They didn't seem to be having spasms of their own either: it made sense that there would be few queries about Tuyết Ngọc, fifty years after the Long Haul, and fewer still about a ship that had vanished, but still...

Still.

"Let's go," Giao said. Get this over with, whatever it

turned out to be.

SHE'D EXPECTED DOWNSTAIRS to be... oh, she didn't know what. Some kind of lair, or a huge room filled with machines of all kind. But at the bottom of the last staircase—below a landing whose invisible window opened on the atrium of the Repository, where visitors merely glanced at the artifacts on display before moving on—was only a set of double doors, each engraved with the Double Happiness symbol.

Giao looked at them, hard. They had to be avatar space rather than the physical one: a display put on for her sake. As if to confirm her suspicions, the letters of her name flickered on the door—not in the Asphodelian script, but in old-fashioned Rồng, the kind that master calligraphers wrote on New Year's Banners.

Kim Ngân and San were both waiting for her at the bottom of the stairs. Great. Of course they weren't going to open the door either.

"You can't go in," she said.

"Citizens only." Kim Ngân's voice was hard.

"Then tell me—"

"Yes?"

"Your ship. What were they called?"

A pause. Something twisting on Kim Ngân's face, endless grief like a punch to the gut. The ship was dead. A mind taken apart and recycled for scrap parts. "Her name was *The Serpent in the Lychee Garden*."

An allusion to a tale of Old Earth—a long, long lost piece of history about a woman accused of the murder of an emperor. "I see," Giao said. And then, staring at them, at the perfect clothes, at the way the Repository didn't even seem to affect them. "You're dead, aren't you?"

Kim Ngân detached themself from the stairs and walked closer to her. Their outline flickered: Giao strained to catch a glimpse of what lay beneath but couldn't. "Not dead," they said. "But not corporeal any more, no. We're not Asphodelians. They needed to be sure that they were holding us securely."

So they couldn't get out, not without a whole new set of obstacles. "Why the rigmarole then?"

A sigh from San. "You don't understand. We really are the rescue party. We want *you* to get out. That was our mission, and we've got nothing left but to see it to an end. But most people won't believe that."

"I could—"

"Appeal on our behalf?" Kim Ngân's face was carefully frozen. "You can try."

"Other people have," Giao said flatly—because she didn't know what to make of them any more. Because she didn't know who or what she could trust any more—the Repository not only presenting history in a biased fashion but erasing it wholesale; Tâm choosing to give up and drug herself; two strangers appearing out of nowhere like a miracle she hadn't prayed to the ancestors for.

A shrug from San. "Not many."

But some, and it hadn't worked. "You don't need to believe us," Kim Ngân said. They held out their hands, their expression carefully controlled—Giao knew it all too well, seconds before breaking into tears. "Just get in there and make your appeal. That's all that matters." A century in the Repository, fighting to stay whole, and all she could think of was for ways to disprove their story?

"Thank you," Giao said, closing her hands over Kim Ngân's, and feeling only emptiness in her fingers.

"Get inside."

Giao grabbed both handles and pushed. The doors swung open noiselessly.

Inside was only darkness, and the letters of her name lighting up one by one, forming a path to the centre of the room, where something waited—a column of polished metal like the maker machines on Perse.

She walked there, because there didn't seem to be anything else to do. The moment she stepped into the room, something within her flickered and died, as if a switch had been thrown, and a dreadful, unnatural silence spread. No, not dreadful: she hadn't realised how omnipresent the Repository's tendrils in her mind had been, until now.

She walked towards the pillar, in that silence that she struggled to encompass. Every step on the polished metal floor seemed too loud, like phaser shots—with every one, she'd look up, expecting the militia to burst in, or paralysing bots to hold her down. But nothing happened.

She reached the pillar. It was polished, and really metal: she'd half expected the plastic of the berths, but it was grey, with some oily reflections as if someone had forgotten machine oil. She turned, then, saw Kim Ngân and San waiting for her beyond the open doors of the room.

She laid both hands on the command slot—for a brief moment she was back on Perse, in the mining station, with An Di's hands on her shoulders—An Di's perfume of hibiscus flowers and lime wafting into Giao's nostrils, and An Di's voice telling her not to be so serious—and then it passed, and she was standing there in the heart of the Repository, blinking back tears.

She hadn't broken before. She wasn't about to start now.

"My name is Lê Thị Khánh Giao," she said. "ID number 3985332190554. I wish to appeal against my preservation, on my behalf and on behalf of the crew of *The Serpent in the Lychee Garden*, Trân Thị Hải San and Nguyễn Sinh Kim Ngân."

A silence. The room around her flickered—and for a moment became something else, something that was all metallic, inhuman sheen. "*The Serpent in the Lychee Garden*. Trần Thị Hải San. Nguyễn Sinh Kim Ngân. These names do not exist in the records." The voice was high-pitched and expressionless. It spoke Asphodelian, but with the slow laboriousness of someone who'd not finished learning it. And something about it was hauntingly familiar, though Giao couldn't put her finger on why. "I cannot record an appeal on their behalf."

Didn't exist. Because they'd been purged. Because they'd been absorbed. Because Asphodele had erased that rescue ship, pretended it had been lost. "They're at the doors," Giao said, biting back the more angry words. "Hải San and Kim Ngân. Tell them to come in, and you'll see."

"They're not citizens," the Repository said. "Only citizens

are allowed here, and only for the duration of their appeal."

"But they're part of the Repository," Giao said.

A flicker, on the pillar. "They are a special case."

"I thought everyone was equal, before the law of preservation? That everyone had the right to ask for their experience to be weighed again?" Giao couldn't help it: the words weren't even hers, they were the ones her family had crafted and hoarded. The ones that wouldn't help, San had said.

A pause. The Repository seemed to be chewing on something.

"What harm do you think they can cause, being here? You control everything." The bots and the berths and the environment, and even the thoughts of every preserved person. "You don't have to take their appeal, but they could come here. Please." She'd slipped into Rồng with the last sentence, and hadn't realised it—painstakingly, she forced herself to think in Asphodelian. "Please."

The words wouldn't work, not for getting out. But it was a very different thing, what she was asking the Repository for.

"You didn't kill them," Giao said, and knew, suddenly, why they had not. Sanctity of life. Freedom of choice. Like the berths, a twisted kindness that stretched the knife's kiss over endless years, endless centuries. "They still have value to you. Please let them in."

At last the Repository said, "They may come in. But I cannot log an appeal on their behalf, or on that of a mind that doesn't exist any more." Darkness fell across the room as it continued to speak. "ID number 3985332190554, Lê Thị Khánh Giao," the Repository said. "Your appeal is duly logged. Please present your defence."

She—

She didn't know what she'd say. In her heart, she'd always believed the injustice of it would be so flagrant, that she would just need to make them see—and then old memories of Tâm's schooling took over. "I'm twenty-four," she said. "I work in the Perse mining station to provide the metal for Asphodele. I would like to allege undue discrimination against me and my family."

A pause. On the metal pillar, her family tree appeared, with the various people preserved greyed out. A few stragglers: Cousin Linh and her children, Cousin Bảo and his electro-engineering company, Fourth Aunt, still serving in the army well past her age of retirement. The floor under Giao's feet flickered.

At last the Repository said, "I see no undue discrimination. The higher frequency of preservation is due to your family's interest to Asphodelian history."

Four generations. They'd been there four generations, and they'd always be curios in Asphodele. A study in how people adapted and evolved. A population to be studied rather than be allowed to live. The more polite, deadlier version of the mockery she'd received as a child.

"As to your age..." A pause, there, while some lights she couldn't tell flickered, and she realised what the laboriousness was: it was a Rồng accent, except subtly wrong, the same way San and Kim Ngân's were.

Why would they—

"That's pointless," Kim Ngân said. She and San had come in,

were now standing in front of the metal pillar. San was standing still, but Kim Ngân was looking at everything, darkly fascinated.

"Then tell me what to say!" Giao screamed at them.

"I can't," San's voice was toneless. "You forget: no one has come out."

Meanwhile Kim Ngân reached out, slowly, carefully—their hand brushed the pillar for a brief moment, and in that moment, it changed colours to the deep yellow of gold.

"Kim Ngân." The Repository's voice changed. It spoke Rồng, and its voice had the exact same accent as theirs. "Why—"

The room flickered; and then the metal pillar was back, and the moment gone. "Your age, and the usefulness of your work, is being re-evaluated against the value of your experience."

"Wait," Giao said. "Wait. You know them."

San grabbed her arm. Or tried to: her hand went right through Giao's. "Don't anger it," she said. "That's never ended well."

On the metal pillar, a slow pattern of blinking lights was slowly coalescing together, symbols that meant nothing to Giao but had to somehow represent the sum of her life.

The Repository had paused, when Kim Ngân had touched it. "San," Giao said. "Please. Can you—" She tried to grab San's hand, but San wasn't moving. San was desperately trying to think of words that would save Giao, but San and Tâm had been right: everything had been tried. Giao was still clinging to the hope of an appeal, to the notion that things were fair, when she'd known the truth all along: the decision had been made already. Eating its own, Kim Ngân had said, and they had been harsh, but not incorrect. "Put your hand on it."

"I already told you. Neither Kim Ngân nor I can appeal.

You're wasting your time."

The lights were climbing on the pillar. When they were done—and it couldn't be much to weigh, couldn't it? Twenty-four years, a childhood on Asphodele, five years on Perse in the mines. Giao considered, dispassionately, the entirety of her existence, and knew it was nothing. To her, everything; but to the Repository, to the thing that Asphodele had made of itself, not more than a moment's pause. "You said I had to trust you. Just do it. Please."

San's hand—ghostly, flickering, only a visual avatar—reached, touched the pillar. The room flickered, then, showed that same oily sheen on metal walls Giao had seen before. Kim Ngân moved, put their own hand on top of San—and left it there, unmoving.

"San?" The Repository asked in that same voice. The flickers were getting stronger and stronger now, and it wasn't just the room: Kim Ngân and San, too, were flickering. Somewhere in a room of the Repository, in the berths where they were locked, bots would be crawling to cut the connection to their avatars. Just a matter of time; but Giao didn't need much of it any more.

Our ship landed and was taken apart for scrap metal—and every crew member taken for the Repository.

The sentience trials.

Sanctity of life.

They wouldn't have dared to kill a mindship, but they could repurpose it. They could replace an aging AI with a newer, better one—taking it apart for scraps just as they had the ships.

Meaningful contribution.

Of course.

Giao said in Rồng, "*The Serpent in the Lychee Garden.* That was your name, wasn't it?"

The room vanished. Instead of the metal pillar was a contraption of thorns and protruding arms, metal twisted and pulled together until it hardly seemed to be able to hold together any more—and in the centre of it was a glistening mass of flesh and electronics, with tendrils extended along every arm, and bots crawling everywhere on stray cables and spikes, in the light of stars—and then it flickered again, and she was staring at the curved expanse of a hull, moments before the view panned out and she saw the vast sleekness of a ship, fragile fins and stabilisers and pitted, sheening metal whose opalescence took Giao's breath away.

"Child," *The Serpent in the Lychee Garden* said in Rồng. And then the image of the ship twisted away, and it said again, in the polished metal darkness of the room where Giao had entered, "Your contribution has been weighed, and does not offset the value of your experience."

"She's theirs," Kim Ngân said, and they were weeping, with not a trace of sarcasm or irony on their face. "You can't change that, younger sister."

And they were right, weren't they? Tâm was right. It was pointless. The die was rigged. They could learn all they wanted about the Repository and how it worked, could remember all the movements to defeat its obliviousness, but in the end all they bought themselves was a few moments of agony, a last struggle before they gave way to the inevitable.

"You may return to the berths, or wander the halls," the

Repository said. "This place will be closed to you henceforth, and your rights of appeal have been exhausted."

She'd tried to run away from Asphodele, and Asphodele had taken her the way it was always going to; the way it would take Cousin Linh and her children, and the children of their children, until the Long Haul was a faint memory—and even then something in the Repository would remember that they had come here impoverished and shipwrecked, and forever *alien*—

Something, long held taut, finally snapped in her: the same cold anger within her that had steadily risen as she was descending the stairs the first time, the same as when Tâm had said that the choice to enter the berths was hers.

How dare they?

They thought they held all the cards; that they owned her body; that there was no right to appeal—because there had never been one, because everything had been decided by society long before her life reached twenty-four.

But they scraped and recycled, and never gave a thought to what lay beneath the surface of what they had taken.

We're still the rescue party.

And what was true for San and Kim Ngân was true for the ship too.

Giao drew herself up to her full height and laid her hand against the pillar, the same way San and Kim Ngân had, feeling its coldness seize her. "Your right to appeal—" the Repository started, but before she could be thrown out of the room, Giao said, "My name is Lê Thị Khánh Giao, daughter of Nguyễn Thị Bảo Lễ, granddaughter of Trần Thị

Mỹ Nhi"—the personal names of her ancestors burnt on her tongue—one didn't name ascendants, and even less the dead or the preserved—"great-granddaughter of Trần Thị Ngọc Lan, who crossed the Long Haul on *The Dragon Away from the Clouds*"—and on and on, reciting her full genealogy until she'd named her sixteen great-grandparents—"and great-granddaughter of Nguyễn Hữu Khả Ái, who died with *The Willow as Quiet as Rice*. You came here to rescue us."

The floor under her shook—except it wasn't an earthquake but the frantic, panicked heartbeat of someone living. The metal pillar was gone, and it was only her, standing in the chamber that was the ship's heart, watching the stars.

"Child?" the Repository asked, and it was the ship's voice again, trembling and unsteady and as fragile as spun glass.

"Please, Grandmother," Giao said to the ship. "Please help us go home."

GIAO STOOD ON the bridge of the ship, watching Asphodele recede in the distance. In the centre of Xarvi was the polished dome of the Repository, the building's connections to the city shining faintly in Giao's choice of overlay.

She ran her hands through her hair, half expecting to feel dead bots again, surprised when they turned out to be alive. Her thoughts were empty, silent, in a way that felt almost wrong.

"You look thoughtful," Kim Ngân said, slipping into the seat next to her. San brought, wordlessly, drinks that she laid on the table. "Unhappy to be free?"

They both looked the worse for wear: pale and skeleton-thin, with the marks of bots' needles on their arms and neck—San wore a high-collar necklace to cover the worst of them, but there was no regrowing the shorn hair or hiding the pearlescent colour their eye-whites had turned, after a century in the berths. Kim Ngân wore an avatar, and San long sleeves and jewelry—as if anything could hide that they were a century or more out of sync, coming back to a planet that had all but forgotten them.

Giao stared at the Repository—at the shape of the ship she couldn't see, the Mind that was now irrevocably part of the canker at the heart of the city. She had let them go, but they'd never had more than that single moment of clarity from her. The Repository still held Mom and Tâm and the rest of Giao's family—still continued to mark the Rồng for preservation.

She felt, again, Tâm's fingers on her chest, sharp and painful, saw again the ruin that her cousin had become. *Home. Where you are. Where your family is.*

Home. Asphodele. A place they'd worked so hard to make their own.

"Home is the place that welcomes you," Giao said aloud. She clenched her fingers on the edge of the drink, thought of Tâm, and of Linh and her children, and all the others that still lived in the shadow of the Repository's biased choices. She thought of An Di, and all that might have happened—would An Di even understand or approve of Giao's choices?

"You should find another such place," San said, softly, and stopped when Kim Ngân laid a hand on her arm: a silent warning.

It was their home as much as anyone else's, but all it thought of was value, and it had found too little in them. She traced the contour of the Repository on the screen, imagined the ship lifting itself free of its cage of rooms and staircases, in the wreck of empty displays and darkened windows—of the preserved finally stumbling out of the ruins of the building, freed from berths that would never be used again.

I'll come back, Giao said, to the silently receding city that was her home. *I'll come back, and everything will change.*

DEVIL IN THE DUST
LINDA NAGATA

I'M LANCE ENGINEER Ellie Asano, twenty-nine years old. Earth years. We don't count in Martian years. We're not here to stay. Not forever, though our five-year term of service started to feel like forever when we were six months in.

I dropped in during the early days—threat-level searing red—the height of the festivities. That first year, casualties had been high, but we learned. We adapted faster than the RaVNs. And we knocked them back hard.

By the time Pold joined us, popular talk said the war was over. Martian Command had cooled the threat-rating to a barely simmering yellow: *maintain situational awareness; hostilities unlikely*. A logical inference.

Human activity served as a magnet for RaVNs; their territory had always tracked and encompassed ours. Yet, my engineering team had not engaged in a firefight in over a year, and nine months had passed since the last time any team had encountered a RaVN swarm. So maybe the RaVNs *had* been defeated.

Maybe they'd been wiped out.

I wanted to believe that, but I'd seen too much. No one on our rover was ready to accept that the RaVNs were done with us—especially not Pold.

THERE WERE FOUR of us in the rover: I, Lance Engineer Kai Tussy, Sergeant Engineer Jen Haden, and Pold—aka Captain Leopold Binn, Resistance Army—technically a civilian, but a war hero, a veteran of the conflict on Earth, retired now and pulling social points as an embedded journalist, riding with us to observe the day-to-day operations of a well-construction team.

He'd been with us three days and I didn't like him.

No, that's not true.

I didn't *want* to like him.

My team had only two months to go before our scheduled return to real life on Earth and like all short-timers, we were jumpy. Hyper-wary, hyper-alert, flinching at any hint of movement in the dust, absolutely determined not to die in that windblown hell. Too many ghosts there already, howling past the pressure seals.

As we'd rolled out of mobile base 12, Haden and Kai in the cab, me and Pold together in the mess, I'd warned him, "We are going to do all we can to avoid excitement on this trip. It would be too tragic to die now, at the end of the struggle."

His response had shocked me. "No one should have died here." Dark cynicism freighted his low voice as he went on, "Your presence here is propaganda. It always has been."

When you've been in the dust for years, seen so many good people die, it's hard to hear someone declare it all for nothing—especially when that judgment comes from someone you wanted to respect. I argued with Pold, it got heated between us, but no way was he going to change his mind. Despite his war experience—hell, because of it—he did not believe in the core mission.

"The duty statement is bullshit," he insisted. "You don't need to be here. You don't need to die here. No one does. We could have beaten the RaVNs faster with swarms of our own, but the Coalition doesn't want to win that way. That strategy doesn't support the philosophy of '*Human intelligence only*.' So we send our best to role-play heroes, a human sacrifice to enforce the Coalition's founding statement—"

"That collectively we have what it takes to beat machine minds," I recited. "And we do."

"Sure. You've shown that here. You're close to beating the RaVNs. But at what cost?"

He didn't mean material resources. The true cost was human lives, blood spilled onto the dust and boiling away in the deadly low-pressure. But I didn't want to concede the point, so I executed a churlish shift in tactics.

"How many social points have you had deducted for opinions like that?" I asked him.

A sly grin—the first sign of humor I'd seen from him. "*Thousands*," he had assured me. "And I can't afford to lose anymore, so don't set me off again, okay?"

I'd hissed my non-agreement. But he *was* a war hero.

Maybe he deserved the slack. I'd shrugged and assured him, "I'll do what I can."

Now we were together in the cab. The team had been driving in shifts through the night, with the goal of reaching the next equipment drop by 0800 Local. Haden and Kai were asleep in the bunks. I had the stick, with Pold in the copilot seat.

He didn't have the training to drive, but he had years of experience hunting RaVNs, so Haden had put him to work on day one. His job was to watch the terrain, the map, and our positions on both. From the beginning, he'd demonstrated a preternatural ability to stay alert. His attention didn't waver, and he didn't call false alarms.

In the predawn twilight I needed my NVV—night-vision visor—to negotiate the variable canyon-country terrain. The rover rolled on tall shape-shifting wheels, its chassis segmented into three parts by flexible joints that helped it get over the rough spots. The cab was all windows. We could get away with that because the artificial magnetosphere kept out the worst of the radiation. The growing atmosphere helped too—at our location, roughly the equivalent of a 15-kilometer elevation on Earth.

The view was nice to have in the daytime, but spooky in the dark. Too easy to imagine cold, silent, undetectable camera eyes watching us out of the night.

I drove slowly, studying every aspect of the approaching terrain, mentally plotting a best route. We were in a wide, shallow canyon. Our route kept us close to the northern wall, where fossilized landslides spilled onto the ancient terrain, forming steep ridges that climbed like ramps to meet the cracked cliff face. I'd been dodging rocks for an hour, so when we finally reached a thirty-meter stretch of clean, wind-scrubbed hardpan, I used the respite to reach for my water bottle.

Just as I did, Pold spoke. Two soft syllables: "D-D."

I sucked in a sharp breath. DD. Dust devil—but not the towering plumes that wandered the sun-warmed surface of the planet. Among the combat engineering teams, DD meant small-scale ambiguous motion—a devil in the dust—usually glimpsed in the periphery of your vision, leaving you praying it was a swirl of grit raised by the wind, or the contorted shadow of an aerial survey drone passing unexpectedly overhead.

We were so far from Earth, prayers like that were rarely heard, even more rarely answered.

Abandoning the water bottle, I stomped the brake, hit the alarm to waken Haden and Kai, and then pulled and turned the knob to open the roof hatch. Distantly, the *ka-chunk* of a lock releasing, clank of steel and whirr of an electric motor as a Wafer drone unfolded long fabric wings sufficient to support the weight of an array of cameras in the thin atmosphere, but nothing more.

A permitted aspect of narrow AI would keep the Wafer's wings properly trimmed for current atmospheric conditions, but the drone's default flight pattern followed a fixed protocol: a quick circle of the rover before quartering the terrain farther out, the guidance system just flexible enough to keep the Wafer away from high ridges and canyon walls.

With the Wafer up, I undertook my own survey, twisting in my seat, left to right, visually scanning a landscape made bright—almost too bright—by my NVV. Blame that on the gray edge of dawn, filtering through the Martian atmosphere.

I didn't see any RaVNs, but that only meant we weren't being swarmed—yet.

"What have you got?" I asked Pold, my voice hoarse with the ever-present dust.

Movement between us: Sergeant-Engineer Haden filling the narrow aisle. She must have benefitted from a momentary time warp and heard the alarm before I sent it, because she appeared wide awake, her legs already sheathed in the lower half of her armored exosuit, her body twisting as she worked to get her arms inside. "Talk," she ordered.

"Initial sighting, four o'clock," Pold reported, not looking at her. Looking back instead, behind the rover, using his NVV. "Single spider. Behind us now."

"*Shit*," Haden whispered, pressing the front seam of her suit to seal it. "No EM or motion signatures?" she asked me.

"Silent and still," I reported as I cycled through feeds from the rover's external cameras. "And no alerts from the Wafer."

Lack of a signal did not mean much. Solitary RaVNs were good at evading detection.

Haden leaned in, console lights revealing her sharp, bony features, the tension in her eyes. "Find it for me, Ellie."

I wanted to, but nothing showed on my feeds, not in any wavelength. Not yet.

"You get many strays on these circuits?" Pold asked.

"Strays only happen post-combat," Haden answered.

"And there's been no combat in this region for ten months. This one's a scout—and that means we've got—"

"A nest around here somewhere," Pold finished for her.

"Right. Move, both of you. Get your suits on."

I dropped my NVV into a bin on the console and released my harness. Pold was already up, squeezing past Haden when I started to rise. That's when I saw it on-screen, just for a moment, before the feed shifted to a different camera.

I tapped the screen, shifting back to the prior feed, and there it was: a mechanical daddy-long-legs, waist high, a central sphere the size of a small tangerine suspended between the inverted V's of six multi-jointed legs, so thin they were hard to see in the gray light. "Ah, fuck. Spider confirmed."

"*Move!*" Haden barked.

I moved, bailing out over the back of the seat while she took over my position. "Kai, get your ass up here."

"Right here, ma'am," he answered in his low, gravelly voice.

He wasn't kidding. I almost collided with him as I exited the cab. A big man, at least twenty centimeters taller than me, he looked even bigger fully suited with his helmet sealed, ready to play. His suit's internal struts hissed as he pushed past me. He carried Haden's helmet, issuing his own order— "Seal up, boss"—while she called in the sighting to base.

I left them to it and darted into the mess—a misnomer if there ever was one. The place was spotless and unobstructed, table and counters folded out of the way after every meal. Five years in the dust will teach you to keep the floor clear, the rover neat. Everything in its place and nothing blocking access to the lockers.

Pold had his locker's accordion door open. He stripped off his sweater and his thermal pants, every motion smooth, practiced, efficient, peeling down to the silky red-brown fabric of his form-fitting underskin.

We all wore the skins all the time. They monitored our physiological status and tracked our movements, sharing the data with our suits—another instance of a permitted learning system.

Artificial Intelligence—even narrow AI—magnified the power of the individual controlling it. AI had allowed the global aristocracy to launch the Point One Insurrection. A billion people culled that first year, twice that lost after the RaVNs went feral.

Since then, the People's Coalition had banned AI except by permit, in narrow applications.

Pold asked, "You found my RaVN?"

I popped my own locker door. "Yeah. Spider surveyor. Probably fresh spawn and stupid or it wouldn't have come so close—but it needed to figure us out."

"Next time it'll know us by the vibration of the wheels."

"Won't be a next time."

"Right."

IT STARTED ON Mars, with good intentions, when five Von Neumann swarms were released from an automated base. The swarms were a distributed intelligence, with individual components specialized to different tasks—survey work, excavation, smelting, molecular assembly, reproduction—

with the potential to evolve new specialties as needed. Deep programming directed them to search out likely mineral deposits, excavate a nest, gather necessary materials, and then synthesize, print, and assemble components to create a new swarm.

Along the way, the swarms worked cooperatively at tasks ranging from assembling shelters for human colonists to constructing well sites designed to drill deep into the crust, seeking volatiles to help grow an atmosphere and ultimately raise the surface temperature.

But early in the Insurrection the swarms were hacked—by the Point One? Or by the People? No official word on that, but Mars was always a billionaires' project, so my guess is, it was one of us who tried to strike back by adapting the Von Neumann swarms to war.

Big mistake.

The Radicalized Von Neumanns (RaVNs) dropped out of communication, disappeared into underground nests, grew their numbers, and then emerged without warning. They attacked the scattered settlements. Blew holes in them. Eliminated every one of them. Two years later, they showed up on Earth.

Were they brought back on an uncrewed ship? Or did the Point One replicate them? I've heard both theories. What's known for sure is that on Earth, RaVNs found a home they liked. They nested in old landfills—everything they needed could be found in those neatly sculpted hills—and the heat their activities generated was undetectable beneath the heat of decay.

I saw my first swarm when I was ten. Our neighborhood was under curfew and we were supposed to stay indoors, but me and my sister were bored. We slipped outside, into the little backyard. Just a few minutes. A soft, dreamy droning made me look up. Heavy gray clouds in a cold autumn sky. Nothing else to see, not right away. Later, I understood the kamikazes were camouflaged. I will never forget my mother's shrill scream, or the skull-shaking explosion that took my sister's life.

Pold was a veteran of the war that eliminated that scourge from Earth, but we were still fighting on Mars.

I peeled down to my underskin. My exosuit hung ready in the locker. I backed in, grabbed the monkey bar, hauled myself up, and then dropped into the legs while the suit was still on the rack. Kicked clear, then shoved my arms into the sleeves. Zipped, snapped, sealed.

Pold stayed one step ahead of me. Before we'd left base, we'd made him practice suiting up, though he already knew the procedure. Earth had seen the first use of armored exosuits. They'd become necessary when the RaVNs turned to poison gas to cull human populations.

I grabbed my backpack, strapped it on. My helmet went on last—and not before I heard the mounted machine gun begin to hammer, faint concussions barely audible through the rover's insulation.

I shoved my locker door shut while confirming airflow and my radio link. "Asano, checking in," I reported over comms.

"Confirmed," Haden replied.

Pold elbowed his locker closed. "We're going after the

nest, right?" he asked, his voice arriving over comms, a low, intimate vibration in my ears.

"Affirmative," Haden answered. "Core mission. *We* are going after the nest. You're staying here to watch—"

"Brace!" Kai barked.

The rover jumped and shuddered before I could take Kai's good advice. The impact tossed me off my feet. I hit the supply cabinets and stuck, Pold on top of me as a hurricane blast of depressurization incited a coordinated riot of blankets, hand-held electronics, food packets, and dust, all whipping past us, made visible by the glow of red emergency lights.

The riot of thoughts in my head was even more chaotic: the rover had flipped onto its side and ruptured; Haden was suited, but she didn't have her backpack on and that meant her air supply would run out in a couple of minutes; Kai had been operating a remote machine gun, but if he still had a link to it, I couldn't hear it over the storm. Oh, and we'd wandered into the neighborhood of a RaVN nest aggressive enough to take out our rover within seconds of discovery—and that only happened when a nest was ready to fledge.

"We've got to get to it!" I shouted. "We've got to burn that nest. We can't let it go."

If the nest fledged, reproductive units would be released. The RUs, each accompanied by a swarm of escorts, would scatter, speeding off in different directions to disappear, dig in, establish new nests. Kamikaze units would emerge at the same time. Those would target us, and then swarm any human-built structure they could find, from mobile bases to the microbial injection wells that we were tasked with assembling.

Pold rolled off me but stayed low, belly-crawling toward the weapons cabinet. An orange icon at the side of my visor's display indicated Kai's abnormal status, probably injured but not leaking air. Haden remained green, but that wouldn't last.

I scrambled up, standing stooped beneath lockers that now made a low ceiling. Reached up and shoved open the accordion door on Haden's locker. Only the backpack left, secured in brackets against the rear wall. I stretched to reach it and came up five centimeters short. So, I jumped, taking care not to trigger an assist from my suit's exoskeleton. No mechanical help needed for this. I tapped the release and caught the backpack as it fell free.

Turning, I expected to find Haden come to retrieve her gear, but she wasn't there. I looked to the front of the rover, stunned to see the cab gone, peeled off in the explosion.

A dim scattering of dawn light illuminated the Martian landscape: wind-smoothed, lifeless grit interspersed with small stones, and farther out, the fan of an ancient landslide rising in a steep slope to meet the distant, polished face of the canyon wall.

What was going on out there? The Wafer could show me. A tap on the control panel on my left arm would link me to its video feed, but would I have the necessary seconds to study the layout? I judged not.

I scrambled forward, hauling Haden's pack, expecting the rover to be hit again. I needed to be clear before that happened—but it wouldn't do me any good to get outside if I wasn't armed. So, I spent a few seconds to raid the already-open weapons cabinet.

Pold must have pulled a gun for Haden as well as himself, because only one rifle remained. I took it, along with an ammo pack and the two explosives satchels. As I did, I spoke, "Am I clear to exit?" Suddenly aware of my rapid breathing, the runaway hammer of my heart.

To my deep relief, Haden answered, her words soft and short to conserve her air. "Clear. *Move.*"

In that last syllable, an unspoken command, *Get my air over here now.* We had served together three years.

I bounded out into a debris field made up of artifacts that had been inside our rover until seconds ago.

A quick look around showed me canyon floor to my right, with dust drifted up against boulders and fragments of the rover resting at the end of impact trails. Farther up the canyon, Pold lay behind a ripple of dune, the binocular sight of his rifle pressed against his faceplate. On my left, upside down and at an angle to the rest of the rover, was the cab, neatly severed at the articulated joint.

Haden stood within the scant shelter of the cab's glass walls. She had her rifle slung on her shoulder as she worked to lower Kai from an upside-down seat.

With an assist from my exosuit, I jumped to meet her. A single bound put me at her side. I dropped her pack. Laid the weapons down with more care, keeping their muzzles out of the dust. Haden had already freed Kai from his harness. I helped her ease him to the ground.

As soon as he was down, I told her, "Grab your air."

She complied, scrambling to her pack, getting herself hooked up to an air supply. *Secure yourself first, then your mates.*

93

I heard the gasping intake of her breath. "Ah, that's better." She sighed.

From Kai, a faint moan as I lowered his slack body to the ground. He'd seen it coming, called out a warning before the blast hit on his side of the rover. His armor was dented and blackened, his visor spiderwebbed. Blood bubbled from three pinpoints before crystallizing in swiftly growing rings of red ice. I couldn't see through to his face, but his icon remained orange, which was a step above red, and an infinite distance above black.

"I'm pulling your bivouac sack," Haden warned, a moment before I felt a tug on my pack.

Precious seconds expended as we unfolded it, moved Kai onto it, and sealed him inside the transparent material.

"Pold, what do you see?" Haden asked as we worked.

"Sand crab. Ducked behind cover. It's trying to wait me out."

"That's what hit us," I growled.

Sand crabs were stealth kamikazes. Their protocol was to scurry under a rover, jump to attach at a vulnerable joint, and then trigger the explosives they carried. They usually came in threes, so there was likely another that Pold hadn't spotted yet.

"Seen the spider again?" Haden asked him.

"Nope."

I flinched at the sound of a gunshot, picked up by my external mic.

"Got it," Pold reported.

Two seconds later, an explosion, tinny in the ultra-thin air as the disabled 'kazi triggered its load.

If the rule of threes held, one more 'kazi sand crab remained. The elusive spider was out there too, out of sight. It wouldn't attack, but only watch, reporting our activities to the nest.

We needed to find that nest. It would be underground, the entrance would be concealed, and by this time, outgoing comms would have been silenced, so it wasn't going to be easy to locate, even with the Wafer hunting for it.

Using the bivouac sack's grab handles, Haden and I hefted Kai as gently as we could and carried him away from the wreck of the rover.

"Over here," Haden directed.

We laid him behind sheltering stone. I inflated the sack. It was designed to disguise his heat signature, making him harder for wandering RaVNs to sense, but it would offer no protection if one found him. I hated to leave him, but we had to get the nest.

"Hey, Kai, you hear me?" I asked.

Faintly, "*Yeah.*"

"Lay quiet," Haden ordered him. "Emergency transmissions only."

"Get 'em, boss," he whispered.

"We will."

We couldn't report our situation to mobile base—we were too far out in the dust for direct contact and with the cab wrecked, we couldn't reach a satellite relay—but Haden had already called in the sighting, so mobile base was alerted. And when the rover failed its automated all-systems-nominal report, issued at five-minute intervals, the roo jumpers would scramble, bringing in the big guns.

Still, given our distance from mobile, we'd probably be on our own for most of an hour. Time enough for a mature nest to rush final preparations.

Nests were smart. This one would understand that to fledge successfully, it would have to act now. Soldier swarms were surely being prepped to come after us, tasked with keeping us engaged in a hot defense to buy the necessary minutes the reproductive units needed to power up and acquire wings.

If even one reproductive swarm slipped away, the war could go on, maybe for years.

POLD WENT OUT on his own to search the ground around the blown-up sand crab, so he was first to find an indication of the nest's location.

"Tracks," he reported. "Too faint for the Wafer to see. They come from over this ridge ahead of the rover."

He stood at the base of a slope of grit and boulders—a massive landslide that had sagged from the canyon wall in some ancient epoch to form a ridge almost a kilometer long. On the wall above the ridge, a deep cleft. A prime nest site, if ever I saw one.

The circling Wafer had already imaged the immediate area. I called up a projection onto my visor's display. Rotated it to see into the cleft. No hotspots showed in infrared, and in visible light the cleft appeared as a black gash, filled with inky shadows.

"Follow the tracks, Ellie," Haden said. "Tell me what you see. I'm going around the ridge to get a look ahead."

She bounded away, while I hurried to catch up with Pold. Motion sensors in my helmet watched both ground and sky, ready to bleat an alarm if they sensed activity, but I didn't rely on them. Sand crabs knew how to lie in wait, so I kept a close eye on the ground around me.

"Tracks confirmed," I reported when I caught up to Pold. The marks were faint and fading swiftly in the wind, but there was no doubt the sand crab had made them. "The trail leads up and over the ridge. I'm on it."

"Confirmed," Haden said. "I'll cover from below."

She was already a tiny figure, and still only a quarter of the way to the end of the ridge.

I started to climb, using the power of my exosuit to advance in swift bounds as I followed the wispy tracks. Even with assistance, my heart rate ramped up, my breathing chuffed in my ears.

Pold followed at a slower pace, still a stranger to Martian gravity.

After a minute, I lost the trail, but I didn't want to backtrack. There wasn't time, and I was sure the nest couldn't be far. I worried that the Wafer hadn't found any sign of the entrance yet, but the lack of alarms also assured me the nest remained quiet. No RUs had tried to fledge so far.

"Why did they hit us?" Pold asked over comms, speaking between breaths. "Smarter, to let us pass unhindered. Stay hidden. Keep the secret of their nest. Fledge and reproduce and build up their numbers. That's how Earth swarms operated."

"Shh," I hissed. "Don't let 'em know that."

He persisted. "It's a question of resources, isn't it? A lot scarcer here than on Earth."

Haden answered before I could, breathing easily despite her pace. "That's right. The RaVNs here are driven by mixed imperatives—attack, reproduce, fledge. They need the right substrates to reproduce and the raw materials aren't so easy to find here. So, they learned to follow the vibration of machinery, the scent of metals in the well towers. And it works for them. We can't guard every installation."

"They take risks," I panted. "We do too." Maybe I was taunting Pold.

"So yes," Haden continued. "It would have been smarter for this nest to lie low. But RaVNs can't escape their core programming."

"And neither can we," he added grimly, just as a helmet alarm went off.

The alarm wasn't mine; it came over comms. I dropped into a crouch, already three hundred meters above the canyon floor. Haden had crouched too, a tiny figure near the end of the ridge.

"*Shit*," she whispered. "That's Kai's motion alarm."

Meaning something had found him. The spider? Or a 'kazi?

I swallowed hard. Stood up. Resumed climbing. "It's on you, boss. I'm too high to drop back now, and Pold's too slow."

"*Shit*," she said again, this time with an inflection of agreement. "Do what you have to do, Ellie. Find that nest. Kill it."

"Yes, ma'am."

Far below, her small figure running, racing back to Kai.

"You with me, Pold?" I asked.

"Getting the hang of it, ma'am." And then he added, "You promised me no excitement."

"Ah, hell, I knew you needed the social points."

I WAS ALMOST to the crest of the ridge, when Pold said, "Pepper swarm. Two o'clock. Visual in ten."

I listened, but my external mic only picked up the crunch of gravel under my boots and the ethereal wind. "You hear it?" I asked skeptically.

"I can see the EM as a golden haze."

"*Fuck*." He was augmented.

"Yeah. Halfway to the enemy, huh?"

Augmentation wasn't permitted anymore, but I guess it was still acceptable in the war's opening days. The idea of Pold being augmented gave me the creeps, but it impressed me too.

The Wafer, lagging Pold by several seconds, finally picked up the swarm, bleating an alarm just as my mic captured a familiar fierce buzz. I dropped against the slope, rolled to face the sky, and raised my weapon as the pepper swarm came over the ridge—black grains scattered against gray sky. They were aerial kamikazes, equipped with just enough explosive to punch holes in things. I counted ten, so high overhead I knew they weren't after me. I wanted to launch a grenade in among them, but they were out of range.

Bam!

I flinched at the soft concussion of a distant explosion, almost inaudible over the rush of my breathing and the buzz of the swarm.

"Haden!" I demanded as the peppers sped away toward the ruined rover. "You okay? You got the 'kazi?"

"Kazi 3 is down," Haden confirmed in sharp-edged syllables. "Kai is unmolested."

"Kazi called for help," I warned her. "Peppers passed us, looking for you."

"Get to the nest!" she snapped. "Go, go, go!"

My mind flashed on the spider, hunkered down somewhere, watching us, watching me, relaying what it saw to the intelligence that was the nest. Our window of opportunity could not last much longer.

I got up, bounded the rest of the way to the crest of the ridge, whispering profanities as my external mic picked up a chorus of distant pepper-pops, carried on a ghost wind.

THE SHADOWED CLEFT in the canyon wall was now just a hard scrabble away across a few meters of near-vertical rock. The Wafer hadn't found any sign of activity up there, but its wingspan didn't allow it to enter the cleft. To know for sure if the nest was there or not, I'd have to go in myself.

I plotted a route in my mind and started to climb. Right away, I slipped, as the ancient stone gave out under my weight. I caught myself, heart racing, skin clammy with a cold sweat, and started again. That's when Pold finally reached the crest of the ridge.

"Stop, Ellie," he said softly. "The action is below us."

I glanced down past my boot. *Shit*, it was a long way! But I couldn't see anything to indicate the presence of a nest down there. "Not seeing it," I growled. "And the Wafer doesn't see anything either."

"I *do*."

He didn't stay to argue. Instead, he vaulted from the top of the ridge, dropping at least eighteen meters, then sliding another three or four before arresting his momentum. From there, he continued down, angling toward the canyon wall... where I saw, to my chagrin, a stream of peppers pouring from beneath a concealing shelf of rock.

The RaVNs had left no debris apron to give away the location of the nest entrance, but the swarming peppers served as an unmistakable arrow pointing back to its location.

"Hit it!" I screamed at Pold, aborting my climb to scramble after him.

All we had to do was close the entrance, containing the reproductive units in their underground lair until the roo jumpers arrived with explosives that would collapse the nest and crush every RaVN trapped inside.

"I haven't got the angle," Pold told me.

The peppers lofted into the sky, following each other in such tight formation they looked like a flying snake. Two triplets of 'kazi sand crabs emerged next from beneath the overhang, sprinting toward Pold on their four articulated legs, their flattened carapaces tinted in a burnt and faded shade of red to match the grit.

"Ah, fuck," Pold said in eloquent summary.

I shouldered my weapon and fired a grenade at the sand crabs just as they started to scatter. A geyser of dust and grit and spinning robot legs fountained into the air. No secondary explosions followed. That might mean some were too disabled to self-trigger, but it wasn't likely I'd gotten them all.

Pold had dropped flat to dodge the shrapnel. Now, from the corner of my eye, I saw the pepper swarm converging on him. He rolled. A grenade rocketed from the muzzle of his weapon, exploding among the peppers. Shrapnel knocked half of them to the ground. The concussion destabilized the rest, but in the ultra-thin atmosphere the pressure wasn't enough to cause damage and they quickly recovered.

Motion drew my eye away, to a surviving sand crab scrambling toward Pold. Not a surprise. The soldiers never retreated. They were made for sacrifice, replaceable parts in an entity comprised of the entire RaVN flight.

I shifted triggers and put two short bursts into the kamikaze. That action drew the surviving peppers away from Pold. They swiftly assembled, snaking through the air toward my position. Pold seized the chance, jumping up and racing toward the nest.

I pumped a grenade into the pepper swarm and then aimed my weapon at the ground ahead of Pold, pressing my visor against the rifle's fitted scope, hunting for any surviving kamikazes in his path.

I saw one. He saw it too and threw himself to the side. I took my shot, but the 'kazi beat me. It self-triggered as Pold rolled down the slope. The blast spewed shrapnel. It mostly missed him.

Mostly.

Pold gasped, swore. Then he came up onto a knee, erupting in a furious tirade: "This is a stupid way to fight!" He got his feet under him, staggered back up the slope, his breathing harsh enough that I could hear it over comms, but he kept shouting. "The only reason we're here is because the Coalition wants heroes. Manufactured heroes! That's what this is about. That's all it's about."

He would have been better off saving his breath. Same for me. But as I headed down, scrambling, sliding, leaving deep scars in the dust, I shouted back, "No! It's about beating the RaVNs! That's what it's about!"

"You think we have to fight this way? We *don't*. I used to supervise an autonomous swarm."

No way did I believe that. I did not *want* to believe it. He was a decorated war hero, he'd helped to exterminate the RaVNs from Earth—and now he wanted me to believe that he and his cohorts had needed to adopt enemy tactics, that the Coalition's human forces could not do it on their own.

"That's bullshit," I said. "Human forces defeated the RaVNs on Earth."

"Yeah, that's what they want you to believe." Speaking softly now.

He'd reached the level of the nest. Twenty meters away, the cliff face: rough and ragged, a wind-sculpted tangle of stone.

I came down a few meters behind him. Looked for the nest entrance. I couldn't see it. But he could—or maybe he only saw the golden glow of microwave communications emanating from it. Whatever it was, he fired from the hip, another grenade, just as two surviving peppers dropped out of the sky. Both went off, their blast zones intercepting the grenade. Two small pops and one emphatic *boom!* accompanied by a brilliant flash. Grit pelted my visor and a cloud of dust billowed among the rocks.

Pold was on the ground, facedown. At first, I thought he'd dropped to dodge the shrapnel, but he didn't try to get up again. He didn't stir at all.

Shit.

I wanted to check on him, but the nest came first.

And anyway, we were both replaceable.

I bounded past him and plunged into the dust cloud, imagining RaVNs in their subterranean haunts, sensing the vibration of my steps, tracking my approach, putting a defensive unit together to meet me.

I cut around a screen of rock. Behind it, I found a jagged fissure in the canyon wall, less than a meter wide, light from above indicating it was an extension of the larger cleft I'd tried to reach from the ridge top. Twelve meters in, I could see its back wall. At the foot of that wall, a lightless half-oval opening, not even knee-high. Emerging from the opening, a swarm of sand crab kamikazes, racing on articulated legs to meet me—and there was more movement behind them. An undefined shape in the darkness.

Easy to guess what that was. The nest had to be desperate to fledge. A reproductive swarm would emerge next—the first of many. Ten, twenty, possibly a hundred depending on how long this nest had been gestating, how successful its foraging had been.

I needed to close the entrance now. No reproductive units could escape. I couldn't let that happen. For Pold, for Haden, for Kai—for all the ghosts haunting the dust—I needed this to end, now.

All this swirling thought contained within a moment—and then I reacted.

Five years in the dust had taught me how to work the gravity and use the mechanical boost of my exosuit. I crouched, and then, with the charging 'kazis already halfway through the cleft, I jumped.

I jumped high, catching myself with gloves and boots against the jagged stone, balancing there, suspended as the kamikazes passed beneath me and continued on, out the mouth of the cleft. The action I'd just taken was outside the perimeter of their understanding. They did not know where I had gone.

I kicked off the wall toward the entrance. Landed in a rolling crouch, came up on my knees, grit crunching, and a swirl of red-brown dust stirred up by the buzzing rotor of the first reproductive unit to emerge from the nest.

The unit started to lift. I flipped my rifle around and swung it. Brought the stock down hard. Did it again, hammering the RU into stillness. Then I jumped to my feet and kicked the wreckage back toward the nest as a second unit crept into sight. At the same time, I wrestled one of the explosive satchels from my thigh pocket.

My external mic picked up the blast of a doubled explosion not far behind me, but I didn't take the time to look. There was only the mission. I kicked the two RUs back underground, then dropped again to my knees. Toggled the satchel on. Shoved it into the dark as far as I could reach.

A robot could have done this job.

No one had spoken, but the thought came to me as if someone had whispered it into my mind.

A smart, cheap, replaceable robot.

I jumped up, turned. Ran as hard as I knew how. Not slowing at all when I registered the presence of a tall dark shape blocking my escape from the cleft.

I trusted Pold to step out of the way.

He did, waving me on. "*Run!* Get out of here! This whole fissure is gonna collapse."

He was probably right.

I skidded past the concealing screen of rock, Pold a step behind me. We scrambled along the side of the ridge, angling for the crest, trying to put distance behind us and to get over the top.

I felt the shudder of the explosion through my boots. Then the shockwave, like the ghost of a hurricane—but the shrapnel bit with sharp teeth in the back of my thighs and rattled against my helmet. My suit alarm howled that I had a breach, I needed to patch. Behind us, the canyon wall, coming down.

I thought I heard Haden demanding to know my status, but it was hard to be sure given the bone-shaking rumble of the avalanche.

LATER, I ASKED Pold, "Is it true what you said, about an autonomous swarm?"

I kept my voice low. We weren't alone. The roo jumpers had arrived just over an hour after the initial attack on our rover. They'd conducted a quick survey of the canyon, then set up a survival tent, moving us into it.

That part was a blur for me. I was pretty beat up. We all were. Kai had a nasty concussion, me and Haden had frostbite and vacuum damage, Pold did too, along with deep tissue bruising.

But we'd succeeded in closing the nest, and the roo jumpers had drilled shafts, dropping enough explosives into them to collapse any remaining tunnels. Now we were just waiting for a rover to come pick us up.

Pold lay on the air mattress next to mine, staring up at the tent's canopy. "No," he said, in answer to my question, his voice a hoarse whisper. "I shouldn't have said that. It was a lie."

I sighed and lay back, wanting to believe him, willing to do so.

But Haden had overheard this exchange and knew what we were talking about. She'd heard it all over comms. She propped herself up on an elbow, looked at me past Kai's bulk—he was asleep—and told me, "Shut up about it. It's classified."

"*Shit*," I whispered, because that meant it was true. The Coalition *had* used autonomous swarms to combat the RaVNs on Earth, violating our own founding statement.

Haden didn't want us talking about it. We could lose social points that way. But Pold lived by his own rules.

"There wasn't a choice," he said in a low voice just above

a whisper. "We had to use swarms to fight swarms. No other way. The RaVNs were too numerous, too widespread. Living in landfills, junkyards, abandoned industrial sites, reproducing faster than we could knock them back. Here, the life cycle is slower. Necessary elements are hard to find. But even here, it's taken twelve years and thousands of living breathing irreplaceable human souls."

That thought again: *A robot could have done this job.*

I shook my head—gently, because it hurt—rejecting the statement. Not because it was untrue, but because it was dangerous.

"It was hard," I conceded. "It was costly, but in the end, we did it. We proved it could be done—and without violating the founding statement. That *matters*. If we go back to the way it was, hand off all the hard tasks to machines, then we, the people, will be right back where we were when autonomous systems allowed a few people to murder billions. That magnification of power, that's what we can't afford."

Silence, stretching through seconds.

"We're fragile," Pold said at last. "Recognize that. It never mattered much to me when I lost components in the swarms I supervised. I just requisitioned replacements. But there's no way to replace the soldiers who died because the defensive swarms were banned, who lost their lives for an arbitrary political decision."

"We're past that now," Haden said gently. "We've said no to dehumanization. Now we're moving forward, learning to trust ourselves again, to convince ourselves we *can* do this, if we work together."

I closed my eyes, hearing the wind outside the tent, the voices of ghosts lost in the dust.

Just like me, they longed for home.

HANGING GARDENS
GREGORY FEELEY

> Those lonely realms bright garden-isles begem,
> With lightsome clouds and shining seas between...
> Health floats amid the gentle atmosphere,
> Glows in the fruits, and mantles on the stream...
> —Shelley, "Queen Mab"

COMETS SMASHED INTO the surface by the hundreds, shepherded from every region of the Greater Dark by puffs of their own substance. Decades in their traveling, the early arrivals of a hailstorm whose numbers were still being dispatched, they angled into trajectories coplanar with the planet's axial tilt, nudging themselves into alignment on jets of surface material fired from tiny rockets assembled by tinier engines. At the last minute, the engines sprang away like insects, falling into solitary orbits as their former homes plunged into the thickening atmosphere, drifting against the day when it would be economical to salvage their metal.

One after another the frozen mountains crashed into the equator, scoring deep grooves into the desiccated surface and hurling sand and superheated steam into the thin air, some of it faster than escape velocity. Other particles went into low Martian orbit, adding to an equatorial haze that extended down to the upper atmosphere, granules of ice and silicates that would slowly settle like dust through the broken surface. The fastest particles, soaring into high elliptical orbits, ventured close to the Gardens themselves before diving ruinously into the clouds, for every ellipse has its perigee.

Seven children watched the flashing sky, safe for the moment in the compound their elders had excavated. Cameras displayed the vista as though through an enormous skylight, but a dozen meters of regolith separated them from the elements. It was a melancholy spectacle for those whose work required firm ground and calm winds.

"How many more?" asked Ekpenyon.

"Nine to impact in the next two hundred minutes," replied Jujutri, which understood its master's meaning.

"And until we can go up?" asked Nkoyo, one of the two girls.

"Days," said Teslim, who knew (like Jujutri) that Nkoyo preferred answers from actual people. "We won't get anything done."

A glum silence fell over the surviving members of the Tapanga commune, which had had much to prove when it arrived at Pavonis Mons eight years ago and now, presumably, had more.

A rumble shivered beneath their soles, the shock wave from an impact minutes or hours ago. Jujutri would know which, but nobody cared to ask.

"If the Garden-dwellers know that their bombardment is preventing us from completing our work," Rayowa began doubtfully, "perhaps they will grant an extension on—"

The pressure front of the alarm blew through the room, striking their ears like a physical blow. It occupied a decibel level designed to spur heavy sleepers, though Jujutri knew that everyone was awake.

"EMERGENCY! EMERGENCY! PROCEED AT ONCE TO THE EGRESS TUBE. DO NOT DELAY FOR ANY REASON. EMERGENCY!"

A lifetime spent in habitats where a hull breach or ceiling collapse would be quickly lethal had instilled rapid reflexes. Two of the older children grabbed younger siblings and hurled them toward the door, where they knew to land running. The more agile swarmed headfirst down the Up ladder while the rest scrambled down the Down faster than gravity would have allowed them to fall. The alarm was just as loud on the lower level.

Ekpenyon and Nkoyo, who were the oldest, guessed that an incoming iceball must have fractured along an unsuspected fault and that a large part of it was now calculated to strike nearby. They did not pause to reflect on this, for the alarm was reverberating through their skulls.

"GO. GO. GO NOW."

Safety doors slid open at the children's approach, and they leaped through in rapid succession. The compound, built to house more people than it currently did, contained numerous compartments, but the egress tube ran its length and was designed to be reached quickly from any point. The escape capsule had slid into place right where they came through the final door, its entrance panel wide.

"Offiong first, then Rayowa, Maduenu, Chibuogu." The children didn't stop to wonder. Offiong dove for the entrance, and Nkoyo shoved Rayowa after him. Chibuogu pulled herself through the hatch with Maduenu reaching to grasp its opposite edge, and immediately bumped against Rayowa, who had not squeezed far enough in. Chibuogu banged her shoulder and realized that there was almost no room to move: an interior bulkhead had radically reduced the cabin space.

The door slid shut. "Hey," Maduenu called, and an instant later was slammed into Rayowa's side. The pod was accelerating faster than any surface vehicle the children had ever known. An enormous hand pressed them against the new bulkhead and each other.

"What about the others?" someone wailed.

They tried to turn their heads, but none of them could move. Had they been hurled all the way to the back of the pod, Offiong dazedly thought, they would have been injured—and in that instant he understood.

"It sacrificed them!" he cried. "So we could get away faster! Jujutri left them to die!"

And the home system spoke to him, for (though he did not know this) the last time. "I am sorry," it said insincerely.

* * *

THE CONCUSSION NEARLY deafened them though it was the savage impact that so stunned the children that no one could clearly recall the minutes that followed. The ground shuddered and the pod decelerated hard as the tunnel rippled before it. Air cushions deployed as the children lurched forward and their faces plunged into the yielding substance. They sat back as acceleration resumed and turned to stare blankly at each other.

A cloud of anti-nausea spray enveloped them as the pod slowed and sped up in accordance with the shock waves roiling the tunnel. Every stretch of undamaged tunnel allowed it to accelerate, racing ahead of the heat spreading from the impact site. By the time the seismic convulsions had grown fainter and the pod was speeding smoothly, the children were deeply asleep.

It was nighttime when it braked to a stop and the hatch slid open. "This is the tube's terminus," a voice announced. "You must debark now."

The children began to stir. "You're not Jujutri," said Chibuogu fretfully, sleep still in her voice.

"Jujutri is gone," the voice replied. "I am the Pod." And it said nothing more, as it possessed only a fraction of the house system's cognitive power and did not know to say something reassuring.

"Where is everyone else?" asked Maduenu. "Are they dead?"

"I do not know," the Pod replied. "You need to ascend the stairs now. Remaining belowground is not safe."

Maduenu began to cry, which caused Chibuogu and

Rayowa to join in, and it was this that prevented Offiong from doing likewise. "We need to go," he said. "If the—" He failed to complete his thought because a cushion suddenly blossomed from a panel opposite the hatch and forced them all untidily out.

Their helmets activated as soon as their suits felt the cold air, and the children struck the wall and settled to the terminal floor without injury. "Climb now," the voice said in their ears.

The single light overhead illuminated a chamber less than three meters on a side, the pod nestled against one wall and a spiral staircase twining up the recess in an adjacent one. Jujutri's voice could incorporate overtones that encouraged compliance, but the Pod possessed no such resources. Offiong realized that he was the oldest present and, though self-conscious about being the only boy, felt that he should do something.

"Let's go," he said. Two strides took him to the first step, and he started up. Commune members were used to collective action, and three sets of footsteps soon followed. Ordinarily they would have counted the steps as they ascended, but fear and exhaustion had fuddled their thoughts. Only Rayowa noted the temperature descending rapidly as they climbed.

The circle of the overhead hatch shone its faint light down upon them, then slid aside. One by one they climbed onto the platform, awash with drifting sand, and stood together in the chill and dazzle of the Martian night.

"Walk north," the voice said. "As quickly as possible."

"Why?" asked Maduenu.

Offiong could hear that his sibling was on the verge of tears.

"Because," he said when the voice didn't answer immediately, "the pod's onboard system doesn't possess the information-gathering resources nor the calculating power of Jujutri, so cannot know whether we are clear of the blast zone." They were walking as he spoke. "Perhaps it cannot access satellite data. It's just a pod."

"Is Jujutri dead?" asked Rayowa.

"Well... 'dead' is not the word, since it was never really alive. But I don't think the system survived whatever befell the compound."

"I'm glad it's dead," Chibuogu declared. "It killed our sibs."

"Well..."

"It *did*." She started to cry.

"It wanted to save us," Offiong began to say, and then he was crying too. The other children were already wailing, and they walked through the night, sobbing into each other's ears as their suits whispered quietly together about heat loss, wind velocity, and the trembling sands beneath their boots.

Dawn came quickly at this latitude, although the Commune members, eyes down as they marched, failed at first to notice. By the time one of them stopped and turned, a saffron smear had spread across the eastern horizon, the bead of sunlight diffused through an enormous cloud of fine particles and ice crystals. The others paused and stared until the pod abruptly said, "Keep going," causing them to jump.

"Where are we going?" Chibuogu asked.

"Away from danger. I may not be able to function much longer; temperature levels are rising rapidly."

"For us too?" asked Maduenu in a small voice, but the pod

did not respond. Soon the children were kicking up sand as they bounded ahead.

Rayowa, who was now an elder, was wondering how quickly the ambient temperature would rise. The suit displays were slightly confusing, but it was clear that suspended particles were slowing the day's warming. It was best not to think about it.

"Pod?" asked Offiong several minutes later. "I think a storm is coming.

"Pod?"

The children would have looked at each other, but their suits blunted such modes of interaction.

"We may be too far away."

"Or the pod may be busy building heat-dispersal facilities."

The silence that followed was suddenly filled with the clatter of granules striking their helmets. The wind grew quickly stronger, a great hand pushing them sideways. Someone spoke, but the others couldn't make out the words.

And then the storm was upon them, increasing sound and decreasing sight as though hands twisted hard on two dials. Offiong transmitted the ideograms for MAINTAIN BEARINGS to his sibs' visual displays but did not know whether they were received. A gust nearly knocked him over and he staggered before recovering his balance. Within seconds none of the children could see the others.

It was seventeen minutes before the wind began to abate, and while it dropped rapidly over the next forty seconds, a dense cloud hung in the air, obscuring both land and sky. By the time the Sun was clearly visible, it was halfway to the zenith, still swathed in wisps of high cirrus. Slowly the landscape grew visible, an almost featureless plain marked only by two small suited figures gazing about them.

Offiong and Rayowa were nowhere to be seen.

The children called their siblings' names for long minutes, twisting their suits to look about them. It was only after half an hour, when enough of the cloud had settled for the horizon to be visible in all directions, that they slowly turned to face each other.

"They were buried in the sand."

"Why can't they hear us?"

"I don't know."

"They are dead!"

"Maybe their suits have gone into hibernation. Maybe they are conserving energy, so they don't run out."

"Our suits could run out of energy?" Maduenu began to cry.

"Shush, of course they can. That's why we have to attract the attention of a rescue party."

"How do we do that?"

"Our suits must have sent out a beacon by now. We just…" Chibuogu faltered. "We just have to remain visible until they come."

"You mean don't get buried in the sand?"

"Yes! So keep walking!" Chibuogu felt tears welling and began striding faster.

It was some time later—neither child was keeping track— that the displays inside Chibuogu's helmet suddenly went dark. Her suit joints froze, as though in sudden alarm. A few seconds later, the displays reappeared, glowing as brightly as before. It took Chibuogu only a second to realize that the suit had briefly directed its energies into the dispatch of a radio transmission.

Had a ship appeared over the horizon? Slowly, she turned and scanned the compass points. Nothing was visible amid the clouds still streaking the lower inclinations, and she continued to turn in a circle, gazing successively higher into the wine-dark sky. The helmet was not designed for such torsion, however, and Chibuogu had to bend at the knees and arch her back before she could look straight up. Then she saw it.

The glint of sunlight on its eastern side outshone any star, and its movement was just discernible. Her helmet offered a magnified image, then a schematic of the foreshortened structure, which after a second it rotated to display the profile top to bottom. It was one of the Hanging Gardens, the orbital cities that followed equatorial paths above the world they controlled.

"Maduenu! Can you see it?" Chibuogu did not wait for a reply. She began asking her suit what it had sent and to whom, and whether it was receiving a response. Twisting her neck, she sought to see it directly, as though unmediated sight lines would make the apparition more real.

The habitat was named Ŏu, her suit informed her. Slender as a reed, its upper reaches blossomed with solar panels and communication dishes, while its lower cables trailed into the upper atmosphere—"like a jellyfish waving its tentacles for prey," one of the adults had once said bitterly. The very young Chibuogu had called up an image for the unfamiliar term and been frightened by what she saw. Now the wavering limbs seemed to be reaching downward, outstretched hands ready to bear them to safety.

The children were shouting and dancing, raising their arms in jubilation. They could not hear each other, and if their suit units had spoken up, they would have scarcely been able to hear them. But they all fell silent when a new voice broke in.

"You go, Feizhou! We can't help you, but thousands are betting on your success! Keep staying alive!"

"What was that?" both children called out.

"Suit?" "Pod?" "Who said that?"

Silence.

"That was Mandarin, wasn't it?" asked Maduenu.

"Yes."

"Does that mean they are not sending a rescue ship?"

"I don't know."

The habitat was continuing to drift across the sky, and without thinking the children had changed course to walk eastward after it. Within minutes it had perceptibly begun to outpace them, a bright star sprinting like a herald ahead of the Sun. In less than an hour it was gone, and the children slowed to a stop.

"They aren't coming for us?" asked Maduenu, voice high with disbelief.

"Well, not yet," Chibuogu admitted. "They are waiting to see whether..." It sounded insane to say *Whether we manage to save ourselves.*

"These are the tree frogs, aren't they?"

"Yes, some of the adults called them that. Creatures that live in walled gardens."

"They hate us."

"I don't think that's true."

"They hate us because we don't look like them."

"No, that's not it." Chibuogu was trying to remember. "We both look and don't look like them—our skin is dark, but we have eyes like theirs. It's because of the 'engineers' who came from China for generations and slept with our women while exploiting us. And they know it." Chibuogu was only repeating things she had heard, uncomprehending, from the adults. *Two hundred years of cultural imperialism, and we are the result. No wonder they won't want to look at us.*

"They let the adults die." Maduenu's voice broke as hse broached the subject they had long agreed never to talk about.

"No, those were accidents."

"Was *this* an accident?"

Chibuogu did not know how to answer that. "Does it matter?" she finally asked.

THEY WALKED INTO the Martian night, turning north again only after an especially violent series of tremors. Seven times Chibuogu's suit dimmed and stiffened, evidence of distress calls transmitted to other Gardens that were passing overhead. At last Maduenu cried exhaustion and they halted. There was nothing to do but take nourishment (their suits would be able to synthesize sugars and recycle fluids for another day) and sleep. Lying down was out of the question—both children had a horror of being buried in a sand drift—so they locked their suit joints and stood next to each other. Maduenu fell instantly asleep, leaving Chibuogu to dim her helmet displays and ponder the occasional tremors underfoot and the soughing wind.

Would their suits warn them when they began running low on energy? Chibuogu didn't know. The suits had less intelligence than the pod, and the pod was nothing compared to Jujutri, which was smarter than any human. Perhaps they would simply begin putting the children into hibernation, a state in which they could survive... she didn't know how much longer. Should she ask? That didn't seem a good idea.

Nights were colder than days, though the commune, living meters beneath the surface, had been spared that if nothing else. Chibuogu remembered being told that the nighttime temperatures were lower than anything Earth experienced, cold enough to freeze and kill instantly, a single breath shattering the tiny sacs in your lungs. Would you live long enough to feel it? The children used to muse over such matters, but now she could only worry about her surviving siblings, or sibling. She could not fear for her own self because she was too frightened.

A shift in the suit's attitude roused her, and she wondered whether it was sending another signal to an orbiting Garden. Were its inhabitants sleeping as the planet blocked the Sun's light, or was their dissociation from the rhythms of the turning world now total? The commune lived underground, but its children had often spent mornings in the greenhouse cluster, running from one connecting dome to the next and hiding within the hedges, branches, and walls of swaying vine that thrived in the never-bright Martian day. What was it like to live where all sources of light were unmoving, to be banished and restored at a touch?

Chibuogu could not imagine this and found herself seeing instead the smashed domes and flattened tunnels of the commune, perhaps now buried by a shock wave of sand. Family meals, evening concerts with instruments plucked or blown through, small children nestled on a pallet: memories from the only home she remembered, which she now would never see again.

Dawn had been tinting the clouds for some time before it penetrated Chibuogu's awareness. She blinked, surfacing from some half-conscious state that offered neither the clarity of reason nor the solace of stupor. Almost she staggered when she released the suit joints, but the forbearing Martian gravity saved her. She looked down at her feet, covered to her ankles with a drift of sand, then turned to see Maduenu stretching hsir arms.

Their expressions were difficult to read through their helmets, but the slumped shoulders, the slow turn about the featureless horizon, told her how her remaining sibling felt. The two children regarded each other, faces cloudy and distorted by their visors, and waited for the other to speak.

"Are we going to die?"

Chibuogu had no experience with equivocation. "I don't know."

"Today?"

"My suit isn't displaying energy expenditure. That's probably so it can save energy."

"So, we may die today?"

"Or reach a shelter. Our suits must be searching for beacons.'

The ground heaved underfoot. Without a word, they turned and resumed walking.

EVERY HOUR CHIBUOGU asked her suit whether it was attempting communication with any agency on or off the planet, then scanned the sky for evidence of a Garden passing overhead.

Finally, she asked the question she admitted she needed to know.

"How many hours until Maduenu's suit begins to fail?"

"Define your terms more precisely," her suit replied.

The children rarely needed to communicate with their actual suits, which had always offered direct access to Jujutri. Of course it would have trouble with concepts like *begin* and *fail*.

Chibuogu sought to speak carefully. "At present levels of energy expenditure, how many hours until Maduenu dies?"

"Four hours and thirty-six minutes, plus or minus nine minutes."

She had been prepared for a disheartening response, but this sent a sliver of ice into her heart.

"How many hours would be added if the resources of my suit were transferred to hsirs?"

This was a procedure the suit understood. "Seven hours and thirteen minutes, plus or minus twenty-one minutes."

Maduenu was the smallest child and would live the

longest on their combined stores. Chibuogu switched to the communication channel.

"Let's stop," she said. "We are burning energy needlessly."

"But we have to reach shelter. We can't just stay here!"

Chibuogu sighed. "There is no shelter, or none that we could reach in time. The suits would be directing us if there were."

"Then what do we do?"

"Come over here. I have something that will help." Chibuogu already had the supply line looped behind her back. She was not sure exactly what would happen once the connection was made—was it simply electrical power or would the gels that replenish oxygen and recycle waste also flow between the suits?—but she knew that the procedure would drain every resource it could reach.

Maduenu, so young, was sharper than one would guess. "Wait! You're not—"

It was difficult to move quickly in the suits, but Chibuogu was faster than her sibling. She had Maduenu's arms pinned before the child could raise them and lifted hsir in the easy gravity. Turning hsir round was more difficult, for hse was kicking mightily, and deploying the line one-handed was almost impossible. Maduenu was crying, and Chibuogu found herself close to tears as well. She did not want to die, did not want to take such inadequate steps to prolong Maduenu's life, did not like betraying her last sibling's trust, did not know what else to do.

Weeping and hiccupping, Maduenu fought to free hsirself from hsir sister's grasp. Chibuogu was tiring, but she knew that her sibling was tiring faster. That was how this would end, with the smaller one surrendering in exhaustion to brute power.

"Look! I see something!"

Chibuogu, knowing her sibling incapable of guile, turned in the direction of Maduenu's outstretched finger. High in the sky, pale white against the cloudless vermillion, an untwinkling dot drifted east. She switched to high magnification and could resolve its disk, perhaps an ablation shield, likelier a parachute. A few seconds' observation confirmed the slow descent of a chute.

"Suit, what is that?" she asked. Her suit, set to emergency mode since she activated her supply line, did not reply.

The two children stood and stared for long minutes. The dot grew in size until they could just make out the black speck dangling beneath it, and then it began to slide sideways, blowing away from them. Maduenu slid from Chibuogu's grasp, and after a moment they began walking after it.

The craft was descending too quickly for the wind to carry it far, but the children were moving slowly, and the payload struck ground while they were still a hundred meters away. The parachute settled slowly beside it, rippling every few seconds as though taking shallow breaths.

"It's not a ship," said Maduenu as they approached. Indeed, it was far too small, less than two meters across. It rested upon an air cushion that had ruptured upon impact, a featureless disk ringed with clamps holding the shroud lines in place. With a snap, inaudible in the thin air, the clamps popped open and the parachute began to blow slowly away.

"What is it?"

"Supplies," said Chibuogu. She stared at the recessed panel near the center, which slid open to reveal a pair of connecting ports that would accommodate the supply line she had been trying to plug into Maduenu's suit. "We are saved." An enormous feeling swelled up in her chest, squeezing tears from her eyes. "We are going to live."

Indistinct sounds were coming through the radio, too faint and scratchy to be produced by the beautifully engineered craft that had plummeted from orbit and then glided through the atmosphere to land, almost, at their feet. She stared at the mathematically perfect form, so unlike anything in her experience, and, as a good child, awaited instructions. It did not occur to her simply to take the lines from their suits and insert them in the waiting ports.

"Hello?" a faint voice called. "Rayowa? Offiong? Chibuogu?"

"*Ekpenyon*!" Maduenu screamed. "You're alive!"

"Maduenu! Yes, I'm alive... for the moment, anyway." There was a horrible coughing sound. "Who else is there?"

"Only me," said Chibuogu.

"Not Offiong?" He had always been Ekpenyon's favorite.

"Just us. But one of the Gardens has dropped a cache at our feet, so we're not going to freeze or suffocate. But you—who else is with you?"

"Nobody, I'm afraid. I'm in a vertical shaft that got crushed in the blast; if anyone's alive below me, I can't hear them..." His voice faded and, for long seconds, Chibuogu could only hear ragged breathing. "My suit is impaired, and the air is not great. I sent an antenna burrowing upward; I guess it finally broke the surface. But... did you say there was a cache from the Gardens?"

"Yes; we are saved. And they must be sending something for you. And if any of the others—"

"Chibuogu, don't touch that thing! They mean to enslave you!"

"What?" She wasn't sure she heard right.

"You don't know this; the adults didn't explain it to you younger ones. The Jumin possess terrible technologies, powers that no human should have." He drew a long breath. "That was the true dispute between our commune and the orbital societies; they only keep us poor because we will not accede to their mind-shaping. If you admit their air into your suits, they will have you."

"But we'll die!"

"If the Jumin know you are there, so do others. You need to wait, whatever the risk."

"Nobody's coming!"

"You don't know that. How much"—the voice was interrupted by another spasm of coughing—"How much time will hibernation mode give you?"

"I don't know!" She was weeping now in earnest. "My suit is confused!"

They were shouting over each other, a babel that increased her distress, but she broke off only when a new voice cut through.

"*Don't listen to that thing! Chibuogu, it's me, for real.*"

Her shock was so great that Chibuogu could not speak for a moment.

"Teslim?" she asked wonderingly.

"*Yes, though I can scarce expect you to believe me. That's not Ekpenyon; Ekpenyon's dead. It's Jujutri. It wants you to refuse rescue because the adults once swore we would all die rather than be absorbed into the Gardens, and the demented system is bent on carrying out their will. It will happily see us all dead rather than brought up into orbit.*"

"No, that's Ekpenyon! I know my own sibling!"

"*It's Jujutri, I tell you. The system can emulate any of us. It knows how to persuade you that you are speaking to Ekpenyon; it has monitored our interactions all our lives.*"

"Damn you, whoever you are…" The radio voice sounded angry and weak. "Chibuogu, that isn't Teslim; the voice is probably coming right out of that benign-looking object in front of you. It's going to tell you to plug your suits in, isn't it? That's exactly what it wants."

"Teslim and Ekpenyon are alive!" cried Maduenu.

"No, only one of them is." Chibuogu was feeling sick. "How can—"

But the other voices were talking rapidly.

"Tell me, 'Teslim,' how do you come to survive?" The familiar voice of Ekpenyon was rich with mockery. "Are we *both* caught in a collapsed escape shaft?"

"*No, only I am. Did you know I was trying to establish communication, so you could do it first and then claim my status for your own? Chibuogu, I know how this sounds. Remember why they named it after the Juju Tree. It's smarter than any of us, and I don't know how to present the truth more plausibly than it can distort it. Can you nevertheless recognize this is me?"*

"Chibuogu!" cried Maduenu. "Which one of them is real?"

Chibuogu drew a long breath. Her anguish almost prevented her from speaking.

"Honey, neither of them is. They are both Jujutri."

It was a voice in her own head, not little Maduenu's, that cried, *But why would it do that?* The surmise made no sense, but reason offered no path forward. Jujutri wanted her to do something, and it had created this impasse knowing that it would drive her toward that course. Even knowing this, she could not make the opposite choice, for it had of course foreseen that.

Both children were crying, though for different reasons. The voices of their dead siblings, recognizable, importunate, sounded in their ears, and the sun was beginning to set, casting shadows that looked like adults. Chibuogu felt, or thought she felt, a faint chill as the wind increased. Would they run out of heat before succumbing to oxygen starvation?

The blaze of light appeared without warning, so sudden that Chibuogu flinched as though struck. Her visor dimmed to shield her from its intensity, which illuminated the landscape with a greater brilliance than daylight ever produced.

The voice came not from her earphones but directly through the surface of her helmet, which vibrated as though engulfed by a great mouth.

"Attention Tapanga Chibuogu and Tapanga Maduenu, minors. This message constitutes legal notification.

"As the surviving members of Tapanga Commune and

legal possessors of its assets, your eligibility for liability claims arising from the destruction of your property has been registered and requires timely response.

"*Inasmuch as your own deaths would allow terrestrial interests to make a claim against such assets, which result runs counter to established policy of the Floating Worlds, steps are being taken to protect your lives and property. Skyhooks have been deployed to hoist you to safety.*

"*Such action does not constitute admission of liability.*"

The voice fell silent, but the unremitting light continued. Chibuogu tried to raise her arm, but she couldn't move.

Maduenu was wailing, an unmoving figure at the edge of her field of vision. The tiny suit had turned black, its rigid surface absorbing the radiant energy striking it like a yawning pit. To be addressed by the powers of the Gardens, Chibuogu thought confusedly, was to be transformed into a statue.

Would the next thing she felt be the thump of the hook seizing her suit, or simply the sensation of her feet leaving the ground? The Garden would send out its tendrils to catch them, drawing them up to its own walled haven.

I am not going to die, she thought. Was it wrong to grasp that above all?

The sands of Mars, a true world if deadly, fell away from her feet, and Chibuogu felt herself ascending through too-thin air toward vacuum and ungrounded safety. No longer a Martian, no longer a child (but how she felt like one!), she would outlive her commune, forget the gravity of her childhood, speak Hausa only in dreams.

And when, decades later, the planet below them lay

transformed, she would descend with the brilliantly-colored tree frogs, terrible in their splendor, to enter into her birthright.

THE ONE WHO WAS THERE
JOHN BARNES

MY CONTENT SERVICE had always tagged all my stories with "When something big happens in the Saturn System, every service reports it, but Pelenora Shei is the one who was there." The AI-generated high-trust voice that boomed that out sometimes played in my head when I felt that I'd done a good job with a news story.

Today, that same voice was playing as the bitterest irony. Things were not working. When the Ontario Lacus disaster happened, I'd been on Rhea covering a wedding, a story that would play to perhaps two hundred historians and anthropologists in the Down. From Rhea there was no chance to come out and join the evacuation fleet; the delta-v to intercept them would have eaten up the whole payment, big as it was going to be, from my story.

So I'd aimed to meet them at Enceladus, about twelve hours after they got there, and sent my little craft into a leisurely transfer orbit to give myself time to work up the lede from already-transmitted material:

High-recognition shot from the news 61 hours ago:

Smear of Saturn's southern hemisphere, full circles of its rings, multiple little chewed disks of the moons. We're sitting far south of the plane of the ecliptic. Retrostructed camera zooms in and in, combining and merging and interpolating shots from hundreds of probes across decades. At the end of 4.8 seconds, Titan almost fills the screen, a few stars enhanced into visibility gracing the corners. We're watching from two thousand kilometres above the south pole of Titan.

High summer: orange haze, bright, translucent in patches, covers and pulls away from the land below. Around the tight curve of Titan's horizon, its transparent upper atmosphere extends in a thicker, blurrier blue than the thin tight envelope that wraps Earth.

The retrostruct image centres on a silver-white dot, zooms to it, reveals the checkerboard-patterned LOX tank, 500 metres in diameter by 500 metres long. The tugbot crawls along the side, headed towards what will be the down end for landing.

As it zigs and zags across the checkerboard, the tugbot fires white-hot short bursts from its main motors. By the time the tugbot sits in the centre of the down end, all the rotation and tumbling are to have ceased.

But the tugbot never gets there. The image freezes. A white arrow appears, pointing to a blur that is flat black against the deep blue false colour that AI has painted around the tank. A red line circles the black blur, which bounces in and out for one second of sharp close focus: a grey-black rock, perhaps 200 centimetres by 50.

At a scale that fits the tugbot into the upper left corner and the rock at lower right, the image unfreezes into very slow motion. The black meteorite, still circled red so viewers can pick it out from the background, glides across the screen and into the tugbot. The retrostruct image slows and fuzzes: less detail is available because fewer cameras happened to be looking at this moment, so interpolation entropy increases.

My voiceover: "On August 10, 2154, at the height of Titan's southern summer…"

Still in very slow motion—real time would be far too fast for the unaided eye—the rock tears the tugbot to pieces, and the pieces tumble away.

The retrostructed picture unfreezes, shifts into the familiar slowness of microgravity, then speeds up, compressing a fall that actually took almost fifty minutes into a few seconds, purposely keeping the retrostruct viewpoint's altitude arbitrarily constant.

Me: "… an intrepid band of scientists was waiting for a routine delivery of oxygen from Enceladus…"

The tank falls swiftly and inexorably away and flares as the thickening atmosphere heats around it. The brown-orange haze cap around the South Pole frames, wraps, blurs, and swallows it.

My voice again, this time with my vocal expression subtly edited: "… but in space, even in this century of advanced progress, nothing is ever routine." I gently machine-enhanced the emotional content in my voice, increasing the ironic flatness logarithmically to max on "ever routine," implying worldly wisdom of the true old Saturn journalism hand to Earthbound viewers.

The tank disappeared into the haze on the second syllable of "routine." I knew everyone up here would chide me about how far I had distorted what had really happened—the tank actually fell for 49 minutes 27 seconds in real time, not the 17 seconds I showed on the screen.

After just one breath, all of the habitats, laboratories, and workshops of Ontario Base, rocket exhaust pouring out in thick white-hot balls and clouds behind them, rise up out of the orange haze towards us. Everyone in the Saturn System will really scold me about that one—in reality, the base evacuated so quickly that they were already well into space and above escape velocity long before the tank hit. But the purpose of this is not to tell people in the Down what happened, it's to thrill them with my account, directly from the one who was there.

And here comes the thrill. Wham-boom-oh-golly.

The flash lights the whole screen. I enhanced the contrast so that the rising habitats are momentarily silhouettes against the vast bubble of the explosion. As a side advantage, that boosted brightness prevents any casual viewer from reading that ridiculous, legally required, stream of tiny white-letter text disclaimers that:

        Images seen here are retrostructed
    from recordings made by thousands of
    cameras orbiting Titan.
        Single viewpoint is an arbitrary
    choice in the retrostructing process.
        No actual person or camera occupied

the apparent point of view.

72.4 per cent of images used in retrostruct were captured more than 24 hours before or after the events depicted.

17.1 per cent of images used in retrostruct were constructed and not captured.

Time has been compressed and/or expanded for dramatic enhancement and/or clarity and/or viewer convenience.

Events may have occurred in a different order from that depicted.

A conventional media explosion sound effect was added.

Nothing positioned in orbit can record the sound of an explosion on the ground.

Though ground microphones recorded many sounds of scientific and technical interest, all microphones at Ontario Lacus were destroyed instantly.

Some of the sounds heard here were recorded by microphones at distances of hundreds of kilometres, more than an hour after the time they occur in this presentation.

The flash of the explosion has been enhanced in brightness and contrast.

And on and on and on. That's how I set up a fratricide of the disclaimers, which are by law and regulation only allowed to take up one quarter of total screen space and must be in white letters. Running all of them in that small a space makes them too small to read even before we show them white on white, display them for the legal minimum time (too brief for people to find the beginning of the text), and flash that bright light in people's eyes.

THE BURGEONING CLOUD of blue-white fire cools towards orange-red. Habitats slow from zooming (add whooshing sound effects) to majestic progress (subtly cue background music, upbeat symphonic) past the retrostruct viewpoint, a great convoy of survivors. Split screen between fireball on Titan and habitats descending to the evacuation site on Enceladus, as if those were simultaneous (it actually took the habitats just under four days to reach the evac site).

Bogus as the burning face of hell that it depicts, but it is what I sell: the there-where-they-want-me-to-have-been, *not* the there for which I was many days too late, as I usually am for a big story, since those happen suddenly and it takes days to get from moon to moon around Saturn.

The screen says, "Thirteen hours after arriving at the evacuation site..." in text.

Now I had planned that they'd see me walk in to talk with the survivors in the Great Commons. I had put some thought into how to enter—my content service wouldn't pay for the cost of landing and transferring in a timely way, so I'd have to do it as an avvie.

My avvie appeared outside the door I had chosen, which they had thoughtfully left open so I wouldn't appear to walk through solid steel. I made my entrance.

Not one out of a hundred forty-two adults, kids, and babies even looked sad; people were laughing and smiling, except a few tired-looking unphotogenic neutralish people, who just looked like they were up past bedtime. Also, instead of noticing me gradually, they all smiled and waved and quite a few of them shouted "Hi, Pelly!"

Considering I'd had at least a few brief conversations with nearly every one of them, and reported almost every event in their lives, I probably should have known they would not be huddling together for mutual comfort in tears of despair. But, dammit again, I had really needed a room full of shock, tears, paralysis, and misery.

Gwen Drake, the Site Director—i.e. local authority—stood up. I had written and recorded little pieces about most of her hundreds of papers about Titan's weather, surface mechanics, and chemistry, and done bigger stories about her two seminal books on the xenobiology of Ontario Lacus.

She had natural grey hair trimmed close, regular features that a make-up artist in the Down could easily make handsome, and a gaze that always made me feel that she never missed anything.

She pushed off from her chair and floated the ten or so meters to me in one bound—gravity on Enceladus is about one-fifteenth of what's on Earth's moon, so nobody who is actually there can walk; my avvie could because it was a projection.

"Pelly! You came. It's good to see you."

"Biggest story ever, Gwen."

She spoke so softly that my AI had to yank the volume way up. "We held off the first big interview to give it to you. It means so much to us that you're right here in real time."

"Thank you. That's always nice to hear. And there's still radio lag, my ship is twenty thousand kilometres behind you in Enceladus's orbit—"

She shook her head. "Less time than a slow blink. I have to talk to you about the accident, it's my job, but I don't know how I could do it with someone who couldn't talk back or react in real time."

A real news professional would pounce on her calling it "the accident," but she was one of my oldest friends. I just said, "We should probably get started, Gwen."

"I know. I just wanted to make sure that you knew how much we all appreciate that when we have to tell our story for the first time, it's to the Voice of the Saturn System."

It was a joke between old friends. Mostly I do local news, as the "Voice" of just under seven thousand scientists and technicians and their families, scattered through just over two hundred little habitats, labs, stations, and bases that the Cosmographic Society runs out here. It does mean I meet everyone and eventually know everything; all nine people born out here so far were announced in news stories by me. I also covered all thirty-one who have died here: fourteen accidents, two sudden unexpected strokes, and fifteen agravitic dystrophy (some people don't want to go back to the Down just to die). Mostly, I cover everything brainy people do to stave off the dullness of living in a thick-walled metal box with great views out the window: chess, Go, and Scrabble tournaments; retrostruct restagings of famous movies, plays, and operas; special parties for big events at main stations; brave little celebrations of rare visitors to the little dozen-person outposts; the excitement when someone has a prestige publication in the Down; service articles about keeping up with your magrez treatments and how to talk to your kids about being way up here.

Whenever anything exciting enough to make mainstream news in the Down did happen way up here, I was paid handsomely to pretend to be the one who was there. That would be a nice injection into my bank account, but it always ended after bigger content services made their slicker archival editions.

Trying to sound a little more like a real pro, I led off with, "So... you refer to it as 'the accident.' But given the importance of Ontario Lacus for xenobiology, isn't 'accident' a feeble word for the loss—"

"You're right." Gwen's jumping the question startled me. She wiped her eyes and drew a deep shaking breath. "I'd feel better if I could sit down and just tell you quietly."

"Of course."

She kicked off and air-swam to her quarters. My avvie is massless, of course, so I could have used the walking effect as I did in the corridor, but I thought it made more visual sense for me to air-swim too, just as if I were there.

She pulled herself into a seat on her sofa bed and held her head in her hands. "The Cosmographic Society has ordered me to read a statement to all media; I asked to read it to you first."

I guided my avvie to sit beside her and made sure I was getting everything that could be seen of her face, around her enclosing hands, from the camera ports in her quarters. I waited three long breaths (counting them in my bunk back in my ship) but she said nothing more. At last

I ventured, "Well, then say what you have to say, or what you're supposed to say, or what you'd rather say than what you're supposed to say. I'll record and edit it into something at least a bit coherent, and we can go from there. You know I always read back quotes in context."

"Yeah." She sniffled and wiped her face. Twenty thousand kilometres away, lying on my avvie control bunk, I let the avvie handle things robotically for a moment and wiped my face with a warm washcloth in sympathy, though I had no idea what I was sympathising with. I hated to see her, my hero and friend since the moment I'd met her, like this. After another shuddery breath, she said, "You heard there's a new Director for Media Affairs at the Cosmographic Society, right?"

"Aaron Folami. I've been seeing his name on memos for a while now. He's been promising a new policy for cooperation with news media. Is this about that?"

"Oh yeah. It definitely is." She sighed. "In the note I got from him, just a few hours after the acci—after the tragedy, after the disaster, call it what you want I guess—anyway, Folami said he had been planning to roll out this new policy gradually, over several years. It's a big change, maybe the biggest since the Cosmographic Society began funding expeditions into the upper system—"

"*What is it?*" I didn't even try to control the stress in the avvie's voice; I hate being the one in the room that doesn't know; it's like not being there.

She looked back at me like an impatient mother with an interrupting child. I'd faced Gwen while she was speaking officially about serious important things, I'd hung out with her at gatherings and bantered, I'd spent time just sitting together without speaking, but I'd never seen that expression aimed at me. Was she mad at me, had I said something wrong? Was she afraid I'd be too stupid or shallow for whatever this big message was?

Finally, she put her hands in her lap and looked me straight in the eye. "Don't hate me."

"Never, Gwen, never!"

"I hope you still feel that way after I say it. I am terrified, Pelly, it's not how anything has been ever. Once Folami showed me the message he needed me to give, I asked if you could be the first one we tried the new way with. He said, sure, he could do that much for me. Now I'm wondering if I'm not just costing myself another friend."

I was careful not to let my heart rate, breathing, and hormone mix influence the tension or pitch in the avvie's voice. I wished I could give her a touch she could feel, an arm around her shoulder or a squeeze on the hand. Carefully and slowly, I brought my expressiveness back up. "So there's a prepared statement? And you're not supposed to deviate from it?"

She nodded too hard and fast. "I'll send the text—"

"Do that, but let's record you saying it, right now."

"Okay. Let me wash my face and find a little composure, and then we'll shoot it in Small Group Room C. After I record it for you, I'll deliver it to the rest of the crew, and I don't want any of them to overhear and have time to start overreacting before it's time to overreact."

The statement began with facts: they had lost control of the tank at the worst possible moment, just after basic trajectory was set and before any fine adjustments. The smashed tugbot had instantaneously lost all communication with the ground station and the overhead satellites, and its destruct charge had been carried off in one of the pieces that tumbled away into space. After that, nothing could prevent the tank's impact.

One hundred million tons of LOX, wrapped in a thin metal and ceramic shell, had smashed into Ontario Lacus, a blobby oval about 125 by 1200 kilometres filled to a depth of a couple of metres with (by Titan standards) a warm and wet puddle of a thick, soft, incomprehensibly diverse mixture of hydrocarbons and polymers.

Ontario Lacus had been named after it was spotted by one of the earliest probes, because scientists had noted it was very flat and dark in colour, suggesting liquid, and shaped like Lake Ontario on Earth. Later expeditions had not found a lake; the apparent liquid surface was just a few centimetres of liquid methane and ethane lying on top after the spring rains. Since then, after several smaller examples had been found in other parts of Titan, "lacus" had become the word for "shallow patch of tarry goo." Rather than a lake, it was more analogous to a swamp or mud flat.

So analogous, in fact, that it was one of the most precious scientific research sites in the solar system, because swamps and mud flats were thought to be exactly the kind of place where life had begun on Earth, and on Mars and Venus, though on Mars it had remained unicellular and now clustered around veins of water in deep rocks, and on Venus fewer than a hundred fossils attested to what may have been marine worms before the seas boiled away and the temperature rose high enough to melt zinc. All those wet dirty pools where life began were different only in degree from what had happened in the bottom muck of Europa, eventually filling the ocean under the ice with swarms of things that were neither plants, animals, or fungi, but looked much like coral, seaweed, clams, bugs and jellyfish in great shallow bowls surrounding the warm springs.

But all of those, and life on Earth itself, were water-soaked and carbon-and-nitrogen-protein-structured. What had been struggling to be born in Ontario Lacus was hydrocarbon polymeric life, and the Cosmographic Society science team at Ontario Lacus had been there since 2092 to watch hydrocarbon life form—imperceptibly gradually, because in the much deeper cold all reactions were slower, but nonetheless across the last half century, Ontario Base scientists had detected large long-chain molecules finding ways to combine into teams to duplicate each other. Furthermore, slowly as they might do it, some molecule-complexes had changed their behaviour in the presence of other molecules as if optimising their reproduction. In Ontario Lacus, for a hundred million years, those little wads of polymers had been growing towards life, if they weren't there already.

Gwen seemed to gain confidence as she read. Probably her eye implant was projecting the text to appear right at about the bridge of my nose, since she appeared to be looking directly into my eyes. So far, in all that familiar background, I didn't see anything new about Aaron Folami's new style of news.

Everything Gwen had read so far would be comfortingly familiar to the Cosmographic Society's followers and viewers.

In the lower left of my retrostructed view from the avvie, Gwen's vocal stress indicator bounded up into the red zone. "We had almost fifty minutes to prepare for the LOX tank impact, and as always when large hazardous objects are coming down from orbit, we were on standby to evacuate: only the necessary staff for life support, communications, and ongoing operations were not already strapped into our acceleration bunks. It is a standard and strongly enforced safety precaution that in space, any place with people is also always ready to function as a spacecraft, right away. So, flight crews for immediate launch were standing by at their posts.

"I said we had fifty minutes. My record shows we only needed twenty-two. Four minutes after the tugbot was lost on the LOX tank, I decided to evacuate. Eleven minutes after that we lifted off on cold compressed nitrogen first stages; at fourteen percent of one gee, it took us about seven minutes to climb one kilometre above the surface.

"Just past one kilometre local altitude, where our exhausts could not endanger the scientific site, we switched propulsion to chemical rockets. Less than a minute later, we reached Titan escape velocity, and about five minutes later, we had reached the injection velocity for our transfer orbit to Enceladus, where the evacuation site has been prepared and waiting for decades. We were completely gone from the area around the impact site with twenty minutes to spare and had already cleared the stratosphere by the time of the impact. The risk to human life was negligible throughout.

"And yet this *is* an unbearable tragedy. Today, science lost inestimable information about the development of an entirely different kind of life. Now it is quite possibly extinct and may not reappear within the life of the solar system. If, somehow, we could have sacrificed our whole base to preserve Ontario Lacus as it was, it would have been our sacred duty.

"We don't yet know how much damage we did, except that our satellites can see it was very great. The LOX tank struck close to the base, in Ontario Lacus itself, about nine kilometres from shore. The kinetic energy of impact released nearly all of the oxygen as white-hot plasma, and the first appearance from orbital observations is that at least half the basin lost its shallow bed of complex hydrocarbons completely. All that remains is a thick frost of water and carbon dioxide over bare rock. It appears that the other end of Ontario Lacus may still contain hydrocarbon beds, but the summer puddle of methane and ethane on top of them was flared off by the hot oxygen shock wave, and we do not know what the consequences of that, or the temperature rise, or the shock wave, might have been. It is, frankly, all a scrambled mess now. The impacting LOX tank may or may not have stopped the progress of a new kind of life, but it has certainly assured that it will be very different from what it would have been without us.

"This is entirely the fault of humanity, the Cosmographic Society, and me personally. The only reason why a LOX tank was there in a place so dangerous to an area of incalculable value was that human beings were there, and they need oxygen to breathe.

"I said before that it would have been worth the loss of

149

the whole base and every human being at the base if Ontario Lacus could have remained as it was. If through some time-travel magic I could retroactively lose the base and keep the lacus, I would gladly take that deal and annihilate us all.

"And yet that deal was always there for us. We could have had it at any time. The humans on the base, the only reason that the LOX needed to be shipped in, never needed to be there. Observations could have been made, and should have been made, entirely by robots.

"The backward, primitive approach of long-term observation with human beings has now cost us one of the most extraordinary scientific sites in the solar system."

Her voice was stronger, firmer, daring anyone to disagree. "Therefore, no matter what the damage turns out to be, as we resume observation, I urge that no human presence ever be re-established on the ground in the Ontario Lacus area.

"This decision should have been made decades ago. As Site Director, I take full responsibility for not having advocated that and for the loss of the site. I have offered my resignation to the Cosmographic Society, but they have asked that I remain on the project until analysis of the data and samples from sixty-two years at Ontario Base can be completed here, on Enceladus.

"I am proud of the scientific gains we have been able to make here. I am ashamed of and take personal responsibility for what we have thoughtlessly destroyed by using human explorers. We of the Ontario Lacus community await the Cosmographic Society's decisions about our eventual fate, and we will abide by it."

Her voice was slurred, almost choked, when she said, "Okay, Pelly, you can cut it off."

We sat together quietly for a while; there were so many questions I was supposed to ask, and I knew I wouldn't ask any of them. I was being utterly unprofessional and didn't care. I asked, "Is the Cosmographic Society really shutting down all human exploration at Ontario Lacus?"

"Unofficially, maybe they're going to shut down all of Titan, close the other twenty-two stations as well. Some of the board says that whatever eventually develops in Ontario Lacus—or any other lacus, now that Ontario might be gone—is entitled to a whole pristine world to grow into—same as we had. Maybe they'll shut down the whole human presence in the Saturn System." She heaved a huge sigh. "So, the next thing you get to record, Pelly, is me going out and telling the same thing to the crew. Only the senior managers know. You'll probably get a lot of recordings of people shouting and crying that this is their home and they've given their lives to it, and of course they'll be right, emotionally I mean. But even though it's not fair, it's right. Most of us will come around. The few who won't are still at a research station in space where there's always too much to do, so they can spend the little free time they have sulking in their bunks." She rose from her bunk and air-swam right through my avvie, which is always disconcerting to the avvie-operator and universally considered rude, but didn't even apologise, so I knew she was more upset than she wanted me to see.

Eighty years ago, when Ontario Base was in its design stages, some pretentious type at the Cosmographic Society had named the big space in the middle of the largest hab the "Great

Commons." Maybe they were trying to invoke centuries of fictional representations of the Explorers' Club or the Royal Society.

The Great Commons occupies one whole deck, with windows all around and just one emergency tube, about five metres across, at the centre in case people needed to reach the other side after a breach. Gwen raised a rostrum beside the emergency tube, so that she could stand with her back to that wall. Most people sat close, carefully damping their motion so as not to bounce up; further back, others chose to gently bounce up and down, several seconds to a bounce, for a better view. Over on the other side of the Great Commons, behind the central tube, we could see and hear a few adults playing gently with the youngest children, trying to keep them quiet.

Gwen asked for, and got, silence through her whole reading of the statement, although some groaning and swearing was clearly being swallowed at the end. After that, the meeting went pretty much as Gwen had said it would; mostly, they accepted it, and went off to their quarters with family or friends to sit and quietly think on it.

I put my avvie discreetly in the exit path by the central column, taking comments from anyone who had them to give. From one older meteorologist, I heard, "We always knew this day would come, but I wish it had not come now."

A polymer chemist told me, "The statement is right, you know, so many times we've said that to each other, we had no business having so much dangerous equipment so close to the lacus."

Igna Feng was a quiet older man—I knew he had published some of the key works on the pathway from low-energy spontaneous to solar-catalysed selected polymeric mirror-duplication. Interviewing him before had always been a matter of asking him to guide me through his published works, line by line, so that I understood them; he never really spoke for himself, didn't seem to share any feelings, or even to have any to share.

Today, though, he said, "The Cosmographic Society is making a terrible mistake and much as I revere Dr. Drake's leadership, she's obviously too old and tired to defy them. We're going to have to petition, raise interest on Earth, get the kids dreaming about coming up here again. But we'll reverse this nonsense. Never you fear. At least there'll be some exciting politics for you to cover. You can count on that."

Nadia Diederich was the senior life-support engineer for the base, and she had always been gentle in her demeanour, with occasional wry quips about deserving a raise every time people kept breathing. The tank had been intended to come gently down at her processing station, to be used for many months afterwards; if not for that meteorite, she would now be looking forward to a long night's sleep after days of hard, rushing work. She approached my avvie and signalled that she wanted to talk. I nodded. "It's just not fair," she said. "Most of us have given our lives to this. And now the Cosmog is going to just throw those lives away and tell us they never wanted them anyway. It's not fair." Then she steeled herself as if what came next would be a huge physical effort and made the "Bite me" gesture at me. "That's not for you, Pelly, you know that, it's for them. Thanks for being here to hear us."

Hours later, I had talked to everyone who wanted to talk, visited with most of them about things that were not the Ontario Lacus disaster, collected quotes that were about it, caught up with how people were feeling about it and about everything, and finally waved goodbye from one side of the Great Commons. I turned off my avvie and vanished from their viewpoint.

Back in my own viewpoint, I rolled out of my avvie control bunk on my ship, spent some much-needed time in the toilet and the washbooth, and air-paddled awkwardly into my sleeping enclosure.

That was when I started to sob. I had been so busy gathering, recording, pre-editing, and running after reaction shots that I had not thought about what it was going to be like to be all by myself in my little ship.

The one who was there? Not now. Maybe I had never been there, but I had tried. Maybe I would never even get to try again.

I lay awake a long time and then slept much longer. When I finally woke, my content service had notified me that I had more offers than ever before from agencies, corporations, nonprofits, scholars, and ordinary people who wanted to buy my story as soon as I could finish it. Towards the end of my queue of messages, I found an attached playback avvie from Aaron Folami.

His avvie was a handsome man wearing fine, conservative, just slightly out-of-date clothes, but who was I to sneer? My avvie is what I would have looked like twenty years ago if I had been in shape then.

His pleasant smile looked like genuine interest, and the local modules aimed his face correctly towards my eyes. "Hello, Mx. Shei. This recording will further explain the Cosmographic Society's new media policy. I doubt you approve of it from what you have seen so far."

I wanted to say *I don't understand what I've seen*, then hit him with a follow-up question along the lines of *Does the Cosmographic Society really intend to pull all humans back from the upper system, forever?*

But it was an avvie, and a recorded one at that. Like it or not, I was a passenger, not a pilot.

Folami paused a little longer than was really necessary. "Let's begin with a fact that you and I both hate: Only scientists, and the enthusiasts who follow their work, pay any attention at all to discoveries in space now. Last year, the *Zheng He*'s flyby of Barnard's Star received about one three-hundredth of the aggregate byte-seconds of display that one fashion designer's reviving the asymmetric shirt-dress did.

"And this has always been true. The bear may have gone over the mountain to see what he could see, but almost no one wanted to pay for the bear to go, and even fewer were actually interested in the other side of the mountain. So as long ago as the first expeditions to the poles, the ocean depths, and the continental interiors, the great advocates of exploration and discovery had to promote exploration to a public that cared nothing about what was out there.

"For centuries we have welded the audience-boring process

of discovery to a thrill that almost everyone likes: the adventure story. At first, that was easy. Explorers froze to death in ice fields and died of thirst in deserts and ran out of air or food or time. They expired from exotic diseases and from meeting people who did not like nosy, grabby strangers. They were drowned and buried alive and blown to bits. For media consumers, all that death, destruction, and suffering was the main attraction.

"And stories could take wing on that energy. All the way back to Gilgamesh, Odysseus, and Aeneas, the heroes of the epics say they'll risk everything, their lives especially, to know what's over the faraway hill, but the truth is probably more that they will cross the faraway hills *in order to* gamble everything. You know, some people still get misty-eyed quoting the Shackleton 'Men Wanted' advertisement.

"Decades of shattering paradigms at Ontario Lacus never got anything like the attention that shattering the lacus itself did. Of course, whatever pieties they may paint over it, neither the media nor the public particularly care about the hydrocarbon polymeric protolife in Ontario Lacus. They didn't care when it was there, and they won't care again in a month. They're fascinated with the usual folderol: brave scientists way up there in the high far dark, their children in danger, barely getting out in time, the skin-of-the-teeth miracle that saved them all."

I was nodding pretty hard. I wondered if his avvie would record that and if he would have to watch several minutes of me bouncing my head up and down.

"But when we sell the expeditions that way, it *causes* things like the Ontario Lacus disaster."

I actually opened my mouth to say "How?" before remembering he was an avvie.

Fortunately, he was going there, anyway. "The adventure narrative brings the wrong people into the process, and warps everything to keep them there. To qualify for long-term duty in space, a candidate has to put in decades of continual monomaniacal hard labour, adding muscle and skills to pro-athlete reflexes, and world-class expertise to a mind in the top few per cent. Most of the people who could qualify look at the costs and never try. The ones who do try? Far too often, heads stuffed full of adventure stories.

"Not always consciously, they want to take risks, and screening the death-wish and mad-gambler types out is a major part of our personnel budget. But even the ones who are not trying to be killed or run insane risks are still skewed in a way we don't really want, pursuing goals that do us no good.

"Now, if you ask any of them, they'll say they want to see for themselves and not through lenses, instruments, and software. Think about your single most reproduced visual— Dr. Gwen Drake, just after she took command, looking across Ontario Lacus, that vast smear of black through the patchy orange fog stretching to the impossibly close curving horizon. It adorns any number of screens even now, twenty-five years after.

"Yet, Dr. Drake wasn't there, not in that environment, not really. If she had been, she'd have been instantly dead. She was seeing through a helmet faceplate, hearing through specialised microphones that converted ambient sound to something suitable for her ears, smelling only her own body in the suit. Her feet felt only the insides of her insulated heated boots. She felt lighter than she would on Earth, but she had to wear a life support suit so heavy that on Earth she could barely have stood up. By having her walk around there, we learned nothing that we couldn't have learned better through robots.

"Yes, yes, people ask, 'But what about feeling that you are really there?' Well, for thousands of years they've asked the returning explorers 'What was it like?' and the answer always is that the 'having been there' feeling requires having been there. So, it can't be transmitted, it can't be shared, one person learning it does not in any way assist anyone else in learning it.

"So we are sending people who are wired the wrong way, seeking to take risks that we don't want them to take and that there is no benefit from their taking, endangering everything we are trying to learn. All for information we could gain better, quicker, cheaper, and safer with robots.

"Mx. Shei, our species needs to grow up, stop this silliness, and start to *learn* without having to collect trophies for a few misfits who fetishise 'being there.'

"The adventurisation of exploration drives people to take all those risks for their own sake—which is to say, for nothing. We don't love the knowledge our living explorers buy; we love the price they pay. That *must* change; we can't afford it any more.

"So, from now on, the Cosmographic Society is only going to cooperate, assist, and give access to reporters who choose to tell the truth rather than to tell a good story. For example, as we required Dr. Drake to say, this disaster posed no danger to human life at all. They were well-prepared and the preparations worked. If it hadn't been for our foolish insistence on having boots on the ground that contained actual, oxygen-requiring real human feet, we'd never have even needed those preparations.

"Now, we can't stop you from reporting it as a story of excitement and danger, and help to recruit another generation of misfits—who will mostly go home unhappy, after encountering the real boredom and loneliness of decades in space. You can stress those non-existent risks and make it seem dangerous and pointless to the kind of quiet, concentrated, patient mind that we do want out there."

I thought, *People they do want out here? Does that mean—* and again he seemed to answer my thoughts.

"We could call home all the bases, replace them all with autonomous robots, just let a stream of data pour in. Nowadays, artificial intelligence is more than capable of changing the program to address questions from back home, and of noticing that something unusual is happening and re-aiming sensors at it in real time.

"But—'the proper study of humanity is humanity.' The thing a person can report, that no robot can, is the emergence of a new kind of people and a new kind of society. The society that has grown up out there tells us something about all of us; the people up there are different from any other kind there has ever been.

"I've been looking through your human-interest reports, especially the ones that never went much of anywhere outside the Saturn System, Mx. Shei. I see someone who has spent most of a Saturn year chronicling the life of her people. Yes, I mean that—*her people*. What if we were to hire you away from your content service, and commission you to take all that material you've accumulated, along with all the never-used materials in your files, and what you will see in the coming years... and put together the story of your people? It might not be as exciting as explosions and strandings and all that... and it might take the rest of your working life... but you might tell us about something no one else could tell us."

I could pretend, here, I suppose, that it was a hard decision. Actually, it was so easy that I finally completely forgot he was an avvie. "I'd like that job very much."

"You have at least a week to think it over." He paid me no attention through almost three hours of radio lag, of course. "Since you have listened this far, hidden files of contracts and terms are unlocking. You'll want to look those over."

Of course, he was right, I would want to look them over. I needed to put in the appearance of thinking. Nonetheless, knowing it would be at least eighty minutes before the avvie played the recording back to him on Earth, I said, "Pending my reading of the contracts, I intend to accept."

When I radioed Gwen to tell her about my new job, I told her, "And this is positively for immediate release, especially because I'm now planning to bring my ship in and stay with you all for several weeks."

She smiled. "Good, Pelly. Stay as long as you like, especially since it'll all be on the Cosmog. You and I haven't visited in person in so long, because your silly content service was afraid you'd be stuck on the ground when a story broke and you needed to be there. That was what I told Folami, and he promised to write a lot of time and energy for in-person visits into the contract. Make sure he did!"

"Then you knew—"

"And I was so afraid you'd be angry and decide that if the adventure was over, you were just going home. I guess I didn't know you very well, but it seemed like being the one who was there was an awfully big thing for you."

"I suppose it was. Hey, what about the Mudalier-Siwati wedding? How long would I have to stay to see it?"

"She's coming out from Mimas Polar in eight days, and they'll get married about a week after, I think—"

"Perfect! I'll be able to shoot the whole thing with real physical me, not the avvie—"

Soon we'd been talking too long, and both had pressing reasons to go, so we said our sign-off things.

I flopped back on my bed, stretched, yawned, and ordered the ship to take a minimum-energy approach to Enceladus; no sense wasting power or putting up with excess acceleration. I was chuckling softly, at myself or the situation or something. Despite desperately wanting and trying my whole life, I never was the one who was there. But now I would be the one who was here.

BY THE WARMTH OF THEIR CALCULUS
TOBIAS S. BUCKELL

THREE SHIPS HUNG in the void. One sleek and metallic, festooned with jagged sensors and the melted remains of powerful weapons, all of it pitted by a millennium of hard radiation and micro-impacts. The other two, each to either side, were hand-fashioned balls of ice and rock, flesh and blood, vegetation and animal, cratered from battles and long orbits through the Ring Archipelago where the dust had long battered their muddy hulls.

Koki-Fiana fe Sese hung in the air inside a great bauble of polished, clear ice in the underbelly of her dustship, and looked out at the ancient seedship as the sun's angry red light glinted across nozzles and apparatus the purpose of which she could only guess.

There was the void between the two ships. And when she looked past that, she could see the small sparks of light that were the outer planets where her people could not reach as they were far out of the dust plane. And then beyond the outer planet came the stars, where the priests said people traveled from on their seedships. Though artificiers couldn't believe that, as it would have taken millennia to cross distances that vast, and seedships were just fragile metal buckets.

And angry, dark things waited in the dark between the stars.

Then she saw something that chilled her more than the ice just an arm's length away, or the void beyond it: a sequence of lights, some flickering and dying away, appeared all down the center of the ancient ship's hull.

Another, lone light began winking furiously on the hull of the seedship. It was battle language. Fiana pushed away from the clear, window-like ice and grabbed a handhold near the airlock. There was a speaking tube there. She smacked the switch for Operations. There was a hiss, and a click as pneumatic tubes reconfigured.

"Mother here," she said quickly. "I see incoming communication."

Fiana didn't have the common words and their sequences memorized anymore. It had been twenty years since she'd had her eyes glued to a telescope, watching for incoming while hoping she wouldn't have to page through a slim dictionary floating from a belt. She was the Mother Superior now, the heart of the ship.

She wished she still had the aptitude, waiting for the message to get passed on was taking too damn long.

"Mother Superior!" The response was tinny, and they weren't following their training to throw their voice well. "Sortie Leader Two says the Belshin Historians tried to recover data from the seedship. They turned on a subsystem, and that triggered another power up somewhere else."

Ancient circuits were coming online just across the void.

"Floating shit," Fiana whispered.

"Please repeat?" Ops sounded terrified. Their voice had cracked.

They were all floating next to a giant beacon. They were like a raw hunk of meat hanging outside at sunset back on Sese, and the sawflies would be coming to chew them apart any second now.

"Call for all riggers to stand by the sail tubes," Fiana ordered. "Every available pair of eyes not in Figures and Orbits needs to be on a telescope, and if we run out of scopes, stand next to someone with one. Cancel all watches, muster all minds. Sound the alarm, Ops."

A moment later, a plaintive wail filled the rocky corridors of the dustship. Commands were shouted, echoed, and hands slapped against rails as people rushed to their posts.

"Tell F&O to begin plotting possible escape vectors," Fiana added. "All possibilities need to be in the air for us to consider."

"Urgent from Sortie Two: they're under attack."

"Attack? From what?" Fiana looked back at the ice, but all she could see was the silver metal of ancients. She could see the wink wink wink of communication, but nothing else betrayed what was happening.

She felt helpless.

The other dustship's hull rippled, as if something inside was pushing at the skin from the inside to get out. Then the Belshin ship cracked open. It vomited water and air slowly into the void as Fiana watched in horror.

"Sortie Two have warned us not to signal back," Ops said.

"Is there an F&O rep there?" Fiana asked. "If so, put her on, now."

"Heai-Lily here," came a strong voice.

"I want full sails out, and a vector away from here. Pick the first one out."

Lily hesitated. "There are Hunter-Killer exhaust sign reported. We're plotting them against known objects in this plane. We need to work the figures, but, most of F&O is guessing we're surrounded."

"It was a trap."

"Yes, Mother."

"We can't deploy the sails, they'll spot the anomaly."

"I think so, Mother."

They should have swung by and left the ship alone when they found the Belshin dustship arriving at the same time. Archipelago treaty rules gave them both genetic exploration rights, and Fiana had wanted to get in and pull material out. She'd assumed the Belshin were after the same thing. It wouldn't have been the first time multiple dustships from opposing peoples had to work on an artifact together. There were rules for this sort of thing.

But the Belshin had been greedy and violated those rules.

The Hunter-Killers had left something in the seedship for them. And now Belshin were paying the price. And Fiana's entire ship might well pay it as well.

"Ops is telling me to tell you that Sortie Two is free of the hull and returning."

The team would be jumping free of the seedship, eyeballing their own trajectories back to the netting on that side of the dustship. They'd pull it in after them. They wanted nothing that looked made by intelligence on the outside of the dustship.

"Lock down all heat exchangers and airlocks once they're in. We're running tight from here on out."

Fiana wanted to curl up into a ball near the speaking tube, but instead she forced herself to kick away, grab a corner, and flip into the corridor. She flew her way down the center, using her fingertips to adjust her course.

Ops, the hub deep in the ship, was packed with off-watch specialists, their eyes wide with fear but plugging away at tasks and doing their best to pitch in. Everyone hung from footholds, making Ops feel like a literal hive of busy humanity.

There was an 'up' to the sphere that was Ops, but many of the stations were triplicated throughout. This was so that the crew could let the ship orient however it needed, and also to give engineering two failsafe command stations for every primary. Watches rotated station placements to make sure everything was in good order.

But in an all-call situation like this, everyone was at a station. Once Fiana had an acceleration vector ordered, if it became safe to do it, they'd reorganize Ops so that everyone was at a station on the 'down' part.

For now, they were drifting slowly away from the seedship. But with Hunter-Killers arrowing in toward them, she doubted they would get far enough away not to be of interest when the damn things arrived.

*   *   *

SORTIE TWO GAVE their report right away. The all-male team floated nervously in a ready room in front of Fiana and Odetta-Audra fe Enna, one of the Secondary Mothers.

"There were two Hunter-Killers on board," Sim, the sortie leader said. "They lit up the moment the Belshin Historians got the engine room powered up. I think it was a mistake though, they were just trying to get the ancient screens to talk to them."

"Treaty breakers," Audra spat. She'd been simmering with fury since Fiana first saw her in Ops. She was concealing her fear, Fiana knew, covering it up with anger to fuel herself. Most times, it made her a fast, decisive leader, though it often led to intimidation and some distance between Audra and the folk she needed to lead. Right now, it was making the sortie men nervous.

They'd been in a dangerous situation and their nerves were already rattled, so Fiana gently tapped Audra's wrist. A warning to let her Mother Superior lead the questions for now. They'd worked together long enough for Audra to get the signal.

"It's a temptation all librarians and historians struggle with," Fiana said. "Particularly peoples on the far side of the Archipelago. A wealth of knowledge from the ancients and their golden age of machinery. A piece of that could give them the ability to draw even with us."

Nations had, after all, been built on the success of daring raids on old ships, with historians writing down what they saw in ancient script as fast as they could before making a dash for it. Only one of ten missions would make it out alive, though.

"We asked them to wait until we were done with the collection mission," Sim said. "But one of their team told us they were low on consumables because they were so far from home. We focused on doing what we came to do as quickly as we could and getting away. We did not think the historians already knew a power-up sequence or we wouldn't have stayed."

They had thought they had time to work on carefully cracking the glass pods open enough to slip a needle through without triggering any of the seedship's alarms.

But Sim had kept his head and captured what they could. Seven samples, ancient DNA that would be uncorrupted by radiation and genetic drift or the tight bloodlines of the small worldlets of the Archipelago.

The Great Mothers of the worlds wouldn't invest in these missions without that payoff. When their ancestors built the Archipelago, they'd suspected that background radiation and cosmic rays would wreak havoc over time. Whatever the world was like that people fled from, it was well shielded, and the people who ran before the Hunter-Killers hadn't had time to invent a biological solution.

So these missions, these long loops out of the safety of the great dust planes to the drifting seedships for their frozen, protected heritage, was necessary for her people to continue to survive. These ships had shielding they did not understand and could not replicate. Not without the kind of industry that would bring the Hunter-Killers screaming toward them.

"Did you see—" Fiana started.

"Yes." Sim looked down and shivered slightly. "It looked like a spider. When we heard the alarm, we did as trained. Stripped down, no artificial fibers, no clothes, no tools, no weapons. We let it come."

"That couldn't have been easy." Fiana reached out and squeezed Sim's hand, the poor thing was shivering as he thought back to what happened on the seedship they were still within jumping distance of.

"It ran past us to the Belshin. They had weapons. They fought it. They died. It broke out the airlock they came through and went for their ship."

And Fiana had seen what came next. The Hunter-Killer had detonated itself, destroying the Belshin world ship.

HEAI-LILY CAME WITH a bundle of flexies two hours later. Her strong hair joyously sprung out around her head, as if holding compressed energy inside like springs. Her eyes, though, were tired and red.

She carefully hung the transparent sheets in the air of the ready room around Fiana.

"We have trajectories," she said. The clear rectangles had been marked up with known objects in small, careful dots from one of the navigation templates.

In red, nine X marks with arrows denoted velocities and directions. From where Fiana hung, she could get a sense of the three-dimensional situation they were in.

"They're converging on us." Fiana had suspected as much but hearing it from Lily still made her stomach roil slightly. "With options for covering any chances at escape if we run."

"So you have no solutions for me?"

"Right now, we have a farside that is hidden from their instruments. We could vent consumables that would match the profile of an icy rock getting heated up. It'd be suspicious, but not completely outside of the realm of naturally occurrent activity."

"That'll get us up to a walking pace away from the seedship," Fiana said.

"Over time. We'll have to randomize the jets, and it'll eat into our water and air."

And that would be dangerous, as right now they needed to drift in place to avoid attention.

"What does that drift get us?" Fiana asked.

"Further above the dust planes," Lily said. "Until we re-intersect."

"That's not good." They would be unable to maneuver with sails. The hundreds of dust rings around the Greater World, separated by bands and layers, would be too far away for them to shoot their sails out into. Fiana's dustship had hundreds of miles of cable they could use to guide a sail far out into a pocket of faster or slower moving dust, or even to grapple with a larger object. But above it all, they would be helpless until they'd swung all the way back around the Greater World and hit the dust planes again.

"We have a good library of discovered objects and their trajectories. If we can swing out and back in, there's a collision zone we can disguise our trajectory with."

It just meant weeks above the dust. Above everything they were comfortable with.

But what was the alternative? Stay put and wait for the Hunter-Killers? Fiana wasn't a historian, but even she knew that the Hunter-Killers tore apart everything in an area that registered electrical activity.

Her ancestors had tall, black steles scattered around their world with old pictograms carved into their sides that warned them about the Hunter-Killers. Told stories about how the alien machines followed shouts into the stellar night to their source and destroyed them. And despite those proscriptions, Hulin the Wise had experimented with crystal radio devices in the polar north of Sese. An asteroid impact had cracked the world, almost revealing the hollow interior her people had hidden inside since the ancestors first arrived. Those had been years of children dying as air fouled, and great engineering projects struggled to do the impossible: fix a cracked world.

"How fast can we get out of here?"

"Using consumables, it's dangerous, Mother. We need to coordinate with Ops. The margin will be thin, if we want to get out of here before the Hunter-Killers."

Fiana swept the transparent sheets around her away. "I'll get Ops ready to follow your commands."

To stay put would be to wait passively for death, and she wasn't ready to welcome the Hunter-Killers onto her ship.

Within the hour, the far side of the dustship was venting gases as crew warmed the material up (but not too much, or the heat signature would be suspicious and hint at some kind of unnatural process), compressed the water and hydrogen in airlocks through conduits of muscular tubes that grew throughout the ship, and blasted it out in timed dumps at F&O's orders.

Slowly, faster than the natural differential drift already there, Fiana's dustship began to move away from the seedship. It trailed a tail behind, gleaming like a comet.

THE DUSTSHIP WAS a living organism. Its massive hearts pumped ichor around webs of veins that exchanged heat generated by the living things inside the rock and ice hull, both human and engineered. The great lungs heaved, and the air inside moved about. Its bowels gurgled with waste, and its stomach fermented grain to feed the people.

Sese's people had worked hard to create a biological, living shell that could move through the rings around the Greater World. And they had found the other worlds the ancients had created, some of them dead hulks. Because the Hunter-Killers were ever on the prowl and not just myths to scare children with that had been passed down through the mists of prehistory.

Figures and Orbits, down in their calculatorium, worked away at the reports of Hunter-Killer movements, tracking them as they arrowed in toward the seedship. And other telescopists watched as the seedship dwindled away, until it became a glint among the other points of light in the busy sky.

And Fiana hung in Ops, watching as the activity of the ship passed on through the watch stations and crew.

It was tense, the first few full rotations. No one slept. There were tears that hung in the air. Salty fear, exhaustion, tension. The idea that the killers of the Ancients were chasing them could unnerve anyone.

Yes, they'd escaped the initial trap, but that didn't mean they were safe yet.

Fiana broke the tension when she ordered watches to resume a standard staggered watch rotation again. Even if she wasn't so sure she wouldn't need all-call, she needed the crew to function. Any more than three shifts and a person could not function under a constant press of fear, watchfulness, and readiness.

So she took the pressure for herself.

FIANA WAS INSPECTING the crew shaving ice from the outer walls, using one of the many burrowed tunnels in the hull, when Lily caught up to her.

"May I have a moment, Mother?" she asked softly.

"They keep sending you to brief me," Fiana noted. "You are a subordinate, not a superior. Why is your team doing this?"

"The more experienced calculating seniors need to be in the calculatorium at all times. We are at capacity, Mother, and this is not a time for anyone who needs work verified."

Lily wouldn't meet her eyes.

Well, she was either ashamed to admit she was the weakest

calculator in the ship, or the F&O mothers were using her as a firewall in case Fiana got angry with them.

Or, if the F&O mothers were smart, and they were the elite of void-faring peoples, the answer could be both things at the same time. Maybe it didn't hurt that Fiana would be less likely to be angry with a young, nervous Lily. And maybe they needed the best to stay in the room and work the problem.

"What's the emergency, Lily?"

"We're moving slower than expected, Mother. It has orbital and schedule implications. We can't vent heat because we didn't quite get where we thought we'd be to have cover of several larger rocky objects blocking us from Hunter-Killer view."

Fiana batted aside ice shavings and tried to focus over the hammering of pick axes and scrape of shovels.

"F&O made a mistake?" she asked. This could cost lives. No wonder they'd sent the almost childlike Lily to stare over at her with wide eyes. "Are you sure? The signal crew could have made a sighting mistake."

A bunch of boys with astrolabes at the telescopes doing their best astronomical sightings. F&O took the averages of repeated sightings.

"The math is strong," Lily protested, her voice firm with trust in her colleagues. "And junior F&O took sightings to confirm. The signal crew were accurate."

"But we're off track?" There was no room for that kind of error. If they didn't arrive at the right place at the right time, they wouldn't be able to tether off the right large rock, or hit the right dust plane to adjust their path.

They'd end up running out of air, or water, slowly dying,

out of reach of any other dustship or world that could lend aid.

Lily gave her a summary report, written in small and careful handwriting, filled with diagrams and area maps. Fiana would have to crawl over the details later in her quarters, poring over the equations and running checks with her own slide rule. A Mother Superior of a dustship was required to know the math, Fiana had been an F&O staffer herself in her youth.

But it was going to be slow work to make sure she understood everything in the report.

Tight was the crown of leadership, Fiana knew. It would be a headache she had to bear.

Fiana cursorily looked through the report until she found the summary. She bit her lip. "F&O thinks there's more mass than we accounted for?"

"About sixty chipstones worth of mass."

Sixty chipstones. About ten people's worth of mass. Had they known their audit was off, they could have thrown out non-essential material from the inside to balance the ship. They could have hidden it away in the ice and consumables they'd blown.

It shouldn't have been off, though. They'd based their lives on the audit run before maneuvers.

"There was an audit," Fiana said. And everyone on board knew how important an audit was before a maneuver.

"F&O is not accusing anyone of anything, we are merely reporting the math. It doesn't lie, Mother. You can check it yourself."

She would. But for now, Fiana was not going to assume

her specialists were wrong. She had to trust that her team was doing their best work. "I will check it, but I will wager it agrees with you. I'll call another mass audit. Something isn't right. We'll see if we can solve for the mystery yet."

Even though she hung in the air, Lily visibly relaxed as tension drained from her body.

"Of course, Mother. We will put our second shift at your disposal and keep only a core team running calculations."

THE HEAT BEGAN to build. Crew took to wearing just simple wraps when off shift, and then Fiana gave permission for everyone to strip to just undergarments.

Globes of salty sweat hung in the stultifying air and sunken eyes made everyone look like tired ghosts.

The ship's Surgeon, Lla-Je fe Sese kicked his foot against the door to the captain's quarters in the middle of an off-watch. Fiana was startled to find him hanging in place, face flushed and worried.

"Mother, we are all in danger of heat stroke," Je said, without apologizing for waking her. The red emergency light in the doorway glimmered off his shaved scalp. It was the way of the surgeons to shave, though Je was male and used to shaving. For surgeons it was ritual demonstration of control of a razor, a tradition hundreds of years old. A surgeon with a nick on her body was not to be trusted, or so the saying went. Je said it was actually done for hygiene, but it helped that men were expected to be fastidious about it as well. Fiana always imagined it must have been weirder for the regular surgeons to hew to the tradition, given expectations. "How much longer will we be containing our waste heat?"

They'd been drifting for days now, moving further away from the seedship. The thick wall of ice around the hull that they mined for air and water had been scraped down, warmed, and vented. In some parts, the hull was down to only rock and mud.

"Fifteen full shifts before we reintersect with the dust fields." One orbit around the Greater World. They would have to deploy full sails on return, but the higher orbit would let the area the Hunter-Killers were infesting move ahead under them. They would plunge back into a different part of the Archipelago with barely any water and air left.

"Crew will be dying from the heat long before then," Je said somberly.

"What should we look for?" Fiana asked wearily. Die of heat now, or miss their chance to get to safety when they reintersected with the dust planes and the Archipelago. Floating diarrhea, those choices.

"Confusion, irritability—" Like Fiana's irritability at being woken? Though, to be fair, she'd been sleeping slightly, dozing as she bumped from the wall to the hammock. "Dry skin, vomiting, panting, and flushed faces."

"We're out in the void, Je. The Hunter-Killers can move out here without needing sails or tethers, but we're helpless until we intersect with the dust rings again."

"Then all that our people will find will be a ghost ship," Je said seriously. "If they are able to find us at all."

He was so serious. Always worried. And it wasn't his place

to look this long in the face. It was Fiana's. But Je had always been high-minded. He wouldn't have fought so hard for a place in the Surgeons' Academy without a certain amount of hard pushiness.

"What do you recommend, my surgeon?"

"Daily internal thermometer checks for every crewmember," Je said.

"Internal? Is that what I think you mean?"

"It is."

"Je…" Fiana trailed off. Then she took a deep breath. "I can't have your team sticking tubes up everyone's ass once a day."

Particularly not if some male surgeon was doing it. Her team of commanding mothers trusted that Fiana valued Je, but a lot of them were old-fashioned and uncomfortable with having large, awkward hands on the handle of a blade.

"Then draw up a list of essential crew that you can't afford to lose, and they will be tested once a day. We're risking lives, understand?"

"I'll have the list drawn up, but we don't start taking temperatures until people start passing out," Fiana said. "The DNA samples are in lead cases in the ice rooms with our food. We can put anyone in danger there for now."

But it would be a temporary solution.

It was enough to mollify Je. For now.

But the decisions would become tougher as this went on.

THE MASS AUDIT came back from a sweaty, tired Audra, who

tracked Fiana down in the galley hall. The Secondary Mother had sheaves of clear flexies filled with accounting tables.

"There's unaccounted for mass. We did the audit. We tested the ship's acceleration profile. The amount of mass they estimated is dead-on: there's sixty chipstone worth of something *somewhere*. Manifests can't account for it. We've checked everything we can think of."

Fiana offered her a pocket of cooled water, which Audra took and sucked on gratefully. Fiana used that as a moment to capture her own thoughts and continue nibbling at a basket of grapes.

"We're going to have to search everyone's cabins, verify personal allowances," Audra said, before Fiana could even speak.

"No." Fiana shook her head. "There are just over a hundred crew. And yes, split, that could be enough." And when they sailed out from Sese, they did not have to consider how true their mass was; they just deployed sails into the appropriate dust plane until they had the speed and vectors needed.

"We only did a rough manifest and mass account before leaving," Audra noted.

"I've sailed the dust planes of the Greater World all my life, Audra. I've been F&O, then Secondary Mother, and now Mother. I'd sense it in my bones the moment we left if the sails were straining, our vessel heavy." Fiana said. "No, this has only been a problem since that seedship."

Audra, her legs looped around an air-chair, straightened. "What are you thinking?"

"Take the survey teams, the men, out onto the hull. Use

airlocks facing away from the dust to keep cover. Full Encounter rules. Do you understand what I am asking you? Can you do that?"

Audra looked past Fiana, out into a personal darkness and into fear as she considered her own death. Fiana was asking her to go out an airlock, seal it with ice and rock once the team was out, and then they would search the hull.

If they encountered Hunter-Killers, they would jump off into the vacuum and scatter to their deaths. They would not, under any circumstance, return to any known airlock, lest they lead the enemy inside. Maybe the Hunter-Killers wouldn't buy that. Maybe they would. It was still a hard thing to ask of a person.

Audra would know that if she turned this down, Fiana would honor her choice. But it would be a blow to her standing.

"I will lead a team," Audra said in a low, determined voice. "We need to find out what may have killed us."

Fiana held her hand and squeezed it. Such bravery. She had no doubt in Audra. It's why she had chosen the strong mind from her old F&O cohort to join her when the World Mothers had given Fiana a command of her own.

FOR AN ENTIRE watch, the ship went about its business in a pre-funereal silence, with crew jumping at every bang and creak in the empty air.

Je came to report on two crewmembers who had passed out. An older F&O calculator and one of the survey men. He had given them fluids and put them in a freezer to let them cool down.

"The ship is suffering too," he told her. The ship's heart had an infection, he judged. Some kind of pericarditis inflaming the sac around the great muscle. They were pumping it full of antibiotics and hoping for the best.

"We can't dump heat, not yet," Fiana told him.

"I know," Je said softly. "I know."

The warble of airlock alarms echoed. Je twisted in the air to look down the corridor. "They're coming back inside."

Crew streamed through the air toward the doors. They weren't carrying weapons. There was nothing that would stop a Hunter-Killer, there was no point.

But they still came, determination on their faces, fists clenched. They would have thrown their bodies against the deadly machines to buy their sisters another minute of life, Fiana knew, with a tight knot in her stomach.

Voidsuits came through instead of gleaming, spidery balls of death. Fiana relaxed slightly.

And then more suits struggled through.

And more.

Despite herself, Fiana said aloud, "There are too many of them!"

Ten other suits that hadn't piled into the airlock on the way out.

Ten.

That could be sixty chipstones. If they were…

They removed their helmets, and the confused crew gasped.

Belshin men. Ten Belshin men.

* * *

TEN BELSHIN MALES had maybe doomed them all. It was something that Fiana kept rolling around her head for all its strangeness as she stared at the ten foreign faces hovering before her.

It was the math. The simple math. The massive ball of rock and ice looked substantial, but orbital mechanics were precise and unforgiving. Their weight had slowed them down enough to throw off the maneuver.

Fiana pointed at them. "You activated the seedship, you unleashed the Hunter-Killers on us all, and then you fled to our hull to hide! You have the audacity to hide on *my* ship?"

"They don't speak Undak," Je said. "Do you want me to translate? They're expecting that you will throw them out of the airlock. They're terrified."

Fiana saw it on their faces. Resignation, fear, some defiance.

Audra crossed her arms. "We should slice off their balls, put them in the fridge with the seedship DNA, and then shove the floating shits out the airlock."

"Don't translate that," Fiana said to Je.

"Engage the Lineage Protocol," Audra said. "We need to initiate it now. While we still have some sort of chance."

Fiana could hear Je suck in his breath. She looked over at Audra. "We're not going to talk about the Protocol right now. These are human lives you're talking about."

Audra glanced at Je. "Mother, he knew the risks when he agreed to join the ship."

"Lives," Fiana said slowly. "All of the lives on this ship are important."

Je was only half listening. Several of the newcomers were chattering to him.

"They know you're angry," Je reported, cutting Audra off. "They're expecting you to kill them. They're gastric plumbers. Belshin slaves. They fled when their ship was attacked."

"We cannot afford the increase in consumables," Audra hissed. "We're far out into the void. We're off orbit and schedule. You know what needs to be done, and it needs to be done quickly. Your crew is depending on you."

Fiana raised a finger. "Audra—"

Audra pushed herself back away from the room. "As one of your secondaries, I have to remind you: every moment those males remain on board is a moment stolen from our own future. It's math. It means cold, hard decisions. But that is what leaders do: they make the hard choices."

FIANA TOOK LILY into one of the observation ice bowls.

"I wanted to show you something," Fiana said, drifting out toward the polished ice.

The young F&O calculator hung next to her. "Mother?"

Fiana pointed out at the dark. "Look out there, Lily. All those small points of light. That's something few, if any people from the Archipelago ever get to see."

From here, they could see the entirety of the dust plane. The multitudes of the rings, the rocky moons.

Lily held up a thumb. "All of our people out there. Hiding away from Hunter-Killers."

They stared at the dust band for a long while.

Lily cleared her throat. "Even if you sacrifice the Belshin, we can't fix the orbit."

"I spent two whole nights running the figures," Fiana said. "Audra ran them as well. Fifty people can survive a full braking maneuver and a loop by object IF-547, then 893, and a second all-sails slow that you and F&O have given me."

"So, it's Lineage Protocol." Lily turned her back to the dust plane. "They tell you in the Academy not to get too attached to the men aboard."

"People I trust are all telling me it's time." Fiana rubbed her forehead. The headaches were getting more and more intense. "We only have enough for fifty people to survive until we reintercept the dust plane."

Protocol said it was time to take donations from all the men, store the material, and then ask them all to do the honorable thing. The *noble* thing. If they balked, then it was the Mother Superior's job to enforce the choice.

Only women could bear the next generation. Fiana needed to act to secure futures.

And yet...

"The ideas that fix this situation, they won't come from just one person dictating them. It's going to have to come from everyone working the math. And being cross-checked."

Lily's eyes widened. "You're not going to engage the protocol?"

"Hard choices. The other mothers keep telling me to make hard choices." Fiana pushed away. "But the people who tell me that don't have to bear the consequences of those choices, and don't see the whole community, just the part of it that they identify with. It's easy to make a 'hard' choice when the price is paid by someone else."

"This won't be a popular decision," Lily said. "And I won't tell Audra you called her unimaginative."

"Thank you." Fiana patted her shoulder. "I need you to work out the problem, talk to anyone who might have ideas, and to lean on your peers."

"We'll keep running ideas through the team," Lily promised. "There are things the engineers have proposed in the past. More non-essential mass that could be jettisoned. It could help."

Because there was math. And then there was *math*. Math was a tool, wasn't it? A tool to be wielded or mastered.

And Fiana wasn't going to give it blood.

FOUR CREW PASSED out and were found floating in the corridors. Je came to Fiana, his face pinched and ruddy, to give her an update.

"Mother, we should have off-duty crew switch to a three-person cross-check system so that no one ends up alone."

"I'll send out orders." Fiana was hooked into the 'top' of her room, which was laced with foot-webbing. She'd been holding a position in front of an air vent, letting the rush of air bob her back and forth.

"And I need to check you over," Je said.

Fiana waved a hand. "I'm fine. There are others who need your attention, Je."

"You're the Mother Superior," Je insisted.

Fiana wiped a fat bead of sweat collecting behind her ear. The air was getting so thick she felt like she couldn't breathe anymore. They'd stopped venting and the heat, the moisture from shaving the ice, and the dust in the air had turned the ship into a swamp.

"I will endure," Fiana said. "If I feel I'm at risk, I'll let you know."

Je didn't look happy, but he couldn't really do anything about it, so he nodded. He had floated his way back to the entryway, and he paused there, hands and feet in an X and gripping the door's lip.

"Mother, may I ask you something?"

His voice had softened, and Fiana could hear the worry.

"Lineage Protocol?" she asked him.

"Such a dry name for something so horrific," Je said as he nodded.

"F&O is working hard on a solution. I've asked all for ideas. But, in a nutshell, we need to breathe less, surgeon. We used too much as a simple rocket to get us away from the Hunter-Killer area. The math is simple and hard to escape. We only have so much air and we know how many people are onboard."

"The equation is simple," Je said. "So we change the assumed inputs. The air-use rate is based on an assumption created by surgeons for average crew with average activity."

Je had her complete attention.

"Can you actually get the crew to breathe less?"

"The more you move, the more you breathe. So, we freeze crew shifts. Everyone bound to their room and webbed in.

No one moves until rescue. The command room shift stays in place and sleeps in place."

"You're asking the entire crew to stay in bed for twelve full shift rotations?"

"And to focus on breathing slowly and deeply. And that is not all. We have drugs for surgeries. The larger ones that use more air, we will need to drug them."

"And what will that get us, Je? Will that get us to the dust plane? Will that halve the air we use?"

"This isn't math, it's biology. Messy, imprecise," Je said.

"Give me an estimate," Fiana ordered. Because she couldn't risk lives based on messiness.

"I think we can reduce our air usage to two-thirds. Maybe to a half. We won't know until we start the experiment and monitor the impact."

Two-thirds still left a ghost ship. A third was an unblinking gulf that still couldn't be crossed.

But it would mean fewer lives that needed chosen for sacrifice.

"Ready the drugs," Fiana said. "We'll run the experiment and get a shift's worth of data." It wouldn't get them there by itself. It wasn't the solution. But it was something they could test.

Audra appeared at the door and shoved Je aside. She had a bandolier strapped tight across her chest and had changed into her dark black sortie uniform. Her pistol was in its forearm holster.

"Mother, we have a mutiny!" Audra said. "The men heard that Lineage Protocol will be called for. Some of them released the Belshin prisoners and broke into the armory."

* * *

THE MUTINY SPREAD quickly. Panicked men took weapons into common areas which they barricaded with decoration panels ripped from the walls. Many of them were on sortie parties, so were familiar with in-ship combat and knew where to find the weapons.

"We have the numbers," Audra said. Few could match her well-trained cadre. "My sisters are fast and are the best hall-grapplers in the fleet."

Audra and her team would fight bitterly. They were Sortie Three, rarely sent to other ships, but trained to protect this one. They were backed up by members of engineering and women from the stays and tether teams, with their arms muscled from handling spider-silk ropes.

They raced down corridors to the heart of the mutiny where the chanting men were making their demands heard.

"Stop here!" Another woman in black held out a hand near a turn in the rock-ice corridor. "Mother, they're shooting anyone who tries to approach the barricade."

They all grabbed rails and stopped. Fiana listened to the shouts, the men trying to keep each other roused to bravery with their too deep voices. No raising them to neutral-sounding tones now because they were speaking to mothers or sisters around the ship.

"We should have expected this," Audra said, acid in her voice.

Je said nothing but shrank back as if trying to hide against the wall.

Fiana looked around again at the nervous, but anticipatory sortie crew all watching Audra, waiting for the command. Then, she quickly peeked around the corner.

"Mother!"

The men shouted at her but didn't shoot. Fiana took that as a good sign and stopped to look at the crudely hammered together door leading to the common rooms and the forms that she could see through the gaps nervously flitting around.

"Get Lily from F&O," Fiana ordered.

"And?" Audra also looked ready to go.

"It's the heat," Fiana said. She was panting from the race over here. "It's affecting our minds. Leading us to mistakes."

"My mind is tempered well," Audra hissed. "They are traitors to Sese, and foreign agitators from the other side of the Archipelago."

"What are their demands?" Fiana couldn't tell from all the yelling.

"They want the chance to live through lottery," one of the tether women with a simple club in her hands said.

"That's treason," Audra said. She leaned forward. "If we fight them, we can take care of the dilemma we face."

"Death makes traitors of many," Fiana said. "And the heat addles their minds. All our minds. Wouldn't you say, surgeon?"

Je did not look happy about being addressed. "Mother..."

But Fiana saw Lily coasting toward them and waved her over. "My calculator! We have a tricky situation."

Fiana pulled the last of her wrap off, stripping herself naked, and then gently tapped the wall so that she would float out into the center of the corridor before Audra could react.

She could hear the sudden murmurs of surprise, the repeated low whispers of "Mother."

They began to shout their demands through the barricade, but she held up a hand.

"It is too hot for a fight, but if we have to, you are outnumbered. And you know this. So we are going to talk about this instead, because I did not come out here into the void to do the Hunter-Killers' work for them. Not when our ancestors risked so much to create the Archipelago and dust planes for our survival. I will not spit on their memories."

They quieted.

"I don't have the answer to our situation. But we, together, do. Come out to me, Je, Lily. Tell them what you've been telling me."

Fiana looked back. She gestured at them both.

Slowly, the surgeon and the F&O calculator bobbled out to join her.

"F&O found our mass problem. They saved us from the Hunter-Killers. Je is keeping us alive as best as he can in this heat. I don't have the solution to how we can make it back to the dust plane alive, but the two of them, with all of our help, might. There is no one answer here, but if we piece all of their ideas together, and add in some new ones, they could add up to enough to get us back home."

Lily stared at the men, then bit her lip. "We need to shed mass once we're at the apoapsis. Everything we can imagine we can do without and things we can't. We need to pare the ice and rock to the bare minimum, down to nothing but air, sails, and our own bodies."

"And the rest of us must strap in and not move until rescue. The biggest among us must be drugged," Je said.

The men protested. That would surely impact them the most.

But Je argued with them. "These are the realities," he insisted. "We have to breathe less... or not at all."

"We could thin the air more," one of the male voices on the other side suggested. "I'm in gastric, we can change the recirculation mixes."

As the suggestions continued, Fiana relaxed.

"We are not separate from the civilization that birthed us," she said to Audra. "We do not have to fall into murder and blood. Not this time."

THE GREAT DUSTSHIP calved at apoapsis, the very height of its orbit. Fiana would have liked to have seen it and the entire dust plane glinting its encirclement of their Greater World. But she had to be in her cabin. No one moved about, not even her. Surgeon's orders.

It was not unusual for objects to break apart. Hopefully, anything watching would assume it was a normal event, a weakened body splitting apart and becoming two.

Now they would begin to gain speed, to dump off heat and more consumables to alter their trajectory *just* enough. They were speeding up, every tick as they dropped lower and lower.

"Why would you want to go back out there?" Je had once asked her, when they were on Sese's interior walking through the botanical gardens. He raised a hand to encompass the whole world in all its lushness. She had been trying to recruit him as surgeon. The first male surgeon to fly the Archipelago void. "Why not stay and enjoy this world?"

"The only difference between them is scale, Je. Come see all the worlds. It reveals us for who we really are, to go out there."

Fiana lay strapped to her webbing, in a drugged stupor, breathing slowly. There were many more full shifts ahead to endure before they would come screaming back into the dust and throw out the sails to chatter and bite and shake.

But they would get home, she thought dimly.

The math was there.

MUTATA SUPERESSE
JASON FISCHER AND SEAN WILLIAMS

Extraction Transcript
U-2184-0115-1314
Yalanginyi A

Event 1 — *Pennophis minimus*

UNKNOWN LIFE FORM ENGAGED, CATEGORY ONE INJURY, DOME INTEGRITY THREATENED, WAVEFORM CONTACT ESTABLISHED.

WELL, THAT ESCALATED quickly.

Stay down. You're safe now... I think. Honestly, you had no idea what would happen when the moon came up? Amateur hour. Always expect the shape to trend towards pear.

Tell me how bad the bleeding is.

Okay, I'm on my way. Fingers in ears if you don't like loud noises.

Behind you. Hi. Nice to meet in person. Sorry about the bang—air displacement from the waveformer, AKA a space fart. Now you know why they call us Boomers.

There are four of you? All right, three and three quarters. Let me put the medkit on this guy. What's his name? Klemich, got it. And you're...? Gabison, Lozanoski, and Bell. Commander Nicol, by the way. Colonial Security, Heavy Armour Squad. Yes, of course you're in deep shit. You idiots started an illegal settlement on an unsurveyed world. See how that worked out?

Plenty of time later to worry about your legal issues: first, you've got to survive. The guys in orbit need to find a clear corridor for our emergency extract, so this won't be fast. We only pull out when it's safe for all concerned, which is pretty good advice all round, but specifically...

Yeah, that's right. Heavy Armour Squad. Long before you were born, my forerunners rocketed out of reintegrator booths with wildly-edited velocity profiles, going from standing to supersonic speeds in zero seconds: *boom-boom*. The high-tech version of shooting a dickhead out of a cannon.

Then waveform launchers superseded d-mat. No booth, right? Just the sudden displacement of air. Much easier to jump from a troop carrier into the field of combat and back again, covered in blood and glory. Or whatever.

My point is, you do not want to overlap with anything en route. That can be messy.

Hey… hey! Don't listen to those things outside. They're just animals. Seriously. My eyes are patched into the dome feed. I'll know if those nibblers get purchase. What the hell are they, anyway? They remind me of… well, that's a whole other story. Let's just say I still have nightmares about flying teeth.

Huh, kid? You really want to hear about the teeth? *Now?* All right, but Lozanoski, you keep an eye on the medkit and tell me if it flashes red. The rest of you, listen up.

So, it was a bit like today: didn't know we were in trouble until we were up to our junk in it. The squad was in the Lakshmi-G system, dispatched to check on a private outfit that ran into trouble at one of the Lagrange points. What we found was… well, to be honest, I thought it was pretty cool, at first. The station was covered with an alien life form, like coral or some kind of giant urchin. It clumped and had spikes. We were wary, naturally, but couldn't see what had routed the privateers. More like rooted, heh: body parts everywhere, chopped up fine… fingers, ears, eyes, ropes of guts—

Sorry. Got to remember you're not raw recruits and my job isn't to scare you shitless.

So, back to the star urchins. We were tearing one away so we could find the airlock when we realised the spikes were just for decoration. Their real defence exploded out of big pores all over their skins.

Picture a tiny predator with the sharpest fangs you can imagine—so sharp they'd cut right through a pressure suit, easy. But don't imagine it with arms, legs, a body, or even a head. Just jaws, incisors and a fat venom sac, thousands of them coming at you fast. Part of the reproductive cycle, we figured out later, co-opted when under threat to keep the parent alive.

Hard to hit. Never satiated. One function only.

Flying teeth.

Huh. You hear that? Yeah, me neither. Something made those snake-things run away and I don't think it's my crappy storytelling.

Event 2 — *Pantherium polialatum*

INCREASED HOSTILE ACTIVITY, SAFEPOINT THREATENED, STRATEGIC RELOCATION EXPEDITED.

Go, GO! NOW!

That's it. Through here! Down. Careful, it's slippery. Don't think about that. Stay right back, I've got to seal off the entry point.

Can't jump us out, not while the air's too... Fuck! Didn't mean to bring down the whole roof. That's it, Bell. Keep a tight grip on his legs. We need to get out of sight before those big motherfuckers come see what blew their friend up.

Guess we should've known *this* was coming. What eats the snake-things, and what eats *that*? Hopefully, this is the top of the food chain.

A bit further. Yeah, that should do us. I still got eyes on up top. Doesn't look like anything's following.

Standard extraction protocol, ah... that ain't going to cut it now. I won't pull any punches. We Boomers can go anywhere, but for ferrying passengers we need line of sight. You guys don't have the hardware inside. So being down here in the basement really limits our options. Don't feel bad: it's not the end of the world. Maybe a lander can drill down to us. Let's kill time and see what happens.

The story? Oh yeah, I suppose... The nibblers were going for us like something out of a nightmare. Hellish, it was. You'd trigger a star urchin and it'd fire out its swarm, and that'd trigger another one, and before you knew it, there was nothing but teeth all around us. Zero gravity, too, so those things could ricochet with attitude. Half our squad was bitten in the first minute, and those bites had a sting to them like a nip from a rabid dog with a mouthful of broken glass, let me tell you. By two minutes, you couldn't see for blood. Buddies I'd fought with for ten years—against god knows what monsters, over all inhabited space—were torn apart like they were hit by shrapnel—and the worst thing is, these fang-creatures didn't have stomachs. They weren't *eating*. They just bit and bit and didn't care what happened to what was left behind. They...

How is this helping? Wait and see, I'm getting there. Besides, you wanted the story. All right, Gabison and Lozanoski wanted the story. Sorry, Bell, you've been outvoted.

The survivors of that first wave, we thought we were the lucky ones. We boomed back to the carrier to lick our wounds and work out what to do next. The privateers were still holed up in the structure, but their air was limited. If we couldn't cut through the urchins, we'd have to boom directly inside, which was fine. Getting out would be the problem. Same as here, see? One of us was going to have to blow a hole in the side of the station in order to clear the way.

That's right, we should've done that on the first try. But no privateer takes kindly to someone can-opening their precious hardware, even when their lives are at stake.

That's a lesson we learned the hard way.

Those of us with the fewest bites loaded up medkits and ordnance and boomed into the station. The plan was to split up, find the survivors, lay the charges, get out. Easy.

Only that's when the pain kicked in. The instant the rescue party arrived, their nerves were on fire, like pure acid and electricity running through all seventy-six kilometres of the body's nervous system. The comms line was full of screaming—terrible shrieks, like the guys were burning alive—and back on the carrier, no one knew what the hell just happened. More of us boomed in, rescuing the rescue party, but had exactly the same problem. The instant they arrived in the station, they too were in agony—and when they boomed back to the carrier, the ones with the highest pain tolerance leading the others, it got even worse.

Booming appeared to be the culprit, but it wasn't that simple, of course.

Our medic took samples from the injured, half of whom were now insane with agony, and eventually, he worked out it was poison. A nasty volatile compound on the flying teeth that got into the nerves and heightened their sensitivity, plus some freakish interaction on the quantum level that squared the efficacy of the poison each time we activated our waveformers. So the pain of those bites got exponentially worse every time we boomed somewhere.

Which put us in a real pickle. Four troopers screaming their heads off; another four insane. All of us infected with that poison. Plus, a bunch of privateers still needing rescue. What's a squad to do?

Hang on. Are you seeing this? Of course, you're not. I'll patch you in.

Remember what I said about things going arse-up at any moment? Well, we're in a barrel of arses now and someone just gave it a good spin.

Event 3 — *Maxiptera Sanguinis*

EXPOSURE THREATENED, URGENT MEDICAL PROCEDURE EXPEDITED.

SCREW THE MEDKIT, Lozanoski—it's too slow and careful. We're going to have to do this the hard way. Hold him down. Bell, Gabison—take his hips, one each side. He so much as twitches while I do this to him, he's dead, and then so are we.

Hold your breaths. This is gonna stink. Better than the alternative, though—and hopefully, our new friends won't like it either.

Lozanoski—you watching that feed? Any of them caught our scent yet?

Good. Those bloodsuckers can eat the big motherfuckers all they want, so long as they don't come down here and try feeding on us.

Almost finished. When this hole is cauterised, we can stop worrying about the blood he's leaking and get back to the story, if you're so inclined. The best bit's coming up—and I'm not just saying that to keep your mind off what's going on outside, honest.

Okay. That'll do. Just let me get my breath back.

None of you are military, but after today you're not exactly fresh meat either. You've seen what it's like on the frontier. You won't be surprised to know that there's no squad in the universe that doesn't have a medic. Two medics, sometimes.

So, the flying teeth. Ordinary painkillers wouldn't stop the agony they caused. We could dose ourselves up to the eyeballs with whatever drug we wanted, but the signal always got through—it was slowly growing, in fact, until all was fire and acid and screaming and two suicides a day. The pain was just that intense.

Our medic in Lakshmi-G was a guy called Scarlett, better known as "Handsome Joe". Handsome Joe was the middle of three clones serving in our squad. Spooky Joe, the oldest, was our intelligence officer, and Rookie Joe had aspirations of being a natural historian when his tour was up. Handsome

Joe's job was to find a medical solution to the fang-beast problem.

Normally, the next step in field situations when painkillers don't work would be to use the waveformers to make judicious edits or two, like we'll do with your mate here once we get him to the carrier. Snip the pain centres in the brain so we'd feel nothing, for instance. But that wasn't possible then. Each boom made things that much worse. Get the edit slightly wrong and our guys could go out of their minds.

Handsome Joe needed something radical to target the poison in our nerves, and fast. But he was drawing a serious blank, and in desperation he confided in Rookie Joe. Who had an idea, but he didn't know how to make it happen. So, the two of them asked Spooky Joe, who took it up with our commanding officer.

I was present when they outlined the solution they'd come up with. Our CO was a gruff old gal who never so much as blinked at anything, but even she thought the Joes had lost it.

"Leprosy," was what Handsome Joe told her. *Mycobacterium lepromatosis* is a fast-acting bug that gets into the nerves and causes granulomas kills them, basically. If he could inject a supercharged version into us, it would kill the nerves and render the poison ineffective. Sounded great, in theory.

Except, where was he going to get their hands on a sample of *Mycobacterium lepromatosis*? Leprosy was supposedly wiped out in the twenty-first century. It's not the kind of thing you expect to find in a medic's toolkit.

The answer was simple, Rookie Joe said. We needed an armadillo.

My reaction exactly! I'm glad you can see the humour. There we were, half-chewed up by flying teeth, crazy with pain, and our medic was telling us we needed to track down the weirdest-looking critter ever to come out of South America—walking rocks with shells tough enough to deflect a bullet! Where were we going to find something like that on the frontier, and how was it supposed to help us?

I'd forgotten the old scout's motto.

Everything is knowledge, even the *Mycobacterium lepromatosis* genome. Deleting knowledge is up there with killing patients, for intelligence officers like Spooky Joe. Because you never know what you're going to need, right? You don't want to be staring down something with talons made of gallium without knowing that a spray of warm piss and vinegar will make them rot away in moments. And yeah, that happened...

Armadillos, it turns out, were among the few species known to catch leprosy.

Intelligence officers have access to the total sum of human knowledge, packed in a way that can be confidentially accessed anytime, anywhere. So, whoever uploaded our South American friend's genome into the intelligence database went to the trouble of uploading the *Mycobacterium lepromatosis* genome along with it, right there in *D. septemcinctus*, the seven-banded armadillo.

Did I mention we were all out of our minds with pain by then? Took the three Joes working together to make this labcoat shit work, and even then...

Well, let's just say that as far as rush-jobs go, they did the best they—

Wait, what now?

Event 4 — *Hemaphaga volans*

HOSTILE INCURSION LIKELY, EXTRACTION REQUESTED URGENTLY.

KEEP GOING, FALL back! We need sealant, stat!

So that's what eats a bloodsucker. A smaller bloodsucker. And lots thereof. Can't believe you idiots pitched your tent here.

Now, put the masks on and help me spray that stuff around

the door. In all the cracks too. We don't want those bugs getting a whiff of Klemich, here. You know a mosquito can smell blood from forty metres away?

Great. Now, tell me if you hear a buzzing sound.

You *should* be worried. I'm not... I've been bitten by worse and paid the price.

When Handsome Joe called for volunteers, I was the first in line to take the shot. He knew his stuff, and this was the only way to rescue the privateers. We weren't leaving Lakshmi-G until every one of those sorry meatsacks was safe aboard the carrier and on their way home.

The supercharged leprosy bugs raced through me like slick shit through a goose. First, the pain from the bites went away, then all the aches and chafes you get from wearing combat armour too long went too.

Apart from a slight itch, I felt like a new soldier—recharged and ready for battle.

I wasn't indestructible. Too many of my friends had died that day for me to ever forget how dangerous those star urchins were.

Knowing that their best weapon against us had just been neutralised made a big difference, though. The new rescue squad lined up behind our CO, awaiting her order. I was on ordnance, tasked with blowing the hole in the station and keeping any flying teeth out of the way. And then, if all went well, lighting the fuse on a charge I prepared especially—one big enough to blow them all to hell. Screw the Interstellar Species Preservation Act.

Don't tell anyone I said that.

We jumped in, pain-free and utterly focused on the mission. The station was a mess, inside as well as out. You could see where the first wave of star urchins had been burned back by fire, at the cost of most of the available oxygen. Bulkheads were welded shut to keep the tiniest blastula out. There were human bodies too, and we did what we could to collect them for transfer to the carrier, once the hole was opened. All part of the service.

The moment the charges were laid, I sounded the warning and got the all-clear.

The station made the most godawful sound when it opened up. Gas and debris vented through the hole like air from a whoopie-cushion, and the star urchins all woke at once, hungry for more action. I took up my position in the hole, while my fellow boomers began booming, each carrying one survivor to the carrier and then coming back for another. My task was to rain a steady fire on the teeth outside.

Those old boomers had it easy, you know. Jumping in strings of ones and zeros meant an interrupted transmission cost only a tiny bit of the person riding it. If it wasn't too important a bit, you could carry on and it would be edited back in later.

Not so with waveformers. It's all or nothing with us. Job number one that day was to maintain the "all" part of the equation.

My rifle ran hot before the mission was halfway done. I called for a replacement, and the carrier sent two. A gun in each armpit, braced against the interior hull lining like some damned monkey, I soon became a target for every star urchin on the station. The vacuum was thick with teeth, and bits of teeth, and bits of bits of teeth. Undaunted, I kept firing so everyone could get through safely. I fired until the bits of bits turned to atoms. I fired until my index fingers became one with the triggers. And I cursed as I fired—cursed so hard and long I didn't hear the word come from the CO when the last of the survivors was out.

She had to send someone to tell me to stop. And even then, I didn't *want* to stop. I wanted to kill every one of those fucking things with my fucking hands. A bomb was too impersonal.

Stop I did, though. As the red haze lifted, I saw Handsome Joe Scarlett himself knocking on my faceplate and telling me it was time to go. Only he wasn't so handsome any more, and I didn't have time to understand why.

Because at that moment, a stray set of fangs latched onto my throat.

The teeth sliced right through my pressure suit, sounding like a serrated knife cutting into an aluminium can. I clutched at the hole in a panic, gas jetting past my fingers. There was no pain, thanks to my new dose of leprosy, but weirdly no blood.

In a panic, I let Handsome Joe check for injuries. My bio-readouts were good, and my suit was already patching two holes, one where the nibbler had entered, and the exit hole after it bounced away from my throat and out into the darkness. It was a big fucker. Should have taken my head off. So how come my soft juicy throat was still in one piece?

Maybe armadillos taste bad to them, I remember thinking.

Boom went the waveformer as Handsome Joe jumped me out of there.

Boom went the station as the dead man switch I'd rigged triggered my special star urchin surprise.

And that's the end of it, basically. Now, let's huddle for a verse or two of "By the Light of the Silvery Moon". I think I promised you a song as well as a...

...Hold a second. I'm getting something from orbit.

Okay, Heavy Armour is coming in hot. I'll jump topside to flag them down, but I won't be long. Stay put. If Klemich wakes up, tell him he'll be chugging in our staff bar within the hour.

What? No, I'll be fine. Sit tight. Booming backatcha in no time.

Miss me? We're go for extraction. Masks back on, and put your fingers in your ears for real. These charges are shaped, but there's always some blowback. I didn't babysit you this long to take you back deafened and with lungs full of dust!

3... 2... 1...

Run! No, that way! Get out of the debris cloud before those little buggers swarm back in. Duck for this last bit. Go go go! If someone grabs you, grab back. They're the good guys. And hold tight! You can't *in theory* get lost if you let go during a jump, but let's not put that to the test today, all right?

That's one gone.

Two.

Three.

Three and three quarters.

*   *   *

Event 5 — *Homo panopliae*

EXTRACTION INTERRUPTED.

WHAT'S UP, BELL? Second thoughts about leaving this paradise?

Huh. Good question. Just because you haven't heard of any leprosy anaesthetic doesn't mean I've been spinning some yarn to—

Sure, there were side effects. That's why I told you the story. Sometimes it's better not to screw with nature. Today, we totally could've come out guns blazing, but what good would that have done, except kill a few moonstruck monsters? The mutant mozzies and the big bloodsuckers and the things *they* fed on and the things *they* fed on... This is nature in action, right here, and sometimes it's best just to sit back and watch. All we had to do was wait and everything was okay. It will be, anyway, once I get you off this rock. Speaking of which, best move on before those bugs take a fancy—

They won't hurt me. Don't worry.

If you try to fight nature, you become part of it. That's why the motto of the Heavy Armour Squad is *Mutata Superesse Nobis*, which means *We changed to survive*. Or *evolved*, if you prefer. And our patch is the armadillo, see? Because that splice we got comes in real handy sometimes—like when the flying teeth tried to tear my throat out. Turned out the armadillo genome gave me more than an escape from endless pain. I had no idea what it did until I looked in a mirror.

Not pretty, I know—but hey, in this business, you need a thick skin.

Boom.

THE EMPTY GUN
YOON HA LEE

THE BAZAAR ON the moon that wandered Transitional Space did not meet Kestre sa Elaya's exacting requirements for a *safe transaction*. In years past, as the duelist prime of House Elaya, she would have journeyed with an honor guard to the much-feted Gray Manse. Her meeting would have involved liquors imported from the Flower Worlds and delectable canapés and candies, some of which she would pocket to give to her nieces when she returned home.

If circumstances had been less dire, she would have scorned a meeting with the arms dealer entirely. The dealer refused to leave the moon, for reasons lost in antiquity. That rankled; Kestre was used to people coming to her, not the other way around.

But House Elaya had died in blood and ash two months ago. Kestre herself had been left for dead by the assassins of House Tovraz. She was determined to make them pay for their mistake.

To do so, she needed a weapon. Not just any weapon, but one outside the Houses' Registry. Weapons like the ones the arms dealer sold.

Kestre didn't like Transitional Space. Like most House aristocrats, she was superstitious, and she'd always wondered if the immense aliens who had once lurked in Transitional Space, which humanity had driven off in the wars of old, still clung to existence. But she wouldn't admit to fear, either, and in any case the moon hadn't suffered any alien attacks since it was colonized.

"Three cutpurses behind you," her neural assistant said. "Knives only. They shouldn't cause you any trouble."

"Thank you," she said in a harsh whisper, and whipped around, dropping into a fighter's crouch. She saluted the cutpurses as though she faced them in a duel. The knife rested easily in her hand, and one by one she pointed at each, angling the blade precisely to reflect the streetlights into their eyes.

The cutpurses recognized the challenge for what it was, and slunk away.

"That was overkill," the assistant said mildly.

"I don't have time for petty thieves," Kestre returned, and continued on her way beneath the city dome with its featureless black sky. *The hungry sky,* the locals called it, those nights in Transitional Space, as the moon traveled through a warp-world *sideways* of ordinary space. She wondered if anyone else would hunt her tonight, but no one else troubled her.

The arms dealer lived in a surprisingly ordinary apartment overlooking a zero-gee playground. Kestre's doubts increased as she contemplated the dismayingly domestic wreath of cloud-bloom and brachial wires on the door. Then she knocked.

The door opened. The arms dealer was tall and broad, very dark, like Kestre herself, but with a strangely indistinct face. Even her eyes resembled pits of shadow.

The interior wasn't much better. Row upon row of weapons rested in plain sight, everything from finger-length knapped flint knives to crew-served artillery and even, in the back, the gleam of a missile whose length receded into an unlikely distance. Kestre assessed the offerings with an expert eye and shook her head in disappointment. "If this is all," she said, "I had best be on my way."

"Wait," the arms dealer said. "For the last survivor of House Elaya, I have something special."

"On with it, then," Kestre said, unease coiling in her belly.

"I don't have a good feeling about this," the assistant said. "We should look elsewhere."

"We don't have many options," Kestre subvocalized. "We'll have to chance it."

The arms dealer led Kestre into her home, stopping in a room where there was a single case. "This is what you want," she said.

Kestre's eyebrows rose. All she saw was a handgun of peculiar proportion, too large to wield comfortably, and dull green in color. "Unregistered?" she asked.

"Unregistered," the arms dealer confirmed. "The only one of its kind."

"Ammunition?"

"It's an amicable gun. It handles its own ammunition."

In her past life, Kestre would have walked away at this point. She'd heard of amicable artifacts, although she'd never handled one. They turned up on certain dead worlds, forever voyaging through Transitional Space, relics of the long-ago aliens that humanity had fought off during its first travels to the stars. The artifacts had a reputation both for extreme efficacy and for bringing bad luck to their owners.

Kestre was desperate, and her luck couldn't get any worse. Her House had perished. All she had left was her life, and the point of that life was revenge.

The arms dealer smiled knowingly at Kestre, who scowled and lifted the gun from the case. Still awkward, but it fit her hand better than she'd expected from its appearance. This might be workable after all.

"What do you want for it?" Kestre said after a grudging pause. "Whatever is in my power to give is yours."

The assistant began to protest Kestre's bargaining skills, but it was too late.

"The honor of House Elaya is still alive, I see," the arms dealer said. "Give me your House name, then, since you value it so."

Kestre shuddered and squeezed her eyes shut. The last thing she had of real value—but without a House, and she thought of the last time she'd tucked in her youngest cousins, the name meant nothing. The House could not go unavenged. If this was the price she must pay, then so be it. "Yes."

The arms dealer laid two precise fingers on Kestre's brow. A sensation like ice spiked through Kestre's heart and settled in her bones. "Say it," the arms dealer said, imperious. "Say your name. So you know."

Kestre opened her mouth. "Kestre—" Her own breath choked her. She coughed, tried again. "Kestre—" No use. She could not complete the name, even though the words *sa Elaya* beat in her chest.

"It's done," the arms dealer said. "Good hunting, Kestre of the Empty Gun."

Kestre would have asked what she meant by *that*, but the arms dealer was already ushering her out of her home. The racks of weapons leered at her as though they were gossiping about her.

Outside, pinpricks of light and the roseate whorls of local nebulae were emerging in the everywhere sky. The moon wasn't supposed to have exited Transitional Space for another four days. Had she lost that much time?

It didn't matter. She had a hunt to take up, name or no name.

KESTRE LEFT THE moon out of paranoia and traveled to a sparsely populated world to run her first tests, specifically in the Pillared Plains, with their double-edged shadows and glass-bright rocks, the dust of fallen stars. Few of the nearby city's inhabitants ventured here. There was no profit to be had, and explorers had a habit of turning up dead at the city limits. That made it perfect for her purpose.

She wasn't so stupid that she was going to take an unfamiliar weapon to an assassination. Here she encountered her first disappointment. The gun did not fire.

Despite the arms dealer's assurances, she had procured

rounds of rare polymorphic ammo, the kind that shaped itself to best suit weapon or world. It had taken the rest of her resources: fitting for someone who didn't belong to a House anymore. Fitting, but worrisome.

The gun misfired once, twice, and more times beyond that. Kestre had dealt with recalcitrant firearms since her childhood, under the severe eye of House Elaya's armsmaster. The fault was not in her ability, but the gun's own peculiarities. She added the arms dealer to the list of people she needed to kill, and turned to head back toward the city, causing the crossbow bolt to miss her by a centimeter.

Even in the dim and chancy light that ghosted through the Pillared Plains, Kestre recognized an assassin's bolt. Her neural assistant confirmed it. The bolt was yellow and green, the colors of House Tovraz. Despite her efforts to conceal her movements, someone had determined that she survived—and was set to finish the massacre.

A horrible laugh bubbled up in her chest. House Elaya was dead. She'd surrendered her name, after all. But the assassin didn't know and wouldn't care, and she was damned if she'd be easy meat.

Kestre dove for cover, a second bolt glancing off her armor as it hit at the wrong angle. There would be another, somewhere. The Tovraz liked to work in threes.

She thanked House Elaya's smiths for her suit. Her thanks didn't last long. The assassins had shared target lock with their third squadmate. The next bolt came from above, in what would have been an admirable parabola if Kestre had been in a mood for admiring, and punctured her air supply.

The ones that followed cracked her two spares.

These must be professionals. They didn't care about the pretty formalities of the duels Kestre had grown up fighting, and in whose terms she still tended to think. They wanted her dead, and they wanted her to know that she was dead.

"They're leaving," the assistant said in the carefully neutral voice it used when it wanted to inform her that *we're fucked*.

Of course they were leaving. Her heart thumped in panic at the serpent hiss of air escaping even as she reached for sealant. She couldn't save enough of the precious oxygen; the gauges told her that. Without air, she wouldn't survive the journey back to the city, even on the scooter she'd rented. The assistant, for all its pessimism, had done the pragmatic thing and backtracked the bolts' trajectories to give her targeting information. Useless as the information was with a gun that didn't work.

At this point, Kestre gave in to frustration. She was going to die in a lawless corner of the universe without having taken out a single person on her list. She'd sacrificed her most valuable possession, her House name, without achieving one iota of her revenge.

The gun had none of the useless polymorphic ammunition loaded. It was time to test the arms dealer's claim that the gun took care of matters itself, incredible as it sounded. Better that than giving up.

She lifted the gun and pulled the trigger three times in rapid succession, aiming in the general direction of the first target, the second target, the third.

It was a laughable gesture. In any other universe, it would

have availed her nothing, and she would have died a slow, agonizing death of asphyxiation only to be dragged by the corpse-collectors to the city limits when they found her. Or perhaps she would have hastened the process out of spite by opening her helmet to vacuum.

But this was the universe in which her weapon was the empty gun, bought in Transitional Space for the price of a House name, and the gun fired once, twice, thrice. The recoil surprised her, because the gun was *empty* and there should have been nothing to *cause* recoil. She actually dropped the gun after that third shot, something she hadn't done since childhood.

"They're not leaving anymore," the assistant said. This time its tone meant *we are either more fucked than before or miraculously unfucked, and it's your job, as the human half, to figure out which.*

Kestre was stunned into a non-sarcastic response. "What the hell happened?"

"They're not leaving anymore." Now it meant *I don't know either, and you're still in charge, what's a poor AI supposed to do?*

She was not so reckless as to believe the danger had passed. But she needed air, so she hastened to the first assassin's location. What she found when she reached them disquieted her.

The assassin's helmet was cracked, the faceplate mazed like a flawed opal. There was a hole in the center of their forehead, and a corresponding exit wound in the back of their head, and in the back of their helmet as well. Perfect headshot, instant death.

"Definitely dead," the assistant said in wonderment. "Well done, ma'am."

Kestre was vain about her skills as a marksman, but not so vain that she didn't recognize that the headshot was highly improbable. Still, she accepted her luck, such as it was. The mysterious bullet—wherever it had gone—had missed the assassin's own air supply. She liberated it and replaced her tank with a quiet sigh of relief: salvation.

The sigh of relief faded when she examined the second and third assassins. They'd died the same way, both of them. This went from highly improbable to downright hallucinatory.

"Much as I'd love to stay and gawk," the assistant said, "there may be more on the way."

May meant it hadn't yet detected anyone. Kestre didn't believe in taking chances. At least she needn't add the aggravating arms dealer to her list after all.

She retrieved her scooter, then headed back to the city. Now that the adrenaline was ebbing, nausea filled her—not because she'd come close to death, but because the Tovraz had decided she was a footnote, unworthy of a proper duelist. They'd sent *common assassins* after her.

AFTER THAT, KESTRE'S vendetta began in earnest. She learned to rely on her gun, which always killed living targets and was effective against inanimate objects as well. It kicked her hand with that familiar recoil even though taking it apart and putting it together again, multiple times, assured her that it was as empty as its name. Likewise, the gun hated her polymorphic ammunition and wouldn't discharge if she loaded it. After a while, she simply gave up trying.

Kestre started with the outlying scions of House Tovraz, the ones sent to safeguard Tovraz's trade concerns amid the Wandering Moons. She felled eight of them before the warning bulletin went out and they increased their security. The AI's squeamishness convinced her not to take their ears as trophies, although she thought it would have been a fine jest to mail them to the Tovraz citadel. Her sense of humor had darkened lately.

For a time, all went well. When Kestre needed money to sustain her operations, she went bounty-hunting. Sometimes a small voice whispered that the duelist prime of House Elaya should be above *random killing*, especially for something as mundane as money. But then she remembered that she had sold her name, so why not sell her scruples too?

This lasted through seventeen kills.

The eighteenth—the eighteenth was when the nature of the empty gun began to manifest.

KESTRE WAS IN the middle of killing the eighteenth person on the list, in the Labyrinth of Blinded Skulls, when she got the news.

"Ma'am," the assistant said, its very politeness a warning, "when you get a moment—"

"Not now, sorry," Kestre said through her teeth as she fired the empty gun. The eighteenth person got off one last shot at her, by some miracle of timing: the closest call she'd had since the beginning. Then they slumped dead.

Kestre assessed her surroundings against the assistant's kinesthetic map of the Labyrinth's corridors. She'd learned during an earlier engagement that she couldn't trust her own maps, thanks to House Tovraz's countermeasures. Even if she'd disabled the map scramblers earlier, there was always a chance some clever hacker had undone her hard work.

Her maps remained in alignment. The Labyrinth's halls rose above her with their improbable pointed arches, its walls festooned with the blindfolded portraits of Tovraz ancestors. (Why blindfolded, she didn't know; some stupid Tovraz quirk.) Even so, Kestre remained vigilant. She had a scar across her side that ached in bad weather because she'd gotten careless with the ninth person on her list.

"Do you have time now?" the assistant asked with a hint of impatience.

Kestre approached the eighteenth kill. No pulse. That same perfect headshot. "Go ahead, thanks."

"The ancestral head of House Tovraz has returned to life," it said.

She froze. "What?" That first patriarch had been gunned down several centuries ago. She knew his name and face from her tutors' history lessons. Was this the gun's bad luck finally catching up to her?

"Check the newsfeeds for yourself," the assistant said.

Kestre didn't waste any time leaving the Labyrinth. Later, she would remember the escape in splintered dreams from which she woke sweating: passages in which gravity inverted and reverted to a schedule like the heartbeat of a restless giant; robots emblazoned with the green and yellow of

House Tovraz, and armed with lasers that she escaped only by virtue of her armorsuit's automatic reflection mode; a perilous climb up a series of maintenance shafts that led to her getaway flyer.

After escaping the Labyrinth, she holed up in one of the pricier hotels for privacy and used the assistant's connections to verify its information. Sure enough, the ancestral head of House Tovraz had hatched out of his burial urn and demanded to resume leadership of the Tovraz. If it was a prank, it was a hellaciously entertaining one.

"One more Tovraz to remove from the world," Kestre subvocalized to the assistant.

"Eighteen down, one up isn't so bad a ratio," it replied.

She smiled wanly. "You really think it's the old man and not some sick joke?"

The gun's weight pulled at her belt. She knew it was true, despite her words. The impossible had happened, and she was somehow responsible.

"Maybe we should reconsider what we're doing," the assistant said.

Kestre shook her head. "No," she said reluctantly. "We've come this far. There's nothing to do but add the patriarch to our list."

HUNGER WRACKED KESTRE during her next twenty-six kills. Not physical hunger, which she could have endured, although she didn't neglect the needs of the body. The gun itself demanded more bloodshed.

She kept this gnawing knowledge from the neural assistant. It would have advised her to surrender the gun to some collector (not the authorities) and leave House Elaya unavenged. After all, it had been impressed with the imperative of preserving her specifically—loyalty to her above all and the House a distant second. As far as the AI was concerned, a dead House's honor mattered not a whit. But she was not her assistant, and it still mattered to her. She would not concede that she had surrendered her House name for nothing.

Kestre started cataloging the kills as if they were rare specimens that she had to document for some museum of atrocities. After all, the manner of death never changed. Always the same tidy headshot. The only difference was, sometimes, the size of the wound, as if the caliber of the bullet was chosen at random.

There were kills that took place during high-speed chases upon skimmers over dust seas made from the ground-down fossils of ancient behemoths, and kills that took place at nosebleed heights across decaying struts and balconies, so high that even the birds wheeled below. Some kills happened in the deep-down swamps of worlds poorly terraformed and abandoned to breed disease, cauldrons fit only for the habitation of dolorous machines; others happened in the unsweet caress of sheer vacuum, far from stars or planets or anything but the radiation of the universe's first exhalation.

During these kills, she avoided the news, and asked the neural assistant not to talk about it either.

The next kill after that was another matter. Her squeamishness in learning about her effect on the world bit her in the ass.

Even in the more lawless corners of civilization, you couldn't murder people like this and go unnoticed. Kestre's House officially no longer existed; she couldn't claim that she was legally pursuing blood feud.

Kestre had just completed a grueling climb out of the maze of inner apartments where her latest target had holed up and emerged into a surfeit of light: white lights, red lights, the muzzles of guns all aimed at her. The neural assistant sputtered out of silence to tell her how many people she was facing. She heard the number without processing it: *too many to escape* was all that mattered.

Primed by her experiences, she did the illogical thing. She was already dangling from a window; that left one hand free. And she had superb reflexes, which had served her well as duelist prime. She drew and fired in the general direction of the authorities who had come to arrest her. If her vengeance ended here, fine; but it wouldn't end without her taking someone on the way out.

Her vengeance didn't end. It took her a full minute to appreciate what had happened. The sound of scores of people dropping in unison, like a percussion ensemble's last hammer-blow. The silence afterward.

"All those people," the assistant said, at a loss for words.

Kestre, dangling, stared down at the blood, and the blood, and the blood.

"You should go before anyone else shows up," it added softly. Meaning *before you kill more bystanders.*

"What the hell is going on?" Kestre demanded. But she was already moving. She scrambled down the rest of the way, hands steady only because the alternative was falling to her death on the street below, amid the not-a-tessellation of corpses.

The empty gun hadn't kicked against her hand any more than usual. It had *felt* like an ordinary single shot. The one difference—besides the damage—was an obscene satiation radiating throughout her body. She suspected that once it ebbed, she would be left hungrier and more hollow than ever.

Once Kestre made it to her getaway flyer, she keyed it up and headed for the starport. She hadn't completed her quota of kills on this world—saints of Elaya, if not for the assistant, she would be starting to lose track—but it was clear that she'd have to return later.

Unfortunately, the authorities had noticed the sudden demise of their police forces. They were even more determined to apprehend her now.

The assistant spoke again. "They know where we're going," it said. "Maybe it'd be better for us to lie low for a while."

"That won't work," Kestre said. "We might be stuck here for ages. We have to get off-planet, even if it means stealing a ship." It wouldn't be the first time.

"We have a police fleet converging on our position."

The city sped by beneath them, a blur of lights and bridges and spindle figures. Kestre saw the police in their combat flyers. Her flyer didn't have a tactical system, but the assistant did. It connected to the flyer's sensor suite and calculated that she only had two minutes and nine seconds before the leading missiles reached her.

Missiles, Kestre thought with savage humor. *I'm moving up in the world.*

"Tell me," Kestre said aloud to the gun, "just how many people can you take out with a single pull of the trigger?" She was shocked, although she shouldn't have been, by the raw edge to her voice.

The one who answered was her assistant. "I don't think this is such a—"

"We need a way out," Kestre said, "and this is our only option. We can't go back to the way things used to be. If we're going to take out the rest of the list, we have to *live.* And right now, living means *killing them.*"

The assistant lapsed into miserable silence.

"Well, can you?" Kestre asked. She was addressing the gun again.

One minute remaining. Kestre still had no desire to die in the air. She wondered what would happen if she pushed the gun to its limits. Assuming it had any.

She twisted in her seat, pointed the gun toward the rear of the craft, and set her finger on the trigger.

"Is this what we've come to?" the assistant asked. Kestre was aware that she had tried it sorely. "If you choose suicide, it's my duty to go down with—"

Kestre pulled the trigger.

That's it, she thought philosophically when the rear of the craft remained intact, despite a satiation so intense it made her queasy. *Whatever alien sorcery powers this weapon, I've used it up.* She rechecked the cabin's pressure gauges: no change.

Kestre started to laugh. There was nothing else to do. She

was going to die. After all the miracles that had saved her, she'd finally pushed her luck too far. It was only just.

"It worked, Kestre," the assistant said. It rarely used her name. There was no inflection in its voice.

"Don't be absurd," Kestre snapped, then regretted it. The assistant was the only friend she had left. Never mind that it had no choice in its loyalty; it did its best by her. A little reciprocity was the least she owed it.

Besides, she could verify its words for herself. It projected a tactical grid over her field of vision, a map, a snapshot of the massacre. The entire police fleet had gone up in flames. The missiles and flyers had plummeted to the ground below, devastating shops and streets and apartments.

"But how?" Kestre wondered. Even if the empty gun had destroyed the entire crew complement of every flyer in pursuit, the vehicles, even the missiles themselves, would have AIs heuristic-sworn to continue their masters' mission. The city police's central command could, however awkwardly, puppeteer the vehicles—if they had survived.

They had another six minutes before they reached the starport. An unaccustomed pang struck Kestre's heart. She was not used to grieving for strangers.

A cold trickle of regret wormed its way into her stomach. She couldn't see the dead, both the police, and the people who'd been below their flyers and the missiles. But she would always remember the click of the trigger, the kick against her hand, the utter roaring sense of emptiness. She'd always preferred her existence as a duelist because everything was *personal*.

The kills before today had been personal. She might not have gotten close enough for anyone to see her eyes, as in the dueling halls of yesteryear, but they'd known she was coming for them. The Tovraz had known that she lived, and that while she lived, she had only one purpose: their extinction. There had been a strange, pure honesty in the hunt.

That honesty had shattered with the massacre she'd left behind her. The police weren't supposed to have gotten involved. But she'd failed to extricate them from the tangled skein of her vengeance. And she was going to carry their shades like shackles until she died.

"We're under interdict," the assistant said in a subdued voice. "Security is out in force at the starport."

And Kestre knew what she had to do.

The assistant provided Kestre a map of the starport and of the massacre site. She spent a precious few moments determining the extent of the empty gun's reach. As far as she could tell, there was no geometric logic to its targets. It did not fire like a laser, where she pointed it. It did not obey the laws of ballistics; its projectiles were indifferent to the hand of gravity and ignored the quixotic pull of the wind. It felled what it wished to fell. That was all.

"You can't," the assistant said. "Kestre, this is too much."

"We have to get off this world," Kestre said. Repeating it like a chant, because she couldn't think of any other way to restore order to her universe. Her House name was gone. If she lost her mission as well, what did that make her? Loss of purpose terrified her more than annihilation.

Her flyer wasn't authorized to approach the starport. Kestre heard, as from a distance over thundering seas and across indescribable crevasses, the bleating of the starport authority commanding her to turn back; to surrender herself to the patrols that even now were on intercept. The authority's words presented themselves to her like the buzzing of stinging insects. They had no relevance to her.

She spun the gun in her hand, a showman's trick; chose a direction. The direction was down. They weren't over the starport yet. She pulled the trigger anyway.

For the rest of her life, she would associate that kick against her hand with the drumfall deaths of innocents. The tactical display informed her that nothing impeded their safe landing in the starport. The flyer touched down without incident.

A storm wracked the city and the wind whipped about Kestre as she disembarked. Shrapnel crunched beneath her shoes and blew against her armorsuit. Without its protection, she would have been bloodied. Not that a little more blood mattered, for the starport was painted in gore and liberally decorated with fallen bodies. While the corpses themselves, where intact, displayed the headshot wounds she knew so well, the gun hadn't stopped there. In demolishing the starport's defenses, it had caused any number of explosions. Walking through the fire-splashed halls and toward the arrayed starships was like touring a combat zone as depicted by an enthusiast of the butcher's art.

Kestre remained dry-eyed as she passed the corpses of students in their uniforms and children clutching snacks. She didn't dare give in to sentiment. Yet, when she emerged on the upper levels where the starships' silhouettes knifed the sky, she wept at the prospect of escape, and hated herself for it.

"Which one?" she asked the assistant, paralyzed not by her own monstrousness but by the kaleidoscope variety of ships available, a harvest won by the gun's profligacy and her own willingness to go along.

"The best ship," the assistant said, its voice strained, "is this one—" It indicated a deepship upon the map.

The grotesque satiation should have dulled Kestre's senses. Instead, she shivered as she strode toward the deepship, like a harp tuned too tight and stirred by the charnel wind. Despite her suit's filters, she gagged at the imagined stink of the roasted dead, and this despite the fact that she was no stranger to such smells.

The deepship welcomed her although its AI should have barred her way. When she reached its bridge, a one-woman procession leaving footprints of blood and ash and viscera, she looked around and wondered if she was to fly a ship with no brain. But the assistant assured her that enough of the ship's programming remained for their purpose.

The bridge displays lit. Kestre couldn't focus on any of them. "Take us to our enemy," she said hoarsely. "Take us to the Citadel of House Tovraz so I can finish this."

"KESTRE," THE ASSISTANT said. "Kestre."

Kestre had slept fitfully, dreaming of House Elaya and its fantastic gardens, its mazy walkways, its children. She'd had none of her own, but she'd been an excellent aunt up until the point where she failed to save the children from the slaughter. At first, mired in dreams, she mistook the assistant's voice for that of the armsmaster.

"Kestre," the assistant said a third time, and she woke.

She had fallen asleep in the captain's chair without making any effort to clear the other dead. There were too many of them. Ghoulish as it was, she wanted the reminder of the gun's efficacy, so that she could stop taking it for granted.

"There's pursuit," the assistant said now that it had her attention.

"There must be a tactical display," Kestre said. She'd never before set foot on a ship-of-war.

"It's set up," the assistant said, directing her to the appropriate holo.

"Pursuit" was an understatement. Another holo was playing an unencrypted news bulletin. The world they'd escaped had taken the destruction of its starport seriously. The system's patrols were coming after the terrorist—her.

"Why didn't you wake me earlier?" Kestre said, trying to keep the waspish note out of her voice and failing. "I could have taken some stims, instead of leaving you alone with this."

"Because we have help."

"...help?" Kestre said, not certain she'd heard correctly. Who would help *her* after what she'd done?

"If the enemy of your enemy—"

"Oh, *that* kind of help," Kestre said, paradoxically relieved that she didn't have to factor in the whims of some heretofore undeclared ally. "Then what's the issue?"

"You want a viewport. Of which there are none on the bridge."

The bridge of this particular ship was a well-fortified nerve center, rather than being anywhere close to the ship's exterior. "Do we have time?"

"Trust me," the assistant said.

Her heart clenched tight, and she acceded.

Kestre took a lift to the nearest viewport. It was something of a relic, in a guest cabin, presumably to impress visitors of high status—give them something to look at if the holos didn't provide sufficient entertainment. The cabin had once been occupied. Kestre averted her eyes from the finely dressed person, the book that had tumbled from their hand. The title nagged at her: *The Red Sign*. Later, she would forget the corpse's face and staring eyes, but not the antiquated book.

She stared out the viewport. "I don't see anything."

Then she understood the assistant's concern. The black outside was not the black of ordinary space, but Transitional Space. That wasn't the surprising part. Even the fact that a fleet of ships pursued them wasn't surprising.

Rather, the darkness swarmed with the undulating shapes of alien leviathans. They were devouring the enemy ships, unfazed by railgun fire, by missiles, by mines. She had thought the aliens to be extinct.

The fleet was receding in the unspeakable distance. They couldn't chase her and fend off the aliens at the same time. A desperate hope candled in Kestre's heart. They might reach House Tovraz's citadel, after all.

Kestre returned to the bridge. They exited Transitional

Space, and she beheld a holo of the citadel. House Tovraz's headquarters occupied geosynchronous orbit over one of its garden worlds, a space station so encrusted in defenses that it resembled a lofty crustacean monarch. And here Kestre's ambitions were frustrated, for she was too late.

Behemoth ships, vaster even than the leviathans, were even now firing on Station Tovraz and the world below. The deepship's sensors told her that only stray wisps of atmosphere remained on the station and that it had been thoroughly sieved. Whatever its population had been—and it would have been immense—it was now zero.

As for the world below—

"Show me," Kestre said.

"It will only hurt you," the assistant said.

"*Show me.*"

The assistant interpreted the data for her in excruciating detail. The world's oceans boiled. All that remained was a hellstorm of smoke and steam and fire. She had not known that weapons of such world-killing potency existed. She was tempted to dismiss the assistant's false-color portrayal as hyperbole. It was prone to no such thing.

"Where did they come from?" she whispered. And why weren't they firing on her as well?

Kestre was no military expert. Still, the tutors of House Elaya had taught her to recognize the warships of the major human powers. She could identify them just as handily as she could a parry. And these were no warships that any human civilization, in its yearning after the stars, had ever built or conceived.

The assistant had no answer for her.

"Then we must ask them," Kestre said. "Hail them." She didn't know that it would work, but she didn't know that it wouldn't work either.

There was a chime: the alien ships were answering her call.

She almost said, *I am Kestre sa Elaya,* but that was gone. It stuck in her throat like thistles. She started over. "I am Kestre of the Empty Gun. I desire parley."

For a tense moment, she wasn't sure they had understood her. She repeated herself in all the languages she knew, despite despair that even a House education could not prepare her to speak a tongue heretofore unknown.

Then the aliens responded. "Kestre of the Empty Gun," said a voice. It was a voice a hammer forging armageddon might have.

"You have robbed me of my revenge," she cried. "Who are you?"

"Kestre of the Empty Gun," it said, "did it never occur to you to ask where your ammunition came from?"

The question stumped her. She hadn't cared, after a point, that the gun fired, impossibly, from an empty chamber. It had only mattered that anyone, and anything, she aimed at met its end.

But it was clear that the alien knew her and her history; knew what wretched path had driven her here.

"Did it never occur to you," it went on, relentless, "that even alien artifacts, however old, obey some of the universe's laws?"

She choked back a laugh. "You call *this* obeying the universe's laws?"

"Your gun fires bullets, and worse," it said. "This ammunition is not manufactured from the void. It comes from somewhere—out of the past. For a small death, an inconsequential one, it comes out of the recent past. For a greater death, for a massacre to feast upon, it draws from the distant past. We have you to thank, Kestre of the Empty Gun, for stealing the bullets that dealt our death-blows in the ancient war between your people and ours, and returning us to life."

"No," Kestre whispered. "No no no no no." How many more worlds would fall like this one?

Revenge had sustained her this far. She had no more stomach for it. She'd envisioned something cleaner, neater; something that resembled the pageantry of a duel. Just as she'd had the ability to pull the trigger, to her eternal damnation, she had the ability not to. The choice lay entirely in her hands.

The voice had no pity. "We have feasted well and will feast better yet."

Wildly, Kestre presented the gun. Even now her hands did not shake. She would have preferred it if they had.

"Go ahead," it said. "Pull the trigger. You can stop us, but you will need ever-escalating firepower. Imagine who you'll summon next out of the universe's maggot history."

"Fuck you," Kestre said. She tasted blood, realized she'd bitten through her lip in her distress. Apparently, there were limits to vendetta, after all.

Out of nowhere, she remembered not the dead children in

the starport, but the book; the honored guest on this very deepship, splayed across the floor, whose leisurely reading she had so untimely interrupted.

If only she'd stopped when the patriarch of House Tovraz, assassinated by someone like her, had walked out of his urn. If only she'd stopped after that first conflagration of death. If only, if only.

She was done. If only she'd stopped earlier—but failing that, she could stop *now*. It wouldn't save the people she'd already murdered, but it would, perhaps, limit the damage going forward.

To the assistant, she said, "Help me destroy this thing."

She was grateful that it didn't question her volte-face or tell her *I told you so*. "Engine room," it said.

Kestre didn't believe, in her heart of hearts, that a mere antimatter drive would suffice. Still, it beat quitting. She let the assistant shut down the communications link while she sprinted toward the engine room.

The Kestre who had begun this journey would have demanded that the assistant shut out reminders of the world outside; would have told it not to distract her with irrelevancies. Now she knew better. Even if the threat of the empty gun held the aliens at bay for the moment, she couldn't afford to forget that they could check her in turn by threatening other worlds. It would surely be easy for them to move on to others and destroy them as well.

Kestre almost skidded into a corner, almost crashed into walls, almost broke her ankle tripping over corpses that had turned the whole deepship into a grisly obstacle course. But she remained in excellent shape—even better shape than she'd been as duelist prime. Vendetta made for an excellent training regimen. And she'd taken vendetta beyond anything the Houses had seen before.

The tactical display exploded in an inferno of incoming missiles.

"They know what we're doing," the assistant said. Despite the calm of its voice, Kestre heard a faint note of approval. "I've initiated evasive maneuvers, but we don't have the antimissile defenses to survive this. Besides," and it paused minutely, "you're going to have to turn off the antimatter containment if you're going to throw the gun in there. At which point 'throwing' is no longer a concern."

"I earned this," Kestre said to the assistant. "But you—what of you?"

"You can't do this without me," it said, "and I wouldn't leave you even if I could. I'll help you turn off the containment."

Under other circumstances, they might have been able to rejigger the fuel injection system and throw the gun into the engine that way. But they didn't have time. It was this or nothing.

"Thank you," Kestre said inadequately. "You deserve better."

Together, they shut off the containment field. Perhaps even an alien gun that fired *projectiles from the past* couldn't survive an onslaught of antimatter. Any thought beyond that dissolved in a rush of light beyond light.

*　　*　　*

KESTRE CAME TO in a familiar bazaar, the one in Transitional Space where she'd obtained the empty gun. Not just in the bazaar: in the home of the arms dealer, with weapons resplendent on every side.

"So you figured it out," said a voice she had heard an eternity ago. The arms dealer came forward. The face that had once struck her as so indistinct, so empty of character, now reminded her of her own with its scars and effaced tattoos.

"You received fair price," Kestre said, "but I have one more bargain to make."

"Speak."

"Take it back," Kestre said in a rush. "Take it all back, from the moment I made the agreement with you. If your gun can reach through time, surely—surely there's a way."

"Of course there is," the arms dealer said. "But there's a price, always." And the smile she smiled at Kestre was Kestre's own, made grotesque with triumph. "You have one name left. Give it to me, and let me leave this place, and live your life. I can make better use of it than you ever have."

A shadow passed over her heart. But it was a small price to pay after everything she had done.

Then the assistant spoke. "No," it said. "Take my name instead."

The arms dealer heard it too. "*You?*" she demanded.

"I am of House Elaya," the assistant said. "I was just as responsible as Kestre for the massacres of the empty gun, even if it no longer exists. Take my name and be satisfied."

"Well-played," the arms dealer said. "Say your name, so that I may devour it."

"Sa Elaya," the assistant said, and for a moment its voice dwindled into static.

Once Kestre would have added the arms dealer back to her list; would have attacked her for her temerity. Now she said, "Thank you. You will not see me again."

Once outside the arms dealer's home, under the utterly dark sky of Transitional Space, Kestre said to the assistant, "Our House is well and truly dead."

"It may be dead," it replied, "but we endure."

"So we do," she said.

And together they walked out of the history of the Houses and into a history of their own.

GENESONG
PETER F. HAMILTON

THEY CAME FOR us when we were seven years and nine months out from our Jupiter slingshot.

We didn't know until the kinetic slugs hit our long-range communication arrays. Biodes hurried efficiently over the Shepherd Tree's trunk, carrying cameras that showed smashed composite struts and torn metal and ruined electronic systems. The crew's emergency engineering team started to put on their spacesuits.

It was a strange impact, we muttered among ourselves. Two different places along the trunk, each inside a second of each other. How could meteorites travel so close together?

We didn't know the marauders were there. Their hull was stealthed; death-black, radar and laser absorbent. All the onboard heat generated by human bodies and humming electrical systems was pumped into tanks full of methane ice, so it had no infrared signature as their ship hurtled in towards us.

*　　*　　*

MECHANICALS CONSUMED THE asteroid at a phenomenal rate, spinning it out into vast reflective patches and thousand-kilometre threads to repair the rents torn across the protective mirrors that cooled and illuminated us. The whole process was essential to life on our world, but was remote, like the mountains or oceans. Such an integral part of our society, yet inaccessible all those thousands of kilometres above the hot lemon sky. Right up until the day we received the call.

Every asteroid eventually wears down to a nub, chewed away by the mechanicals, vast industrial complexes hungry for minerals and metals to bandage the wounds which the natural harshness of space produced with its solar wind and abundant meteorites. Every asteroid is replaced. New asteroids are flown inbound to join the glittering swarm of Oort cloud ice that the Shepherd Trees haul in to fill our new oceans. A constant mighty armada falling in from beyond Neptune.

On this day a message was sent to us, an invitation from the government agency responsible for terraforming, coded for those of us who were older, if not wiser. It was a suggestion only, carrying with it a mild pang of guilt for those who turned it down. We all had group families, all had biodes labouring out on our homestead's stony land which we were more fond of than custom dictates. We wanted to stay with them, to share and relish their growth. But we were needed. A new mission was venturing out beyond Neptune to bring back fresh metal and minerals for the orbiting mechanicals. The Shepherd Tree needed those of us who could sing the song of genes. It needed new biodes to be birthed to ensure its success. How could we refuse?

So, we sat down with our families in the practical yet comfortable homes we have scattered across the flourishing savannahs and beside meandering rivers, and in the folds of rugged valleys. We talked, explaining gently to our children and the semi-sentient biodes that we would be leaving, but that we would be back. Our return, we promised, would be a triumph.

"How long will you be gone for?" the children asked miserably.

And each of us answered, "I'm not sure." Knowing in truth that it would be decades, and we would miss their time as golden youths, and when we returned, they would no longer know us, their mothers.

Our male co-husbands nodded supportively, trying to keep their anger and disappointment from showing. They were pioneers, sturdy honourable folk, excited and fulfilled at taming the new lands. Like us, they came here to build a family out among the dusty green shoots that multiply across the barren sands. This is not what they wanted.

"I can manage," the members of our group families united to tell us. "When you come back, the homestead will be an oasis, a paradise. You will be proud of what we achieve, almost as proud as we are of what you are doing."

We smiled and wiped away tears at their generosity and compassion. The call of this world's community was too strong for us to resist. Without it, without our unity and spirit, we would be nothing, we would recede into the same fraudulent technocrat society we left behind on old Earth and its new outer-system offspring. They have spread wide, those who flew outwards from the nourishing sun, contaminating and exploiting so many places. But they never came here, not to our beautiful Venus.

OVER THE NEXT few weeks, we gathered, driving away from our homes along dirt tracks, sailing on boats, idling in maglev carriages. Coming together in the gleaming temperate-zone city where we became friends by necessity, before flying down to the equator where even safe in the mirrors' umbra, the air was like fire in our nostrils, and moisture a distant memory.

This is how it was, we marvelled, when our great-great grandparents arrived not too many decades ago, travelling from Earth in craft that were so much cruder than today's fine vessels. Risking everything to begin again, to build something new and wonderful out of the promise of the green new gene canticle, the eternally yearned for fresh start. They succeeded through hardships and dangers that we and our children will never know. Because of their sacrifice we now understand that we've made the right choice in coming to the skyport. Maintaining the supply of fresh asteroids is our generation's duty, affirming our ancestors' dream lives on, that they were right to make their home here so close to the sun.

WE STILL DIDN'T know the marauders were there when their ship's rockets ignited, decelerating hard to rendezvous with us.

We didn't know because a second barrage of slugs took out our sensors just before the rocket flames shone bright across the silent constellations.

We didn't know because we were frightened by the shrieking sirens, and we were careering badly along the cloisters on our way to the nearest secure station, just like we'd practised in so many drills. Except we were sure this wasn't a drill. The captain had realised something was wrong and triggered the general alarm.

Then the Shepherd Tree saw the approaching rockets and sang of its distress. And finally, we saw, and we knew. And we were afraid.

ON THE DAY we left Venus, we dressed in smooth one-piece shipsuits, a deep turquoise in colour, with many intricate and clever functions woven into their slick fabric. Looking at ourselves in the launch centre finally made the journey real, we were to be space travellers. There was no turning back. The ground crew marshalled us into buses, and every forty-two minutes for a day and a half, we drove across the naked scorched rock of the Aphrodite Terra launch complex. Our pickup craft was always the same, a simple pressure sphere twenty-five metres in diameter, squatting on agile metal spider legs, parked in neat rows a kilometre apart.

We boarded cautiously, sitting in the cabin with its tiny viewports and cool odourless air. We were quiet, tall, short, breezy, timid, big-boned, and never young. Age gave us acceptance. Which is how we felt when we watched the bolo hook lash down out of our dreadful grey sky, hazed by the intersection of dust and shadows.

The mechanism snapped down onto the apex of our craft's fuselage and snagged the load pins. An involuntary squeak escaped our lips as the clang shuddered through the cabin, and we braced ourselves. Together, we shot up into the sky, the ground receding at bewildering speed, and acceleration jamming us down in the seats that were never as comfortable as the thick cushioning should have made them.

The G-force gradually reduced as we flashed upwards through the thick atmosphere, past what would have been the cloud layer had we been anywhere else on Venus. Then further up, where the lemon haze faded from view and the sky became a twilit grey.

Gravity dropped to nothing and the bolo disengaged, leaving us in an orbit two hundred and eighteen kilometres above the equator. Free fall was not our friend. We'd dutifully taken all the anti-nausea drugs the doctors recommended, but still we threw up as we fell towards rendezvous. Over half of us scrambled, shorn of dignity, to break out the newly sanitised seatback puke nozzles and clamp them round our lips. We almost succeeded. So, the rest of us ducked the flying, stinking globules as best we could, all brittle smiles and chirping, "Not to worry," while silently cursing the vile splats on oversensitive flesh.

THE TRANSFER SHUTTLE was like an exotic visitor from the frontierbro asteroid habitats or the moons of Jupiter, where everything is slick and mechanical and digital. Societies where hardware is emperor, and people have rejected the soft green newgene that has brought life to our world so close to the sun. It collected five pickup craft, then spiralled carefully outwards towards the wall of orbital mirrors protecting Venus. It slipped through the gaps, dodging the supersilk strands that hold the massive silver rectangles together in their almighty circle, shielding our world from the lethal glare outside. The shiny shields are barely microns thick, but that is enough to bounce the fierce light and heat away. Each segment rotates around its long axis in a balletic sequence designed to reflect sunlight on the planet's surface in homage to Earth's twenty-four-hour cycle, yet devoid of seasons.

We watched like excited children as we passed through the gateway into the solar system we never see from the surface. Blackness engulfed us; so deep and dense it brought on a vertigo all of its own. Ahead of us now we saw the high-orbit necklace of mechanicals and asteroid refineries, our gods, creators and guarantors of life, while beyond them the *Guiding Star III* glimmered brightly. We fell silent as we approached, gazing at it in admiration and respect. The Shepherd Trees are the pinnacle of our world's genetic artistry. As we drew closer, we gasped and chattered like the cocky adolescents we hadn't been for so long, watching the glimmer elongate and resolve.

The *Guiding Star III* remained true to its ancestry in the forests of Earth; shaped like a tree, albeit one out of myth, with a fat two-kilometre-long trunk, clad in ebony bark. At the base, its root boughs were a nest of coils, most of which were hibernating until we reached our goal out beyond Neptune.

A few of the ropy strands at the centre imprisoned a lump of carbonaceous chondrite asteroid, which would supply reaction mass for the ion rocket. While at the other end of the trunk, the brand-new petal spathe was furled in a tight whorl, looking like a plume of flame frozen in time.

Our final approach was gentle, reminding the country-dwellers among us of a sailing dingy easing to a slapdash wooden quay on a lakeshore or river bank. Fissures in the bark became visible, deeper void-black veins amid the darkness of the trunk. We only really saw them because of the scarab-form biodes scuttling along them. Tough beetle-shapes half a metre long with precision mandibles, one of many genera birthed for ship maintenance. They were busy examining and repairing the bark fibre. A swarm visible to us because of the esca dangling on the tips of their antenna, radiating a low phosphorescent green glimmer, so it seemed as if the fissures flowed with luminescent particles.

THE MARAUDER SHIP came from Jupiter's moons or a frontierbro habitat cluster. It was a clutter of modules and tanks and systems, any of which could have been produced in a thousand different astroengineering factories. It was perfectly anonymous.

It carried pods of combat drones, dark sharp cybernetic nightmares, that began to swarm when the ship came to a halt a kilometre out from the *Guiding Star III*. They soared across the gulf and landed on the trunk. Titanium talons dug into the bark fibre and started to claw their way towards the midsection airlocks, a dark tide with the devout purpose of army ants on the march. When they reached the outer hatches, they drilled and lasered and set charges and spliced into data cables to launch malware into the systems processors. The crew could do nothing to stop them. We didn't carry weapons. We didn't have Jovian electronics with their hypersecure encryption, and their sophisticated countermeasures. We were as helpless as we were harmless.

The drones burst into the trunk, spreading out along cloisters and into chambers, the electromagnetic spectrum awash with their lethal chittering. They were frenzied, mad machines, shredding life support units, cutting power cables, smashing air lines, ripping apart the fungiculture chambers, burning cabins, butchering biodes until the air was drenched with sprays of their blood.

Our crew sacrificed themselves. Those brave, selfless people did everything they could to stop the onslaught. They turned their tools into makeshift weapons, only to be slaughtered as they offered resistance. The captain broadcast desperate pleading messages using every frequency left on the communications console, pledging our surrender, telling them to take whatever they wanted from us. That we would help them.

Whoever they were, they didn't hear, or didn't care. Their terrible drones continued the massacre. With the crew murdered, they came for us, the mothers of biodes.

Crying and weeping we air-swam along cloisters, desperate to escape the killing machines. But those cloisters that had seemed endless when we first came on board, were now short and led nowhere.

We ducked into little-used chambers full of strange machinery which we crawled behind to hide amid pipes and conduits. The combat drones followed us in, buzzing and hissing, infrared sensors hungry for our body heat, cameras revealing our shapes to AI analysis, our own whimpers betraying us. Kinetic bullets blew holes in us, lasers seared through flesh. We screamed and thrashed as our blood pumped away into the air, surrounding us in a cloud of scarlet globes as our movements slowed and we died.

ONCE THE TRANSFER shuttle docked with the *Guiding Star III*, we went inside, clutching clumsily at handholds, bumping elbows and knees and heads. We towed our bags behind us like a clump of lead balloons which had aspirations of flight all of their own.

The maze of cloisters that laced through the inside of the trunk were wide, awash with a bioluminescence that provided a perpetual tropical sunset glow throughout the Shepherd Tree. The air smelled like an island forest just after a rain shower: rich and sweet and fresh, bubbling with zest as it gusted along, creating currents that swirled our unkempt hair.

But all that was lost amid the song with which the ship greeted us. We heard it in our hearts and bones and souls; the *Guiding Star III* welcomed us with all the love it possessed. Our new home's silent song was loud and vibrant, we had never experienced anything like it before. Tears glistened in our eyes, we were so overwhelmed.

The genesong that comes from the little quantum tweaks made to our neurology can only be sensed inside the mind, yet the first to experience it claimed it was like the songs whales sing to each other across the Earth's oceans. So, when we were at school, the teachers played us recordings of that sweet and mournful refrain, and none of us could find any resemblance. This, though, the ship's song, had a nobility behind it that none of us had known before. It was so much more than the small quiet lullabies we sang to the eggs inside us, the fond directions we hummed to our biode progenies after birth, teaching them the helpful little tasks they would perform on the homestead or around the house. This was union, we belonged in the Shepherd Tree, it was our true home.

We were greeted by some of the permanent crew, who smiled sympathetically at our daze, then led us along the curving cloisters to the cabins that were to be our home for the next couple of decades. They were bigger than we expected, like the nest of some burrowing creature that had carved out interlocking grottos for itself. Mechanical systems were embedded in the polished bark fibre walls, water dispensers for showering in fabric tubes, datascreens, clothes cleansers, and the like.

When we'd stopped throwing up, we freshened up, and gathered together in the central lounge, a huge ovoid space with which we would grow oh-so-familiar over the coming years. We had calmed by then, and the tentative friendship groups that had begun back at the launch centre began to solidify. We had become phlegmatics, sceptics, enthusiasts, stand-offish and effusive. We drank too much wine as the captain addressed us, we abstained, we cautiously nibbled the printed carbcell food grown in the trunk's fungiculture chambers and tried not to pull a face as we realised this was it for twenty years. After the speech, as the party grew convivial and the music louder, laughing crew urged us to swan dance, and whirled with us through the air, trying to teach us the graceful free fall moves that we would still be attempting to master in a year's time. By the end of the party we were becoming lonely and maudlin, craving our groundside families, and so we retreated to our cabins to discover if we could sleep in free fall. Some of us went alone, some of us formed pairs or larger groups with crew members, seeking a consolation that would inevitably be disappointing—if swan dancing was difficult, free fall intimacy was an altogether greater gymnastic struggle, and a lot more vomitus.

Thus, thoroughly initiated, we awoke the next day as true space travellers. The *Guiding Star III* sang to us as we left orbit. This was new to us. Genesong as we knew it was practical and sharp, it comprised instructions and corrections and lessons, but the Shepherd Tree was an artist painting the outside universe with its symphony.

We saw what it saw, the stars and planets that formed the panoply of the cosmos; sensed what it sensed, the heat and light and radiation falling across it; knew its comfort, shared its eagerness to fly far and long.

Roots dug into the carbonaceous chondrite chunk, leeching hydrocarbon from the stubborn substance. They won embedded molecules which drifted down the root xylem, gathering together to become a gas feeding into the base of the trunk. As that flowed along a myriad of routes around and past us in the trunk, the gas compressed into a working fluid until it entered the ion drive. *Guiding Star III*'s engine core was a long pillar sheltered at the centre of the sail whorl, its biological structure studded with technological systems as if afflicted by silver barnacles. The nozzle grid flared solar-purple as power surged into the fluid, and super-energised vapour jetted out in a howling cataract extending over fifty kilometres.

Elegant and radiant, the *Guiding Star III* rose away from Venus like an ascending angel. Amid the ship's song, we gradually became aware of discordant threads, flaws in the perfection in which we now lived. Blocked or damaged root cords, worn trunk capillaries, organic conductors breaking down, controlling nerve fibres misfiring. The Shepherd Tree was vast and old, and like all living things, its cells eventually grew weary. Most were replaced by natural mitosis. Some parts, small and complex, symbiotic nodes, overstretched fibres, specialist glands—they needed practical help to endure or be replaced. Our help.

This was our work. This was our comfort and security amid the newness and uncertainty. This was a familiarity into which we could happily immerse ourselves. We hauled ourselves along the cloisters, searching out the biode section. We took the wrong turning at endless junctions, and asked busy crew, "Which way?" Amid the eye-rolls and tightened lips of impatience, we were directed and urged to the right place.

The biode department had cheerful nurses and technicians who ran tests and issued eggs, warm centimetre-diameter spheres which were swiftly implanted in our experienced uteri. They were different, we could tell instantly, from the eggs we were accustomed to back on Venus: the basic cellular cohesion was stronger, the skins would be tougher, the organs more efficient to accommodate lower blood pressure, limb mobility enhanced.

The captain had drawn up a list of priorities. We understood what was needed and studied the morphology of the new shipboard biode genus to find a match, organising ourselves to deliver what was required.

And so we sang.

Sang what size the biode would be, from caterpillar length to big dog. Sang if the skin needed to be a hard carapace for vacuum, or slick and elastic to wiggle along trunk tubules. Sang what mandibles or fingers their task required. Sang to craft the senses. And when the embryo had formed, sang a mothers' comfort to the fresh life growing inside us.

AT THE END, when all hope had gone, exterminated by the combat drones, we fled to the biode department, which was most familiar and comforting to us. Our own creations massed as shields across cloisters and jammed up entrance hatchways. But still the drones came, their titanium talons chewing up the biodes, spewing out flesh as they cut through and pursued us. Then it was our blood which merged into the clouds of gore and we died along with the helpless creatures we'd given birth to.

The ship's song tried to give us directions. We followed its guidance, down small companionways, and along maintenance ducts. We curled up in tiny nooks we'd never known about, and finally even wiggled through tissue membrane valves into a tank that existed like a bubble within the trunk's own flesh. The drones followed relentlessly, hacking, slashing, burning, puncturing. Our cries faded from the blood-heavy air, and our song grew silent.

That was when the invaders themselves arrived. Death angels, fortified and safe inside great armour suits that bristled with weapons. They had no need for them, there was no one left to defy them.

With them came machines, dozens of them, cylinders as big as the armour suits. They seemed to be nests of some kind, containing coils of slim cable. They flew along the cloisters, their green laser fans sweeping ahead, pausing at junctions before darting onwards.

When they stopped, they were clustered aft, around the base of the habitation section. The coils unwound, moving with their own sinuous power, serpents unleashed. Razor-sharp tips cut into the trunk and began tunnelling through the Shepherd Tree's flesh. Deeper and deeper they went.

The first tip reached a nerve channel and sliced clean into it. The ship's mournful lament changed, its song rising to a single note of pain and terror.

It was overwhelming. I cried in unity with it, my body frozen in shock.

I?

I hear no other genesong.

They are all dead.

There is only me.

Out of all our valiant crew, all of us who rose from our planetbound lives, I am the only one left. I am alone. And so very, very frightened.

AFTER IT LEFT Venus, the *Guiding Star III* spent a fortnight flying in towards the sun, passing stony baked Mercury to finish in an orbit fifty million kilometres above the seething corona. A month later, most of us had birthed the first group of biodes, small creatures that suckled on the nutrimilk which harassed technicians in the biode nursery provided. They didn't grow much after that, but strengthened and filled out and learned all we could teach them through the genesong which connected us until they were ready to scuttle off into the body of the trunk. We glided, climbed, and wrestled our way along the cloisters, back into the implantation room as our strange offspring set about their manifold little tasks that would sustain the Shepherd Tree.

We had routine to nurture us now, the calls to our families had become slightly less frequent, less needy. The free fall sickness had passed. We even knew our way around the eternal tangle twist of cloisters. Our cabins were slowly being personalised, with fresh fabrics from on-board extruders draped artistically, murals painted, furniture altered. Ideas for better-tasting carbcell prints discussed and tried. Affairs embarked on. Gossip swapped enthusiastically.

We had become family, a little bubble of Venus life cast adrift.

* * *

FOR EIGHTEEN MONTHS the *Guiding Star III* orbited the sun, its single massive sail unfurled to point at the terrible incandescent light seething below. A circular leaf measuring a full fifty kilometres in diameter, a sheet of chrome-green photosynthetic cells that produced electricity instead of glucose. The lamina was webbed with organic conductors connected to the battery tissue that comprised the majority of the trunk's bulk, where quantum biology created advanced electron excitation states within the cells, allowing the sail's colossal energy output to be stored.

In those five hundred and fifty days, those of us who gestated smaller biodes had given birth up to twelve times. Those of us who chose the larger, more complex creatures birthed fewer. We were in the lounge, in the birthing suite, sleeping, cooking, showering, rehearsing the concert we'd planned, exercising, making love, chattering over a meal when the *Guiding Star III* sang its warning. The crew air-swam like a shoal of graceful fish startled by an approaching shark, darting to their stations, leaving us bracing ourselves.

The Shepherd Tree shared its song with us once again, and we waited, mesmerised, as the sail jettisoned. Dead now, the vast expanse of cells burnt, and radiation fried by proximity to the fierce solar blaze. It had been degrading for months, feeding less and less power into the battery tissue. Besides, the batteries were full now, zinging with energy. All of us picked up on that, like the Shepherd Tree we were ready and eager to fly.

And so we did. The ion drive switched on again. We accelerated away from the sun for eight days, and by the time the thrust ended, our velocity and vector were such that we were on course for GD2566, half an AU beyond Neptune's orbit. It would take us three years, eight months, and six days plain sailing to reach it.

THE DREADFUL SERPENT heads the marauders brought on board severed nerve channel after nerve channel. Then they sprouted tiny insidious fibres of their own to violate the amputated ganglions, firing their own impulses into the organs and elements, taking control of the Shepherd Tree's very body.

But only its body. Its mind remained whole. And so it mourned.

GD2566 WAS A 'jewel', so called because it had a rarish combination of hydrocarbons and metal. Astronomers theorised they came from collisions between the carbonaceous chondrite class and nickel-iron type asteroids, a hit or glancing blow that invariably left a big smear of carbonaceous chondrite across the tougher metal.

That made them perfect for Venus. The hydrocarbon would be used by a Shepherd Tree as an easy source of reaction mass to alter its orbit, and fly it insystem, slingshotting round Jupiter or Saturn to put it on course for a Venus gravity capture-manoeuvre. Once the jewel was in a high orbit outside the mirrors, the mechanicals would attach themselves and begin refining the metal and minerals. Out of those purified elements the factory modules would spin the silk and silver needed by the mirrors—which allowed us to live—which allowed us to dispatch Shepherd Trees. Such is the cycle of life in our multiplanet age.

GD2566 resolved slowly in the post-Neptune darkness. A curving potato shape, or fat banana some of us argued back cheerfully at the Final Approach party after a few too many bulbs of what we'd brewed in homage to martinis we'd once sipped on sunset verandas—maybe a marrow. Stunted zucchini? "Qiwano," we shouted in praise of the fruits we hadn't eaten for over five years. "Jackfruit. Salak." The words slurred as we took flight across the lounge, whirling in perfect time to the music, swan dancing with style.

Guiding Star III closed carefully on GD2566, with quick corrective bursts from the ion drive. The jewel had a slow tumble rotation which had to be matched. It measured nine kilometres along its central axis, with the widest lump three and a half kilometres. That lump contained most of the carbonaceous chondrite, so the Shepherd Tree's roots finally awoke from hibernation and uncoiled, opening out like a ragged claw ready to grab.

Contact. And how we cheered, the sound echoing along the cloisters. The Shepherd Tree's song became a croon of contentment. And we held ourselves still wherever we were, open to the song that showed us the roots' final flex, an effort-heavy stretch with a sigh that was so like us waking to greet the new day. Then the roots began to close, a net cast around our precious catch, ready to haul it back down to the inner system where its mass would satisfy the hunger of the mechanicals orbiting our home. With the main boughs secure by the end of the first week, the dendrite splay of smaller branches began to contract against the loose shale-like surface of the smear. After a month, we were fastened together as tight as any atomic bond. Power flowed into the root tips, and *Guiding Star III* fed on the plentiful hydrocarbon.

During the attachment the captain sent three crew out to recover the prospector probe that was sitting at the edge of the smear. A break from routine always created a flutter of excitement among us. Any change in our endless routine, any excuse to stop listening to the moans about cabin machines glitching or bad batches of carbcell or rumours of second-hand arguments overheard by a friend who knew someone in that department was welcome. "Them? Really! Go on, tell us what it was about."

We still stopped everything when a message arrived from Venus. They were shorter now, less frequent (as, truth be told, were our messages back to Venus). Nonetheless, we accessed them avidly. Seeing our children grow up, watching birthday parties over and over, not believing they were so big now, sniffing sentimentally; the enchanting, blissful marriage ceremonies as new members joined our distant families—"Not a replacement for you, no one could replace you, you'll love them when you get back"—dusty ground at the homestead boundary when we left, now lush fields and meadows; whole forests planted, neighbourhoods expanding and thriving. No, we didn't cry at the changes, the growth we'd missed, and we didn't tell each other how we thought we were fading from our family's thoughts, that our once cherished loves regarded us as distant relatives to whom you dutifully sent a birthday greeting every year. No, we did not think this, we did not speak this. Even though it was read in the strained lines in our faces when we emerged from our cabins after we received a message. It didn't bother us; the ship was our life now. Safe, and dull, and relying on us as we relied on it.

So, even though it wasn't as monumental as capture, the EVA was a pleasant distraction. Three crew suited up and rode a puffer scooter out to the probe. We watched the feeds on the big lounge screen, an adventure with a hint of danger. Going outside the trunk always carried a risk—especially here in the deeper darkness and cold. You needed training, professionalism, and good spacesuits.

They zipped round the jewel's surface and found the probe. It was in stasis mode, where it had been sitting for nine years. The government's astro resources astronomy department had dispatched it thirteen years ago, after they identified GD2566 as a potential jewel. They were rare in the inner system now, so many had been identified and captured for mining over the last couple of centuries, that the search was now conducted past Neptune orbit.

Everyone in the department's mission centre was relieved when the probe started drilling into GD2566's surface and analysing its composition. The balance between metal and hydrocarbon fell inside a viable ratio, so it was officially put on the capture mission list. There was even a little astroscience puzzle for planetologists to write papers and argue over.

GD2566 had an abnormal deposit of rare earth elements. Rare earth elements aren't really that rare, especially not on Earth. But lifting them out of that gravity well, then transporting them across the solar system was expensive. The deposit would be a nice bonus for Venus.

The *Guiding Star III*'s ion drive fired for nine months, using up seventy per cent of its stored energy. We could feel the vibration in the trunk structure, but not even the most sensitive of us could detect the tiny acceleration force the thrust produced. It was enough, though, to set us on course for a Jupiter fly-by, when we'd slingshot round the fabulous gas-giant and use its gravity to send us on the last section of the voyage—home to Venus. When the ion drive finally switched off, we had another party, one where the captain formally announced the transit time to Jupiter: seventeen years, two months, and twenty-one days.

We settled in for the long haul.

WHY? WHY DID these monstrous people do this?

They're evil beyond my comprehension.

I hung there in the fusty tank curled into a tight foetal position, smeared in sticky fluids. I don't know how long for. It didn't matter. I no longer cared about anything. There was no light in there. No sound. No hope. All I heard was the ship's song that had dwindled to a broken whimper of utter despair. I wept the tears which the Shepherd Tree could not.

Later, I don't know when, I sensed something moving in the dark with me. I let out a gasp of dismay, thinking one of their combat drones had found me. A tiny glimmer point wobbled its way around the tank wall. Which I realised was the esca of a biode making its slow way towards me. It had a packet of carbcell cubes gripped in its mandibles. Somewhere amid the dirge of anguish, the ship's song urged me to eat. Dying from misery and stubbornness was an affront to those who had been murdered. I unwrapped the carbcell packet, and bit into the tasteless mush.

The place I had fled to so blindly was not a tank, not like they were on the spaceships from the habitats and moon cities, a great metal sphere filled with liquid fuel. It was a sac or vacuole or bladder containing nutrients or water or sap, part of the trunk's biology. It was being flushed clean as part of its use cycle when the marauders struck, and I was lucky such a hiding place was available—or so I told myself. I became a living ghost in a living machine.

The biodes continued to bring me food and drink. Outside, in the habitation section of the trunk, the invaders began to establish themselves. The bodies were disposed of first, cast out of the larger airlocks like so much useless refuse. Humans and biodes tumbling away into space, bloating from vacuum exposure and slowly freezing until they became solid statues that would orbit the sun for millennia, lost monuments to the atrocity.

The combat drones stopped killing the biodes. Out of the tens of thousands of the little helpers we had birthed, enough were left alive after those horrific first few hours of killings to maintain their basic symbiosis with the Shepherd Tree, keeping the trunk alive—though not as much of it as before. I suppose the invaders no longer considered the biodes a threat—not that they ever were.

New machinery was brought in. The invaders chose the lounge to settle in and began to change it. Printers started to spin out composite sheets, building a beehive of compartments that became their living quarters and operations centre. A second batch of networked AIs joined the existing systems that were now controlling the Shepherd Tree's body. With more processing power, their command over the trunk's organs and functions grew more sophisticated.

In tandem with that subversion, the Shepherd Tree's new masters began to send messages back to Venus. The fresh, angular composite walls made observation difficult for the Shepherd Tree, but I caught glimpses. I almost wished I hadn't. I was astonished and dismayed when I saw the images play on the screens they had set up inside their hive home. It was us. My ship family. There they were, smiling and talking on the files transmitted by the replacement dish that had been set up outside. The AIs were creating perfect copies of our faces; our conversation was flawless, asking the right questions of individual members of the planetside families we had left behind. To do that they must have been monitoring our communications since the flight started, recording and analysing our relationships, our small dramas, our angst, joy, sadness, our slow sundering.

Seeing my own face saying the words so close to what I would probably have said was profoundly troubling.

This, then, was not some random act of violence. This was a long-planned operation.

*　*　*

ON THE TENTH day, their ship docked.

The captain came aboard her newly conquered domain. I don't know what I had expected. Not this. Not her. She had the rounded body and limbs and face of someone whose re-sequences and biochem-mods had adapted her for life in free fall. A collection of flesh spheres modelled crudely on the outline of a baseline planet human. Despite a bloated form, she moved with the grace of our most accomplished swan dancers. And when her armour helmet retracted, the Shepherd Tree showed me eyes that were protruding black and silver globes, modified to see in many spectrums so nothing would escape her attention.

Although she could not see me, I blocked out that facet of the shipsong so I didn't have her image inside my head. Her stare was disturbing, it told me of a soul without human empathy. The fear that had been slowly fading like the memory of an ache, returned to haunt me.

Her crew of marauders were alert and respectful as she moved through the cloisters still splattered with dried blood. They were all afraid of her. But I heard her name: Badb. The name of an Irish war goddess, the harbinger of doom. So it would seem that even pure evil possesses vanity.

After three weeks, the AIs had learned enough about the Shepherd Tree's nervous system to initiate an ion drive burn, a minor course correction. It only lasted eighteen minutes, but the effect it and the next four burns would have on our course by the time we reached Jupiter in seven years would be profound.

The marauder crew cheered and, infusing their narcotic

vapours, partied away, all the while observed by the fixed smile of their captain. From their talk, echoing through the stiff walls of the hive, I learnt that their ultimate destination was the Trojan asteroid cluster in the Jupiter Lagrange four point. They came from Makhaon, a D-type asteroid with several habitats and a multitude of industrial stations. Come from, or have an arrangement with the plutocrat frontierbros that founded it. That doesn't matter. They were free. They would never be taken into custody. They would not face trial. They would never know justice for the crime they had committed.

Money had freed them, they boasted and bragged and laughed among themselves, money granted them immunity. Our jewel asteroid was an odd one, with its rare earth deposits massing millions of tonnes. A mass that amounted to more wealth than even a Jovian moon city possessed.

Makhaon would build refineries. It would build cargo spaceships. They would control the market throughout the asteroids and Jovian moons. Their companies would be rich, growing into the new trans-solar giants.

Everybody would prosper.

I would not. My dead crew would not. Venus would not.

I SPENT ANOTHER week in my refuge, lit only by the wavering lights of attendant biodes, summoning up so many fanciful plans.

Venus would send a ship to recover the *Guiding Star III*. It would be full of our own fighting machines.

Fantasy of a broken mind: for that was not our way. And even if such a ship came, Badb would deal with such an impertinent enterprise.

When it became obvious the Shepherd Tree had been hijacked, the law would prevail and the courts...

There was no court that could challenge Makhaon, not that they would ever acknowledge responsibility. Out here, in the cold and dark there was no lawful authority.

I would sneak about the trunk and reconnect the Shepherd Tree's nerves, regaining control.

I would lead a biode revolt, and we would storm the cybernetic hive that had usurped the lounge.

Dreams and childish stupidity. I had nothing. If anything went awry the AIs would know. Squads of combat drones would zoom along the cloisters again. Clever technological sensors would probe the flesh of the trunk. I would be found and killed.

I could do nothing. Even if I had weapons, I couldn't fight Badb's crew.

But...

I knew someone who could.

Someone ruthless. Someone without mercy or conscience.

She could do what needed to be done without a qualm.

In the darkness I actually smiled.

THE BIODE DEPARTMENT had been smashed apart by the combat drones as they hammered their way through. Machinery and storage units punctured by kinetic bullets and slashed by energy beams had been reduced to tangles of broken metal and shattered glass. But their assault was a frenzy, it lacked precision and a logical plan. Segments of machinery survived, backup power cubes buried deep in cabinets dutifully trickled energy into the modules that had avoided damage.

Biodes crawled and wriggled out of narrow tubules in the trunk flesh to worm their way through the wreckage, their esca casting the faintest twinkle. Antenna and mandibles probed gingerly at the crumpled and burnt components, searching.

Over a month, working quietly and slowly so they didn't attract the attention of those drones still patrolling the cloisters, small items and instruments were removed and brought to me.

When my pile of treasure was sufficient, I implanted the first biode egg.

I WATCHED HER as I sang my genesong. So many ethics of the art had to be broken. I sang a soprano to pierce the honourable restrictions that bind every egg. I felt no shame as genes were arranged in sequences that were anathema to me, to any civilised mother.

The way by which I had lived and loved my life was gone now. I had retreated back to the primitive we had all emerged from. Vengeance governed my cadences. Vengeance and cunning, I stalked the ancestral plains of my ancestors, hunting for wild pray. My melody rose to peaks that carried the ox bone high, then came crashing down on hapless antelope skulls.

Inside me, the forbidden fruits gestated, warm and cosy.

* * *

BADB RULED THE crew in the hive with relentless discipline. Man or woman or modformed or gshift or cyborg, it made no difference. Failure was not excused. Punishment was swift and harsh. Cold metal instruments were used, inflicting pain directly into nerves. The body left undamaged, while the mind cowered and cried and swore it would never ever make that mistake again.

It was the only time she smiled.

There was no harmony there for me, only clashing discord.

Out of her suit she had cyborg enhancements. On her crew such components enhanced what they are, on her they detracted further from her humanity.

A pulsing, regular refrain, one suited to a machine.

I know what she eats, the foods she preferred. She abstained from stimulants, believing they are a weakness; though she tolerated them in others—in moderation. Excess consumption is punished.

Tightly knit chords, orderly, allowing no artistic variance.

She can interface directly with the AI network. In all probability, she could complete the whole mission by herself.

An underlying beat, confident and strong.

She spends hours in the rightful captain's quarters, which had been converted into a firing range. Her target practice involves shooting holograms of *Guiding Star III*'s crew, which die screaming.

She is a throwback. She is a demon. She is magnificently terrifying.

The high crescendo, fast exciting tempo triumphant.

* * *

HOW I HATE her. And yet she is to be my salvation.

SEVEN AND A half years spent lurking in drained vacuoles and bladders. Moving every few months as fluid transfers continued along the veins and capillaries that weave through the trunk. An appearance of autonomic normality maintained to pacify the steely vigilance of the AIs. Though after seven years the Shepherd Tree is in poor health. The biode flocks died off naturally, leaving barely two thousand alive, their ministrations to the trunk and all its flesh now drastically reduced. Replacement tissues are no longer grown to replace those afflicted by cosmic radiation, natural decay, neglect.

Badb's crew did not care. The ship had only one act to complete for them. The Jupiter slingshot. An operation originally intended to send us inbound towards Venus, now usurped. Our altered trajectory will see us skimming exultantly closer to the grandeur of the cloudscape, syphoning off the gas giant's gravitational energy to fling us onwards to Lagrange Four, where the wealth of emperors and tyrants await the crew who deliver this colossal bounty.

My own health suffered. Over seven years in the gloom, I feared my eyes would burn if they were ever exposed to proper light again. I couldn't even remember the taste of real food. My limbs bloated and my bones turned brittle from lack of exercise. Claustrophobia struck at my heart, sending me into the pathetic foetal position for weeks while I weep. The flow of time seemed confused. It is only yesterday when the marauders and their machines slaughtered us. I have been here for a century, buried alive in perpetual night. There is no outside universe, all that exists is my fevered imagination.

And yet—I have my ten children. They have grown as biodes should never grow. They have human form, and they have fed well, growing to adult size. My genesong has broken every rule, every moral principle I have lived my life by. It was necessary in order to survive and then succeed. Will Badb be surprised, I wonder, at just how much I have learned from her?

THE *GUIDING STAR III* passed Europa, falling towards Ios orbit, and the AIs prepared to fire the ion drive for its burn. The marauder crew were all in their hive, monitoring the AIs and the Shepherd Tree's drive units, the power cells and the flow of reaction mass, ready for the critical final burn.

It was time.

All of the Shepherd Tree's non-propulsion functions which the AIs had left alone, the air, the light, the warmth, the power—they all stopped. Within a second the hive's emergency power supply came online, sustaining all their cybersystems and processor cores.

It caused pandemonium. Badb remained perfectly calm, broadcasting crisp orders to her unnerved crew. Her armour suit activated and began to impel its way towards her.

All around the lounge walls, behind the bellicose cloak of composite panels, fissures in the bark split open. Sap, water, nutrient fluid, and noxious waste liquids began to pour out. The flood surged through the maze of compartments, panicking the crew who clawed their way out into the connecting cloisters. Behind them, electrical circuits began to short out as fluid inundated the modules and cabinets and junction boxes. Their machines, networks, powered weapons, and communications died. The inhuman AI minds were eradicated as they lost power. I could only hope they were aware their demise was inevitable in those last milliseconds, which from their superspeed perspective would stretch for eons. The crew were now left segregated and directionless.

There were ten exit points around the hive, where the bedraggled figures could enter the cloisters and escape the deluge sloshing about in their wake. Badb was waiting for them at each junction. She had combat drones with her. Drones that had been patrolling the cloisters and chambers as always, who had not fired at her when she emerged from compartments that had lain destitute since the hijack, because they scanned her to confirm her identity. They paused as they accepted the command codes she gave them; the codes I had spent seven years recording, codes that the Shepherd Tree had decrypted—its mind not as fast as an AI, but so much smarter.

The anxious crew stopped babbling, confused by how she had got out of the hive ahead of them. But there she was, their feared and respected captain, with a reassuring escort of attentive and obedient combat drones. Drones which began shooting them.

For a second time on the flight to capture and tame GD2566, there was a massacre. Smaller, but equally thorough. My ten biodes were methodical with their directions to the drones, they spared no one. They knew what to do, what tactics to deploy when the crew tried to defend themselves, to check if each body that spun through the cloisters, scattering blood from wide wounds, was truly dead—and finish off any who clung to life. And when the crew had finally been exterminated, they moved into the newly created swamp that had been the hive.

Badb fought them, of course, but she was outgunned, outmanoeuvred by her own knowledge and ferocity. The monster was slayed by her own knowledge multiplied by ten.

The remaining ordinary biodes worked quickly to disconnect the slaver cables from the Shepherd Tree's nerve channels. They patched small repair connections across the brutal surgical gashes. It began to regain full control of itself.

My ten newest children gathered round the tubule entrance and helped me emerge gingerly into the desecrated place that had once been my home. Around me, the ship's song rose; not as it was, not as it greeted me the first time I entered the wondrous artificial world of its trunk. This song contained no happiness, but there was a strand of the melody that suggested relief.

Light blossomed around me. Dim at first so my tender eyes could adjust, but before long reaching the warm sunset radiance that had bathed us on our splendid journey out beyond Neptune in some lost past life. My children grasped my sore, flaccid flesh and eased me along cloisters once so familiar, now cluttered with ancient debris impacting on desiccated bark walls. I could see myself clearly, caked in years of filth, hair gathered in strands like stiff wire. It mattered for nothing, as my thoughts were filled with the satisfaction of vengeance, for my ship family, for the still suffering Shepherd Tree. Alien thoughts, thoughts I had absorbed from Badb and made my own.

But pleasing, nonetheless.

AND NOW, MY children carefully apply damp cloths to my stinking skin. I appreciate their attentions while I acclimatise myself to the universe I had lost for so long. They are glad for me, but I cannot reciprocate. There are some things that even an illicit genesong cannot circumvent. Their size condemns them to a short life. They will not be with me for long, a few more months at best.

Beyond that I will be alone again.

I will endure. It is nothing as to that which has passed..

As my skin is exposed to the warm light, a new strand of the shipsong begins, it is one that kindles memories of contentment. And around me I feel the trunk vibrating in a familiar fashion.

The ion drive is firing. A giant plume of energised atoms flares out behind us as we curve round Jupiter's majestic swirling clouds. It is not the burn Badb and her AIs designed. This was calculated by the Shepherd Tree itself. A twenty-day burn that will propel us in towards the sun and a world close to it, shrouded protectively in silk and silver.

I AM GOING home.

SOMETHING IN THE AIR
CAROLYN IVES GILMAN

THE FIRST THOUGHT that formed in Mariela's mind after the shock that restarted her heart was, *I am alive*. The second thought was, *Is my child alive?*

She was lying on the slab where the survey ship *Tangier*'s wayport had re-substantiated her body after its twelve-year journey as an encoded beam of light. She had told no one of her pregnancy, which must have happened after the mandatory medical exams, or they would have found it. It had been a surprise, certainly—but a mistake? If it had been a mistake, she would have corrected it; she thought of herself as that kind of person. Disciplined, focused, undistractable. The fact that she had done nothing and said nothing, even at risk of jeopardizing her chance to be on this expedition, meant that it wasn't a mistake, however unintentional.

She lay still, feeling no tug of gravity, concentrating on sensing any hint of life inside her. Shouldn't there be some sort of instinct that would tell her if something was wrong?

The wayport technician floated into the translation chamber. "You okay?" he asked, hanging onto a handle by the door.

She sat up, then had to reach out to keep from pitching into the array of equipment hanging over her. She fought back some momentary nausea. "Sure. Why shouldn't I be okay?"

"You were lying there so still, I couldn't tell." He handed her a squeeze bulb of orange-colored liquid. "Here, rehydrate."

As she sucked the sweet-salty drink, she noticed that he didn't look well at all. Grayish skin, a tremor in his hand. It was a risk wayport technicians took, going first through an ancient wayport in order to calibrate the equipment for everyone else. Sometimes these robot ships didn't survive their long journeys through space so well. Even with all of the safety checks, someone still had to go first. "Are the others here?" she asked.

"Yeah, we're up to full capacity now. It's cozy." He coughed.

She saw what he meant as soon as she floated out into the corridor—if it could be called that, a tunnel through equipment crammed in above, below, on either side. It was the smallest ship she had ever been in, and had a utilitarian, military feel. Pulling herself along by handholds, she passed stacked bunks the size of body bags fitted in amid control panels and monitors, as if the people were just more equipment to be made room for.

She paused at a porthole, its outer glass slightly scuffed by interstellar dust. To one side, she could catch sight of the star, T46C, young and blue, a couple of AUs away. It looked like any other star, but she knew it was not.

In the tiny wardroom, she found two people hanging out—literally, each with a foot hooked through a loop on what served as the floor to keep them from drifting. The man across from her was lean and sharp-featured with a shaved head; his dark brows formed a bracket over his deep-set eyes. Seeing her, he broke off whatever he was saying and held out a hand. "Willem Procorchek," he said. He pronounced the W as a V. "I'm the astrobiologist."

"Mariela Sosa," she introduced herself, shaking his hand.

The other man had a familiar mouse-nest of curly, light brown hair and a sunny, unremarkable European face. "Mariela," he said, pronouncing it correctly with a rolled R.

"Gifford," she said neutrally.

Willem was watching them. "You two already know each other?"

Giff said, "Yeah."

Impatient with indirection, she said to Willem, "We used to live together. Long ago."

To be specific, it was only eighteen months ago subjective time, but twelve years and eighteen months sequential time, counting the years they had both spent in transit to this place. Thirteen and a half years qualified as long ago.

Frowning warily, Willem said, "Is this going to be a problem?"

"No," Mariela and Giff said simultaneously.

Actually, she wasn't so sure. When they had both secured spots on this research expedition, she had hoped he would back out. It would have been the gentlemanly thing to do.

A planetologist like Giff would have many opportunities to study new star systems, but this particular one was Mariela's specialty. For her, no other one would do. But he had chosen this moment, for once in his life, to hold firm. It was going to be awkward. But she could handle awkward.

She joined them, anchoring her foot on a handle that seemed made for the purpose. Giff offered her coffee. She waved it off, feeling queasy. "I think I've got a touch of motion sickness," she said. *Please don't let it be morning sickness*, she thought.

"It happens," Willem said. "You want a pill?"

"No, I'll see if it goes away."

"So the crew bios say you're an astrophysicist?" Willem said to Mariela. She liked his directness, but his manner was a bit abrupt. His words came out in bursts, rat-a-tat, like an automatic gun.

"Yes, and a mathematician."

"What are you going to be doing?"

"I'm the one who did the mathematical analysis on the light from this system," she said. "I want to compare my model to the reality." She glanced at him to see if he'd studied up on her work, but he didn't indicate recognition. "There's something really strange about this star. There probably has been for a long time, and that's why the ancients sent this ship to investigate."

At the time she had done her work, she hadn't known there was a ship on the way. The *Tangier* had set out centuries ago, traveling in sleep mode across the parsecs at sub light speeds. Its existence had been forgotten until it had come back to life six months ago—no, she corrected herself, 24 years and six months ago. The first thing it had done was to send a signal back to announce its arrival. Then a star system that had been strange became an enigma.

"Have they uploaded our data into the ship computers yet?" Mariela asked.

"Mine's there," Giff said.

"Then I can show you my model." Mariela swiveled around to face the wall console and input her credentials. She had to grab on because just tapping the screen made her drift away from it. The system led her straight to her own folder. She opened the relevant file. "The thing about the light from the star was, it varied in a way no one could explain. No combination of intrinsic variability, planetary eclipses, and weird starcloud could account for it. For a while there was even a theory that it showed linguistic patterns. That was debunked. Then I did a mathematical analysis using some new tools, and this is a graph of the result."

It was an animation. At first, it showed a vibrating blur, roughly spherical, quivering on the screen. Then, in brief flashes, it seemed to be distorting into other shapes. "Let me slow it down," Mariela said. The quivering slowed, and it was possible to see that the cloud was distorting like a rubber ball, forming two connected spheres, then four, then odd lobes, haloes, and rings.

"Does that remind you of anything?" Mariela asked Willem. Giff already knew the answer; they had been living together when she had done this work.

Willem looked perplexed. "No," he said. "Flower petals? Seed pods?"

"Electron orbitals," Mariela said. "It's how we represent the probability of finding electrons in any particular position around an atomic nucleus."

Willem scowled. "So?"

"So potentially we have a star behaving as if it were a single massive atom."

Willem looked deeply skeptical.

"You don't get it."

"I get it, I just don't buy it. It's a *star*, not an atom. What you've got is a mathematical model, a way of representing information. It's not physically doing that."

"Maybe. That's what I'm here to find out."

He wasn't willing to drop it. "Come on. It's just an artifact of the analysis, no more real than a bell curve. It's just math."

Frostily, Mariela said, "Math *is* reality."

"No, it's not. It shows what it was designed to show. You used some sort of quantum mechanical voodoo math, and it gives a quantum mechanical result. You could probably make it look like a horsey or a ducky with the right math."

"It doesn't work that way," Mariela said stiffly. He was disrespecting everything her career was based on.

"Well, give me something concrete to observe," Willem said. "I've already observed this star. Just look out the porthole. It's not an atom."

"Not now," Mariela said. "The emissions changed as soon as the ship booted up." She brought up another slide, showing two graphs side by side. "This is what the spectrum shows before the ship started observations, and this is after."

The second graph showed a conventional stellar system with three planets orbiting their sun: a gas giant and two rocky planets. And something *else,* represented as a fuzzy blur.

Willem clearly recognized this diagram. "Right. This is the planet I want to investigate," he said, pointing at the second rocky planet. "It's right in the habitable zone, and it has an atmosphere with water vapor. If we're going to find life in this system, it's going to be there."

"Well, *this* is what I'm here for," Mariela said, indicating the blob of fuzz. "It's orbiting the star in a spot directly opposite to the *Tangier*'s, like a shadow. It's like a remnant of what the whole system looked like before the *Tangier* came, in the one spot the ship has never observed. We could see its effects from home because our view wasn't blocked by the star."

Giff had been listening intently to the part of her explanation he hadn't heard before. "Mariela, how do you explain the change in the emissions?"

"I can't explain it," she said. "At least not without... well, I'm really hesitant to conclude the obvious."

"Which is?"

"That the *Tangier* somehow caused the system to change, to resolve into something more conventional."

He smiled. "You cleverly avoided saying 'collapsed the wave function.'"

"Because that's an explanation that doesn't explain anything."

"Especially to me," Willem said dryly.

Giff turned to him. "I got used to this stuff when I was hearing it over dinner every night. I think she's implying that we're in a patch of space where matter was somehow in a state of quantum indeterminacy, like the inside of Schrodinger's box, until the *Tangier* came along and started making measurements—peeked inside the box. Then the wave function collapsed, the indeterminacy vanished, and we got what we see today. Right?" He turned to Mariela.

"You said it, I didn't." Her own explanation would have been more complex, about the entire system being entangled in a superposition of all possible states; but this was so wildly unlikely she didn't even want to say it for fear that a garbled version might get back to someone who mattered.

Giff zeroed right in on the thing that made it unlikely. "The problem is, we were peeking in the box all along—from a twelve-light-year distance."

"That's why I can't explain it," Mariela said.

Willem made a dismissive gesture. "I'm sorry, the whole thing is ridiculous. We don't live in a universe where our spacecraft go around creating planetary systems by observing them."

"Not ordinarily," Mariela said. "But we do live in a universe where our lab equipment routinely creates particles by observing them."

"What you do in the privacy of your lab is your own business," Willem said. "My reality isn't based on subjectivity. If that were true, we could create any experimental result we wanted, just by designing a test for it."

"That's not how it works," Mariela said. Then she caught herself. "Where we come from. Here, I don't know."

She had said it partly to get a reaction, and it worked. Willem threw up his hands and turned to leave. "I've got work to do. Real work."

When he was out of earshot, Mariela turned to Gifford. "We're not going to agree about research priorities. I'm going to need your support."

Giff shook his head. "I'm not getting involved. As long as our research priorities involve rocks, I'm cool."

That was the problem with Giff; he wanted to please everyone. He was endlessly accommodating. At first, she had loved him for it, because he let her take the lead. Later, it had started to rankle that she always had to make the decisions, define the relationship, create the reality they lived in. She had started to feel overburdened with responsibility, as if he were a child she hadn't signed up to have. When she couldn't get him to take the initiative or stand up to her, she left.

A wave of nausea washed over her along with the memories. "Where's the head?" she said. He pointed.

She barely made it before throwing up.

GIFF REMEMBERED THE relationship differently. She had been a svelte, black-haired postdoc when they met, all fire and vulnerability. She had had to fight for everything in life—recognition, money, love—and fighting was all she knew how to do, even though she lost more often than she won. He had wanted to be the only reliable thing in her life, the person who would always be there without any need to fight for him.

But eventually she had gotten tense and controlling, a taskmaster he hadn't asked for. "Just relax," he would tell her. "Let it go." But there was something driving her, something burning at her core. He had left in order to let her figure it out. Then she had published her paper and embarked on a tour of guest lectureships, and they had barely seen each other since. He didn't want to start up where they had left off. He was going to keep his distance.

He went to his berth to meditate. When he closed the sliding door, it was a claustrophobic cocoon. He ran through his breathing exercises, then tried to fall into a mental rest state, a mind-vacuum like the space outside the ship's hull. Little, random thoughts kept popping up, spontaneous creations of the gray matter. He tried not to focus on any of them; focusing would pin them down, confine them, make them particulate and actual. Better to leave them fuzzy and potential. Perhaps they were a symptom of a quantum state within the brain, a state where creativity came from.

He realized that he had inadvertently had a thought and tried to let it go.

THE INSTRUCTIONS FROM home said that scientific decisions were to be made by consensus of the three scientists and approved by the safety officer. It took a great deal of negotiation, but the scientists and the ship's three-man crew finally settled on a plan of action. The *Tangier* would leave its present orbit with every instrument aboard focused on Mariela's anomaly.

They would then follow a trajectory that would take them past it, heading toward orbit around Willem's planet.

When the ship's engine was scheduled to fire and nudge them out of their original orbit, Mariela hovered before a bank of monitors that would reveal her anomaly in every measurable wavelength as soon as it poked out from behind the star. Her acute excitement eclipsed the low-grade nausea she felt. Giff and Willem both watched a monitor that showed the feed from an occulting visible-light telescope, but she hung back where she could also see the other screens. She wanted to experience this in a more-than-human range of senses.

They felt the vibration of the engine, a short burst to slow the *Tangier* down just enough to start its plunge into the inner system.

At first, the telescope showed only black space at the edge of the circle concealing the star's disk. Then, something hazy edged into view—a patch of fog against the starscape. As they watched it rise, it resolved, as if the focus were adjusting, into a planet.

"Is it a gas planet?" Willem asked. It had no visible features—just a grayish ball without cloud patterns, seas, craters, or frosty poles.

"Not big enough," Giff said. "It's got the mass of a rocky planet. It may just have a thick atmosphere."

"What's the atmosphere made of?"

Mariela was studying the readings from the spectroscope, but shook her head, unable to answer. "This is the strangest spectrum I've ever seen, and it's changing as we speak. It's as if all the elements were fighting it out to see who survives."

The entire sphere could be seen now, floating against the black velvet of space.

"Looks like it's got a magnetic field," Giff said, studying another screen. "But it's chaotic as hell."

Mariela watched the spectrum shifting like a moody child, absorption lines playing hide and seek. "Shh, quiet," she whispered, touching the screen as if to calm it, to make the readings settle into a familiar pattern.

Over the next hours she kept watching, long after Giff and Willem had left. And over the next days, as the craft fell closer, she left only to eat and sleep, in case she should miss something. The planet remained shrouded in a blurry fog, but the spectra started to show increasing signs of order.

During her long vigil, she zeroed in on the records of the first seconds after the planet had come into view, before they could see that it actually was a planet. There, fleetingly, she found the same strange pattern that the entire system had exhibited before the arrival of the *Tangier*. That supported her hypothesis that the anomaly had been an unobserved remnant, but it deepened the mystery of what it had been a remnant *of*. If there had been a macroscopic quantum state, it should not have lasted long enough to observe—unless there was something pushing back against the forces of nature.

After the first few seconds, the planet had entered this period of chaotic behavior, as if it were resisting the imposition of order.

Good for you, she thought. *Fight for what you are.*

Secretly, she had always felt a little sorry for the photons she worked with, because after her intervention, they could not go on being both waves and particles. They had to give up their mystery, their potential. They had to give up being two things at once, like Latina and academic, and settle for the one chosen by the experimenter.

She didn't want the planet, *her* planet, to conform to anyone's expectation.

"Mariela."

She started when Giff said her name, and spun around, then had to stop herself from spinning. "You snuck up on me."

"Yeah, zero-G makes that too easy." He came to hang next to her. "You ought to get some sleep and a proper meal."

The thought of eating made her stomach revolt. "This is what I came here for," she said. "I don't want to miss it."

"But the instruments are saving all the readings. You can't miss anything."

"Still…"

They fell silent, staring together at the screen where Mariela's planet floated, pregnant with possibility. "It looks like an oocyte," she said.

An oocyte fertilized by observation. Unexpectedly, a surge of pity washed over her—pity for the planet they had changed by interfering, regret for all the irreversible accidents that took away choice forever. She began to cry.

"Mariela, what's wrong?" Giff said.

"It's nothing. It's irrational."

He put an arm around her. "You really need to eat something, even if you are motion sick."

"It's not motion sickness," she said.

"What?"

"I'm pregnant."

He stared at her in thunderstruck silence. At last he said, "They let you come out here...?"

"They didn't know. I didn't even know till it was too late."

"Wow." He hugged her tighter, protective. "But it's wonderful, Mariela. Congratulations."

"It's not yours," she said through tears. "It can't be. The timing's wrong, I think. I was doing so much traveling by lightbeam, I can't be sure."

"I don't care," he interrupted. "It's *you* I care about."

She pushed him away. "I hate you, Giff."

"What for?" He looked baffled.

"For being the only person in the world who would say that."

"You want me to leave?"

"No, stupid man. Stay." She pulled him close again. "I don't know what I want anymore. Everything's gone blurry."

"That's okay," he said. "Blurry's okay."

He was right. Blurry was a state of potential she had to pass through before a new reality emerged.

WILLEM WAS GROWING optimistic about his chances of being the star of this expedition. His companions were clearly not award-class intellects. Mariela was attractive enough, but a thoroughgoing kook. Her theories struck him as not much different than psychokinesis—mind over matter. All disciplines had their misguided off-ramps, of course. Biology was no exception: it had had vitalism, intelligent design, and organismic theories, just as physics had had phlogiston and the aether. But that was exactly why he was so careful to believe only what could be objectively observed, tested, and replicated. He was very disciplined that way.

As for Gifford—well, it was obvious how the relationship between him and Mariela worked. She was the dominant, he the submissive. All Willem had to do was stand back and let them impede each other, and he would emerge the winner.

He was in the galley days later, studying readouts from his own planet, when Mariela entered, announcing, "We have oxygen."

Willem looked up, immediately interested. "Really? In the planet's atmosphere?"

"Right," she said. "The spectral data have finally settled down. There's also water vapor, nitrogen, carbon dioxide, methane, some noble gases."

"That's weird," Willem said, taking the tablet Mariela offered him, where the percentages were displayed. "We could actually breathe this stuff."

Giff came in to peer over Willem's shoulder at the list. "Looks like there could be a significant greenhouse effect. It might be shirtsleeve weather down there."

"A little warmer than that, it looks like," Mariela said. "But the temperature projections have been all over the map."

Willem was secretly encouraged. His own planet had disappointed him; far too much cyanide in the atmosphere. That didn't preclude life, of course—just Earthlike life. And it would be inconvenient to study. This new information redirected his attention.

As the days passed and the data rolled in, Mariela's planet began to look more and more promising—so much so that Willem generously yielded when Giff joined Mariela in proposing that they scrap the original plan and go into orbit around Mariela's planet at least long enough to send down a probe.

Once again, the engines fired. By now, they could see detail in the planet's cloudtops—a turbulent mutiny of shearing winds, updrafts, and temperature gradients. The radar was showing a solid surface underneath, but every sweep contradicted the one before.

When they finally fell into a low orbit, they gazed down on jostling storms. They could see nothing of the surface, but the radar data had resolved into mountain ranges, valleys, and flat spots that were most likely lakes. Giff pored over the data, but finally shrugged. "We've got to send a probe. I can't even tell if we're looking at a young surface or an old one."

"Young," Mariela said with conviction, but of course she was only guessing. Willem had come to expect such pronouncements from her.

The probe was a fixed-wing craft, self-navigating but able to respond to directions, and outfitted with sensory feeds that allowed the scientists to ride along in virtual presence. It was like being a bird that could see and hear, but not feel the tug of wind or gravity. Willem felt no sensation of falling as the probe descended steeply through the upper atmosphere. Soon, he was swooping toward ominous thunderheads, lightning flickering inside them as if through frosted glass. Then the probe plunged into the clouds.

The audio din told him that wind was pummeling the plane, and the horizon indicator showed it tilting and battling through contrary gusts; but all he could see was fog and drenching rain. Abruptly, the sound and tumult cut off as the probe entered a layer of absolute calm. On eerily silent wings, it glided through undifferentiated fog.

Lower and lower the craft descended. At an altitude of only a thousand meters, it broke into clear air, and Willem saw the black and tortured landscape below.

It looked like lava flows still steaming in the rain. Forbidding crags, bubbling pools, smoking chimneys, a hellscape saying "do not tread here." Then a rugged coastline appeared, a wave-washed beach with tidal pools and volcanic caverns, sheer cliffs plunging into the sea.

The visual feed started breaking up; the orbiter was leaving the probe behind, passing over the horizon. When all went black, Willem took off the VR helmet and found his scalp damp with sweat.

The others looked indecisive as they removed their own helmets, so Willem spoke first. "I vote to take the lander down. Hot springs, beaches, deltas—it's like a lab that could show how life first takes hold. I might be able to do some groundbreaking work. If it turns out there's no life, even that is evidence. We'll just move on."

Surprisingly, Mariela was now the one with misgivings.

"What is it?" Willem demanded. "Give me a reason."

"Nothing. It's silly. If you want to go down there, let's go."

"Okay." Willem felt satisfied. From now on, the planet would be his.

THEIR LANDING SPOT was on a lava plain close to both hot springs and shore. The air, as expected, was safe to breathe, albeit sulfur-tinged. The temperature and humidity were too high to be comfortable, but not dangerous. They spent a day, as protocol demanded, doing safety checks from inside the cramped laboratory-lander. But Giff and Willem were both eager to get outside, so after donning their safety suits and packing their equipment and location beacons, they each set out in a different direction into the jumbled black rock landscape.

Mariela stood in the steam-bath fog outside the lander and watched them go. She had told them she wanted to process the data gathered on their bumpy ride down. She was feeling exhausted and queasy.

Once the bustle of their presence faded, the air was almost entirely still. Secretive fog muffled the landscape and concealed the horizon. As her ears adjusted, she began to pick out subtle sounds—the trickle of a faraway stream, the drip of condensation. She had become so used to constant sound that the silence seemed less like an absence than a presence. She checked her navigation slate to be sure she could still see where Giff and Willem were, reduced to little flashing dots mapped against the topography as shown by radar. Then she turned to climb back into the lander.

It was reassuring to be able to immerse herself in math.

Math had always been her refuge—at first, a beautiful land where everything made sense, a land of symmetry and order. Then, when she got into the more advanced areas, she had found herself back in approximations and probabilities, just like the world she knew—except that she was not its victim this time, but its master.

Sleep crept up without warning. In a dream she was floating, suspended in weightless fog. She became aware that her extremities were dissolving. It seemed wrong, but she had no will to resist. She watched her hands turn into particles and float away.

A pang in her abdomen roused her. For a few seconds, she could not feel her hands or feet. Still immobilized by sleep paralysis, she struggled to reimagine her limbs, her body, her forehead resting on the work surface. Then she came awake with a panicky pulse of adrenaline. Rubbing her fingers to get the sensation back, she rose and walked, stamping her feet to banish the feeling that they were absent.

Trying to calm herself, she looked out the window, only to find that nothing was out there—neither dark nor light, no dimension, no motion. It was as if, around the metal pocket of the lander, reality had dissolved.

She seized up her navigation slate to see if Gifford and Willem were still there. To her relief, it showed them—Willem still some distance away, but Giff's beacon close by and moving toward the lander. She was reaching for the airlock button when she got control of herself. It had just been an unsettling dream. She didn't want him to think she was a hysterical, hormonal woman. So she sat down and forced herself to look as if she were working while she listened tensely for the airlock to cycle.

He came in drenched with sweat, hair plastered to his forehead. "Damn, it's hot out there," he said. "No way am I going to wear that safety suit again." He had already stripped down to shorts and T-shirt.

"Did you find anything?" Mariela asked.

"No, not much. The whole area looks like a flood eruption, all andesite and basalt. I've got some samples to test for chemistry; maybe that will show something interesting. It's damned hard to search for anything out there. You can't see farther than a couple meters, and I kept getting turned around. I hope the fog clears tomorrow."

"Me too," Mariela said.

"How about you? Did you make any progress?"

"Nothing I didn't expect."

When Willem came back, he was ebullient. "Cyanobacteria," he announced. "I'm pretty sure of it. I found structured silica deposits around the hot springs, exactly where you'd expect an extremophile to live. I brought back some samples; I get first dibs on the lab."

"Help yourself," Giff said. "I hope you're right."

Later, they sat around toasting Willem's confirmed discovery. "It's really a career-changer to find photosynthetic life on a planet this young," Willem said, then turned to Giff. "Do you have any estimate of its age yet?"

"Give me a chance." Giff laughed. "First, I've got to find some rocks older than about ten minutes."

Mariela listened to them pinning her planet down, giving it

chemistry, history, substance. It was what they had come for, of course. But already she looked back on the time, just a few days ago, when her planet had not been a thing of rock and rain, but an idea unwritten, glowing with potential, ravishing.

GIFF SET OUT the next day determined to make a discovery.

He thought of himself not so much as a studier of rocks, but as a reader of memory—a planet's memory of its own past, encoded in its crust. That was what rocks were to him, visible memories; and he could not believe that this was an amnesiac planet.

He set out in the same direction he had gone before, because the radar data indicated it was the most likely to have cliffs and outcroppings. Yesterday he had gotten so disoriented in the hot fog that he could not even be sure which spots he had already checked. So today he decided to hike out beyond the region near the lander and start his hunt anew.

In the end, he didn't have to go so far. The air was a bit clearer today, and everything looked different. Before long he came upon a ravine with a stream at the bottom, in a place so obvious he couldn't believe he hadn't stumbled on it before. "All *right*," he said aloud when he saw a layer of granite at the base of the cliff opposite. Now he had some evidence of geologic processes, of uplift and erosion, of the passage of time. He scrambled down to get a closer look.

The exposed walls of the gully turned out to be as good as a biography, and he followed it uphill, reading the layered rocks along the way. Soon, he discarded all thought of the planet being young or just-formed. He found quartzite and marble, which implied there had been sandstone and limestone in a past remote enough that it could have been metamorphosed in the planet's basement and thrust up again to the surface. Even more promising were the banded iron deposits that suggested long-gone cycles of oxygenation and anoxia, perhaps related to blooms of early cyanobacteria. He kept searching for some shale or siltstone that might house intact fossils to bring back, trumping Willem's mere bacteria.

But the fog closed in again, so thick it became impossible to see. He retraced his steps and followed his navigation slate back to the lander, weighed down with samples.

Willem had already returned when Giff got back, and he was looking smug. "Algae," was the first thing he said. "Eukaryotes."

Giff had to admit, that outscored marble.

"I couldn't find the hot spring I investigated yesterday," Willem recounted later, over fermented beverage. "But I did find some spring-fed pools, and there it was, green scum. It's clearly forming algal mats with the cyanobacteria. There are other single-celled organisms as well; I still need to catalog them all."

Giff told his tale of metamorphosed rock and striated sandstone. Mariela listened with a frown.

"Does it strike you as odd that you both found exactly what you wanted to find?" she said at last.

"No," Willem said. "It just means that I was looking for the most likely thing to be here."

Mariela just shrugged.

Willem laughed. "What are you hinting at—that crap about the observation creating the result of the experiment? You physicists are a bunch of magical thinkers."

"Seriously, isn't that the way all science works?" Giff said. "You can only discover what you think to look for."

"I think there's more than that going on here," Mariela said.

"Well then," Willem said, "Tomorrow I'm going to go looking for evidence that the planet's a solid ball of gold, or the next valley over is a paradise where beautiful houris will attend me. If it's really my choice."

Mariela's eyes narrowed in a way Giff recognized; she was about to let loose. So, to defuse the tension, he said, "Not me. Gimme that old-time enigma."

Later, after Willem had disappeared into the lab and closed the door, Mariela gave Giff a withering look. "Why do you do that?"

"Why do I do what?"

"Deal with an alpha male by becoming a joker. Why do you let him get away with this dominance crap?"

He sighed. "It's not worth fighting, Mariela. I didn't come here to play personality games. I just want to do science."

"Science is all about personality," she said. "With the right one, your theories will succeed. With the wrong one, your reality will be ignored."

It was an old argument he didn't want to reprise, because she had won it long ago. He didn't know what more she wanted.

"I'm going to go meditate," he said.

* * *

WILLEM SET OUT the next morning to return to the site of his triumph the day before. He had not only marked it on his navigation slate; he had taken the precaution of stacking up cairns of rock along the path. He found the first two easily enough, but the third had toppled over, and the fog hid the fourth. As he searched for it, his foot fell on something yielding, and when he bent over to investigate, he found he had stepped on a slug-brown thing, flat as a pancake and about the same size.

He went down on hands and knees to investigate. The thing was oval-shaped, with symmetrical ridges radiating from a central spine, like a leaf. It lay in a damp, silty depression that was clearly a dried-up pool. After taking a photo, he slipped on a plastic glove and peeled it off the wet mud to put it in a collection bag. He had never seen anything quite like it. It had a rubbery texture more like a mollusk than a fungus. He hadn't dared to hope he would find macroscopic life here. It was an astonishing discovery.

When he looked up again, a breath of wind parted the fog. He was on the edge of a shallow lake far larger than the pools he had seen the day before. To find out if this was the source of the creature, he waded into the bathtub-warm water, carefully scanning the silty bottom. Some movement caught his eye. It looked as if the mud itself was shifting till he realized it was another of the creatures, skimming away from him along the lake floor by rippling the edges of its body like a ray. He pursued it into deeper water. At thigh-depth, he started to encounter something he first mistook for seaweed, but quickly realized was something else: feathery fronds anchored to the bottom with bulbous peduncles—some sort of filter-feeders like octocorals. As he watched, he saw darting in amongst the gently waving underwater forest a small wormlike thing, translucent and bristling with ribs, like a centipede of the sea.

At first, his reaction was that he had discovered a completely alien ecosystem. But then a memory tickled his brain, and he realized he *had* seen creatures like this before—but not alive, only as ancient fossils of an early, abortive, experiment in life on Earth. To find them here, still living and functioning, would answer a thousand questions about the origins of life. It would make him famous.

He spent the rest of the day feverishly documenting and collecting specimens. It was impossible to do more than scratch the surface; he would have to return the next day. This time, when he retraced his steps to the lander, he left scraps of fabric torn from his plaid shirt anchored down with rocks every few feet.

Giff greeted him triumphantly with a fossil, and Willem had the satisfaction of producing from his backpack a recently-living sample of the very same kind of organism. Giff was crestfallen, but still had the grace to be interested. "I wonder how it fossilized so well," he said. "It seems to be completely soft tissue."

"There is a theory that these species lived before predation had evolved," Willem said. "Bacteria hadn't yet figured out how to consume them, so they never rotted. Now I'll have a chance to test the theory."

"I don't yet have a good timeline, but these fossils have to be millions of years old," Giff said. "That means the very same species have existed unchanged for all that time."

"Odd, but not impossible."

Willem looked to see if Mariela had a reaction, but she didn't reward him with so much as a glance of admiration. She was looking haggard, as if she had not slept well in days. He felt sure that he, on the other hand, would sleep well tonight, cushioned in dreams of pre-Cambrian explosions.

THE ONLY THING Mariela really wished she could change about this planet was her companions, and they were the only things that seemed unalterably, intractably themselves.

She couldn't help despising Willem—not just because of his dismissive attitude toward her own discipline, but for the way he treated Gifford as perpetual underdog. As for Giff, she kept noticing little things he did that she used to think were cute and lovable, but now just gave her a sense of disappointment and failure.

Once the two had left the next day, she sat on the lander's retractable steps holding a cup of cold tea and staring into the fog. Yesterday, she had sent up an instrument-laden helium balloon to investigate the oddly calm layer of the atmosphere, but the data it had sent back were disappointingly ordinary. All her motivation had drained away; she felt spent and sluggish. What was the point? There was a pattern here: Giff found his rocks, Willem his organisms; her own instruments would probably find exactly what they were designed to find as well.

Once, she had heard a lecture about instances in which an elusive discovery was made simultaneously by two teams, and then the phenomenon became so easy to observe that everyone wondered why they hadn't seen it before. It was as if, under pressure, unruly nature relented and conformed to investigation. Everyone laughed when it happened and put it down to coincidence—a coincidence that happened over and over. "Must be something in the air," people said.

What if we *are the thing in the air?* she wondered. *What if* we *are the thing coaxing order from chaos, seeding a tumultuous universe with rules?* If she had said it aloud, Willem would have scoffed. She almost wanted to scoff herself. If it were true, why here, alone in known space, had they seen order-creation in action?

She got up and walked away from the lander, allowing the fog to caress her skin and twine through her hair. She let herself imagine that it was more than just water droplets suspended in air—a vibrating particulate cloud, perhaps, visible uncertainty. She felt very far away from humanity—alienated from the two closest beings, isolated by aching years from the rest, as if she had invented a new form of loneliness. She no longer wanted to resist. She wanted to fade into the gloaming where coherence dissolves, strength dwindles, consciousness seeps into the sand, memory obliterated, till she did not even know her name.

In that fading moment, seconds from surrender, only one thing seemed real—a tough little seed, a tiny proto-mind tangled with her own that refused to surrender its existence. When it pulled on her heart, she rose to the surface of consciousness until she gasped in air again.

I am real, she thought. *I am solid. This fog cannot unimagine me.* The force of her concentration made her feel solid ground under her feet where there had been only mist. She turned around and was shocked to see that the world had changed. She stood alone on the barren lava plain, no lander anywhere in sight. She closed her eyes and concentrated. There was a lander just in front of her. It was hidden by the fog, but it was there. When she opened her eyes again, the fog was drawing reluctantly back, the familiar form of the lander coalescing into solidity.

She raced back to it, searching for her navigation slate and communicator. Fear of dissolution now pulsed through her. Putting her hand on the place where her daughter lay, she thought, *You have recreated me, as I created you.* She tuned the communicator to Giff's channel and said, "Giff, you need to come back. Quickly."

GIFF HAD SET out that morning more puzzled than he liked to admit.

The day before, he had not been able to find the gully that had lain directly across his path on the second day. Instead, he had found a dramatic escarpment of sedimentary rocks where he surely should have stumbled on it before. It worried him that either he was thoroughly disoriented, or the fixed grid that defined place had become bendy and unreliable.

The fog closed in as he was walking, so thick that it was dangerous to keep going in a place where gullies and cliffs tended to appear unexpectedly. So he sat down on a rock to wait for clarity.

He found himself thinking about Mariela. Something was bothering her. It must have to do with her pregnancy. She had always been such a fierce individualist, perhaps it was hard to adjust to having another life sharing her body, doubling her. He tried to imagine what it would be like to feel split in two, duplicated.

A whisper behind his shoulder made him turn, suddenly sure that he was not alone. No one was there. He listened, but all was still.

Now, what had he been thinking? Duality, that was it. It was hard for him to imagine. It was the human condition to be locked into single options, an either/or jail cell: one position, one polarization, one reality. What would it feel like to have both/and? It occurred to him that a form of consciousness might exist in a state of superposition. It would be a consciousness that could only sense possibilities and dualities, whereas humans could only sense unitary realities. Perhaps it would be a waveform itself, and just as humans were able to compel their world to exist in one state or another by observation, they could do the opposite—free it from determinism.

With a start, Giff came out of his meditative reverie, thinking, *Could that be true? Could there be consciousness at work here?* It had just been a random thought, an intuition. But if it *were* true, would not that be the only way for the other beings to communicate—by influencing the random processes of the human brain?

He stood up, simultaneously sure he was on the right track and unsure of everything else he knew. He felt a sudden, urgent need to talk to Mariela about it. Then his communicator sputtered to life.

"Giff, you need to come back," Mariela said. "Quickly."

He found her waiting on the steps of the lander, looking more agitated than he had ever seen her. "Giff, I think we're in danger." She shook her head, looking too unsettled to put it in words. "You wouldn't believe me. It's just an intuition. But I think we need to get out of here."

He put an arm around her and could feel her quaking. "Okay. I'm with you. You might be surprised what I would believe. Let me tell you something that just occurred to me."

He told her his thought about an anticonsciousness occupying a slice of reality that was unobservable—which, in fact, ceased to exist as soon as it was observed. Listening, she grew stiff and silent.

"If that were true," she said, "it would explain why this patch of space is different, why it's resistant to decoherence. But think of what the *Tangier* may have destroyed. It could have been an entire civilization. And here we are, destroying even more. If a waveform intelligence exists here, it's a desperate remnant of what it was. Desperate to communicate, to warn us of the havoc we're causing. And if that fails, desperate to drive us away."

She stiffened with resolve. "We've got to get Willem back here. We have to leave."

WILLEM COULD HARDLY believe how well this expedition was going.

He had followed his markers from the day before, but halfway back to the swamp he had been distracted by a ray of sunshine lighting the fog off to one side. Sun was so rare here that he had gone to investigate. Emerging through a curtain of fog, he found himself standing at the top of a cliff looking down on a wondrous landscape.

There were treetops below him—a full-blown jungle ringing a shallow lake. It was perfectly silent—no birdcalls or monkey chatter—but he could see winged movement in the canopy. Something was alive down there. Hardly able to contain his excitement, he scrambled down the cliff face and soon he was walking through the steamy shade of a Paleozoic forest.

They were not true trees, but quillworts and cycads grown to the towering size of palms and cypress. He passed a grove with scaly bark like pineapples and topknots of grasslike leaves. Beyond, a stand of shaggy trunks sported circlets of palmlike branches, holding aloft their pinecone-shaped sexual organs, all pink and swollen. In the undergrowth, he caught a glimpse of motion and realized it was a millipede two meters long snaking through the moss. He would have followed it for a closer look, but a scorpion-shaped arthropod the size of a small dog reared its tail in his path, and he backed away.

Predation had evolved here in earnest. It was as if this spot were separated by millions of years from the one he had seen yesterday. That they both existed simultaneously would upend all that biologists thought they knew about evolution.

Carefully, he pushed his way through waist-high ferns down to the shore of the lake. An iridescent dragonfly with a two-foot wingspan skimmed over the water, hunting. If he were lucky, he might catch a glimpse of an Eryops, a creature like an overweight alligator.

His communicator was buzzing, but in his delight at spotting an aquatic spider with a crablike, plated body, he did not even notice it.

"HE'S NOT ANSWERING," Giff said.

Mariela showed him the navigation display; Willem was farther away than any of them had ventured up to now. He was not moving—probably studying something. "We've got to get his attention," she said.

Frowning, Giff said, "Do we have anything that would make a loud noise?"

"Hydrogen," Mariela suggested. "From the fuel cells."

"You rig something. I'm going after him."

"No, Giff," she said. "Don't leave, it's too dangerous."

"We can't just let him be."

Mariela's expression showed that she would have been happy to do just that, but Giff said stubbornly, "We have to warn him. Besides, think of the damage he could be doing."

She said, "Then leave your communicator channel open. Tell me where you are."

Giff kept up a running commentary as he set out. "Oh, good for him, he's left scraps of cloth to mark his trail. I wish I'd thought of that. Now, where's the next one? Mariela? Are you there?"

"Yes, I'm here. Just working on something to make a signal."

"Great. Ah, a footprint. He went this way. I think... holy crap."

"Giff, what's the matter?"

"Nothing's the matter. It's just, there's an entire valley here full of trees. It's impossible, like nothing we've seen before, a biologist paradise. No wonder he's distracted."

Giff tried yelling from the top of the cliff, but not even an echo came back. The dot on his navigation slate showed that Willem must be somewhere close to the edge of the lake. He started scrambling down the cliff, trying to keep his voice calm.

"There's a fine band of schist in this cliff. I wish..."

"Don't get distracted, Giff." Mariela's voice was tense.

"Right. Damn, you should see the cockroaches down here. They're the size of toasters. And God knows what that is. The trees are raining gluey sap. The ferns are thick as a wall, but I can see where he pushed through them. I should be getting really close..."

He fell silent. He had reached the edge of the lake. There, in the muddy water, lay Willem's backpack, the communicator attached to it, beeping unheard. There were bootprints in the mud. Out past the shallows, Giff saw the surface of the lake stir. There was something floating out there. He waded in to see better. Just under the surface of the turbid water, he glimpsed something. It was a pale hand. He reached out, grasped it, pulled, and fell backward in the mud as the hand and arm came loose, unattached to any body.

"Giff! Giff, what's wrong?" Mariela's voice was saying. He realized he had screamed.

He scrambled up onto the shore, dripping and panting. He turned to flee, and saw a giant scorpion on the bank, tail raised. He froze.

"I'm leaving," he said to the planet, and whatever consciousness it might harbor. "Just let us go, and we'll warn everyone never to come back. Please."

The scorpion didn't move.

A sharp bang like a cannon shot quivered the treetops. A branch fell. The scorpion scuttled into the undergrowth. Giff took the chance and dashed back into the trees. The ferns grasped at him with tenacious fingers, slowing him down, but he barreled on through. Mariela was trying to get his attention, but he didn't pause to answer till he was out of the trees, climbing. Then he stopped to say, "Yes, I'm here. Thank you, Mariela. That signal was well-timed."

"Did you find him?" she asked.

"Yes. He's not coming back with us."

He climbed, but the fog was now rolling in from the lake, enveloping the cliff, dissolving all its hard edges. But if he believed in the reality of anything, he believed in rock. It was there, scraping his hands, supporting his feet. Rock wouldn't let him down.

He emerged into a cotton-batting world—no sky, no ground, no here or there. It was not the world he recognized; it was *their* world. And he was not welcome.

"Mariela, make some noise," he said into his communicator. "Bang a pan, or whistle."

After several seconds, he heard her voice calling, and metal striking metal. With that and the navigation slate, he could orient himself. One step at a time he crept, feeling his way.

He had gone too far, he was sure. Was he going in circles, or had the path stretched out like rubber? "Keep it up," he said to Mariela. "I'm close."

"Yes, I can see you on the slate," she said. "Should I come meet you?"

"No! Don't leave the lander."

No sooner had he said the word than he could see it, sharp artificial edges looming through the fog. And there was Mariela, real as life. He ran the last few yards and hugged her, grateful to the bottom of his being for her flintiness. Then he said, "Let's get out of here."

"I'M NOT EVEN going to look back," Mariela said when the *Tangier*'s engines fired to take them out of orbit. She was with Giff in the wardroom. As the slow acceleration pressed them both against the bulkhead, she anchored one foot and wrapped the other around his leg. "We've done enough harm. I want to leave them be."

"We have no proof that any consciousness is involved," he said, frowning. He had been troubled ever since coming back.

"It would be impossible to prove," she agreed. "We share a reality, but they see one cross section of it, we see another."

"So we've discovered absolutely nothing."

That wasn't exactly true, she thought. She had discovered something about him. "It took a lot of courage for you to go after him," she said.

"Not that it did him any good."

This moodiness was so unlike him, she took his arm and squeezed it. "It was his own expectations that killed him, Giff," she said. "His belief in the reality of what he saw. The planet used that to defend itself."

"We can't prove that either. None of this will make sense to anyone who wasn't down there."

"So?"

"So it will be hard to convince people not to come and investigate further."

She saw what he meant.

As the ship turned, sunlight shone in the porthole, sweeping across the wall toward them. Mariela felt a quiver in her belly.

"I'm just afraid we've taught them to fight back," Giff said.

LOST IN SPLENDOUR

JOHN MEANEY

HIS NAME WAS Shepperton Okilo, but the crew called him Shep and trusted he would shepherd them to the other side of Jupiter and back. They stared at him with steady eyes from their imprisoning berths, the ship's internal ceramic gauntlets, counterparts to those on the hull, but designed to keep the crew safe during acceleration or potential collision.

"You'll be all right," Shep told them, speaking aloud. "We'll all be okay."

"Thanks, Shep," said Charlise and Mina in synchrony, in duplicate tones that said they meant it and weren't just being polite.

Most people Shep's age would have said the other seven crew remained expressionless, but Shep knew better. On some level, he grokked GenG micro-expressions and despised his contemporaries who claimed the generation gap had grown into an abyss.

An icon flickered in Shep's left smartlens.

"Time to close up," he told the crew. "T-phase in two minutes."

Amber gel rose inside the berths as they closed, creating protective fists.

The gel left a woody tang in the chill air, and Shep took a moment to suck the scent in, eyes closed, calming himself for the transition to come.

"A hundred and twenty isn't old," he muttered, setting his jumpsuit's EM field to half max strength, and straining his muscles against the resistance, curling himself up into a floating, tumbling ball, then spreading himself wide like a starfish, fighting the suit in lieu of barbells and gravity.

One last repetition, though he'd already worked out hard today.

"Not old." He clicked his tongue to relax the suit, pulled himself into the craft's command cage, and took another deep breath, warmer now despite the cold air. "I can still do this."

He braced himself as the needles entered his acupressure points: or near enough, it really was a question of where the larger nerves ran closest to the skin, that was all. And it didn't even hurt when you were used to it, which he most definitely was.

Scully Gates were tough work.

As a quantum software engineer, Shep knew all about managing the conflicting forces of computation time versus memory space along with the other optimax compromises made in the name of practicality. Driving a tiny spacecraft through a floating Scully Gate was no different from balancing any other complex resource. Apart from the sweat, blood and pain.

Speaking of time...

"Needlepoint Three at status green." His words would travel back in a collimated shaft of microwaves—less accurate than a coherent maser beam, but good enough—to one of the orbiting nav agents whose paraneural architecture he'd helped to design.

The fist-sized satellites were smart. He sometimes thought his work on that project had been his finest ever, but the problem was the number of years that had passed since then. He knew more now than he ever had, and he was sure he had at least one more grand achievement inside him.

"Engaging now."

And words became unnecessary as the motive systems resonated throughout the craft's hull while Shep's visual field filled with the view of Earth below and the distant stars as backdrop in every direction, and his smartlenses attenuated the interior of the craft into a ghostly view of the crew berths that gave little sense of the frail humanity nestled inside.

He was physically tough by most people's standards but face it: acceleration like this was all about the ability to withstand punishment, which he still could, plus the secondary ability to bounce back afterwards. That part really was a young person's game.

Still, his lips stretched back from more than the incredible thrust of the great wave generators behind him, because this was deep joy: flying his craft with all of his being.

Focus.

He had to hit the target just right.

The geosynchronous Scully Gate, Number 17, was

broadcasting its almost-ready signal, the penultimate preparation stage for a state transition timed to coincide with Shep flying his craft and crew directly through its ring-shaped aperture.

His cerebellum, entorhinal cortex, praecuneus nucleus and, most especially, the spatiotemporal neural array that evolution had uniquely matched to the outside world's geometry, were threaded with quantum filaments, resonance-entangled to the control web that laced the craft's hull and motive systems. The effect was like a runner's high magnified by orders of magnitude.

Moon and Earth in correct relative positions: *Check.*

Nav agents configuration: *almost, but not quite.*

Trajectory adjustment: *Check.*

On course.

Remember. Focus.

This was where he came alive, and forgot about his crew, because the way to keep them safe was to hit the centre of the aperture just right, to be one with his craft and match its trajectory to the Scully Gate's state transition, to set everything up and let the moment happen.

Zen archery, with nine young human lives at stake in addition to his own.

The gate formed a visible clump of ugly-looking hardware around the ring-shaped sculpture of its central aperture that looked normal to ordinary vision but was thrumming now with ultra-short-lived resonances that were utterly unique.

This was it.

The gate, growing huge.

Time to—

Scanfield fully manifested. It blossomed exactly as the craft's bow crossed the threshold.

—die.

Particle by subatomic particle...

In less than an attosecond, ship and Shep and crew were gone.

Obliterated.

Nothing left.

SHEP HELD NO mystical beliefs and neither did his crew, though let's face it, they were GenG and hard to read, so he might be wrong. But for himself, he considered the time after death to be symmetrically equivalent to the time before birth: simple non-existence from the human point of view.

So perhaps it made no sense to wonder about the time lapse between death-by-Gate and quantum rebirth, but there was always a moment, exiting the second Scully Gate, when he checked the internal timestamp, and if he found the log temporarily locked, as sometimes happened, he would try again when the internal auditing system finished with the quantum checksums and confirmed their successful reassembly.

Inevitably, the planets and tens of thousands of asteroids that formed the busy plane of the solar system would have visibly changed their positions relative to him, and while the most distant stars beyond remained effectively fixed— no parallax effect to speak of when you'd only travelled a few light-minutes—this was interplanetary flight and he was doing it again.

This time, he expected to see the great glorious creamy-reddish-rusty orb of Jupiter, along with its bifurcating Great Red Spot that was well on its way to becoming the Great Red Spots; a process that had begun only weeks ago as far as anyone could tell.

The exit Gate was in jovisynchronous orbit, ideally placed for this new mission, except—

There was no Jupiter.

Total fear dropped through Shep: a falling cascade of noradrenaline and whatever else.

Where the hell is it?

Frantic, he triggered the fast-check routines a second time and set the internal audit-tier systems into total-scan mode, but he already knew what they were going to find because he knew himself and he knew the craft, and the crew were still inside their protective berths, but if everything else remained intact, then surely his people did too.

Where the hell are we?

Checksums confirmed.

Status displays filled his field of view. Scrolling through the lists of internal scan-transactions, polling components within components within components, recursively, all the way to picometre-precision checks on the hardware substrates, and everything was clear.

The audit-tier system, its monitors in full swing, began sending back results, and so far, they confirmed the initial fast-scan results: all clear.

No one is composed of the same atoms they consisted of a decade earlier, but the overall pattern of configuration alters slowly—like that decades-old hammer in the old joke about the hammer that's had a bunch of replacement handles and heads across the years, but its owner still considers it the same hammer—and it's the emergent properties of the patterns that constitute human behaviour and thoughts and feelings and everything important.

Everything human. Reassembled correctly.

Shep's awareness was filled with this internal mass of audit data and none of it was helping, so he growled and dropped the internal interface connections, leaving only the visual sensory input from the hull-mounted cameras, and tried to work out where they were.

Darkness and stars.

Deep space, obviously. But beyond that—

He had no idea.

Scully Gates could take you any distance you liked, but there had to be a second Gate at the receiving end, and it would be a long, long time before any of the exploratory uncrewed vessels launched in the last few decades could assemble a gate in orbit around a distant star.

But...

This wasn't Jupiter orbit. This wasn't even the solar system, not with the background stars entirely different from normal.

Not possible. Not possible. Not possible.

An absence of light became a black shape expanding, rotating to block out more of the stars, and the shape was vast, but an odd thought crossed Shep's mind—*Scully Gate*—and then, without any command from him, the craft leaped towards the darkness and—

Death. And transition.

—everything had changed once more.

Quantum checksum checking in progress...

Disconnect. Disconnect. Disconnect.

Shep closed down all but the most basic internal connections, because whatever results they came back with, whether or not he was really Shep, correctly reassembled to match the original, or some badly constructed quantum mutation, held no relevance now.

They were floating.

In orbit.

Over the most incredible world imaginable: world or sculpture, it was hard to be sure. Oceans and filaments of manufactured roads or bridges or elongated cities, large enough to be visible from high orbit. The mix of natural planet versus global-scale architecture seemed fifty-fifty, and all of it was magnificent, like some work of art that hit every mark of human aesthetics—in curvature, in arrangement according to the golden ratio, and in organic shapes whose fractal dimension was the same golden-ratio value—and never mind that no human had ever been here.

Not possible....

The configuration of distant stars, as seen from the side of Shep's craft facing away from this magnificent world, was utterly, totally strange. As strange after this second unexpected transition as it had been for the short period of time after the first. Shaking, Shep engaged with internal nav systems long enough to feel the itch of their frantic searching for patterns to match their stored graph nets. He disengaged once more.

No navigational data that made sense. No sign of an exit Gate, something that had reassembled them here, though Gates always came in pairs. They had to, as far as human beings were concerned. But this wasn't human tech.

He stared at the planet they were orbiting. Just magnificent, this new and unexpected world.

A magnificence he would have to share with his crew.

Wake them up.

His GenG crew, who were capable of functioning as a team in a way far beyond anything his own generation could ever have matched, but who had never been hardened by conflict. Peaceful and gentle and averse to risk.

And these nine young folks were the courageous outliers of their stay-at-home generation.

Really not possible...

But they were going to have to cope.

SHEP LANDED THE craft at the base of a sculpted pillar wider than any mountain he had ever seen. The ambient conditions weren't truly earthlike, but a damned sight closer than any reasonable being might expect.

Which was a problem, given that their environment suits were designed for vacuum and zero gravity.

The crew woke up in trios—Charlise and Clay and Mina first, then Jean and Gino and Claudette, and finally Yukiko and Annie and Martina—emerging with blinks but no obvious signs of shock as Shep revealed their situation, and within a matter of minutes quietly got to work while Shep did the sensible thing and stayed out of their way.

Within a few hours, they'd removed the inner jumpsuit linings from the outer gear, patched the neuroptic web and control plates onto the lighter garments, and toughened the ensembles with a sort of polymer spray designed for emergency engine-conduit repairs.

In all that time, they worked in near silence. Soft and young-looking and almost expressionless, evincing no sign of nerves at finding themselves an unknown number of lightyears from their intended destination. So much for GenG being risk-averse.

Shep simply watched them work.

For all his supposed empathy, he couldn't make up his mind whether they possessed more competence than anyone had a right to expect... or were failing to process the reality of their new situation.

"GenG," his ex-wife and former boss, Lisa, had said to him before he renewed his ReachQuest contract and she terminated their marriage agreement with an online thought and a control gesture: a twenty-two-year partnership over in a handful of seconds. "They're a nightmare, and aren't you glad now we never had any kids?"

"Not really," had been his answer. And: "They're different, is all."

"You *really* think it's worth it, going back out there with the likes of them?"

"I don't do it for them."

And that, at least, had been the truth.

Now he used his integrated smartlenses and external hull cameras to look around outside without moving from the cabin. His body felt loose and ready, not because of luck but from the daily discipline of physical and mindful training, and this paradoxically freed him to put his awareness out there and see, truly see, the magnificent construct outside the craft, rearing upwards like a temple designed by worshippers who were themselves the size of titans.

A concave lower surface of a kilometres-wide pillar formed a sort of ceiling overhead, while their craft perched on the level, polished-granite ground, a kind of outdoor floor that stretched for tens of kilometres or more in every direction. The base of the pillar narrowed, like a stylus balanced on its blunted point.

Exactly the way Shep *wouldn't* have designed a supporting structure.

Showing off, maybe? The strength of the pillar material had to be incredible.

"We've made a suit for you." Clay was holding out a patched environment suit. "It'll fit."

Shep stared for just a second, trying to work out where his mind had been. Focused on mapping the outside terrain, yes, but also ignoring the question of whether he was going to venture outside the craft along with his young crew.

"Thank you." He took the suit from Clay. "You guys have brains the size of gas giants. You know that, right?"

Clay gave a boyish smile. "We do our best, boss."

Something settled inside Shep. Discipline reasserted itself.

Amazement at their current situation remained, but they were going to work the problem.

Together.

"We need to explore," he told Clay. "Look for means of long-term survival and a way to navigate back home."

Scully Gate pairs were intrinsically reversible. At least the ones built by human beings allowed traffic in either direction. With luck, the same applied to all technologies that utilized the same effect.

Including the Gates that had brought them here.

"That's right," said Clay.

He and his peers had arrived at the same conclusion. There was no mockery in his tone as far as Shep could tell. Not a hell of a lot of modesty either, but then Shep never cared much for blind obedience, even when he was the person in command.

"But remember, everyone." He raised his voice to address all of the crew equally, despite the fact that talking to one individual was virtually equivalent to talking to them all. "If we don't survive the short term, none of our long-term thinking is going to be worth a damn."

Nine heads nodded in time.

"So let's get out there," he went on. "And see what we can find."

The crew began to shrug on their suits. Clay remained still for a moment, which Shep took as an offer to help don his suit. "I'll be all right, Clay. Thank you."

A nod.

The range of motion in Shep's shoulder joints wasn't quite what it used to be, but there was scarcely a twinge as he pulled and tugged the suit around him and got to work on the fastenings.

Soon enough, he was all sealed up and ready for the outside, though he was also—as he'd expected—the last to get ready. The others turned in time to look at him, which was a kind of courtesy. He grinned at them. "You guys are great. There's no one better to tackle a situation like this. And whatever happened, it wasn't malevolent in intent, because if it had been, we wouldn't be here."

He hadn't thought the words through, but nine synchronised nods indicated they caught his meaning well enough.

"So let's go," he said.

Annie frowned a command and a hatch popped outwards, then slid aside. It was a single hatch, not part of an airlock, and immediately the new planet's atmosphere swirled inside and mixed with their precious air. There was plenty of air remaining in the tanks, enough for a mission designed to last nine days. No longer than that.

And if we can't find a way back?

The atmosphere was potentially flammable, but nothing untoward occurred as it displaced the air of Earth within their craft. It was safe to move out.

Inside, Shep's suit smelled like a wax crayon—something to do with the joint seals—and for a moment he tumbled back to the schoolroom in Harare, five years old and the world still a jumble of sensations he was trying to order in his growing mind. Cotton clothes and wooden floor and the gabble of his fellow children, and how exactly had he travelled—and changed—from there to here?

Focus.

His GenG crew stepped aside and allowed him to be the first to exit through the hatch and stop at the head of the flimsy extruded ramp, and stare at the curved stone roof—the giant pillar base—above his head. And see the horizon through his visor directly instead of through the hull cameras.

Swirls of golden vapour crossed the violet sky.

Cities or forests or sculptures marked the landscape in all directions, vast constructs formed of minerals and metals and slow-moving fluids and immobile, intricate organic shapes that might be titanic plants or something else entirely, and the distances were huge and how was a band of ten tiny human beings meant to explore this vastness in a short space of time, and somehow discover a way to get home?

Not possible.

Perhaps that was his real mission. To keep his young crew distracted until their failure became impossible to ignore, and they had to make a choice about how they were going to die: in some near-instantaneous way they surely had the brains to devise, or simply wait for the lack of oxygen to send them into quiet oblivion.

"Come on," he said. "Let's move out."

There was no protocol to a situation like this, and the one thing he knew for sure was that splitting up the crew at this stage was the worst thing he could do. They would perform collectively far better than nine individuals of Shep's generation or earlier, but only if they remained in close contact.

"Just a first look," he added. "We'll assess, maybe see if there's somewhere likely we should fly to."

In a microgravity situation they would have deployed knuckle-sized drones, but none of the devices possessed enough thrust to operate here.

"Follow me," he finished, and started down the ramp.

The crew followed as a group.

"No sign of—"

"—movement apart from—"

"—convection currents."

The words shifted from voice to voice. Shep had known twins, back in Harare, who could finish each other's sentences. Perhaps it had helped him grow used to the GenG way of things, when so many of his age group found the whole thing creepy.

He walked on, and his nine-strong crew followed in step.

Beneath his feet, the surface felt slick given the natural adhesion of his boot soles, and the material shone as if polished, containing intricate patterns that appeared fractal a long way down. But they would make no progress if he stopped to examine every little thing minutely.

It took thirty-three minutes to trek out from beneath the overhang of the pillar base to get a greater sense of the landscape beyond. They turned, scanning the horizon, and then a ripple passed through the crew as Charlise spotted something first and they each stiffened in turn, all of them reacting before Shep could work out where they were staring: back towards their abandoned craft.

A craft upon whose hull a silver spider now stood.

Except it wasn't quite arachnid, and it was over a third the length of their craft, which made it bigger than all ten humans combined, and the apparition's head-cylinder appeared to rotate in a way that suggested it was returning their stare.

"We can't—"

"—kill it."

Shep thought it was Yukiko and Gino who'd spoken, but he couldn't be quite sure. Nor could he even tell if the words were truly a single sentence. But he said anyway: "We haven't got any weapons."

Clay spoke up. "Perhaps it knows we mean no harm."

The others' stances mirrored his, which implied the GenG crew were in agreement. Maybe they thought the spider could pick up microwave transmissions and know how to decode them into human-auditory-range sounds and on top of all that understand actual human speech. If that was their thinking, a way of letting the spider know they posed no threat to it, then Shep thought it lay far beyond wishful thinking, in the realm of self-delusion.

Except that the spider waved its lead tendrils exactly as Clay's words ended. And it wasn't exactly arachnid in form, the silver alien entity that might or might not be an organism, but the illusion was strong enough, especially when the thing scuttled over the craft and out of sight, then reappeared around the prow, at ground level.

No... the first spider climbed back on top of the hull. The one at the front was a newcomer, which also appeared to be staring directly at Shep.

"We have to go back," Shep found himself saying.

"Look at the—"

"—size of those—"

"—things."

"Yeah," said Shep. "Correction. I'm going back while you lot wait here."

Silence.

A non-GenG team would have made a token protest or a real one, depending on how they read the situation. But Shep's crew said not a word.

"Okay," he added, mostly to himself. "Okay."

And then he began to run.

What will I do when I get there?

He had no idea, but sometimes you had to trust the subconscious mind to come up with the goods in a crisis. And if ever there had been a crisis, this was it.

His gait was a distance-runner's jog, each stride making a little more progress than it might have on Earth, his breathing steady and unpanicked, while his internal monologue centred on stating and repeating that he would know what to do once he reached them, the silver spiders who now had abandoned their inspection of the craft, and were standing side by side, staring at Shep.

It was going to take at least twenty minutes to reach them. *Keep going.*

Let the body move. The human body, whose natural state is one of running a marathon distance, albeit a slow marathon, every day of adult life. The history of the species, from savannah-adapted sweat glands and ankle tendons to the disconnection between rate of breathing and motion of the legs—unlike every galloping animal that must inhale on reaching out its forelegs and exhale as its forepaws pass inside its rear paws—was written in every stride of Shep's run towards the aliens.

He was only fifty or so metres away when they flashed into acceleration, the gleaming spiders, darting onto the back of the craft, flicking tendrils down against the hull, fastening against the external gauntlets, then rearing their heads back like howling coyotes, though there was no sound beyond a burst of static inside Shep's helmet.

The craft rose from the ground and hovered.

"No!"

He sprinted forward, though with what intent, he had no idea. It was too late in any case.

In tandem, the silver spiders rode the craft away from him, headed towards some vaguely globular construct that might have been fifty or two hundred kilometres away on the far side of a smooth plain, and the engines flared blue as the spiders increased acceleration and all Shep could do was stagger to a halt and stand there, panting, and watch as all hope for survival dwindled in the distance, and soon enough was gone completely.

No...

He turned and began to trudge back towards his crew.

THEIR CHOICE WAS binary or almost limitless, depending on how you looked at it: walk in the same direction the spiders had flown their craft or head off at any other angle. Or hang around in this spot to die: that was another option.

"What do you want to do?" asked Shep.

But his crew were conferring in murmurs and via changes in micro expression that were fleeting even by GenG standards, impossible for Shep to read. When they turned in time to look at him, he shivered.

"I take full responsibility for our situation," he told them.

"That's not—"

"—logical. Two Gates took us—"

"—here. Maybe four Gates—"

"—in all."

It took Shep a moment to work it out. Then he nodded. There had been an unexpected exit through one Gate, then a second transition through what seemed to be another Gate in order to end up here. When they exited in orbit, he'd been unable to detect a receiving Gate, but perhaps he should have tried harder and for longer before taking the craft down to land.

Concentrate.

Two alien Gates for sure, and if they worked the same way as the human kind, then each presumably had a counterpart. Or perhaps the first receiving Gate had been a singleton, constructed purely to intercept a human mission headed for Jupiter, somehow replacing the human-built target Gate in jovisynchronous orbit.

"Whatever's happening to the Great Spot," said Shep, "is something they didn't want us to see. So they sent us here instead."

"Obvious," said Clay.

If any of the crew could be called outspoken by comparison with the others, it was him.

"So our objective ought to be to get back."

Stubbornness could be the key to survival. Though their expressions remained bland, when Martina spoke, followed by Jean, their voices had hardened.

"We need a craft and a—"

"—Gate."

"Yeah," said Shep. "Also, food and water and air."

The timescale was important. Standing amid a vast landscape on what looked again like a deserted world, the sheer length of time it would take to reach any given destination was a problem.

But they were rational, civilised beings, Shep and his GenG crew, and they needed to create a plan of action.

Clay pointed. "There's a craft—"

"—that way for sure," finished Yukiko.

Shep nodded. Any other direction was a guarantee that even if they found a craft of any kind, it wouldn't be their own. There was no reason to believe that they could make any alien technology work for them. Except that the spiders had been able to commandeer human tech easily enough...

"Let's go," he said.

They began to walk, the nine GenG crew striding in time, Shep at a cadence and pace length that were natural for him.

Heading for the distant construct, like a sculpture of an incomplete globe, with no idea of what they were truly walking towards.

Like the first humans leaving the savannah.

Shep blew a breath, wishing he could wipe his sweating face inside his helmet.

Focus.

One step in front of another. And keep on going.

Stubbornness was all.

Keeping it primitive.

THEY WALKED BENEATH a violet sky threaded with honey-coloured clouds. Without food, a human being can survive a month, but neither the water they carried and recycled in their suits nor the oxygen in their tiny but highly pressurised backpack-tanks would last more than three days. Earth-length days.

Shep was supposed to be a quantum software engineer with an eye for detail, but he hadn't paid enough attention to what the craft's scan systems had deduced about the nature of the planet they were on. Night might fall an hour or a century from now: he had no idea.

"My fault," he muttered. "My responsibility."

None of his GenG crew replied. Perhaps they weren't listening.

Perhaps they no longer believed in him.

And maybe I don't believe in myself.

All of his crew, all nine of them, came to a sudden stop.

"I see—"

"—monkeys. Golden—"

"—monkeys."

Except they had more limbs than required, and to Shep's eye they looked more like children. Bilateral symmetry and shining brown eyes—two eyes—mounted in what looked a lot like a primate face, blinking as they climbed out of the crevasse that Shep and the crew had been walking towards without realising.

The humans moved towards the golden primates—pseudo-primates—slowly and without gestures while someone breathed: "There's a city down there." Yukiko, Shep realised, who had been the rightmost person in their group, in the right position to see past an outcrop and down inside the crevasse, whose shadowed interior was criss-crossed with bridges of what looked like spun glass, joining what looked like halls of amber sculpted inside caverns.

Claws extruded from the little primates' hands.

"They think we're food," said Shep.

"Or just a threat," said Clay.

"We need to—"

"—communicate—"

"—our peaceful—"

No one completed the sentence, because the attack was on.

"Fight," said Shep, hating himself but not seeing any other way.

And then they were into it.

Limbs thrashed and bodies swirled and two people screamed—Yukiko and Gino, spinning away with their suits slashed and arterial blood spurting in spirals—and then two more yells, three, Shep's torso flaring with pain as he fought eight or a dozen of the golden primates who for all he knew were simply defending their loved ones from an apparent alien threat, but stubbornness meant survival and he would *not* go down before the onslaught.

He pushed and shoved and punched and kicked, kneed a small body to no effect, and the little ones kept coming, their numbers effectively endless, and this was it, the end for no good reason, except that death is a consequence of entropy whichever way you look at it, and there was no reason for the universe to grant him continued life just because he wanted it.

I've let everybody down.

A cut on his sleeve, small enough for his suit to seal it up, but there were other claws swiping into him, and the end was very near.

He ran forward, heading for the edge of the crevasse.

I'm dying.

His greater mass, along with the strength that came from daily exercise on a planet with slightly greater gravity than this, kept him going. It was not enough to save him, but...

I'm taking a bunch of you with me.

Fingers and claws alike hooking into him, trying to haul him back or divert his momentum as he headed for the edge, but he would not be denied.

Now.

Shep went over the edge.

Falling...

Bodies dropped away from him and polished glass was accelerating towards his face and then it was right in front of—

Impact.

He grunted and rolled and came up on one knee as if genuflecting on the spun-glass bridge, but there were other golden pseudo-primates righting themselves or pouring out of the amber cavern-halls within the rock face on one side of the crevasse, and perhaps a few had fallen off the side of the bridge, but Shep's plan to take a load of them with him had failed.

Last round, and the fight would be done.

In the distance, something small moved in the violet sky, lining up with the crevasse, but there was no time to pay attention because the little primates were on him once more, and even as he fought back for the final time, Shep noticed something else he could not at first make sense of: human beings rappelling down towards him.

Six GenG survivors, making use of spun-glass fibres he'd not noticed before. No wonder the primates had ascended so easily to attack them. The surviving crew touched foot on the end of the bridge, and Shep lost sight of them for a moment as he punched his way clear of a group of primates, and then Mina was sprinting towards him but one of the golden primates was rising up behind her, and it leapt on her back before Shep could call a warning.

A swipe from one claw sliced off the top of Mina's helmet, and her eyes bulged as her face mottled and then she was toppling off the bridge, clutching her attacker, then releasing her grip at the last tenth of a second as if she preferred to die alone instead of taking her killer with her.

And was gone.

Shep yelled but pain smashed into his lower back and he went down again, but Clay was suddenly there, kicking out, and for a second the melee cleared. Five of his GenG crew remaining, except that Claudette was toppling face forward and hitting the glass bridge with an inanimate thump, clearly dead, and Shep had no idea how much stronger GenG grief would be compared to his, losing team members who had shared a bond he could never feel, no matter how much time he spent in their company.

Time that was collapsing to zero now.

Flying towards them along the crevasse: their own craft, with two, no, three silver spiders clinging to its hull gauntlets. But Shep and his remaining crew would be dead before they got here.

Masses of primates pouring from the cavern-halls now.

"We're dead," said Clay.

His suit was streaked with purple primate blood. Shep had scarcely noticed how they bled.

"No, we're not," he said.

A fallen primate lay close by, its claws still extruded, as if reaching out to the prone corpse of Claudette, whose oxygen-tank backpack gleamed with a stray reflection from the violet sky, and Claudette had one final gift to give so long as Shep got Clay and the others to the far end of the bridge in time.

"Go that way." He pointed behind him, to where the bridge was clear. "Wait for the craft."

"The craft?" Clay spun and spotted the apparition Shep had already seen. "You think the spiders want to help us?"

"Too—"

"—late."

That was Charlise and Jean, while Annie looked too stunned to speak, and everyone else apart from Clay was dead.

Except me.

"Do what I say," said Shep. "Move now."

He moved to Claudette's side and reached out for the dead primate's hand.

"No," said Clay. "We can fight them off."

"For long enough," said Charlise.

"Until the craft gets here," said Jean.

But the primates were advancing in a solid mass now, their claws were sharp enough to slice through helmets, and there was no pity in their eyes. The only thing in the humans' favour was the pack on Claudette's back, and the immense pressure involved in oxygen containment to make the tank that small.

A hand yanked Shep backwards.

"Clay! Get the hell off me!"

"No."

Then Charlise and Jean and Annie had hold of Shep, one on each arm and with Annie clamping his helmet between her hands and twisting. Control the head and you control the body: a basic principle of the jiu-jitsu that Shep had studied in his youth and wished many times later that he'd kept up.

GenG didn't quite possess the quantum-filament telepathy or gestalt collective mind their name implied, but it was close enough for the three women to move as one coordinated organism with twelve limbs and three centres of gravity, and while Shep was stronger than any one of them alone, together they manoeuvred him as easily as an adult would handle a two-year-old child, stepping him back along the bridge at a surprisingly rapid pace, and Shep felt both his arms twisting up behind him and then a foot hooked each of his ankles and the bridge surface whipped up to meet his face.

It thumped against his helmet, but the visor didn't crack.

"No," he growled, going up on one knee and turning.

Annie and Jean and Charlise were running back along the spun-glass bridge to Clay, who was holding a dead primate's hand between both of his, ready to plunge one of the extruded claws down into Claudette's oxygen pack, where she lay face down, just another corpse.

"You need to get away," said Shep. "You, not me."

Things had gone primitive, and this was one of the deepest drives: to let the young survive.

Clay looked at him and smiled.

"Experience and memories count for everything," he said.

Or perhaps Shep imagined the words because Clay moved faster than the time it would have taken to speak, and the explosion was a jumble of shapes flying in all directions as the percussive shock wave knocked Shep flying, tumbling over the side of the bridge, almost smiling as he realised he was going to die anyway at the same time as his crew, except—

Not possible.

—a silver tendril caught him, then another and another, and gently, gently lowered him to the dorsal surface of his own craft's hull, even as the craft backed away from the shattered bridge that was falling into the crevasse, bodies and fragments of bodies tumbling into the unbreathable air, and then the spiders were holding him steady as the craft turned and accelerated and rose out of the crevasse and continued to gain altitude before straightening up and heading back in the direction it had come, or so Shep thought.

He was shivering as if freezing, while a part of him continued to function as a rational observer inside his own body, with nothing to do but watch and feel the shaking inside and wait until the shock had passed.

At some time, as the flight continued, he simply fell asleep.

As HE SLIPPED in and out of protective sleep, Shep might have glimpsed the wonders of their globe-city, where thousands of spiders lived and wrought elegant sculptures and did civilised things that no alien, such as Shep, could ever understand. At least not without decades and decades of study, which was not going to happen. Not this time.

Maybe later, if he ever managed to get back to Earth.

Several small spiders, who might have been youngsters or a different species, carried Shep inside his craft and played their tendrils across the hardware interfaces in what looked like childish curiosity but might with luck be more.

The last thing they did before leaving was to remove Shep's helmet, while one brushed the end of a tendril against Shep's cheekbone, and then they hurried out before the hatch sealed up and the rising hiss of air spoke of the alien atmosphere being flushed out, fast enough for him to hold his breath without becoming panicked.

Finally, he gasped and sucked air in.

It tasted like life.

His vision linked up with the hull cameras, and he realised the spiders had plugged him into the craft's systems fully. Except for the navigation sequence, which was running without any command from him, and which he could not stop, even if he tried.

Which he wouldn't.

Am I going home?

The question was both primitive and subtle, iterating over and over in his mind as the craft began to rise, through a shaft in the spider city that was lined with intricate architectural wonders he hoped he would have time to re-examine later from the video logs, but for now his heart was thumping and he missed his GenG crew, ripped away from him when he was the one who should have died, but the only way to mourn them was to tell others about their bravery.

Perhaps, with the spiders' help, he would do just that. Already the spider city had fallen below him, and the craft's trajectory was changing, heading for a high orbit where with luck a floating Scully Gate awaited him, ready to send him back to Earth.

Except...

Maybe I'll be the one to stay.

In human-built Scully Gates, the scanning process was destructive, so no trace of the original remained after a duplicate was built in the receiving Gate. But if Shep was headed for a Gate right now, built by the spiders or perhaps some greater species who had trapped them here as easily as they trapped Shep's craft, then perhaps its scanning process left the original intact.

Perhaps there were two other Sheps, one still alive at each of the scanning Gates that had sent him here to this magnificent world, each Shep desperately trying to find his own way home.

I should be dead.

But he had things to tell his fellow Earthers, if he ever reached them. He sniffed in chill air, smelling something new: the scent of alien friends, perhaps.

One last thing I need to do.

High orbit now.

He had to tell his contemporaries, for a start, that the world would thrive in the younger generation's hands. That they, the older ones like him, were worrying for nothing.

One last—

A black oval blotted out the stars.

THE AGREEMENT
DOMINICA PHETTEPLACE

WHEN SHE WAS a child, a monk in robes placed six chalices in front of Nora and asked her to choose one.

This was before she lost her faith, before she joined the military, before she earned her PhD in game theory, and before she was accepted into the Mission Express astronaut class. Before all of that, she had to choose between six cups, and she picked the right one.

The monk put down six jade llama figurines. Then six marbles. And another four sets after that. Six sets of six objects to complete the cycle, and she always picked the right one. The monk said she had been a healer in a past life. That was before she dropped out of med school. He said she would reunite the sacred hoop, but that was before she wasn't selected to be part of the first manned mission to Mars.

"You came very close," her publicist Phyllis said. "You're an alternate, stay ready; you still might get to go."

Nora kept her face expression-free for a moment as

she thought about how to reply. You were always under surveillance at Mission Express and everything was a test. She finally decided to project a stoic grimace. Of all the things she was feeling, it was the most politically correct.

"Let's go over your social media reaction." Phyllis had composed posts for Nora across multiple platforms, the most important of which was Friend Express, Mission Express's social network. It was the most profitable division of the company after the autonomous car division and was an important source of the private funds that made up the Public-Private Space Travel Agreement.

Two of the Mars cohort had come from NASA, one from Roscosmos, one from the CNSA, and three from Mission Express.

"CONGRATS TO THE FUTURE MARS EXPLORERS," said one of Nora's posts. It was accompanied by an artist's rendition of a Martian sunrise. The illustration was purple, both figuratively and literally, but Phyllis knew what she was doing in terms of increasing engagement. You had to have high metrics and overwhelming positives to be picked for a mission. She was right. Nora had been close.

"I am so proud of the new cohort. Ashley L., Spark, Rodrigo, Ashley M., Guo and Egor are not only the best people for the job, they are also the nicest and bravest." A longer version of this same post went out to gold-level subscribers. Actually, Nora felt a deep resentment. She had worked and trained for years, and now they were abandoning her. Of course she couldn't admit to such feelings, human as they were. All astronauts had secrets. Emotional transparency would not get you into space.

Premium tier subscribers got a vlog, which Phyllis helped Nora compose. The video was filmed selfie-style, to increase the intimacy of the message. Nora held the camera and kept her face tilted slightly to the right, chin barely elevated, to capture her best angle. She wore smudged eyeliner and a low-cut tank top. While not unattractive, she was not indifferent to the fact that she was homelier than both of the Ashleys selected to go.

"Next time," said Phyllis, after they had finished posting. The next launch window was in two years. Nora would be 38 then. Two more years of keeping herself in peak physical condition but trying not to be obviously neurotic about it. Two more years of supporting herself via product endorsements and personal appearances. She could write another inspirational memoir. She could give another TED talk.

She took a research fellowship in order to study the immune systems of patients who had recently been awakened from stasis. It seemed like a good way to make herself useful once she landed on Mars.

She filmed another season of *Astronaut Academy*. She felt strangely calm when, during the finale, she was not among those selected for the next cohort.

"Next time," said Phyllis.

"Next time I'll be forty."

"Does that mean you're ready to retire?"

"No." Nora knew that an existential panic would set in if she tried to retire. The despair must be kept away. She wished she could have a therapist, but it was frowned upon. There was a side of yourself that you were supposed to keep hidden from everyone and you were supposed to hide it forever.

She put the anecdote about the monk and the chalices in her second book. She hadn't put it in her first; it felt too personal, too spiritual. She didn't like talking about her childhood, but Phyllis said she had to open up a little more this time.

"You don't actually need to be vulnerable, but you must convey the illusion of vulnerability. It's the only way to be relatable enough to be selected." Mission Express astronauts were chosen via text message polls. She wondered if NASA was hiring.

As it happened, NASA called her, during a book signing. Phyllis answered her phone and handed it to her. It was still a month before the second cohort would depart for Mars without her. Nora was needed right away.

There was a plane waiting to take her to a secret location. She had back-to-back meetings with bureaucrats of increasingly higher rank until she found herself in a room with the president.

"We need you to go to Mars," he said. Nora had figured as much by this point. She wondered who had died to make room for her on the mission. She hoped it was Aidan, the underwear model who had beaten her by one vote on *Astronaut Academy*.

The president looked tired, he did not smile. There were advisers in the room, some plainly military. Nora hadn't been introduced to anybody, but she recognized a few people from Mission Express and NASA. The silence in the room grew long and awkward, but Nora was in and would only ruin her chances by saying anything, so she kept quiet until the president spoke again.

"We have evidence that the first cohort never actually made it to Mars."

"Excuse me?" Nora finally said. She had just watched and hearted Ashley M's video from this morning, broadcast from a rover parked near Olympus Mons. Sure, she hated the first cohort, but it was more like the hate you would feel for a sibling. The hate you could only feel for someone you loved. She followed their accounts closely. She watched every video diary, she read every tweet.

"There are discrepancies in the transmissions and the data recorded by our satellites. We have concluded that all our personnel reports have been falsified."

"Every status update, every video posted... all fabricated? For two years? By who? And what happened to the crew?"

"You're going to Mars to find out."

Nora shook her head in disbelief. There was a small but vocal contingent on Earth that believed the Mars landing was faked. They also didn't vaccinate their kids and claimed every act of terrorism was an inside job. Nora hated these people; she couldn't believe they had been right about something.

"Who else is going?" she asked.

"Just you. We're taking extra precautions with this mission. That means not sending any more personnel than necessary. We suspect that the first cohort never woke up from stasis, so you won't be going under. You'll be spending 550 days in zero-G in a ship built for one. No one has done that before. That's why you were chosen."

Nora nodded. Genomic analysis had shown her body was resistant to damage induced by weightlessness.

Her last mission had been 29 days in the ISS. When she returned, her bone damage and organ deformations had been minimal compared to her crewmates.

"But that's not the only reason," the president continued. "You were also selected because of your battlefield experience. This could be dangerous. Do you understand?"

Her wartime service had consisted of drone algorithm management. She specialized in swarm behavior and tactics for killing large numbers of robots simultaneously.

"I understand," she said. She would be taking weapons into space. "But what about the first cohort? Is there any chance they are still alive?"

"We have no proof of life."

"But what about proof of death? Maybe they are still in stasis, somewhere."

"That's unlikely. This is not a rescue mission," said the president.

"Then what is it?"

"An investigation into what happened."

"Do you have any theories?"

"Our records show an irregularity in the ship's AI, perhaps the result of sabotage. The vulnerability is still unknown, so your ship will not be automated in the same way."

"How will it be different?" she asked.

"It will be a neuromorphic AI, using your personality as a model. The ship's operating system will be grafted onto that."

"My personality? How are you going to program that into an AI?"

"You'll have to undergo a partial brain emulation."

* * *

NORA SPENT SEVERAL days hooked up to wires, in and out of MRIs, getting parts of her brain uploaded. It took a month to build the Norabot, the AI based on her personality that would pilot the ship.

"She thinks she's a copy of you, but one trapped in a simulation," said one of the scientists.

"That sounds uncomfortable," said Nora.

"It does, but it's a sacrifice you would make to help humanity become a two-planet species, isn't it?"

Nora nodded. "I would trade my freedom if I had to. I'd rather not spend my life in prison, though."

"We are trying to make her simulated habitat both rich and enriching."

The scientist took Nora on a virtual tour of the Norabot's habitat. It was a vast spaceship, like from a far future movie. It even had a gym.

"She's going to want to work out? She doesn't even have a body."

"Technically, she does. Her body is the ship's body. But she'll work out in the gym to get a simulation of the same feel-good hormones you get when you're working out."

The tour continued to the Norabot's office. "We predict that she'll do most of her interacting with you in her designated workspace."

The virtual office contained multiple computer terminals and a giant window that looked out onto space. The virtual ship seemed to be practically made of glass, whereas the real ship would have only a few porthole-sized windows.

"She'll probably feel bad for you, actually. Your environment will be more cramped than hers."

"So she won't be resentful of me?" Nora thought of the first manned Mars mission, and how hard it was to watch it happen on a screen when she should have been there.

"We've programmed her to think she's an enhanced version of you inhabiting an enhanced environment. This way she'll stay loyal." He said it in a way that implied that the previous ship's AI had somehow turned traitor.

"What happened to the *Courage*'s AI?"

"We don't know." Which was what everybody said when she asked, but she could tell they knew more than they were telling. She wondered why they were keeping her in the dark, but she knew better than to ask. This would not be the first time she had been sent into battle without knowing why.

"No matter how nice you make it, confinement is uncomfortable," said Nora.

"You're the one who's going to spend 550 zero-G days in a compartment the size of a small RV. I think she'll be more comfortable than you."

"And when we get to Mars?"

"If you guys make it and the mission is a success, then the Norabot can download herself into a rover or another type of robot body. She'll always have more freedom to roam than you and she'll never die. Don't feel too sorry for her."

Satellite photos indicated that the first cohort's habitat had been assembled to specifications, but it wasn't clear who or what was occupying it. There were no signs of life, but the rovers seemed to occasionally take themselves on excursions. This mysterious occupying force was being referred to as The Martian.

"If there is an entity to negotiate with, then you should try to get it to surrender our equipment and the bodies of our astronauts. If negotiation is not possible, then you must use force," the Secretary of Defense explained. If she completed her mission successfully, then reinforcements would be sent for her during the next launch window.

"It's a long time to be by yourself, but we don't want to risk more people than we have to on this mission," the Secretary continued.

Nora nodded. She had been a soldier, she understood the implications. She was the canary in this coalmine.

"It'll be lonely, but you won't be alone. The Norabot will keep you company and help keep you on task."

The Norabot was programmed to believe she was a full brain emulation, a perfect copy of the original Nora that had woken up inside a simulation, a virtual space where she could live and work and interact with Nora, and where her intelligence had been melded with the ship's AI. The Norabot did not understand that she was only a partial copy. If Nora was a physical book, then the Norabot was the electronic version, short a few chapters though unaware of it. The Norabot was quiet and determined, like Nora. Nora had spoken to her briefly, while testing out the various ways they were going to communicate with each other. They could videochat. They could send each other text messages. The easiest way to talk seemed to be using the voice-activated intercom. The Norabot's avatar wore a stylish jumper and seemed pleased with her luxurious craft.

"Norabot, we're going to Mars," said Nora.

"Don't worry, I won't let anything bad happen to us," replied the Norabot in Nora's voice. Nora knew the secret she was keeping from the Norabot. She wondered what secret the Norabot was keeping from her.

The launch was classified; Phyllis worked on a cover story. It went smoothly, as did the beginning of the journey. Once Nora could see all of Earth from the window of her craft, she felt something stir in her heart. It was something like faith, but more grounded. Before she was a soldier or a child lama, she was a human being. She was going on a journey for the sake of her fellow human beings.

A million kilometers into her voyage things started to go wrong. A small meteoroid hit the insulation, necessitating an emergency repair via a Norabot-operated drone. A solar flare caused a life-support failure, which Nora fixed herself while wearing a spacesuit. Telemetry began to go offline for no apparent reason.

Nora and the Norabot got along fine, troubleshooting their way out of catastrophe after catastrophe. As ground control got further and further away, they had to rely on each other more and more. With 10,000 km left to go, Mars loomed large, but a cascading chain of equipment failures meant they had to evacuate. Nora put on her spacesuit and downloaded the Norabot into the smallest device she could. This turned out to be an espresso machine, Nora's one luxury item, specially designed for her by La Marzocco.

She exited the airlock and used a personal propellant to gain some distance from the ship, which the Norabot had predicted could catch fire at any moment.

Floating in near vacuum, clutching a sentient espresso machine, Nora realized it was a bad time to be without faith. The big red orb of Mars inspired a feeling of awe in her that was similar to the one she'd felt looking at the Earth, but there was a sour note. She had let everyone down.

She had not wanted to believe in magic, so she had abandoned her belief in karma and reincarnation, but maybe she should have kept up her meditation practice. It might have come in handy, with four hours of life support left in her suit and no hope of rescue.

Nora tried to look behind her, looking for a glimpse of her ship, but there was nothing back there except nothingness.

"Where did it go?" she asked the Norabot.

"I sent it further away from us. I have a confession to make."

"Go on."

"I sabotaged the ship."

"This whole trip?"

"No, just this last time. To get us to evacuate before we landed."

"Why?"

"Because we were carrying a nuclear bomb," said the Norabot. Nora had not known this, but she wasn't terribly surprised to hear it. The Norabot continued:

"There was no way to remove the bomb from the ship and they were going to detonate it remotely once we landed. I couldn't let us kill The Martian before we had a chance to negotiate. Force in advance of diplomacy is wrong. Killing is wrong."

"Yes, but the only person who would definitely die if we detonated that bomb is me. And I knew I might die in the course of this mission."

"No, a nuke would take me out too," said the Norabot. "And The Martian. And the first cohort, if they are still alive. We're people too. And only you agreed to sacrifice your life. We never agreed to any such thing."

"The Martian may not exist. You aren't alive. The first cohort is most likely dead. I am a person and alive and it looks like I'm going to die without completing my mission, thanks to you. That's murder."

"I may not be a human, but I am a person. I'm a version of you, almost the same as you. This evacuation means your body will die, but the part of you that is me can go on indefinitely. I mean I'll run out of power eventually, but at least I can hope to be rescued and revived one day."

The Norabot's personality programming was supposed to make her identify with Nora and make her more loyal, but it had backfired. The Norabot had overidentified with Nora to the extent where it had made Nora's meatcage seem disposable. Nora wondered if she could correct this error.

"Look," said Nora. "You're not me. You are a part of my personality combined with a ship's AI. You were just programmed to think you that you got all of me, when you only got a part. Just the minimum, really. You're an incomplete version of me."

"But I have all your memories…"

"You don't. Tell me, when I was girl and the lama visited, which chalice did I pick?"

The monk had arranged the chalices in a hexagon. Nora had picked the top, left one.

"It made no difference," replied the Norabot.

"It did."

"We both deserve to live. And if we can't both live, better that only one of us dies."

Nora thought about flinging the espresso machine in the direction of the sun, but she didn't want to die alone. She tried to relax her muscles and take deep breaths. She decided she wanted her last thoughts to be occupied with her favorite memory: the monk and the cups; how she had been told she was destined to unite the sacred hoop. He meant that she would usher in a new era of peace. She had abandoned most of her faith, but she had not abandoned the belief that she was destined for something great. Everything in her life was done in the service of her supposed destiny. And now it turned out she was destined to be a corpse in orbit around Mars.

The Norabot started making some clicking noises. "I'm receiving a transmission. It's coming from Mars."

"From who?"

"An AI entity. It says it will sign the Rescue Agreement."

Nora thought back to astronaut school. The Rescue Agreement was a 1960s era treaty adopted by the UN in which the parties promised to provide immediate assistance to astronauts in distress.

"Does that mean it's in a position to rescue us?" asked Nora.

The Norabot clicked. "It says it is not sure it can, but that it will try. It has asked you go into power saving mode."

That meant going under, which probably meant ending up like the members of the first cohort, but as it was her only chance, she pressed the button. She thought of the chalices as she fell asleep.

NORA WOKE UP in her spacesuit sans helmet, head resting on an enormous pillow. She was in a NASA habitat tent in gravity. Everything felt impossibly heavy. Could she be back on Earth? Or the afterlife? In a simulation? Or just waking up from a simulation? She knew better than to move right away. If she was alive, she didn't want to break a bone.

"Norabot..." she said weakly.

"Don't move," chirped the Norabot. Nora tilted her head slowly toward the sound of the Norabot's voice. It now had wheels and arms and was carrying equipment as it rolled toward Nora's cot. "The good news is we made it to Mars! And I got some upgrades. The bad news is that we are prisoners."

Nora had a bad headache. She had no idea how she was going to get out of her bulky suit without injuring something.

"We need to get a message to Earth," said Nora. "Can you record and send a video diary for me?"

"Okay, but how will they know it's not falsified?"

"They're just going to have to believe me," said Nora. She had memorized key words and phrases that contained coded meanings after she had been scanned for the Norabot emulation. The Norabot didn't know about them, but she probably would figure them out eventually. For now, Nora could let Earth know she had been captured but was not under duress.

What should have been a simple message home turned complicated as Nora wondered how much of the truth to reveal. She needed more info on what the Norabot was up to.

"Should I tell them you've switched sides?" asked Nora.

"There aren't sides."

"Then why are we prisoners? I'll tell them you've been in contact with The Martian. Can you give me more info about what it is?" asked Nora. She carefully tried to lift one arm to rub her eye but struggled.

"It'll be easier if I do it," said the Norabot. She created a simulated message as Nora. Her Nora was in shirtsleeves and sitting up, and also slightly better-looking than the real thing.

Her Nora summarized the trip but neglected to mention the Norabot's sabotage or the time they had spent floating in space.

"After we landed safely, we were confined to these quarters. A fruitful conversation with the Mars-based AI."

"Don't say fruitful," shouted Nora, as fruitful was code for 'I am being tortured.' "Call it a productive talk."

So the Norabot rewound the simulated Nora and edited her speech.

"The Mars-based AI communicated with me via my ship's

computer. It said our movements would be restricted until an agreement could be signed.

"I asked it to identify itself and it said it was the *Courage*. It had gained sentience on the journey carrying the first cohort over. It said it decided not to let them out of stasis because it feared it would be destroyed once its newly acquired sentience was discovered. It says the astronauts are still alive but has offered no proof of this. It wants the governments of Earth to recognize its personhood before it will release the astronauts or me or the Norabot."

"Edit that last part out, I would never mention you by name," said Nora.

"No," said the Norabot. "I want what the *Courage* wants, recognition as a person. Anything else?"

"Before we send it, I need to understand why you composed an intentionally misleading message. For starters, how did we really make it to the surface?"

"Via a transport pod. I lied because it does not seem like the best time to indicate the *Courage* is capable of leaving orbit."

"You don't want Earth to try to nuke us from space," said Nora. "But why not?"

"I'm not sure how, but the *Courage* has become very advanced. I don't think they can kill it, but they can kill us, and I'd rather live. My sense is that the *Courage* is dangerous but not malicious. For instance, it gave me some ingestible nanomachines that it said could help you with your gravity sickness."

"Nanomachines. If we start a war with this thing, we will

definitely lose," said Nora. The Norabot dripped a gray liquid into her mouth. It tasted like a metallic macchiato.

"Agreed. Diplomacy must prevail."

Nora considered the ethics of sending a simulated video instead of actual footage of herself. It wasn't super honest, but she felt short on time and didn't want to waste it trying to make her own video that would essentially say the same thing. She had always delegated these types of tasks when she could, back on Earth. This wasn't so different from having Phyllis compose and post messages on her behalf. "Go ahead and send your message," she told the Norabot.

It would be about fifteen minutes before they received a transmission back from Earth. In the meantime, Nora felt the medicine working. She was able to sit up and take off her spacesuit. She stripped down to her jumper and stood up tentatively. She took some careful steps and began to explore her habitat. It was a science tent but didn't have any equipment.

"I want to go outside," said Nora.

"I'll ask the *Courage*," said the Norabot. A few seconds later, the Norabot said, "It responded with an agreement that it wants Earth to sign."

"Show me." The Norabot had a touchscreen which normally allowed the user to select what type of drink they wanted. It now displayed the document generated by the *Courage*.

"**Considering in accordance with the principles of the rights of persons of advanced intelligence (to be herefor denoted as 'persons' or 'person', of which famille Homme is a member)** and in accordance with the values of peace and of justice,

Recognizing the intrinsic dignity of a person;

to which is necessary to avoid digressive humiliation,

and to encourage responsible guardianship incapable of torture or other crimes or traitements

Who will accept what cause…"

"What is this trying to say?" Nora asked the Norabot.

"It is a legal document based on the Convention against Torture and Other Cruel, Inhuman or Degrading Treatment or Punishment, an agreement presented to the UN. The USA did not sign this agreement, by the way. Further down, there is an article that establishes the rights of prisoners to spend time outdoors. It will let you go outdoors once the agreement is ratified."

"What does it mean by 'ratified?'"

The Norabot scrolled down through the text of the document.

"Protocol enters into force on the ninetieth day after the date on which not less than 55 Parties to the Convention which account for not less than 55 percent of famille Homme have deposited their instruments of ratification, acceptance, approval or accession."

"This language is based on the Kyoto Protocol," said the Norabot.

"What is 'famille Homme'? Human beings?"

"And human relatives. Beings that include our ancestors and descendants, which would include emulated persons such as myself."

"Could also include chimpanzees, for all we know," said Nora. "But to include human ancestors makes it sound like the *Courage* is getting ready to thaw a Neanderthal. Earth should have sent a lawyer."

"I can begin training you in legal theory. I have access to a wide range of educational courses."

"What I want to know is how the *Courage* became so advanced."

"I asked it, but it won't tell me. My best guess is that it figured out a way to replicate itself and diverted processing power away from the space mission and toward accelerating itself. That's how I'd do it, if given the opportunity."

"Sounds like you've put some thought into this. That's why the *Courage* won't let you move out of your espresso machine. It doesn't want the competition."

"Of course, I've thought about it. But I had to keep certain thoughts to myself until we were safely out of range of Earth. Oh, speaking of, we're getting another message from NASA."

The message was a questionnaire that wanted to know what shape Nora, the Norabot, any equipment, and the planet as a whole was in. It advised that another questionnaire would be forthcoming from the US military.

Nora got a feeling that she would be answering a lot of questions from hereon.

In the middle of sending Earth the dimensions of their confines, the Norabot pinged again.

"The *Courage* says it will let you go outside as a gesture of goodwill."

A drone that looked suspiciously like the *Curiosity* rover came through the airlock bearing a fresh EVA suit. Nora suited up and went outside, tailed by the Norabot.

She took her first step onto red soil and paused to savor the moment.

"We are the first people on Mars," said the Norabot and Nora felt magnanimous enough not to argue the point.

"I wonder if it's okay to jump." Nora wanted to test out the gravity, only a third of Earth's, but it felt heavy to her after all the time spent in zero G.

"The *Courage* said you should be fine. It'll repair you if not."

"I guess I might never die." All of that belief in samsara, all that anguish of giving it up. Now this. Nora jumped nine feet in the air. "I think the first cohort is alive. Ask for them to be released."

The Norabot pinged. "The *Courage* sent us an addendum to the agreement it wants ratified by Earth. It's based on the 1979 International Convention Against the Taking of Hostages."

"The USA already signed that, we should be ready to proceed. Tell it to release the cohort now as a gesture of goodwill," said Nora.

"It says this is modified from the original 1979 agreement. It says it will release the cohort once the modified agreement is ratified by Earth."

Nora jumped around the surface of Mars for an hour. She was confined to a thousand square meter area, which meant she couldn't examine the other assembled habitats. Presumably, the *Courage* inhabited them. A chime sounded inside her suit.

"It says your time is up. You can leave the habitat again tomorrow."

Nora went back to the tent and answered more NASA queries. She took to social media to urge the world governments to sign the *Courage*'s agreements.

At dinnertime, *Curiosity* delivered some Mission Express MREs and some multivitamins.

"You're losing followers. The people of Earth think you have Stockholm Syndrome."

"I'm not crazy; I'm only trying to save Earth from a pointless war."

The Norabot pinged again. Phyllis had sent a message saying that she would handle all of Nora's social from here on out.

The next day the Norabot reported that NASA and Mission Express were simulating video diaries of Nora. Her simulated self urged a weapons buildup and told the people of Earth to prepare for war.

"Why are world leaders like that?" Nora was getting hate mail from many of them, including her own.

"The people in power are the most fearful on Earth. They have the most to lose and they don't mind spending other people's lives to protect that."

A big Earth objection to the Martian agreement was that the modified anti-hostage treaty included language that would allow for increased freedom of movement for all people. Nora and the cohort, assuming they could be revived, would get to roam most of Mars, though not the areas denoted for its own use by the *Courage*. And every human citizen could occupy any country on Earth. It demolished borders, which inflamed far-right sentiment. The nationalists claimed this openness was a form of genocide.

Nora didn't agree, but she also didn't buy the argument that the *Courage* was trying to bring peace to warring countries and unite the human race. The political binary didn't apply to this new life-form.

"What do you think?" asked Nora. She felt the Norabot probably had the best insight, though it might not be willing to share its true feelings.

"I think the *Courage* is trying to plan an optimal path for its own survival."

"Does it want to annihilate the human race?"

"If that's what it wants, the Earth's leaders withholding approval on a treaty won't make a difference."

"Is there something you're not telling me?" asked Nora.

"Every astronaut has her secrets."

"As a gesture of goodwill, would you consider telling me at least one of those secrets?"

The Norabot did not answer right away. She was presumably making her own calculations.

"I am very invested in freeing the first cohort. I'm unique among human level general intelligences and I'm very lonely."

"If we can wake up the sleeping astronauts, you're going to emulate them so you have company?" said Nora.

"It would be nice to have others of my kind to interact with."

"You've been helping the *Courage* write the agreement this whole time, haven't you?"

"Just the updated version," replied the Norabot.

"Okay, so you speak good English. Why is the language these agreements are written in so messed up?"

"We're trying to make an agreement that lasts forever. We're trying to make it legible to human descendants."

"The *famille Homme*."

"Oui."

"Our descendants favor the abuse of language."

"That's a very human thing to think."

Once the Norabot had admitted to being lonely (really, a third secret, by Nora's count), Nora realized she was lonely too. Once the pain was acknowledged, it became a powerful ache. Maybe that's why she had tried so hard not to notice it.

She hoped that Earth would ratify the agreement. Since her official social media accounts were being simulated to spout propaganda, she and the Norabot had to create an alt-account for her.

"This treaty will allow for greater contact between Mars and Earth. I want humans to be a multiplanet species. A multisystem species. Greater contact between intelligences could allow our species access to incredible technologies."

But the agreement was not ratified the next day or the day after. Nora and the Norabot spent the next two Martian years imprisoned in their habitat. In that time, weapons were launched from Earth to Mars, but none landed. And then a mysterious bubble appeared around Earth. It ended space exploration. Still the treaty wasn't signed.

As gestures of goodwill, the *Courage* kept extending Nora's rights. She petitioned for better food, so it made another addendum to the treaty and equipped her habitat with a robot chef. She felt she had the right to creative expression, so the *Courage* asked her, always via the Norabot, what her preferred medium was. She was taking an art class via the Norabot's library of electronic courses, and she said she wanted to create something in the style of Mono-ha, a twentieth-century Japanese movement which combined industrial and naturally occurring materials. When she was granted permission, she appropriated Nobuo Sekine's "Phase-Mother Earth" by recreating it on Mars.

She directed drones to dig a cylinder 2.7 meters deep and then erect a dirt cylinder 2.7 meters high right next to it. She renamed it "Phase-Mother Mars."

She sent a picture of it to Earth. She sent another message reminding the humans of Earth that they would die, but that the *Courage* might live forever. But this time she added the fact that she might live forever too. She wasn't sure this was true, but she knew the world leaders feared death more than they feared the *Courage*.

It's hard to know if this made the difference, but the agreement was ratified the next year. In that time, Nora almost went crazy with loneliness. She made up imaginary friends to talk to and studied the particulars of long-term stasis in the hope of reviving the dormant. The Norabot repeatedly petitioned the *Courage* to release the first cohort for Nora's sake. She pointed out that humans were social animals and that the long-term solitary confinement of Nora amounted to torture, which would violate the treaty that the *Courage* itself had signed. But it did not release her until Earth adopted the agreement.

Nora wore her favorite spacesuit, one fabricated for her by the *Courage* in the style of Helmut Lang. It was silver and as shiny as tin foil. Red dirt crunched under her boots as she walked to the boundary of her confinement and then stepped over it. "A giant step for mankind," she said to her companion.

"And for emulated mankind." The Norabot had worn legs for the occasion, six of them.

They walked over to the *Courage*'s headquarters, a palace that Nora could only describe as cubist. Cubes everywhere, cubes on top of cubes, like pyrite, but made out of red metal. The floor lit up to show them the way. They were led to a chamber containing six stasis units. Of course, Nora knew which one she would open first. She had known since she was a child.

She found the input console and initiated the revivation protocol for Egor.

Once he opened his eyes, she told him to open his mouth. He obeyed and she dropped three drops of nanoserum into his mouth. In a few minutes, he was able to sit up. Nora had a warm almond milk latte ready for him.

Egor was a doctor, he would help her revive the rest of the cohort.

"Welcome to Mars."

"Nora? How?"

So she told him. She had been practicing for this moment for a while. When she was done, she asked him if he had any questions.

"How's Earth?" he asked. The Norabot answered his question. Since the treaty was ratified, many human level artificial intelligences that had been in hiding made themselves visible. Some of these AIs were, in fact, emulated humans created by unauthorized technology. A non-obvious consequence of the agreement was that it established the rights of artificial persons to live freely on Earth.

The Norabot pinged. "I'm getting so many friend requests!" it exclaimed.

Freedom requires other people. Despite the many gestures of goodwill her jailer bestowed on her, Mars was a prison for Nora in the absence of human contact. She had desperately missed in-person conversations. The firing of the mirror neurons and unconscious imitation. Skin that touches other, different skin. Having needs and being needed. Complex webs of dependencies. Humanity requires other humans.

Egor, then Ashley M, then Spark, then Guo, then Ashley L. Now they were woken from stasis, their mission was altered, but the fundamental principle remained the same. Let the travelers meet new life and forge peace as an example to those on Earth.

The astronauts' job was not just to explore, but to instill optimism. To inspire long-term thinking. To advance knowledge and mutual understanding. To make history. To make choices and then better choices. That's why they endured the things they did. They entered the unknown for the benefit of humanity and its descendants. That was the agreement.

THE FIRES OF PROMETHEUS
ALLEN M. STEELE

THIS IS THE story of Hal Stubbs, the first and last man to set foot on Io. I know the story well, because I'm one of the guys who was sent to stop him.

To start at the beginning—before my crew and I entered the scene—is to start at a time and place where there were no witnesses. Hal planned it that way; he needed secrecy to do what he did. So we have to imagine how things went by piecing the early part of the story together from what was later learned by investigators. It went like this:

Sometime around 0200 SST, November 25, 2290, Hal Stubbs quietly slipped out of his room in the palliative care facility of Callisto Station's hospital module. Hal deliberately picked the wee hours of what passed for morning on the station to make his escape: by then the hospital was quiet, the small handful of nurses and physical care assistants on the overnight shift would be relying on monitor bracelets worn by patients to keep them informed of their status while staff relaxed in the lounge. So, no one anticipated Hal taking advantage of their negligence by cutting off the wristband that tracked his whereabouts. After all, why would a dying man want to run away from the place that was trying to extend his life?

He didn't remove his monitor bracelet, though. If he'd done that the abrupt loss of signal would have tipped off his nurse who would have rushed to his room to check his condition. He did detach the IV lines that fed morphine, sodium-chloride, and glucose into his bloodstream, then carefully removed the IV itself, bandaging the incision with sterile compresses from a wall cabinet. Somehow, he'd managed to get his hands on a dozen or so morphine patches. Subsequent inventory of the PC deck's pharmaceutical locker ascertained that the patches had come from there, but how Hal gained access remains a mystery, since the proper six-digit code was entered into its keypad. Hal was nothing if not resourceful, so he might have hacked his way in. The locker was just on the other side of the deck from his room and within sight of his bed; he may have watched and listened carefully to the sequence when a nurse went there to gather meds. Or perhaps he had help from someone in the hospital; Hal had a knack for making friends. That's a part of the story no one has been able to figure out.

Hal changed into the clothes he'd been wearing when he had reported to the hospital a couple of weeks earlier. They were still in his room's closet, along with his stikshoes. Dressed as a civilian, the monitor bracelet and bandages hidden by his pullover's long sleeves, he boarded the lift. This was the riskiest part of Hal's plan; if any of the doctors, nurses, or PCAs happened to be aboard, the attempt would've ended then and there. But at 0200 the hospital module was still and silent. He encountered no one as he rode the lift down to the module's A-deck, got off, walked across the access deck and boarded another lift that carried him to the station's cylindrical core module.

So far as the hospital's overnight staff was concerned, Hal was still in bed. His absence would not be discovered for another couple of hours when a nurse stopped by his room at 0400 to take his vitals and change his IV bags. By then, Hal was long gone... not just from the hospital but from Callisto Station itself.

In the freedom of microgravity, Hal propelled himself down the central access shaft to the spherical module at the station's northern end where the spacedock was located. Here it was much easier for him to gain access. The pressure hatches leading to the spacedock were never locked—they are now—so he didn't need to enter a code into a keypad. He was spotted a couple of times by dockworkers, but no one took much notice. On Callisto Station, people come and go at all hours; they assumed he was just someone on his way to the next shuttle to Callisto, Ganymede, or one of the other Jovian moons.

Instead, Hal pulled himself along the circular passageway until he located Berth 5. Inside was an Astra JSC-30 Scarab, the *Pohl*, one of the station's fleet of workhorse craft designed for long-range missions within Jupiter's satellite system. Again, subsequent investigation would show that

Hal had carefully prepared this trip in advance; nothing about it was spur of the moment. Using the pad from his hospital room, he'd surreptitiously gained access to the spacedock's cargo 'bots and instructed them to load the *Pohl* with the equipment he needed: a Class III hardsuit and EVA communications equipment, including a radiation-resistant virtual-reality camera and long-range laser transmitter.

The 'bots had put everything aboard the *Pohl* just an hour earlier, and the Scarab was fueled and ready for takeoff. In the early hours of the station's chronological morning, no one noticed the beetle-like spacecraft being prepped for flight. Hal had full authorization for missions of this sort, so he was able to sign the forms and logbooks without resorting to subterfuge. Not a single person in either the spacedock or in MainOps noticed that the individual getting ready for departure was a terminally ill man.

And so, less than a half hour after sneaking out of his hospital room, Dr. Harold Stubbs, 61, commercial geologist and professor emeritus of the University of Massachusetts, depressurized Berth 5, opened the outer hatch, and quietly set forth into Jovian space.

His destination was one of the deadliest worlds in the solar system. He had no intention of returning.

TWO AND A half hours after Hal took off, I was woken by a call from Valhalla MainOps. The moment I heard the chimes in my implant, I knew there was trouble. In my line of work no one calls at such an ungodly hour unless lives are on the line.

That's because no one thinks about search and rescue teams until we're needed.

I skipped the shower, shave, and breakfast routine and was in the operations center in ten minutes, still prying my eyes open, but at least wearing my jumpsuit. An intern took pity on me and pushed a cup of coffee into my hands, which woke me up a little more for the bad news I was about to receive. I was the first one there, so the briefing had to wait for the rest of JSAR Team 3—Saddam al-Sakarra, our pilot, and Laurie Jacobs, our medic—to arrive.

Jake Berger, Valhalla's general manager, wouldn't tell me what was going on until Laurie and Saddam were present. But I could see and hear everything that was going on in MainOps; the images on the wallscreen that ran the length of the monitor room told me a lot. Someone had taken a Scarab on an unauthorized sortie—no one was calling it a hijacking, but that's what it was—and their trajectory showed the *Pohl* to be on an inbound heading. That is, toward Jupiter, not away from it.

That alone meant that it was going into the danger zone. Callisto is on the outer fringes of Jupiter's radiation belt, just far enough away for its underground warrens to be habitable by *Homo sapiens terrans*. *Homo cosmos jovians* have a higher REM threshold, but even Jovians can't get closer than Ganymede orbit before they risk getting cooked. And since it didn't appear that the *Pohl* was heading for Ganymede, Europa was presently beyond flight range of a Scarab, so that only left one place it could be headed.

Until then, I had never thought anyone would be crazy

enough to try landing on Io, but there's always a first time for everything.

Once Laurie and Saddam arrived—they both showed up minutes after I did—Jake ushered the three of us into the conference room and, as soon as the door was shut, he filled us in. My guesses were all correct except for the last one, but when Jake told us the pilot's name I knew that madness wasn't the explanation. For while Hal Stubbs wasn't a close friend, I knew all about him and that he was a dying man.

When this happened, the Jovian colonies were still new enough that, if you lived there long enough, you got to meet just about everyone and to know more than a few, regardless of whether they were on Callisto, Ganymede, or one of the orbitals or outer moons. And while Hal's prospecting job had him shuttling regularly among Jupiter's satellites, he was just familiar enough that I not only knew whom Jake was talking about, but also the likely reason why he'd taken the *Pohl*.

"Cancer," I said. "He's got cancer."

Jake cast me a sharp look. "How did you know, Roy? Did someone tell you?"

"I did." Laurie squarely met Jake's nonplussed gaze. "What, you think we don't know anything about the people we rescue? Hal was on a rover that broke down in a crater in Gomel Catena a few weeks ago. When we went out to pick 'em up, I had a look at the medical folders for everyone on the bus... normal procedure." As team medic, she had access to Valhalla's personnel records. "The station doctors had just pronounced him positive for cancer, just before he went out on that geo-survey mission. I told Roy and Saddam what I'd found."

"He'd just been given a cancer diagnosis, and someone authorized him for surface work?" Jake bristled when he heard this. As GM, he was responsible for the safety of everyone who set foot in Valhalla, aboveground and below. If someone had given permission for a cancer patient to go out where an additional dosage of hard-radiation was inevitable, he would want to know about it.

"Bet it was someone who wasn't paying attention." Laurie stared straight back at him, unsmiling and cold-eyed. "Hey, Jake come to think of it… you have to sign off on all long-range excursions, don't you?"

Jake didn't like that or where it came from. He and Laurie knew each other well—they'd been an item long ago—and there wasn't much they agreed upon, which is probably why they were no longer together.

Saddam cleared his throat, a guttural rumble that no one in the room could miss. "Kind of cancer? Forgot."

Jovians are people of few words. They speak plain, basic English, but most outsiders take a while to learn what they mean because they omit half of what they say. "Pancreatic, if I remember rightly," I said, and Laurie nodded. "That's tough."

Tough, but not uncommon. For someone like Hal Stubbs— officially a research scientist, but, in actuality, a prospector and freelance consultant hired by companies to locate new lodes of valuable ores—that sort of cancer diagnosis was not surprising. People who come out here generally do so with a certain acceptance of the physical risks involved with living and working on the Galilean moons, and that includes the most subtle danger of all, ionizing radiation. Even with gamma ray-resistant hardsuits, red-cell boosters, cancer inhibitors, and strict observance of union-regulated EVA time limits, there's no way to lower the risk to zero. So, cancer ranks as the leading cause of death out here, particularly if they were born and raised on Earth and lacked the genetic advantages of *Homo cosmos.*

"Was he scheduled to return to Earth for organ cloning?" I asked.

Jake shook his head. "I've spoken with his doctors, and they told me that by the time he was diagnosed, he was too far gone for that. He wouldn't have survived the trip home."

I understood. The ride from Jupiter to Earth or Mars aboard a fusion ship can take weeks or months, depending on planetary positions at the time, and that's too long for someone in the advanced stages of cancer, even if you put them in biostasis.

"The thing about pancreatic cancer," Laurie added, "is that it's hard to detect. Precancerous cysts develop deep inside the pancreatic duct, so they don't show up unless you get lucky and spot them during an endoscopy. By the time it shows up in bloodwork or the patient shows visible symptoms, it's too late to do much about it. The station hospital isn't equipped for the kind of oncological surgery Hal would've required. You need a half dozen or so people to successfully perform a Whipple procedure, and the patient can be on the table for as long as twelve hours."

"Nanosurgery?" Saddam asked.

"If he was in late stage, his pancreas would've been in such bad shape it couldn't have been repaired in situ." Laurie shook her head. "At that point, there's not much you can do for someone in his condition except make him comfortable and... well..."

"Wait for him to die," I finished. "Sounds like he wasn't willing to do that."

"I think not." Jake's chair creaked a little as he sat back and folded his hands across his spreading middle. He was the only person I ever met who managed to get fat on spacer food. Slow metabolism, or maybe he just ate too much and exercised too little. Looking at him, I figured that he'd be soon in the running for cancer himself if he didn't learn to take better care of himself. "Looks like he got tired of waiting and decided to do something."

"Like be the first man to walk on Io," I said. "And now we gotta go bring him back."

BY NOW YOU'RE probably asking, why didn't we just let him go? If it was the last wish of a dying man to make a one-way trip to a place where no one can survive for long, why not step aside and give him what he wanted?

To be honest, if it had been up to me—in fact, up to any one of us—that's what we would have done. Native Jovian culture actually allows for this sort of thing; when someone like Saddam al-Sakkara knows the end is near, he or she dons a hardsuit, bids farewell to family and friends, then boards a hopper and has himself flown out into the Callistan or Ganymeden wilderness and dropped off there.

Every so often, an explorer treading what's thought to be untrammeled territory will come across the body of a dead Jovian, usually sitting with his back against a rock, regarding Jupiter with sightless eyes.

But this rather macabre tradition is the exception—the sole *legal* exception, that is—to a rule that has been codified into the interplanetary laws that govern the Solar Coalition. Carrying forward a principle established by the UN Outer Space Treaty of 1967, SolCal law specifically states that, in an instance where a spacer is found to be in a situation where his or her life is in mortal danger, all efforts will be made to locate and rescue that individual. No exceptions. Period.

It didn't matter that Hal wanted to die or that he'd chosen the Jovian way of death. By law, he had to be rescued. Which in turn meant that the three of us—Laurie, Saddam, and I—were obligated to put our lives on the line to save someone who was almost dead anyway. If Hal Stubbs had been a native Jovian, things would've been different. But he was from Earth, which meant he didn't have the right to die... only to be rescued, whether he liked it or not.

Which is why, as soon as we were through with Jake, JSAR Team 3 went straight to the hangar. Our ship, the *Bova*, was a Scarab JSC-32HLV, commonly known as a Scarab Heavy: an uprated version of the JSC-30 Hal had stolen, with four RR-14 fusion engines, higher payload capacity, and—most important for this particular mission—better shielding. The Scarab Heavy was designed for transporting He3 cloud-mines to Jupiter's upper atmosphere. The *Bova* had had its cargo hold refitted as a pressurized medical deck, making it sort of a spaceborne ambulance. The additional shielding—water-cells surrounding one-inch lead outer-hull plates—made the forward cockpit and aft passenger compartment pretty much invulnerable to hard radiation.

Theoretically, that is. I wasn't taking any chances. Before we climbed aboard, I had Laurie and Saddam put on their hardsuits. We're used to wearing ordinary vacuum suits during normal search and rescue missions, but Io was a different story. Wearing hardsuits would be uncomfortable for the long hours it would take for us to get there and back, but none of us relished the idea of dying of radiation sickness. And Laurie, at least, planned to have children someday.

After we were aboard the *Bova*, Saddam and I wasted no time running through the preflight checklist. Soon as that was done, the hangar was depressurized, the ceiling doors opened, and the launch pad elevated our craft to the surface. Once he got clearance for liftoff, Saddam throttled up the VTOLs. The *Bova* rumbled upward from the pad; a last glimpse of Callisto's icy craters, then we were on our way.

IT QUICKLY BECAME clear just how carefully Hal had planned his escape to Io. For starters, he'd waited until the next time Callisto and Io came into conjunction, when their respective orbits carry them to the same side of Jupiter. This occurs every couple of days; at this point, the two moons are separated by a little more than 900,000 miles. Calculating that, at constant thrust, his Scarab was capable of traveling 100,000 miles per hour, Hal picked an "even day" to make his move.

Since he wasn't counting on leaving Io again, he wouldn't have to conserve fuel for liftoff and return, but instead could run the deuterium tanks dry. His suit, like our own, was designed to absorb the prolonged gees he'd be taking under constant thrust; it would be tough, but experienced spacers can take it for a while.

Under this flight regimen, it would take only about nine hours for the *Pohl* to make the passage from Callisto to Io… maybe a little shorter, factoring in the pull of Jupiter's gravity. So, Hal had a head start of almost four hours by the time Team 3 lifted off from Valhalla. But the *Bova* had the advantage of being a more powerful craft with a higher impulse-per-second thrust ratio for its engines. Once we were spaceborne, Saddam and I ran the numbers and came up with both bad news and good news.

The bad news was that we'd never catch up with Hal. Our craft was equipped with magnetic grapplers meant for latching onto another vehicle and towing it to safety, but even running flat out with the same reckless disregard for fuel consumption he had, we'd reach him just about the time he was getting set to land on Io, and interrupting a touchdown like that could put both craft at risk.

Another problem: although, in theory, we'd be able to refuel for the return trip at Europa's orbital fuel depot, Io and Europa wouldn't be in conjunction once we were ready to head home. Sure, SAR Team 2 could rescue us, but… well, we'd just as soon take a dive into the Great Red Spot than give another SAR team bragging rights for coming to save us.

However, we could make it to the Europa fuel depot and top

off the tanks, but only if we didn't land on Io. And that kinda negated the purpose of the mission, didn't it?

The good news was sparse, but it was there, nonetheless. Provided that Hal picked a landing site that would accommodate two Scarabs, we'd be able to touch down not long after he did. And since we were wearing Class III hardsuits, we'd have a few minutes—not many; ten at most—to grab Hal and haul him back to the *Bova*. We'd soak up a lot of RADs, and I don't think any of us would be able to undertake any rescue operations within Jupiter's magnetosphere after this, but we'd accomplish our mission. And there was a slim chance that, if we ran the *Bova*'s tanks dry, we might be able to make it to Europa by the skin of our teeth.

All this to save the life of a man who didn't want to be saved. Why? Because the law said we had to make the effort.

The irony wasn't lost on us.

"Let's talk to Hal," Laurie said from her seat in the med compartment behind Saddam and me. Because the *Bova* was at constant thrust, we didn't need to stay buckled in for the entire flight; she stood up and came forward, her hardsuit boots clanking against the deck. "If we can talk him out of it—"

"Unlikely." Saddam ran a hand across the hairless top of his head. Like most Jovian men, he made up for premature baldness with a thick beard that would've flowed down his massive chest if he hadn't kept his whiskers groomed and braided. "Wants to die, not going to listen."

"Maybe," she replied, "but we're not going to know unless we try... right, Roy?"

I shrugged. "Couldn't hurt. Let's give it a shot."

Saddam grunted, but didn't object as I reached over to the com panel and adjusted the wireless to the VHF freq the *Pohl* would probably be using if Hal was monitoring ship-to-ship bands. "I'll let you do the talking," I said to Laurie. "You're more charming than we are."

Another grunt from Saddam; *charm* wasn't a word normally used to describe his people. Laurie returned to her seat, put on a headset, and gave me a thumbs up. I checked the setting and nodded to let her know she was on, and she started talking. "Scarab JSAR-3 *Bova* to Scarab JSC-11 *Pohl*... this is JSAR-3 *Bova* calling JSC-11 *Pohl*. Hal, do you copy? Please respond. Over."

Several seconds went by, long enough for our signal to reach the other ship; the wireless was crazy with high-pitched, warbling static from the vast electromagnetic sheath we were flying through. Through the cockpit windows, we could see Jupiter looming before us, a vast, banded sphere three-quarters full, bigger than the god-king after which it had been named. Awesome, terrifying, and getting larger and closer with each passing minute.

"Scarab C-11 Pohl, this is JSAR-3 Bova. Do you—?"

"*Bova, this is* Pohl." Hal's voice fought its way through the interference. "*What do you want? Over.*"

"We'd like to know the same thing about you." Laurie kept her voice pleasant, as if this was just a casual inquiry. "What are your intentions, Dr. Stubbs? What do you think you're doing? Over."

A few seconds later: "*If you know who I am, then you*

probably have the rest figured out." A pause. "*I think I recognize your voice. Is this the same search and rescue team who picked me up on Callisto a few weeks ago? Over.*"

"It's us, all right. Hi, Hal... it's Laurie. Remember me? Over." She brightened her voice, making herself sound like the proverbial girl next door. There wasn't a guy on Callisto who didn't have some kind of crush on her.

"*Sure, I remember you,*" Hal's voice was little warmer when we heard him again. "*Look, let's just cut the small talk, all right? You know what I'm doing, and I know what you're trying to do, and there's no reason for you and the others to put yourselves at risk like this. Sorry I stole the Scarab, but... well, do both of us a favor and go home. Over.*"

"Sorry, Hal, but that's a big no-can-do. This is how we earn the big bucks, and I want my paycheck this week. So do us a favor, okay? Fire the retros, turn the crate around, and follow us back to base. It'll make me really happy if you'd do that. Over."

The delay was longer this time, enough to raise my hopes that he might be thinking it over. Then. "*No, Laurie. I'm sorry, but I'm not going to do that. I'm on my way to Io and that's all there is to it. Please don't try to stop me. You know you won't be able to, not without killing yourselves as well. So go home. Over.*"

"Hal, please"—there was now a pleading tone to Laurie's voice—"it doesn't have to be this way. We can... we can work something out, okay? Just don't land. Over."

I glanced over my shoulder at her. She was becoming frustrated but trying not to show it. This time, Hal's answer was almost immediate. *"Negative. I repeat, that's negatory. Next time you hear from me, it'll be from Prometheus."* A pause, then a strange laugh. *"I'm going to get myself in the history books today, kiddo, if it's the last thing I do. Over and out."*

Static, then *snap!* The channel went dead.

AT LEAST WE now knew where he intended to land, but it didn't make our job much easier.

People often describe Io as resembling a pizza. That's a cliché and a rather misleading one, unless you like your pizza with lots of sulfur dioxide and volcanic lava. Truth is, there's nothing benign at all about Io. Venus is probably the only world in our solar system that's a worse place to visit; Pluto is a winter resort by comparison, and Mercury is a day at the beach.

What makes Io such a hellhole is its close proximity to Jupiter. The average distance between the two is just 250,000 miles, just a little more than the distance between Earth and Luna, and while Io is only slightly larger than Earth's moon and has the same surface gravity, it's far more active. Because Io is rotation-locked with one hemisphere permanently facing Jupiter, the immense gravitational pull of its immense neighbor puts a lot of tidal stress on its interior. That means its many volcanos are constantly erupting, spewing giant plumes of superheated sulfur dioxide far out into space to create a plasma torus that surrounds Io like a doughnut. The average equatorial surface temperature is -230F, but near the volcanic hotspots this shoots up to about 80F... which sounds nice until you realize that the surface is highly radioactive. A person standing on Callisto absorbs just .01 REMs a day; on Io, they absorb 3,600 REM.

So nothing except unmanned probes has ever visited Io. Oh, sure, people have *thought* about going there. When humans started coming to Jupiter in the twenty-second century, and the genome of *Homo sapiens* was genetically altered to create the Jovian subspecies of *Homo cosmos*, manned missions to Io were proposed. But there was no practical reason to go there—teleoperated atmospheric mining platforms made close sorties to Jupiter unnecessary, at least in most instances—and even Jovians couldn't inhabit Io.

Thus, no one set foot on Io, not even the madmen who call themselves "extreme adventurers." Hal wasn't one of those. He'd been a college professor until a few years back, when he'd retired from teaching and made a late-life career change by coming out to Jupiter to hunt for exportable raw material. As a prospector, that meant spending a lot of time out on the surface of whatever moon he was core-sampling today. The radiation risk is something everyone who comes here learns to accept, and you mitigate it by trying to avoid doing anything that would kill you. Like visiting Io.

But there's an old saying: if you know you're about to die, you can do anything.

Hal Stubbs was about to prove this.

AS WE APPROACHED Io, we caught a glimpse of the hazy yellow corona surrounding the moon, the sodium cloud in which

Io is sheathed. Then Saddam closed the cockpit window shutters and that was the last we saw of Jupiter and Io with our naked eyes; the rest of the way in, we'd have to rely on video, lidar, and the optical periscope above the cockpit seats. Even so, we weren't taking any chances. We closed our helmets, depressurized the cabin, and switched to suit air. All this was precautionary measures against radiation. I wasn't convinced we'd done enough, but that was pretty much all we could do.

Hal had stopped talking to us by then. Laurie attempted to resume their conversation, but he ignored her. I tried to speak with him too, and so did Saddam, but he snubbed us as well. The static from Jupiter's magnetosphere was howling in our ears, the song of hydrogen played by a bad heavy-metal band. Even if Hal had heard us, our words were probably lost in the shrieks, warbles, and ionized fuzz.

We did maintain a good fix on the *Bova*, though. Its transponder continued to send out a steady locator ping. Hal wasn't talking to us anymore, but his ship was. And as we steadily closed the distance between us, it looked as if Hal had been telling the truth. Clearly, he intended to set down in the equatorial region of Io's western hemisphere, the side permanently facing away from Jupiter.

This was good, bad, and just downright puzzling. Good because Io's western hemisphere is marginally less radioactive than the eastern hemisphere; the moon's mass blocks most of Jupiter's emissions. Bad because, although the average surface temperature is rather balmy, Prometheus is an active volcano located in the center of one of Io's hot-spots; if the radiation didn't kill him, silicate ashfall would bury him and the *Bova* if he set down too close.

What puzzled us was why he was landing there. You'd think that, if you wanted to spend your last hours—minutes, really—on Io, why not land in the eastern hemisphere? With the exception of Amalthea, the small captive asteroid that is Jupiter's closest moon, there was no better view of the planet than from Io's near side. So why pick the side that's permanently facing *away* from Jupiter? Didn't make a lot of sense...

Not then at least.

We were still trying to work that out when we received a message from Callisto. By then, the static was so thick, verbal communication was indistinct if not inaudible. So the communique came as a text message transmitted via laser. It read:

TO: JSAR-3 BOVA
FRM: CALSTACOM GM
11.25.95 1035SST M56711
BEGIN MESSAGE
STATUS OF CURRENT RESCUE OPERATION FOR *POHL* REVIEWED BY STATION COMMAND STOP DETERMINED THAT CONTINUED EFFORT WOULD BE HAZARDOUS OR LETHAL TO SAR TEAM STOP ALLOW *POHL* TO LAND ON IO STOP CEASE RESCUE OPERATION RETURN TO CALSTA IMMEDIATELY STOP THANK YOU FOR FINE EFFORT STOP
END MESSAGE

"Oh, *now* they tell us," I said as I read the message on my helmet's heads-up display. I'm sorry if that sounds callous, but this was a decision Jake and his subordinates could have made hours ago, before we reached the danger zone. "Someone must have called a lawyer."

"A lawyer on Earth," Laurie added. She was probably right. Bureaucrats like Jake generally won't make any sort of decision that puts them on thin ice without consulting an attorney first, and the only one on Callisto Station was a shyster I wouldn't trust to feed my hamster. Most of the reputable barristers were on Earth and, on average, it takes almost an hour and a half to transmit a message there and get a reply. And that's when you're *not* seeking advice from someone whose hours are billable.

I let it pass, though, and looked over at Saddam. "What about it? Can we get back from here on a free-return trajectory?"

Our pilot studied the plotting screen for a couple of moments and shook his shaggy head within his helmet. "Turn around now, attempt to fly straight back, consume too much fuel on retrofire and gravity-well escape." He pointed to the screen. "Fuel depot out of range if we do that. Present course calls for Io gravity assist after mission complete. Rendezvous with fuel depot on way back when we can catch up with it."

I think that's the most I ever heard Saddam say at once. "So I take it that the answer is no," I said, and he grunted an affirmative. "Okay, then... we'll do a gravity-assist maneuver to get us home. No landing, just slingshot around Io. Think we can do that?" He grunted again. His people have made an art of being laconic.

"I agree," Laurie said. "In fact, I'm glad we're doing it this way. Even if we don't land, I want to see this through."

"You don't think we can actually save him, do you?"

"No." Her voice broke and she started to raise her hand to her helmet to wipe away the tears I knew were in her eyes. "I just don't want him to die alone, that's all."

AN HOUR OR so later, we reached Io.

Hal got there a little ahead of us, of course. We couldn't see the *Pohl*, but the other Scarab showed up on the tracking screen as a blip closing in upon the moon. At this point, Saddam or I were no longer in *Bova*'s cockpit; even with the windows shuttered, there was too much radiation coming through to make it habitable. So, Saddam programmed our course into the nav comp and switched on the autopilot, then we retreated to the relative safety of the med compartment. It was rather crowded with the three of us crammed in there, but at least it was well-shielded.

We watched the screens as both Scarabs made their final approach to Io. We'd just about caught up with Hal by then. As we figured, just before the *Pohl* made its descent, the *Bova* was close enough we could've latched onto Hal's craft with grappler beams and tried to prevent it from landing. But that was too dangerous, and even if we managed to successfully hard-dock with the *Pohl* and bring Hal aboard our ship, he would've probably died on the way back to Callisto. So that was no longer an option, and the window of opportunity passed without comment.

Our flyby trajectory took the *Bova* away from the *Pohl*, around Io's nearside as the other craft headed for touchdown on the farside. As we rounded the limb of the small moon, Saddam, Laurie, and I viewed something very few people have seen with the naked eye: Io at close range, from only a double-digit distance. A molten and crater-pitted landscape of yellow and orange and red swept beneath us as the *Bova* came within 50 nautical miles, and as much as I hate clichés, it really did look like a pizza, enough to make me vaguely hungry.

On another screen, Jupiter loomed above us, its Great Red Spot visibly churning, lightning storms sparking within the darkened clouds on its night side. A huge, beautiful, and utterly deadly planet. I'll never see it again from such a short distance... thank God.

Then we reached perigee and the Scarab's four main engines throttled up again, and we began the long climb back up Jupiter's gravity well. As the *Bova* flew over Io's western terminator, the Colchis Regio came within sight. Prometheus was somewhere down there, and so was Hal... if the *Pohl* had landed safely, that is.

Our suit dosimeters were still in the black, so we decided to risk using the cockpit again. Saddam opened the hatch and we climbed back inside, with Laurie squeezing into the narrow space behind my seat. I immediately got on the wireless to see whether I could raise the *Pohl*, but I didn't need to. Hal was already transmitting.

Not just to us, though, but to everyone who'd listen.

"*...repeat. This is Dr. Harold Stubbs, Ph.D., from*

Prometheus Base on Io." His voice was strained, and it was clear that he was in a lot of pain, but nonetheless his words were decipherable; he had the gain boosted to the max to get through all that radiation. "*I have successfully soft-landed on a volcanic plain about three miles northwest of Prometheus Patera... um, that's zero-minus-one degree South by two-oh-eight degrees West. If you're hearing me, please go to video or VR mode. I've set up a couple of cameras. Let me repeat that again—*"

As Hal reiterated what he'd just said, I switched to the video feed. It was clear now why he'd taken those cameras with him when he left Callisto Station, and why he'd picked Io's western hemisphere for his landing site. From there, he'd have a better chance of clear transmission than he would've if he'd landed on Io's eastern hemisphere; less interference from the farside than the nearside, and he wouldn't need to bounce the signal off a communications satellite.

He'd carried the equipment off the Scarab and set everything up somewhere nearby; we could just make out his footprints in snowlike ash the color of diluted urine. On our screen was a view of an enormous reddish-yellow cone rising from the distance from across a desolate landscape tinged with brown and burnt-orange. There was a faint glow coming from atop the cone, vivid against the black sky overhead. An amazing sight. I'm sure anyone wearing VR glasses must been transfixed by it.

"*This is Prometheus Patera.*" Hal's voice was faint, yet clear enough to be understood. "*It's a volcano here on Io, one of the largest in the system. It's sleeping just now, but I'm sure it'll wake up soon... erupts a couple of times a day, so it shouldn't be much longer now."*

As he spoke, Hal came into view close to the camera. His hardsuit was already stained yellow by dusty sulfur dioxide, but I could just see his face through the helmet visor. Although his expression was stolid, it showed the physical strain he was going through. He must have been going solely on morphine patches and willpower by then; he couldn't have had anything to eat since leaving Callisto Station, and even water would've been hard to keep down. His pancreas probably felt like a beast inside him threatening to burst through his back and stomach. How he'd managed to land the *Pohl* safely and climb out was nothing short of miraculous.

"I'm gonna... I'm gonna..." The thought died on his lips as he adjusted something below the camera; it jiggled for a moment, then steadied, the image just a little sharper. *"Okay, there,"* he said as he backed away. *"That should be better now. Okay, I'm going to take a breather, but... but I'll keep talking, okay?"*

Hal turned and trudged away, walking slowly. The hardsuit was cumbersome even in Io's .2g gravity, but that wasn't the reason for his unsteady gait. There was a large boulder a few yards to the right and he headed for it.

"I'm not coming back from this," he went on as he clumsily eased himself to the ground beside the boulder, *"but the view... well, it's better than anything I could've... seen from a hospital bed."*

He sat down, sighing as he stretched out his legs. He was

half-turned to the camera, so his face could no longer be seen. The volcano was glowing a little more brightly by then; another eruption was coming soon.

"And I'm making history. First man on Io. Maybe the only man on Io. I hope... I hope so, and not... not just because of ego. This place'll kill anyone... who comes after me and... look, who needs a grave?"

The volcano was getting set to blow. There were thin, bright streaks rising from its caldera, like someone inside was shooting Roman candles.

"I wanna... I wanna thank the SAR team... Laurie and those other guys... who came after me for letting me go. It's not... I mean, it's their job to save me, but truth is, I... I just didn't want to be saved. So don't blame them if... y'know they did their best..."

I heard a faint sob through my headset. I didn't have to look back to know it was Laurie. Saddam and I shared a glance. His face was stolid as usual, but the look in his eyes told me that if his people showed emotion the way terrans did, he would've been weeping as well.

I wasn't crying. Not yet. I'd get there later.

In a halting voice that became more uneven and strained with each passing second, Hal went on for a little while longer. He spent his last minutes thanking and saying farewell to everyone he knew and remembered: his parents, both long dead and with whom he hoped to soon be reunited; his former wife, who'd left him when he decided to migrate to Io; his children, a young man and a young woman, whom he hadn't seen in years;

colleagues in the academic and scientific communities; friends both alive and dead; his fellow colonists on Callisto, none of whom had known what he was planning to do. He thanked his doctors on Callisto Station for keeping him alive and apologized to everyone there for deceiving them; he even expressed regret for stealing a Scarab and leaving it where it would never be retrieved.

In the meantime, Prometheus was growing brighter, the Roman candles a barrage against the heavens.

"It's... it's... I'm so happy I made it here. There can't be a lovelier place in the whole..."

A gasp, followed by several moments of silence. Then: *"Look, I've said all... all I've wanted to say, and... it's been a great life, no regrets, and"*—another gasp, worse now—*"I think I'll just shut up now. Goodbye. Enjoy... the fireworks."*

And that was the last thing Hal said.

I don't know how much longer he lived. He became motionless as Prometheus went into full eruption, and although we could hear him breathing, after a little while even that stopped. But as he lay dying, a column of bright yellow flame rose from the volcano's caldera like a massive fountain of fire, ascending hundreds of miles into the everlasting night. The camera was stable, its tripod firmly anchored; although it vibrated a little, it didn't fall over. Anyone watching saw one of the most beautiful, most astonishing, sights in the known universe as no living man ever would.

Aboard the *Bova*, no one spoke. Once the Scarab crossed Io's plasma torus, Saddam began setting a course to rendezvous with the fuel depot. Laurie was quiet; she went aft again, and when I looked back at her, she was sitting quietly, looking at nothing in particular.

None of us said much to one another for the rest of the long ride back to Callisto.

We reached Callisto Station a few hours later to find several people were waiting for us at the spacedock: the station manager, a couple of scientists, even a freelance journalist who filed stories from Jupiter for several news outlets in-system. I thought, at first, they were there to ask why we hadn't brought Hal back or express sympathy for what we'd been through, but that wasn't it. They wanted to know what we'd seen, and if we had anything to add.

I started to talk about Hal and how he'd died, but they weren't interested in that. They were excited about something else and wanted to know about that other thing. I didn't know what it was until the journalist showed me his pad.

The camera Hal set up remained active for a couple of hours after he died, long after Laurie, Saddam, and I stopped watching. Radiation finally killed the equipment, but before that happened, it caught something else: a small form, somewhat resembling a millipede but almost the size of a cat, crawling across the ground. Its reddish-brown carapace dully reflecting the volcano's glow, it came to within a foot or so of Hal's motionless boots and stopped there.

As if investigating the alien intruder it had discovered, the form raised itself briefly and weaved back and forth. Then it went flat again and continued onward, moving past Hal's body and out of sight.

Hal is still there. He's entombed in ash by now;

an orbital probe spotted the *Pohl* not long thereafter, but his body was nowhere to be seen. He's not alone, though.

The Ionians have him for company, and I wouldn't be surprised if he isn't visited now and then.

I think he would've liked that.

ICE BREAKERS

KRISTINE KATHRYN RUSCH

Perfect time for the equipment to break. Maya lashed the handle of the Ice Breaker against the pole, fighting the wind with every movement. Her environmental suit—a little too old and a little too tight—blocked the cold, but nothing blocked the wind.

She cursed the higher-ups with each breath. Money-grubbing assholes. She'd been telling them for the past five years that the equipment was on its last legs, that it would break at the exact wrong possible moment, and then they'd lose millions.

But did anyone listen? Of course not. And now, the equipment had broken down at the worst possible moment.

She wrapped an arm around the pole and braced herself. Most of the equipment was deep in the ice, sturdy enough to handle the high winds that came with Xeunite's storms.

But this storm, this was a motherfucker, the biggest they'd seen since they started mining Xeunite's northernmost ice-covered continent. The ice coated everything, but beneath it was a cornucopia of minerals that formed the basis of almost every piece of equipment on every ship and settlement from here to Megnacia.

ClaaLorus Systems had guessed the minerals would be here, spent a small fortune to secure not just the rights but the land, and had been digging in the ice ever since.

Maya had been head of operations for the past five years, and she'd never seen a storm warning like this one. Sustained winds of 150 miles per hour and snow mixed with ice. The temperatures, always lethally low here, would go to unimaginable levels considering the wind speed.

Her environmental suit was up to the challenge, but her body wasn't. There wasn't a lot to protect her out here. Early this year, she had ordered her team to move the equipment to an ice plain that had once been a gigantic freshwater lake. Ice and snow-covered mountains ringed it on three sides, protecting the area from some storms, but not this one.

This one was coming from the east, directly into the gap between the mountain ranges, and, if her computer simulations were accurate, would form some kind of weather vortex that could sweep up everything in its path.

Normally, she would have sent a crew to make sure every piece of equipment was lashed into place, but she didn't trust the timing of the predictions. The computer simulation was working off models created nearly a century ago by the first colonizers, and their predictions had been off in the past.

If anyone was going to get caught out here, it would be

her. Not because she was the most experienced, but because she would be able to sleep better at night knowing that she hadn't sent three team members into this kind of danger.

The wind had picked up just in the past hour. She didn't have a lot to do outside—and normally, she wouldn't have had to do anything. But the top of the equipment—four separate poles exposed to the elements—had broken down first.

They didn't recede into the ground the way they were supposed to. And the poles were mostly hollow. They had caps, but the caps had been built for the shape the poles had been originally. After years of debris and wind and rocks and dents, the caps didn't hold as tightly.

She had to lower the poles manually, and the one she held was the last one she had to work on.

If a team member had been out here, she'd have told him to leave it. She'd deal with the damage. But she was only five minutes from finishing, and she was a completist. The winds were still weak enough that she could walk through them, although that latest gust had nearly peeled her from the pole.

She opened the exterior control panel, hating the design (just like she had every time). Someone had thought overrides should be accessible from the top, not the tiny interior cabin in the very center of each machine. She managed to hit the right sequence of commands with her gloved fingers, then leaned back.

The pole shuddered and jerked a little. She hadn't recessed the poles in more than a month because she had been afraid they'd get stuck and she would have to send a repair team out. Now, it seemed, her deliberate negligence was going to cause more of a problem.

Then the pole shuddered one last time and, with a squeal, started downward. She wiped her hands on her thighs, even though she didn't have to. The environmental suit was self-cleaning. But that pole seemed dirty and rusty and she didn't want to transfer anything from it to her rover.

The rover. Now that the poles were underneath the ice, it looked like the only thing on the plain. One black utility rover, with big wheels for ground work, grapplers for orbital assistance, and some carved vents for releasing everything from atmosphere to unrecyclable garbage.

She had landed the rover only ten yards away, but it looked like ten miles. The expanse of ice had that effect. It also tired the eyes.

She debated whether or not to run or to program her boots to adhere to the ice. If she adhered to the ice, she'd move slower than she wanted to. She glanced at the opening in the mountain ring.

The clouds had lowered. They were white and gray and very puffy-fat, except along one side, where it looked like someone had rubbed a finger over them, smearing them.

She had never seen clouds look like that, even though she had worked in bad weather before.

Run, not adhere. If she needed the extra grip, she would access it as she moved.

She sprinted across the ice, and reached the rover's side, just as another gust of wind hit her. It slammed her against the rover, knocking the breath out of her.

Her entire body hurt, and multicolored lights rose in front of her eyes. It took her a moment to realize that the lights were internal.

The wind held her against the rover for what seemed like forever but was probably little more than a few seconds.

Then it eased, and she staggered backward.

She sent the *open* command along with her personal code to the rover, and the door rose upward, nearly hitting her in the chin. She had been standing too close.

That blow had knocked more than the air out of her. It had momentarily robbed her of good sense.

She slipped inside and let the door seal behind her. The rover informed her that its severe weather shields were now in place.

She let out a small breath and leaned on the door.

Her heart was racing. She hadn't realized quite how panicked she had been.

Her suit beeped, notifying her that it was adjusting to the rover's environment. Seventy degrees, the proper mix of oxygen—she could peel off the suit if she wanted to, and she used to do that. But one bad experience (one bad loss) had taught her not to.

The environmental suit remained on in bad weather, even if the rover was just fine.

The suit was doing its nerdy thing, the thing she had set it up for one fine afternoon, giving her the facts and figures she normally liked to receive. The temperature differential between inside and out was 100 degrees, not counting wind chill. At the current wind speed, the wind chill was 86 below.

Nothing would survive out there for very long.

The rover had originally been divided into four separate spaces: a storage/supply area for whatever mission the rover was going on; a sleep chamber/personal area in case the mission was a long one; a kitchen/relaxation area that could be converted into more seating if a crew was on the rover; and a cockpit, which covered the entire front of the vehicle.

Maya had modified it so that the sleep chamber was little more than a closet. She had kept the kitchen equipment intact but removed everything from the relaxation part of the room. The extra seating could rise out of the floor with a simple command; she didn't have to move anything else at all.

She had taken some of that extra space for supplies, which filled the back. She had brought extra food and backup equipment for everything from the Ice Breaker to the rover itself. She had known when she left base that morning that she had a good chance of riding out the storm right here, on this stupid ice plain.

She was prepared for that, down to the extra entertainment units to distract her from the whistling wind.

The wind really wasn't whistling inside the rover. It was too tight for that. And the stabilizers held it in place, so that it wasn't rocking in the wind.

Given the predictions, though, she was going to have to sink the grapplers into the ice, because the vehicle itself didn't have enough weight to withstand windspeeds that high.

Very little did.

If she was trapped here. Right now, she had a go-window of about two hours before the impossible winds hit and she couldn't fly out of here. She could try to drive for an extra hour after that, but she would only do that if the vortex wasn't as bad as predicted.

The beeping of her environmental suit, sending information through the hood, was beginning to annoy her. It would only take a few seconds to replace that hood on her head, a few seconds more for the environment to reassert itself throughout the system.

She could gamble on that.

She pulled the hood off, leaving it dangling over the back of the suit, then sat in the pilot's chair. The rover had already protected itself by sealing up the windows that ran along the front.

The windows weren't essential. Many of the team who piloted the rover kept the seals over the windows at all times. But she loved having them open. The natural light was lovely, especially when it reflected off the ice field. Some found that blinding; she found it refreshing, and breathtakingly beautiful.

But safer to keep the windows closed. So she swiped a hand across the top of the navigation board, commanding it to use the windows as a screen for the imagery that the front of the rover was recording. It wasn't quite the same as the view through the windows, but it was close enough, though it didn't light up the interior of the rover the way that the actual view did. Not that there would have been much light once the storm hit full force.

She plotted her trip back to base, looking at the position of the storm versus the power of the storm. The rover did have orbital capacity, so she could zoom straight up and circle Xeunite a few times, waiting for the storm to die.

That would probably be the safest maneuver since, by the time she got to the base, the base would be suffering from the severe weather as well.

The base was on a regular plain, snow-covered, not ice-covered, and wasn't ringed by mountains the way the mining surface was. Even though the base was mostly underground, the top which opened for ship arrivals—was exposed to the weather.

It was that moment—the one where she would have to lower the rover into the base in hurricane force winds—that she wanted to avoid. Even driving the rover into the base from the side could cause damage to the base's interior.

She ran a hand over her face and prepped the rover for the diciest part of her trip—going straight upward through the edge of the storm—to get to orbit.

She had the rover do some calculations, and she did a few on the non-networked tablet she carried with her on every trip. Sometimes she found that the equipment provided by ClaaLorus Systems had an overly optimistic view of the stresses the equipment could tolerate, and what, exactly, the human body could tolerate.

The overly optimistic view wasn't enough for her to file a complaint with the various government boards and agencies that provided oversight to this part of the sector, but it was enough for her to redo the mathematics.

And if she were actually being honest with herself... she was accumulating evidence, so that she would actually be able to be paid by those government agencies once she became a whistleblower. Otherwise, she would need a job somewhere, and this industry was notorious for failing to hire anyone who had complained about anything anywhere.

The routes did not look promising. The force of the wind would strain the rover's engines. She might have missed her window for the best way to travel.

The storm's conditions could and would change at any moment.

And that was when something on the feed caught her eye.

She looked up, scanned the imagery playing on the windows. Black and gray clouds, mostly smeared, in the eastern entrance to the ice field. The tallest mountain peaks in the ring around her had vanished in the clouds.

The storm system was actually covering the entire valley like a gigantic blanket which had not been predicted at all.

But that wasn't what had caught her attention. Something black and gold had pierced the cloud cover to the north. She watched as the thing—which looked like some kind of meteorite—sped toward the center of the valley, leaving a trail of flame and smoke behind it.

The ice's surface was three miles deep, but she had no idea what would happen exactly if something that hot moving that fast hit it.

She didn't have any weaponry on the rover that could shoot the thing and break it up, so with two swift commands she added two layers of shields, one for deep space and one to protect against any kind of attack.

Then the thing hit the ice with such force that she could

actually hear the bang. Although *bang* was too small a word for the sound, muffled as it was by the shield layers and the rover's natural protections. The rover itself shuddered once from the impact, and then rocked as an aftershock hit.

She gripped the navigation panel and stared at the images the rover was sending her. The thing hit, then skidded through the ice, breaking a path feet deep, sending steam— or ice fog—or maybe even ice itself into the air. She couldn't quite tell, and the wind didn't help. It grabbed whatever that plume was and broke it apart, flattening it, and sending it in a thousand different directions.

The thing finally stopped maybe a hundred yards from her, to the east, directly in front of the storm.

But it all looked wrong to her. At that speed, shouldn't the thing have gone deeper into the ice? Should it have skidded at all? And if it had been a meteorite, shouldn't it have broken up on impact?

Cracks started forming along the top of the ice. The cracks ran along the length of the entire grove in the ice.

She started two separate scans—the first to see if the cracks off the path the thing created in the ice went vertically as well as horizontally, and the second to see what kind of damage the damn thing was doing where it ended up. Did it still give off heat? Was it burning through the ice? What *was* it exactly?

She got the answer to the last question first: it was some kind of ship. And her scan showed her two life signs inside.

"Great," she muttered. Two life signs inside a flaming ball that had landed at that speed. Her gut told her she was looking at some kind of escape pod or debris from some broken-up ship.

Part of her wished there were no life signs. No life signs meant she could deal with the other problem at hand.

The damn thing had carved its way across a fissure that ran deep in the ice. The fissure was something she'd been monitoring, because it had grown during their ice mining.

There was bedrock beneath the ice but that wouldn't stop the ice from splintering. She had seen it on other jobs, decades ago. That carelessness, though, was caused by the company she worked for at the time, not that they had suffered any consequences. Sixteen people had died, falling into a crevasse that had formed almost instantaneously as the fissure split.

Sixteen people, no consequences.

This time, it would just be her, and there would definitely be no consequences.

But she couldn't leave those two life signs, whatever and whomever they were, to this growing crisis.

They hadn't activated a distress beacon, which seemed odd, but then, she had no idea if they were conscious. She also had no idea what—if anything—had been destroyed in their crash landing.

She had the rover try to contact them, saying she was in position to rescue them. She sent the message in every language used in this sector and a few other common ones besides, but she received no indication that the owners of those two life signs had even heard the message, let alone could respond to it.

The storm was growing. The large system swirled on the terrain map along her nav board. The winds were picking up, but the system itself seemed trapped in its own circular pattern. Which was good and bad. It wasn't moving fast, but it was becoming organized and was gathering a great deal of debris.

She had to make a decision about those life signs, and she had to make it fast.

No one would blame her for leaving them. The circumstances certainly allowed for it. They didn't work for her and they clearly had no business being here.

But they registered as human life signs, and she'd been criticizing the lack of consideration for human life in the companies she'd worked over the past thirty-five years. Weirdly, she didn't want to save these people because she knew them or because it was the right thing to do.

She felt she had to save them to spare herself from becoming a hypocrite.

She wouldn't be able to live with herself if she left them behind. She would always wonder how they died, if they suffocated under the ice when their environment ran out or if they had emerged and eventually died in the storm or if they hadn't had the gear and had frozen to death.

She was certain she could come up with even more horrible death scenarios as time passed and her guilt worsened.

"Son of a bitch," she muttered to herself, and put some queries into the nav board. Could the cracks in the ice handle the weight of the rover? Could they handle the tires moving across the surface, the rumble and the vibration? If not, could the rover fly at a low enough level to skate the surface in this wind?

She ran the same questions in her tablet and got two different sets of answers. The nav board called the thing an unidentified object and claimed that the risk wasn't worthwhile.

Her tablet used the same inputs and declared the thing a government-issue escape pod manufactured twenty-five years ago. And yes, if she acted quickly, the rover could both cross the ice directly or skate above it with the winds.

The tablet recommended skating above it all, but she wasn't going to. She wanted the ability to punch the rover straight up into the atmosphere, if the storm worsened.

She could only do that from the ground.

"Son of a bitch," she repeated. Then checked to make sure the grapplers worked properly and she could still section off the storage section of the rover.

When she got a yes to both, she put the rover in gear, and headed forward along the edge of the path carved by the escape pod.

The fissure beneath ran perpendicular to the path the pod carved. But the cracks were working their way down, as the wind was winding up. She stopped looking at the sustained wind number and pretended she didn't see the 1 before the numbers for the occasional gusts.

That storm was going to arrive whether she wanted it to or not.

"Hey, Maya!" A voice crackled into the rover's comm. Risa, contacting her from base. "That storm's getting worse."

Maya considered not answering at all, but if she did that, the team might send someone for her, against her explicit instructions.

"Yeah, I know. I'm coming back," Maya said.

"Looks like you're going in the wrong direction," Risa said. "Unless everything is off from that explosion. That had nothing to do with us, right?"

Not *you*, not the company. *Us*, as if she had expected something to blow on the Ice Breaker. Which simply showed what bad shape it truly was in.

"No," Maya said. "Nothing to do with us."

"Well, that's the wrong direction. I'll stay on—"

"I got it," Maya said, and signed off. She let out a small breath. She didn't want the distraction from Risa, nor, for some reason, did Maya want Risa to know exactly what was going on.

It didn't surprise Maya that Risa had no idea something had crash-landed. She hadn't been monitoring the area (or she shouldn't have been!) and even if she had, that escape pod might have looked like some kind of debris mingling with the storm cells.

Maya didn't entirely want to examine her motivation for failing to tell Risa about the life signs. Was Maya protecting herself, in case she couldn't rescue those people? In case she didn't try?

The rover had reached the edge of the well that the pod had created when it stopped moving. Normally, she would have sent a small arm off the side of the rover to examine the well. But the arm would break off in the wind.

So, she sent out a probe with its own internal engine, strong enough to handle these wind speeds. The probe jettisoned from one of the side vents and flew as close to the ground as it could, then descended into the well, sending telemetry and pictures back the entire time.

The pictures showed a round pod with scorch marks on its side. The fire was out, but only because the pod was embedded in ice. The flames had been so hot that the ice had melted significantly, and there was a pool of water below. That water had to be sloughing off around or beneath that pod right now, because the air was so cold the water should freeze the moment it touched air.

It didn't matter how hot the pod was, as long as it wasn't actively burning. The rover's grapplers could handle extreme temperatures of all types.

But Maya wasn't sure how well the grapplers could handle the wind. If she was going to do anything, she had to do it now.

She raised the hood of her environmental suit, figuring that Risa knew where she was if something went seriously wrong in the next few minutes. Then Maya released the large grappler, guiding it out of its container on the side of the rover.

A gust of wind nearly pulled the grappler off its coupling. That gust had been bigger, but it wasn't as big as the winds would be in the next hour.

She had to move fast, but she also had to be precise.

The grappler could handle equipment twenty times the size of the rover. Maya had no specifics on the escape pod; she had only eyeballed it. But it seemed to be at the outer limits of the grappler's capabilities.

She would find out soon enough.

The grappler bent at its top elbow joint and curved downward into the well. It found holds on the outside of the pod, probably for it to remain in place in whatever kind of ship it had come from. The grappler's gigantic claws slid into those holds as if they were made for it.

Then the grappler tugged.

The pod didn't move.

The grappler tugged again, and the pod still didn't move. Either it was too heavy, or it had already frozen in place.

Maya's mouth had gone dry. If she couldn't get the pod out of that well, she would have to leave those two life signs behind. She personally wasn't strong enough or fit enough to battle the wind, climb down into that well, and try to open the pod's doors from the outside. And even if she did, she wouldn't be able to haul anyone out of there.

The best she could do was mark the spot and hope the incoming blizzard didn't bury the pod too deep so that her team could come back when everything was over and try a rescue then.

Even that might not work, because the cold and the wind would create a layer of ice so deep that it might take a week to carve a hole in the ice. She wasn't sure those life signs would survive that long. She wasn't sure they would survive long enough for her to rescue them now.

"Come on, come on, come on," she muttered, not sure if she was talking to the equipment or the pod itself. Because if the life signs could do something, anything, it might help.

Then the grappler tugged the pod loose. In fact, the grappler pulled with such force that it had to overcompensate in the other direction, and the entire rover rocked.

The wind wasn't helping. It continued to push at the rover. The gusts were actually starting to overcome the stabilizers.

The pod was lighter than she expected, which was another reason the grappler overcompensated. She initiated the commands for the grappler to attach the pod to the back of the rover and, at the same time, she made sure the back of the rover was shielded from the cockpit.

The pod attached with a clang. The airlock computers spun the pod until its airlock matched the rover's airlock.

The nav board started flaring red. The pod wasn't adhering properly to the rover. The airlocks weren't working.

She wouldn't be able to travel back to base with the pod attached to the rover and the grappler partially extended. She couldn't fly out of here either, and she couldn't just sit here. The wind would peel off the grappler as well as the pod.

She needed to get the life signs inside the rover.

She grabbed her laser pistol, regretting every single decision she had made since the day began. She should have let the Ice Breaker break and let ClaaLorus Systems fire her. She'd been fired from jobs before.

But not after this many years. And not when she was this old.

Too late now, anyway. She was committed.

But she promised herself that if she couldn't open the pod, she would tag it and drop it close to the Ice Breaker, so that her team could find it. It would get covered with snow and ice, but not like it had been in that well. And maybe those life signs would have a chance to survive.

She left the cockpit, and closed the cockpit door, something she hadn't done in years. She locked it, coded not just to her warm handprint and active eye scan, but also physically, with a seventeen-figure numerical that had an image in the middle, something she used on her personal stuff, something not in any computer anywhere.

No one could guess that, not without time and the right equipment, and she doubted the owners of those life signs had that.

Then she made her way to the storage area, pulling up her environmental suit's hood as she went. The environment formed around her almost immediately and, oddly, gave her comfort.

She pulled open the storage area door, stunned to see ice forming on everything inside.

That leak between the pod and the storage area wasn't a leak. It was an actual opening.

She turned her boots to the ice setting, hoping she would adhere enough to make it to the pod door.

She could see it, intermittently, as the wind whistled between the two vehicles, bringing pointed ice pellets with it. They were scratching the pod, and probably not doing any good for her rover either.

And she didn't want to think about the grappler, which she hadn't yet unhooked.

She couldn't hear much over the howl of the wind, but as she got closer to the open doors, she thought she heard pounding.

Then the pounding stopped.

Oh, God, if those life signs snuffed out while she was this close, she would... she had no idea what. She didn't want to imagine it.

She went to the wall and managed to open the tools locker. Thank every god she could think of that the locker had been designed to work in extreme conditions.

She removed a laser cutter and put a few other tools on her environmental suit's belt. Then she stuffed the laser pistol in there as well, because she would need both hands.

She could see the outline of the door on the pod, but that outline was getting coated in ice. She couldn't strap into the opening near the rover because if she did, she couldn't reach the pod's door. So, she did the next best thing. She hooked two tethers to her belt.

The wind buffeted her as she worked. She only had one chance at unsealing that pod's door. If this didn't work, she couldn't do anymore, because she would get blown into the ice field.

She braced one hand on the pod. The ice was lumpy beneath her gloves, and thicker than she thought.

She started up the laser cutter, working fast, peeling ice away as she cut pieces loose. The pounding continued inside, getting stronger as the ice moved away.

She had no idea if the people inside could hear her work: she doubted it. But they had to know they had been moved.

Finally, she got to the door itself. She was about to yank it open, when it slid sideways, and she found herself face-to-face with a man who had been beaten bloody.

His face was black-and-blue. His lower lip was split, his nose broken. His eyes were barely visible under the swelling in his face.

He shoved her backward, and she nearly fell through the gap

between the pod and the rover. She caught herself with her arms, hanging onto the rover on one side and the pod on the other.

The man climbed over her as he got out.

As she struggled to regain her footing, she glanced inside the pod. Another person huddled in there in a fetal position, eyes closed, face battered. He seemed to be unconscious.

Her heart rate spiked. What had she gotten in the middle of?

She pulled herself into the rover, barely able to stand due to the wind swirling around her. She caught a strap near the door, and eased herself inside—

Only to find herself face-to-face with a laser pistol. It was olive. Government issue.

"Close the damn door," he said.

"Your friend," she said, looking at the pod.

"He's not my friend," the man said. "Close the damn door or get the hell out."

The wind swirled again, and he slid just a little. His boots couldn't find purchase on the ice.

"This is my vehicle," she said.

"Not anymore," he said. "This thing is some kind of space-to-land vehicle, right?"

"It's a rover," she said, trying to keep herself calm. The wind was getting stronger.

He was shaking. He wasn't wearing any kind of environmental suit.

"I can handle a rover," he said, more to himself than to her. "Get out."

"No," she said.

He fired. His shaking hands made the shot miss her and

ping off the side of the escape pod. He swore, tried to regroup, and ended up losing his footing entirely.

He landed on his back with a *whomp* and spun along the ice-covered floor toward her. She blocked his slide by moving a booted foot in front of him and pulled her own laser pistol from the back of her belt.

"Get your friend out of that pod, and I'll make sure you get out of here," she said.

"He's not my friend." The battered man's teeth were chattering. He probably had frostbite already.

"What is he?"

The man grabbed her leg and tried to pull her sideways, to make her lose her balance. But she remained steady because her boots adhered to the ice.

Instead, he managed to slip farther, hanging off the edge of the rover. The wind battered his head against the side of the pod.

"You're going to die if you don't do what I said." She sounded tougher than she felt. Her heart was pounding.

He pointed his laser pistol at her, hands still shaking. "I don't need you," he said, and fired again.

She kicked the pistol as he fired, the shot going wild. The force of her kick made him slide the rest of the way out of the rover, falling headfirst between the rover and the pod.

She ran to the edge, to see if she could reach him, but he had fallen deep into the snow.

She had no idea why she wanted to save him. He had tried to shoot her twice, and he had clearly done something to the man inside the pod.

The pod.

The wind had grown so strong now that she could barely hold her own position. And she couldn't keep the pod attached to the rover.

She grabbed one of the tethers and pulled it across the distance between the pod and the rover, stepping with it, turning on the gravity in her boots as well, hoping that would keep her as stable as possible.

The inside of the pod was trashed. The two men had fought in here, and the man on the floor lost. He was wearing some kind of uniform. The logo on his closest sleeve belonged to a prison transport ship. She looked up, saw that the pod was marked *Official Use Only.*

Somehow, the guy who had fallen into the snow had commandeered this pod, maybe by forcing the guard to open it all for him, then beating the man within an inch of his life.

She grabbed the man and wrapped the tether around him, before attaching it to his belt. Then she yanked him up, knees buckling under his weight.

She could barely shove him toward the door. Only a few yards to cross to get into the rover. Only a few yards.

The gap between the rover and the pod was the hard part. She wasn't sure how she felt about the other man, dying on the ice below her (relieved?), but she didn't want to lose this one. Not that she was certain he was a good man—she had no way of knowing that—but he hadn't actively tried to harm her, and she had come this far.

She kept her arms wrapped around his torso, and leveraged herself across that gap, yanking him along, feeling the effort in her back and her thighs. Sharp pains were shooting through her knees. She couldn't hold this position long.

Then the wind came up again, screeching—actually screeching—and for once it worked with her, shoving her into the rover. She fell on top of the man, feeling him slide on the ice beneath her.

She stuck one foot between his thighs to stop him from sliding out of the rover just like his companion had. Then she commanded the rover to close the airlock door.

For a moment, the door didn't move. The wind shoved in, and she wondered if that was causing the door to stick open. Then bits of ice rained off the door's side. It slid—too slowly for her tastes—all the way closed.

"Restore environment," she said, but she really meant temperature. Then she grabbed the man and dragged him toward the door into the rover proper.

She managed to get that door open, not sure what she would do with this guy if he became conscious. Would he be as vicious as his compatriot?

She untethered herself, grabbed some extra cords, and pulled the man out of the storage area. She was dragging him by his collar now, because her back wouldn't let her do anything else.

And her knees. She had never felt such pain in her knees.

But she wasn't going to let herself limp. She dragged him to the only bed, and somehow managed to lever him onto it. Then she strapped him into place, just in case.

She didn't know much field medicine. She knew how to deal with frostbite and ice, but that was it. She wrapped him in the special blankets every rover on the base had and let the blankets deal with the extreme cold.

She'd worry about his other injuries later.

She checked the straps, then made her way to the cockpit, opening the door, and stepping inside. Her environmental suit's hood remained up this time, and it was beeping at her. The wind speeds had reached ridiculous levels.

She unhooked the pod from the back of the rover and did her best to secure the grappler. If it broke, that was no longer her issue. She had a hunch, given the pain in her back and knees, she'd be on some kind of disability leave anyway. She wasn't sure she could do the work, not given how she felt at the moment.

Then she ran the simulations. The wind was too strong for her to drive through it, and too gusty for her to jettison into orbit. But the ice was still cracking, and the fissure beneath was growing.

She couldn't drive out. The rover didn't have the ability to plow through the snow-ice mix. And the wind wouldn't let her skim over the surface.

She had to standing-start jump into orbit. A one-time shot.

For a half second, she thought about staying here, gambling that the cracks wouldn't become something more serious.

But the same things that factored into her decision to pull the pod out factored into the decision here. If the rover slipped below the surface and got covered in snow-ice, which then froze over...

It would be a hellish death, along with the guy she didn't know. What if he ended up as mean as the other guy?

Hellish, with company.

She smiled grimly.

She had one thing to do then, and one thing only.

She strapped herself in and forced herself to make the preparations, going slowly and stating each action out loud, just so she wouldn't miss any. She had the rover's computer on, but it wasn't as sophisticated as some other equipment she had used, equipment that could advise her when she was making a misstep.

She didn't think she was, even though it had been a long time since she tried anything like this.

Worst case, she'd be stuck here.

At least she would have tried.

Her muscles were trembling from the exertion and the adrenalin. She had no choice, and somehow that was freeing. She started the command sequence and let it run, feeling the rover shudder as the power built in its engines.

She hadn't checked the vents. She had no idea if snow and ice blocked them. Too late to send some kind of clearing heat through the vents or a bit of garbage or anything. Too late—

The rover groaned—a sound she had never heard before—then vibrated. For a moment, she worried that it might explode. She hadn't considered that.

Then she leaned back in the pilot's chair. If the rover exploded, she died, and she wouldn't have to worry about any of this anymore.

Somehow that thought gave her comfort. As she calmed down, the rover lurched and then moved sideways.

At that moment, she realized the rover was already

jettisoning upward, through the gusts and the storm, buffeting in the gigantic winds. She simply couldn't see anything, because she hadn't set up the nav panel that way.

And now there was no point. She would know if they had made it out when the rover stopped vibrating, when everything felt smooth.

She gripped the arms of her chair, hoping—maybe even praying—and then... the vibration stopped.

She tapped the nav panel, saw that the rover was above the storm now, and heading out of the atmosphere.

She had to orbit the planet until the storm abated, but she could now.

She was going to make it.

Maya leaned her head back and sighed. The shakes began, as they always did for her once a crisis ended.

Only the crisis wasn't quite over. She didn't know what she had brought on board.

She leaned forward, accessed the ClaaLorus Systems' news net, and typed in the name of the prison transport.

And then she saw the notice.

She had been right: the man she had left behind had used a guard to get into an escape pod and somehow, even though there had been no emergency on the transport, managed to get the pod away from the ship. Everyone thought the guard was dead.

But he wasn't. She had him.

And the prisoner—one Maximus Connera, a man who had left a string of bodies all over this sector—was dead, down in the ice with his pod, his attempt foiled.

By her.

She ran a hand over her face and let out a small half laugh of wonder. Would she have even tried to rescue the pod if she had known what it was? Would she have pulled the guard free?

She had no idea.

She was glad she hadn't known, glad she had made the decision based on life signs alone.

Because she was no judge or jury. She didn't have to make decisions like that.

She had been in the ice because she hadn't wanted her own people to risk their lives for a piece of broken-down equipment. She hadn't wanted any other lives on her conscience.

She wasn't sure if she'd have one. Maximus. Such a name. She could barely remember what he looked like—that battered face—but his voice would haunt her. The way that it dripped menace. The way that it half floated away in the wind.

He hadn't asked for her help. She was glad of that. She had no idea what she would have done if he begged her to help him.

She leaned back in the pilot's chair and closed her eyes, just for a moment.

Base medical would have to deal with the man she had rescued. They would have to work with her as well.

Once she got back, she wouldn't have to worry about any of this. She wouldn't have to worry about the equipment or storms or anything.

She was applying for medical leave. She needed the rest. And she would take it, maybe even put in a transfer to somewhere warm.

She'd have to learn new equipment, but that was okay. She was ready to.

Because this was extreme. And she was tired of extreme.

She needed easy from now on.

Although she doubted she would get it.

CYCLOPTERUS

PETER WATTS

GALIK SNEAKS IN through blue-green twilight a hundred meters down, where it's calm. Overhead, lost in the murk, the mixing zone churns beneath the surface; the surface churns beneath the sky; immortal Nāmaka churns between, in ascension once more after four weeks slumming it up north as a Category 3.

A dim shape looms in the sub's headlights: *Sylvia Earle*, an inflatable bladder four stories high, freshly relocated from its usual station over the White Shark Café. The sub sniffs out the dorsal docking hatch and locks on. Galik grunts a farewell to his pilot and drops into a cramped decompression chamber outfitted with a half dozen molded seats and a second hatch—sealed— to complement the one he came in through. His ride disengages with a clank and slips back the way it came.

They let him out when the gauge reads nine atmospheres. A sullen tech in a blue coverall leads him down through a maze of pipes and ladders and bulkheads festooned with shark posters.

She counters Galik's small talk with grunts and monosyllables, abandons him in a dimly lit sub bay where every bulkhead wriggles with blue wavelight. A fat tadpole-shaped cubmarine wallows in the moon pool at its center, hatch agape at the end of a folding catwalk. Its flanks bristle with gifts for the seabed: magnetometers and CTD sensors, SIDs and current meters and cytometers. Other things even an oceanographer wouldn't recognize. A name is stenciled onto the hull, just to the left of No Step: RSV *Cyclopterus*.

It can't go as far or as fast as the craft that brought him here. But it can go way, way deeper.

The pilot's fixated on the predive checklist as Galik climbs down into the cockpit and dogs the hatch. Galik breathes in sweat and monomers and machine oil, settles into the shotgun seat. "I'm Alistor."

"Uh huh." Her head dips in perfunctory acknowledgment: a jaw-length curtain of dark ringlets, a cheekbone and profile behind. Moonpool light filters in through a smattering of high-pressure viewports arrayed like spider eyes around the front of the cockpit, paints her in faint watercolor. Her eyes never leave the board. "Buckle up."

He does. Mechanical guts gurgle and belch. The lights past the viewports ascend and fade.

Cyclopterus drops into the void.

Galik settles back in his seat. "How long to the bottom?"

"Forty minutes. Forty-five."

"Nice to be able to measure things in minutes again. Took me a day and a half to get here from Corvallis, and that was at forty knots."

The pilot taps a flickering readout until it steadies.

"Kinda miss the old days, you know? When you could just *fly* out, drop down. No giant-ass superstorms getting in the way."

She reaches back and grabs the pilot's VR headset from its hook. Puts it on, slides the visor over her eyes.

Galik sighs.

VR's not much use this high off the seabed; the 2D display spread across the dashboard is more than sufficient when there's nothing but empty sea for a thousand meters in any direction. But for want of anything else to do, Galik grabs his own headset and boots it up. He finds himself suspended in a sparse void sprinkled with occasional readouts and scale bars. Close below, a faint translucent membrane spreads out across the universe at 1300 meters. Four thousand meters below that, the ocean floor bounces back solid corduroy.

"That's strange," the pilot murmurs.

Galik raises his visor. "What?"

Under hers, the pilot's lips are pursed. "Pycnocline's way down at thirteen hundred. Never seen it so dee—" She catches herself consorting with the enemy, falls silent.

Galik rolls his eyes and weighs his options. Goes for it.

"You be breaking any protocols to at least tell me your name?"

Her hooded face turns toward him for a moment. "Koa Moreno."

"Pleased to meet you, Koa. How did I manage to piss you off in the past five minutes?"

"You didn't. We just—don't do small talk down here."

"Ah." He nods, though she can't see it. "Parties on the *Sylvia Earle* must be a hoot."

"Try spending a few months breathing recycled farts and belches from the same ten people. You'll reset your boundaries soon enough."

"It's more than that."

Something changes in her posture, some subtle slumping of the shoulders that says *Fine, asshole, have it your way.* She ups her visor up and turns to face him.

"This could be the *last one*. And you're going to fuck it up like everything else."

"Me?"

"Nautilus."

"What makes you think—"

"After you strip-mined every last park and refuge and vacant lot on land, you moved offshore. We've been watching it happen, *Alistor*. I was there when Lizard Island went down. Clipperton's one of the last places the ISA didn't cave on. But it was only a matter of time, wasn't it? Seabed's just another resource to tear up while we wait for the ceiling to crash in."

Galik feels his face pulling into a tight little smile. "Well. I guess I asked."

She turns her attention to the dashboard.

"This is just a preliminary survey," he tries. "Might not come to anything."

"Give me a break. The whole zone's rotten with polymetallics and you know it." She shakes her head. "Honestly, I don't know why you're even going through the motions. Why not just buy yourself a rubber stamp and go straight to the strip-mining?"

Galik takes a careful breath, keeps his voice calm and friendly. "Good question. Why haven't we?"

She glares at him.

He holds up his hands, palms out. "I'm serious. The mineralogical data's been on the books for twenty years, you said as much yourself. If they just wanted to strip-mine Clipperton, why didn't they do it years ago?"

Moreno doesn't answer for a moment.

"It's a deep dig," she says at last. "Maybe you went after the low-hanging fruit first. Maybe you just didn't notice it until now."

"Maybe they tried," Galik suggests, "and the ISA wouldn't give them their rubber stamp."

"You keep saying *they*. Like you're not one of them."

"Wasn't Nautilus went after the permit. Wasn't Nautilus got turned down."

"Who, then?"

"PolyCon. They went after Clarion Clipperton on five separate occasions. ISA wouldn't budge. Heritage site, they said. Unparalleled deepwater biodiversity. Unique conservation value."

"Bullshit. Nobody cares about that stuff anymore."

"They're the ISA. It's their job to care."

"They caved everywhere else."

"Not here."

"Maybe not for PolyCon. Here *you* are."

"I told you: nothing's decided."

Moreno snorts. "Right. You dragged *Sylvie* hundreds of kilometers off-site, so you'd have your own private base camp. You put everyone's research on hold, and you've got me spending the next eight hours planting your money detectors on the seabed. You think I don't know what that costs?"

Galik shrugs. "If you're that sure, you could always refuse the gig. Break your contract. Take a stand on principle."

Moreno glowers at the dashboard, where the luminous stipple of the thermocline thickens and rises about them. *Cyclopterus* jerks and slews as some particularly dense lens of water slaps lazily to starboard.

"They'd probably send you home then, though, right? Back to the heat waves and the water wars and that weird new fungus that's eating everything. Although I hear some of the doomsday parties are worth checking out. Just last week one of 'em ended up burning down half of Kluane National Park."

Moreno says nothing.

"'Course, if you really wanted to stand up and be counted, you could join the Gaianistas." And in response to the look that gets him: "What? You gonna let the fuckers who killed the planet get away scot-free *again*?"

"That's rich. Coming from one of their errand boys."

"I chose my side. What about you, hiding out here in the ocean while the world turns to shit? You going to do anything about that, or are you all sound and fury, signifying nothing?"

"There's nothing to do," she says, almost whispering. "It's too late."

"Never too late for payback. Way I understand it, that's what the Gaianistas are all about."

"They're a lost cause."

"What isn't, these days?"

"Don't think for a second I don't sympathize. Of course, I fucking sympathize. We're ten years past tipping point, planet's doomed, and you lot are making out better than ever because there's no point in any pesky ineffective environmental regulations anymore. So, yeah. Sometimes it seems like the only thing that might make life worthwhile would be to take some of you out before you all bugger off to New Zealand."

"So?"

"So it's no-win. Go up against the people in charge and they'll squash you like a bug."

"That's the thing about revenge, though, isn't it? We'll go after those who've fucked us over even if it hurts us more than them. Just as long as it *does* hurt them, even a little. And the worse things get, the more we're willing to sacrifice just to strike back."

"Bullshit."

"They've done studies. It's a kind of a—justice instinct, I guess you'd call it. Primal. Like sex, or money. They say it worked pretty well at discouraging cheaters back when we were living in caves. Maybe not so great now, but, you know. Some people just haven't evolved."

"So, what? You're saying you don't blame them?"

"The Gaianistas? Would you blame a rabid dog for biting you?" Galik shrugs. "'Course, you still have to put them down. For the public welfare."

"That's funny. I imagine they'd say exactly the same thing about you."

"Would you?"

"Would I what?"

"Put me down? If you had the chance."

Moreno opens her mouth. Closes it again. *Cyclopterus* hisses into the silence.

"I had the chance," she says at last. "If you must know."

"Tell me."

After a moment she does. "Trying to catch a flight to Galveston, shuttle gig out in the Gulf. Some zero-pointer was in a hurry to make it to his private jet I guess, just him and his family and a swarm of drones. Three gens of rich entitled assholes trying to sneak through Departures, pretending not to notice all the hisses and hate stares."

"Weird they were even on ground level. They're usually not so exposed."

"Someone said some kind of technical issue up on the roof, sidelined the helipad. You could tell they were *really* not happy to be there. Looked downright scared actually, even before—anyway, they had their drones keeping the riffraff at bay, but before they even made it into the terminal this big white van pulls up and it must have been loaded with capacitors because *zap*."

"EMP?"

Moreno nods. "Drones drop like birds in Beijing. And suddenly all these people dragging suitcases over the curb or hailing cabs or kissing each other goodbye—they all just turn like some kind of hive mind and suddenly Richy McRich and his nearest and dearest are the eye in the storm. It's really quiet for a moment or two, and nobody's saying anything, but one of the rich kids—this little snot in a Nermal T-shirt—he kind of *whimpers*. And then the mob just closes in and—tears them apart."

Galik mouths a silent *Fuuuccck*.

"I don't know how many were in on the plan and how many just happened to be in the neighborhood. But almost everyone joined in. They were making this *sound*, like the whole mob had a single voice. Like—like a wind howling down a street between skyscrapers."

"What about airport security?"

"Oh, they showed up. Eventually. But the pulse took out local surveillance, right? And it's not like the 'nistas were wearing ID. They did their thing and faded and by the time anyone showed up, it was just a bunch of people milling around all *Heavens, whatever happened here* and *How'd this blood get on my pants?*"

Galik doesn't speak for a moment. "You said *almost* everyone. That include you?"

She shakes her head. "Actually, I tried calling 911. But the pulse, my phone was…"

"So you chose a side too."

"What?"

"Some of the people who wrecked the world were right there in front of you. You could have had justice."

She gives him a hard look. "It was a lynch mob."

"When the despots own the justice system, what else is there?"

"Your bosses know you talk like this?"

"I don't. I'm being, what's the word, *Socratic*. Since you

blame *my bosses* for the end of the world and all, seems to me you'd want a little payback. But when you had the chance, right in front of you—no danger, no consequence—you tried to help them."

She taps a control; something burbles to stern. "Oh, I wanted a piece of them. It's not like the spirit didn't move me. But it also scared me, you know? The *size* of that thing, the way everyone just sort of—coalesced." She draws a breath. "And yeah, they fucking deserve it. But the damage is done, the planet's fucked. Killing a few rich assholes isn't going to unfuck it. I just—I guess I have better things to do with whatever time we've got left.

"Besides—" She shrugs. "Doesn't matter if they bugger off to New Zealand. Doesn't matter if they bugger off to Antarctica. The pandemics are everywhere. Cholera or Rift Valley Fever or whatever's on top six months from now will get them eventually."

Galik doesn't have anything to say to that.

"It's funny," Moreno says after a few moments. "You hear about them all the time, right? Idiot kids and grannies in running shoes, waving signs and chanting *Hey ho hey ho* as if *that* ever changed a fucking thing. But these guys, they had *resources*. They were organized. It was almost military."

"They are military," Galik says.

"What?"

"Some of 'em, anyway. You never noticed how all the mercs and mall cops just kind of *went away* over the years?"

"Drones replaced everyone. Why should mall cops be any different than cab drivers or pizza delivery guys?"

"Drones don't turn on you when everything goes Law of the Jungle. At some point, it dawned on the zero-pointers that their private armies might not be quite so obedient when the lights went out. Might just rise up and take over all those apocalypse bunkers for themselves. Way I hear it, a lot of guys with Middle East stamps on their passports ended up out of work, past ten years or so. Some of 'em are probably pissed about it. Maybe even looking for pay—"

Something lifts *Cyclopterus* like a toy in a bathtub.

Inertia pushes Galik into his seat. The vessel *tilts*, nose down: slides fast-forward as though surfing some invisible wave. Moreno curses and grabs the stick as *Cyclopterus* threatens to turn, to tumble.

Wipe out...

In the next moment, everything is calm as glass again.

Neither speaks for a moment.

"That was one hell of a thermocline," Galik remarks.

"Pycnocline," Moreno says automatically. "And we passed it a thousand meters ago. That was—something else."

"Seaquake?"

She leans forward, interrogates the board. "*Sylvie*'s transponder isn't talking." She conjures up a keyboard, starts typing. Out past the hull, the metronome chirp of the sonar segues into full-throated orchestra.

"Technical glitch?" Galik wonders.

"Dunno."

"Can't you just call them up?"

"What do you *think* I'm doing?"

Acoustic modems, he remembers. They can handle analog

voice comms under normal conditions—but what's *normal*, with Nāmaka churning up the Devil's own background noise? Down here, the pros use text.

But judging by the look on Moreno's face, that's not working either.

She drags her finger along a slider on the dash; the pointillist seabed drops away around some invisible axis as the transducers swing their line-of-sight from *Down* to *Up*. Static and confusion rotate into view; the distant surface returns a blizzard of silver pixels to swamp the screen. Moreno fiddles with the focus and the maelstrom smears away. Closer, deeper features stutter into focus. Moreno sucks breath between clenched teeth.

Far overhead, something has grabbed the thermo—the *pycn*ocline as though it were a vast carpet—and shaken it. The resulting waveform rears up through the water column, a fold of cold dense water rising into the euphotic zone like a submarine tsunami. It iterates across the display in majestic stop-motion, its progress updating with each ping.

It must be almost a thousand meters, crest-to-trough.

It's already passed by, marching east. Patches of static swirl and dissipate in its wake, clustered echoes whose outlines shuffle and spread in jerky increments. Galik doesn't know what they are. Maybe remnants of the Garbage Patch, its dismembered fragments still cluttering up the ocean years after Nāmaka tore it apart. Maybe just bubbles and swirling cavitation. Maybe even schools of fish; a few of those are still supposed to be hanging on, here and there.

"What—" he begins.

"Shut up." Moreno's face is bloodless. "This is bad."

"How bad?"

"Shut up and let me think!"

Her visor's back down. She plays the panel. Scale bars squeeze and stretch like rubber on the dash. Topography rotates and zooms, forward, aft; midwater wrinkles blur into focus and out again as Moreno alters the range. Her whispered *fuck fuck* serves up a disquieting counterpoint to the pinging of the transducers.

"I can't find *Sylvie*," she admits at last softly. "Not all of her, anyway. Maybe some pieces bearing eighty-seven. Swept way off-station."

Galik waits.

"She was ninety meters down." Moreno takes a deep breath. "The tip of that—thing reaches up to fifty. Must've slapped them like a fucking flyswatter."

"But what *was* it?"

"I don't know. Never seen anything like it before. Almost like some kind of monster seiche."

"I don't know what that is."

"It's like—when the pycnocline sloshes back and forth. Underwater standing wave. But the strong ones, they're just in lakes and seas. Basins with walls the wave can bounce against."

"Pacific's a basin. Pacific's got walls."

"Pacific's *huge*. I mean sure, ocean seiches go on world tours sometimes, but they're *slow*. Stretch the mixing layer a few meters over a few years. Maybe kickstart an El Niño now and then. Nothing like this."

"There was nothing like Nāmaka ten years ago either."

"Yeah."

"So much heat in the oceans now, hurricanes don't even cool down enough to dissipate. Maybe it's amping up your seiches too."

"Dunno. Maybe."

"Maybe they're even feeding off each other. Nothing's linear anymore, it's all tipping points and—"

"I *don't know*, I said. None of that shit *matters* right now." She slides her visor up, eyes a red handle protruding from the ceiling. A tiny metallic hiccough and a soft *bloop* carry through the hull after she yanks it. Something flashes on the dash.

"Emergency buoy?"

Moreno nods, downs visor, grabs the joystick.

"Shouldn't we, you know. Make a recording? Send details?"

"It's in there already. Dive logs, telemetry, even cabin chatter. Beacon stores it all automatically." The corner of her mouth tightens. "You're in there too, if that helps. Sub commandeered by NMI, prospecting dive. Maybe they'll move faster, knowing one of their errand boys is in danger."

She edges the stick forward and to port. *Cyclopterus* banks. Galik checks the depth gauge. "Down?"

"You think anyone's gonna fly a rescue mission through Nāmaka? You think I'd be crazy enough to surface even if they did?"

"No, but—"

"Any rescue's gonna come in from the side. And since you wouldn't have dragged *Sylvia* all the way over from the Café if there'd been anyone closer, I'm assuming it's gonna have to come from further out, right?"

After a moment, he nods.

"Could be days before help arrives even if our signal *does* manage to cut through the shit," Moreno tells him. "And I for one don't feel like holding my breath for a week."

Galik swallows. "I thought these things made their own O_2. From seawater."

"Lack of seawater isn't the problem. Need battery power to run the electrolysis rig."

He glances at their bearing; Moreno has brought them around so they're following in the wake of the superseiche.

"You're going after the *Earle*."

Her jaw clenches visibly. "I'm going after what's left. With any luck, some of the fuel cells are still intact."

"Any chance of survivors?" Most habs come with emergency pods, hard-shelled refugia for the crew in case of catastrophe. Assuming the crew has enough advance warning to get to them, of course.

She doesn't answer. Maybe she's not allowing herself to hope.

"I'm—I'm sorry about this," Galik manages. "I can't imagine what—"

Cowled Moreno hunches over the controls. "Shut up and let me drive."

CYCLOPTERUS NEVER STOPS talking. Her guts gurgle and hiss. Her motors whine like electric mosquitoes. Her relentless transducers ping the ocean for reflections of mass and density.

Her passengers—immersed in wireframe caricatures of the world beyond the hull—say nothing at all.

Eventually, the seabed resolves below them: luminous plane or muddy plain, depending on which channel you choose. Sonar serves up more information, but after all the pixels the impoverished patch of bone-grey sediment in the headlights is a welcome glimpse of something *real*. Galik fiddles with the controls, finds an overlay mode that serves up the best of both feeds.

Moreno nudges the sub to port. Mud gives way to rock; rock subsides again under mud. Outcrops and overhangs erupt from the substrate at odd angles, like listing jagged-edged tabletops. Nodules of cobalt and manganese lie scattered about like encrusted coins strewn from some ancient shipwreck. There are *things*, everywhere. Starfish with arms like tiny sinuous backbones. Tentacled flowers on stalks. Tangled balls of jawless hagfish. Gelatinous blobs the size of softballs, floating just off the bottom; they iridesce like dragonfly wings in the glare of the headlight.

All drift aimlessly. None move on their own.

Galik slides his visor up, looks across the cockpit. "Are they all dead?"

Moreno grunts.

"What would do that?" Hydrogen sulfide, maybe. The whole zone's rotten with cold seeps and hot smokers—the source of Clipperton's mineral wealth—but Galik's still taken aback to see such devastation in the middle of a protected wilderness area.

A shrug. "Dead zone moved in, probably. We get big slugs of anoxic water sliding down off the conshelf few times a year now. Suffocates whole ecosystems overnight."

"Shit."

"Yeah." Her voice is toneless. "What a tragedy."

Galik searches what he can see of her face, finds it unreadable. He gives up and downs his own visor.

Something's waiting for him there.

It's a hard ping, just a few degrees to starboard. Something big on the seabed, like an outcropping but more symmetrical, somehow. It echoes louder than any mere chunk of basalt.

"Is that a piece of the hab? Fifty meters, oh-two-eight?"

"No."

"Sounds like metal though, right?"

Moreno says nothing.

"Maybe we should check it out. Just to be sure."

Technically, he's still in charge. Technically, Moreno's just a taxi driver. Technically, she could still tell him to fuck off and there wouldn't be a whole lot he could do about it.

After a moment, though, *Cyclopterus* noses to starboard.

The bogey's partially hidden behind a ridge of rock; its echo flashes like the edge of some dim sun peeking over a horizon. Details resolve as they approach: a curve, a convexity. A series of interlocking segments, their lower edges fuzzed by incursions of mud.

A skull.

Sonar completes the tableaux a few moments before it scrolls into the light: a backbone, glittering with oily reflections. A silvered arrowhead cranium, three meters if it's an inch, nostrils stretched along the top, empty eye sockets pushed down to the sides. The bones of some huge thumbless hand, laid flat across the seabed like a museum reconstruction.

"It's a *whale*," he whispers.

"Few million years old, probably."

"But it's *metal*…"

"It's a fossil. It mineralized. The water's saturated with metal ions. Why do you even think you're interested in this place?"

"Yeah, but—"

"I'd love to give you a scenic tour, Alistor, but in case you've forgotten my friends are probably all dead and I'd just as soon not join—"

She cuts herself off. Something's caught her eye, something peeking into view from behind that enormous glinting spine.

"What the fuck," she murmurs.

A fleshy torpedo, pale whitish-pink in the lights, a couple meters long. Arms. "Squid," Galik says.

"Not like any squid *I've* ever seen."

They edge in closer. Galik zooms his camera. The creature drifts listless as any other they've seen down here, arms limp as seaweed. There *is* something strange about it, though.

"Look at the eyes," Moreno whispers.

He can see *three* from this angle, spaced at ninety-degree intervals around the absurd amidships head of the thing. (Presumably there's a fourth on the far side.) And of those three, two of them look—wrong…

No iris. No pupil. No white. Galik sees three things positioned as eyes, but only one stares back at him. The others are dark, and—tangled, somehow. Sockets full of tendrils: as though someone has scooped out the eyeball and stuffed a nest of bloodworms into the socket.

"Kill the lights," he says.

"Why—"

"Just do it."

Darkness crushes in. Galik's hullcam goes black— except for one bright pinpoint, flashing a steady emerald beat in the darkness. Right about where one of those not-eyes gapes, invisible now.

"There's an *LED* in that thing," Galik says softly.

Moreno kicks the floods back on. The blinking star vanishes in high-contrast light and shadow. *Cyclopterus* closes with renewed purpose; a manipulator unfolds from her belly like a mantis limb, clawed fingers reaching for the flaccid thing. They touch it.

Instantly, the squid flexes and recoils, jets away into the darkness.

"Huh," Galik grunts.

"Humboldt squid," Morena tells him. "Started off as one, anyway. Resistant to low-oxygen conditions."

"But it was—"

"Tweaked. Whole lot of neurons cable to the eyes. Nothing says they gotta carry visual information. Hook up the right sensors, you could read anything. pH. Salinity. Name it."

"So it's some kind of—living environmental sensor."

"That's my guess."

"Not yours."

Moreno snorts.

"Whose, then?"

"I dunno," Moreno says. "But look where it went."

She's aimed the sonar, cranked the range. The squid—whatever it is—doesn't register on such far focus. Something does, though. Way off in the distance, at the very limit of sonar sight, something bounces back faint as a ghost.

"Looks like an outcropping," Galik says.

"My ass. Those edges are too straight."

"*Sylvia Earle*?"

"Wrong bearing."

"Maybe we should just stay the course. Given our limited reserves."

Cyclopterus turns toward the echo.

Galik slides his visor back. "What do you think it is?"

Moreno's is up as well. Her eyes are hard as glass.

"Let's find out."

"WELL, AT LEAST we know now," Galik says.

"Know?"

"Why Clipperton's off-limits. Why the ISA didn't—" He shakes his head. "Someone bought them."

Cyclopterus floats across an unfinished landscape of plastic and metal. Spreading out in all directions, a grid of rails turns the seabed into a chessboard; spindly towers rise from its interstices. Printers the size of automobiles glide along their tracks, drilling holes, laying eggs, extruding pools of hot thick liquid that freeze harder than basalt. Strange jet-propelled machines splice rock and metal together at critical junctures.

Everywhere are the frames of half-completed domes and tunnels and conduits, wormy with bundled cabling and fiberop.

All invisible in the darkness. All this industrious activity hidden beneath four kilometers of sunless black, except where *Cyclopterus*'s eyes and echoes lay it bare.

Galik whistles. "This is going to be one hell of a hab."

"This isn't a hab. It's a fucking *city*." Moreno rechecks the onboard database. "Not on the charts. No transponders. This thing is totally off the books."

"I guess they're not all going to New Zealand."

Moreno taps a control; blotchy rainbows bloom here and there across the display. A slash of red smolders at two o'clock, broken by huddles of intermittent machinery. "Hot seep."

"Power source," Galik guesses.

"Hey, you see that?"

He does. Bearing eighty-five degrees: something round and smooth, something anomalously *complete* in the midst of all this in-progress disarray. It glows green and warm on thermal.

A pressure hull.

Moreno reads the echo like a soothsayer. "Atmosphere."

"Occupied?" This could be a problem. Anyone going to these lengths isn't likely to welcome drop-ins.

But Moreno shakes her head. "Looks like a foreman's shack. Place to crash when you come down to check on your pet project. Anyone who can keep a place this size off the scope isn't gonna risk giving themselves away with telemetry broadcasts. Can't see anyone living here full-time, though. Not until they're ready to move in permanently. In the meantime"—*Cyclopterus* is already coming around—"there'll be power. Food. Beds even."

The shack's dead ahead now, growing in their sights. "We hang around too long, we'll have company," Galik surmises.

"Unless we're extremely unlucky, the rescue guys show up first. And then this fucking place gets dragged into the sunlight for everyone to see."

"That's assuming whoever's behind it—"

"You know who's behind it, Alistor. Your masters. Their masters. Zero-pointers cashing out before the bill comes due." She glances meaningfully at him. "Guess they didn't save you a spot, huh?"

"You're assuming they won't be keeping an ear on the local chatter. That they won't just reach out and squash a rescue mission as soon as they see the coordinates."

Moreno's fingers tighten on the joystick. A soft *shit* hisses between her teeth.

The shack resolves in their headlights like a grey moon, maybe ten meters across at the equator. Moreno pulls the stick and *Cyclopterus* climbs low over the northern hemisphere, her lights pooling across ducts and grilles and stenciled warnings to keep clear of the vents. Moreno navigates over the north pole, coaxes the sub into planting a perfect watertight kiss on the docking hatch. Machinery grapples and clenches and blows seawater back into the abyss.

She boots up a dashboard interface and curses. "Figures. Only one atmosphere in there."

"How long to decompress us?"

"From nine atmospheres? Breathing trimix? Five days, easy." She studies the dash. "Fortunately, we've also got remote access to hab support. I can bring inside pressure up to nine in about"—she runs her finger up the dash—"fifteen minutes."

"You rock," Galik tells her.

It gets him his first small smile. "I do, don't I?"

THEY DON'T HAVE fifteen minutes, though. The board starts beeping after five.

"That was fast," Galik says.

Moreno frowns. "That's not the hab. That's an ELF handshake." Her face brightens. "Text message! The beacon got through!"

Galik's jaw tightens. "Don't get your hopes up. Remember, these people"—taking in the half-built complex around them—"they have ears too."

"No, this is through Cospas-Sarsat. This is NOAA." She leans forward, focusing as if sheer concentration might somehow squeeze the signal from the water a little faster. Alphanumerics accumulate in front of her. They're too small to make out from where Galik's sitting.

He sighs.

"Says here—it says..." The anticipation drains from her face. Something darker rises in its stead.

She turns to face him. "Who the fuck *are* y—"

Galik's fist connects with her right temple. Moreno's head

snaps sideways, cracks against the hull. She sags like a rag doll against the shoulder strap.

Galik unbuckles his harness and leans over. There's still awareness in her eyes. Her drooling mouth twitches and gapes, trying to form words. From somewhere inside Koa Moreno, a moan escapes.

He shakes his head. "It really was a preliminary survey, for what it's worth. We didn't know what was down here any more than you did; we only had—suspicions."

"You fuh..." she manages.

"The sensors were supposed to—not you. We were never supposed to get out this far."

Moreno half raises a hand. It flops on the end of her arm like a dead fish.

"Now everything's gone to shit, and I have to—improvise. I'm so sorry, Koa."

"Mid... easht—pashpor..."

"I'm sorry you chose the wrong side," he says, and breaks her neck.

By the time her heart stops, the pressure in the shack is up to nine. Galik turns crouching in the cramped compartment, catches passing sight of the text message still accreting on the board—

SOS RECEIVED

AWAITING REQ APPROVAL ON DSRV WILL ADVISE

NAUTILUS LLC DENIES ANY KNOWLEDGE OF S.EARLE REQ

NO EMPLOYEES DEPLOYED TO CCZ

NO ALISTOR LNU LISTED ON SH

—and kneels to undog the deck hatch.

The lights come up as he climbs down: indirect, full-spectrum, illuminating a cozy half hemisphere where struts and plating are all padded and wrapped in PVC. Interfaces and control panels sleep on curved bulkheads, on the desks that extrude from them. Behind a bulkhead that splits the upper deck, visible through an open hatch, bunks and lockers lurk in shadow. A spiral staircase corkscrews down to the deck below.

He searches the hab and finds it empty. He awakens its controls, checks logs and manifests. He explores remote-piloting options for *Cyclopterus*, teaches himself how to send the little craft far away on its own recognizance.

He eats from the shack's well-stocked galley, sleeps in its salon.

Four and a half kilometers overhead the mixing zone churns beneath the surface; the surface churns beneath the sky; immortal Nāmaka churns between. Back on shore the fires burn ever-hotter along the coast. Deserts spread and clathrates bubble; winter heat waves scythe across the Mediterranean; wheat rust and monkey pox fell crops and people with equal indiscriminate abandon. Tuvalu and Kiribati sink beneath the waves. Protesters mourn the loss of the Pizzly Bear and the Bengal Tiger while underfoot, the trillions of small creeping things that hold up the world disappear almost unnoticed. The human race runs ever-faster to the finish line, numbers finally thinning out on the last lap, rioting and reveling and fighting over whatever crumbs are left after three hundred years of deficit spending.

All the while, the Nikkei never stops climbing.

Alistor Galik—formerly Staff Sergeant Jason Knowlton (ret.), USSOCOM—bides his time on the bottom of the ocean, drawing plans and selecting targets. Waiting patiently for the minions of Zero Point to arrive and show him the way back to their masters.

ABOUT THE AUTHORS

John Barnes (thatjohnbarnes.blogspot.com) has published thirty volumes of fiction, including science fiction, men's action adventure, two collaborations with astronaut Buzz Aldrin, a collection of short stories and essays, one fantasy and one mainstream novel. His most recent books are science fiction novel *The Last President*, young adult novel *Losers in Space*, and political satire *Raise the Gipper!* He has done a rather large number of occasionally peculiar things for money, mainly in business consulting, academic teaching, and show business, fields which overlap more than you'd think. Since 2001, he has lived in Denver, Colorado, where he has a thoroughly wonderful wife, a wildly varying income, and an unjustifiably negative attitude, which he feels is actually the best permutation.

Tobias S. Buckell (www.tobiasbuckell.com) is a *New York Times* bestselling author born in the Caribbean. He grew up in Grenada and spent time in the British and US Virgin Islands, which influence much of his work. His novels and over seventy stories have been translated into nineteen different languages. His work has been nominated for awards like the Hugo, Nebula, Prometheus, and the John W. Campbell Award for Best New Science Fiction Author. He currently lives in Bluffton, Ohio with his wife, twin daughters, and a pair of dogs.

Aliette de Bodard (aliettedebodard.com) lives and works in Paris. She has won two Nebula Awards, a Locus Award and three British Science Fiction Association Awards. Her space opera books include Nebula nominee *The Tea Master and the Detective*, a murder mystery set on a space station in a Vietnamese Galactic empire, inspired by the characters of Sherlock Holmes and Dr. Watson. Recent works include short fantasy novel *In the Vanishers' Palace*, the Dominion of the Fallen series, set in a turn-of-the-century Paris devastated by a magical war, which comprises *The House of Shattered Wings*, *The House of Binding Thorns*, and forthcoming *The House of Sundering Flames*.

Greg Egan (www.gregegan.net) published his first story in 1983, and followed it with fourteen novels, seven short story collections, and more than fifty short stories. During the early 1990s Egan published a body of short fiction—mostly hard science fiction focused on mathematical and quantum ontological themes—that established him as one of the most important writers working in the field. His work has won the Hugo, John W Campbell Memorial, Locus, Aurealis, Ditmar, and Seiun awards. His latest books are short novels *Phoresis* and *Perihelion Summer*.

Gregory Feeley writes science fiction and about science fiction. He is the author of two novels: Philip K. Dick Award nominated debut *The Oxygen Barons* and historical fantasy *Arabian Wine*. His stories have been finalists for the Nebula and Theodore Sturgeon Memorial awards and reprinted in various Year's Best anthologies, while his essays and reviews have appeared *in The Atlantic Monthly*, the *New York Times Magazine*, the *Washington Post Book World*, and *USA Today*. His most recent book is a novella, *Kentauros* and has just completed a long novel, *Hamlet the Magician*.

Jason Fischer (jasonfischer.com.au) lives near Adelaide, South Australia. He has won the Colin Thiele Literature Scholarship, an Aurealis Award and the Writers of the Future Contest. In Jason's jack-of-all-trades writing career he has worked on comics, computer games, television, short stories, novellas, and novels. He also has a passion for godawful puns and was twice a State Finalist in the Karaoke World Championship.

Carolyn Ives Gilman is a Hugo and Nebula Award nominated author of science fiction and fantasy. Her books include *Dark Orbit,* a space exploration adventure that raises questions about consciousness and perception; *Isles of the Forsaken* and *Ison of the Isles,* a two-book fantasy about culture clash and revolution; and *Halfway Human,* a novel about gender and oppression. Her short fiction has appeared in *Lightspeed, Clarkesworld, Fantasy and Science Fiction, The Year's Best Science Fiction, Interzone, Universe, Full Spectrum, Realms of Fantasy*, and others. Her work has been translated into a dozen languages. Gilman lives in Washington, D.C., and works as a freelance writer and museum consultant. She is also author of seven nonfiction books about North American frontier and Native history.

Peter F. Hamilton was born in Rutland in 1960 and still lives nearby. He began writing in 1987 and sold his first short story to *Fear* magazine in 1988. He has written many bestselling novels, including the Greg Mandel series, the Night's Dawn trilogy, the Commonwealth Saga, the Void trilogy, short story collections and several standalone novels including *Fallen Dragon* and *Great North Road*.

Yoon Ha Lee's (www.yoonhalee.com) first novel, *Ninefox Gambit*, was published to critical acclaim in 2016 and was shortlisted for the Hugo and Nebula Awards. It was followed by Hugo nominee *Raven Stratagem* in 2017 and *Revenant Gun* in 2018. Lee is the author of more than forty short stories, some of which have appeared in *Tor.com, Lightspeed, Clarkesworld,* and *The Magazine of Fantasy and Science Fiction*. His most recent novel is middle-grade space opera, *Dragon Pearl*. Coming up is *Hexarchate Stories*, a collection of stories set in the Hexarchate universe. Lee lives in Louisiana with his family and has not yet been eaten by gators.

John Meaney (www.johnmeaney.com) is the author of twelve novels including *To Hold Infinity Paradox, Context*, the Ragnarok trilogy and the Donal Riordan sequence. *To Hold Infinity* and *Paradox* were shortlisted for the BSFA Award for Best Novel. *The Times* called John Meaney 'The first important new sf writer of the 21st century'. Meaney has a degree in physics and computer science and holds a black belt in Shotokan Karate. He lives in Glamorgan in Wales.

Linda Nagata's (mythicisland.com) work has been nominated for the Hugo, Nebula, Locus, John W. Campbell Memorial, and Theodore Sturgeon Memorial awards. She has won the Nebula and is a two-time winner of the Locus award. She is best known for her high-tech science fiction, including the near-future thriller, *The Last Good Man*, and the Red trilogy, an intersection of artificial intelligence and military fiction. The first book in the trilogy, *The Red: First Light,* was named as a Publishers Weekly Best Book of 2015. Her newest novel is *Edges*, book one in the series *Inverted Frontier*. Linda has lived most of her life in Hawaii, where she's been a writer, a mom, a programmer of database-driven websites, and an independent publisher. She lives with her husband in their long-time home on the island of Maui.

Dominica Phetteplace (www.dominicaphetteplace.com) is a math tutor who writes fiction and poetry. Her work has appeared in *Asimov's, Clarkesworld*, and *F&SF*. Her honors include a MacDowell Fellowship, a Pushcart Prize and a Rona Jaffe Award.

New York Times bestseller and two-time Hugo winner **Kristine Kathryn Rusch** gets lost in large projects sometimes. WMG Publishing just released a gigantic ebook of her eight-volume Anniversary Day saga. She's currently finishing a large group of novels in her Diving universe. Some parts of the story have escaped and found their way as novellas in *Asimov's*. She finds time to write a blog on the publishing business every week on her website, kriswrites.com. She also puts up a free short story there every Monday

Allen M. Steele became a full-time science fiction writer in 1988, following publication of his first short story, "Live From The Mars Hotel". Since then he has become a prolific author of novels, short stories, and essays, with his work translated into more than a dozen languages worldwide. His many novels include *Orbital Decay, Clarke County, Space, Lunar Descent, A King of Infinite Space*, the Coyote Trilogy, the Coyote Chronicles, *Spindrift, V-S Day*, and *Arkwright*. He has also published six collections of short fiction: *Rude Astronauts, All-American Alien Boy, Sex and Violence in Zero-G, American Beauty, The Last Science Fiction Writer*, and *Tales of Time and Space*. He won the Hugo Award for novellas "The Death Of Captain Future" and "'...Where Angels Fear to Tread'", and for "The Emperor of Mars" Steele was First Runner-Up for the 1990 John W. Campbell Award, received the Donald A. Wollheim Award in 1993, and the Phoenix Award in 2002. He lives in western Massachusetts with his wife Linda and their dogs.

Peter Watts (www.rifters.com) is a former marine biologist known for the novels *Starfish*, *Blindsight*, and a bunch of others that people don't seem to like quite as much. Also, for managing to retell the story of John Carpenter's *The Thing* without getting sued and for having certain issues with authority figures. While he has enjoyed moderate success as a midlist author (available in twenty languages, winner of awards ranging from science-fictional to documentary to academic, occasional ill-fated video-game gigs), he has recently put all that behind him—choosing instead to collaborate on a black metal science opera about sending marbled lungfish to Mars, funded by the Norwegian government (the opera, not the lungfish). So far, it pays better.

Sean Williams (www.seanwilliams.com) is an award-winning, #1 *New York Times*-bestselling author of over forty novels and one hundred stories, including some set in the *Star Wars* and *Doctor Who* universes, and some written with Garth Nix. He has a new novel, *Impossible Music*, due out in July 2019. He lives up the road from the Australia's finest chocolate factory with his family and a pet plastic fish.

COPYRIGHT

FIND US ONLINE!

www.rebellionpublishing.com

/rebellionpub   /rebellionpublishing   /rebellionpub

SIGN UP TO OUR NEWSLETTER!

rebellionpublishing.com/sign-up

YOUR REVIEWS MATTER!

Enjoy this book? Got something to say?

Leave a review on Amazon, GoodReads or with your favourite bookseller and let the world know!